The Prince's Protégé

The Five Kingdoms, Volume 3

by Deborah Jay

Published by Deborah Jay, 2019

The Prince's Protégé
First Edition. March 28th, 2019
Copyright © 2019, by Deborah Jay
Written by Deborah Jay

Cover art by Ravven
(www.ravven.com)

Maps by Deirdre Counihan

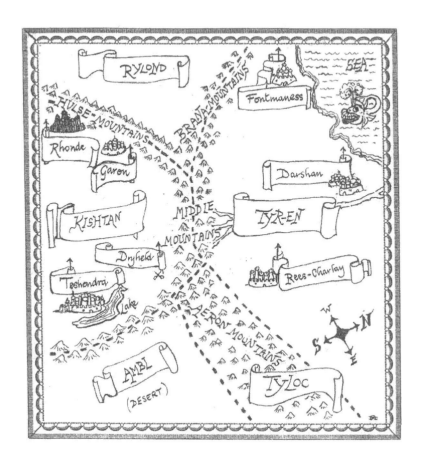

The Five Kingdoms

The Kingdom of Tyr-en

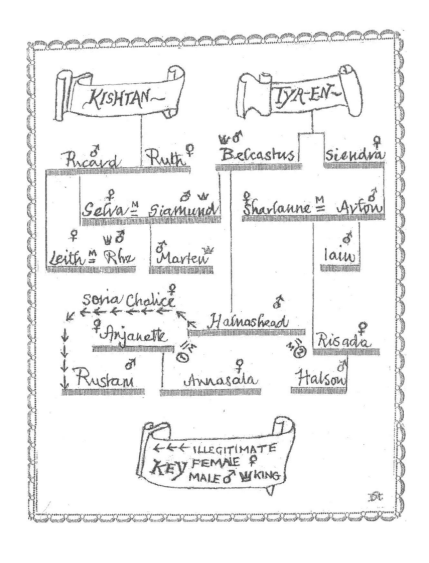

Family Trees of Kishtan and Tyr-en

Prologue

DARSHAN PALACE

The choking air rang with the screams of people scrambling to escape the burning Great Hall. Marten flinched as a sword blade flashed out of the smoke a finger's width from his face. It slammed into the dais beside his knee, metal screeching as it sliced through the chain pinning him to the floor. Abruptly, the pressure on his neck eased.

He heaved himself to his feet with the heavy metal collar dangling a couple of remaining links. His numb legs wobbled, sending him stumbling into the diminutive figure wielding the sword. Raven hair clinging to ice white skin identified his aunt, Queen Leith. Other than staggering, she didn't react, and Marten snatched a breath as her eerie red eyes stared blankly past him.

"What—?" he croaked, throat too sore to form more than a single word. A coughing fit seized him.

The roaring whoosh of flames sizzled overhead and Marten's skin smarted as the temperature rose another notch. His heart raced; how long before the roof collapsed?

Beside him his uncle, Prince Halnashead, rose shakily to his feet, a handspan of metal links trailing from a collar matching Marten's. Without wasting time on words, Halnashead wrapped an arm around his daughter, Princess Annasala, and seized one of Marten's hands. He jerked his chin towards Leith.

Avoiding her magical elvish sword, Marten grabbed the

queen's empty hand and clung to it even as Uncle Hal dragged them into the clouds of acrid smoke obscuring the rear of the dais. There was a doorway there, somewhere, if they could find it.

With a thunderous crash, the roof behind them collapsed. Marten yelped as something hard struck his calf and pain shot up his leg. Heat flared against his back, and he lurched forward, dragging Leith clear of the falling debris even as his knee buckled and he fell forward, saved from tumbling to the ground by Halnashead's strong grip.

"Steady, lad, you're safe."

Blinking watering eyes, Marten peered at their surroundings. Wisps of smoke curled around them, but the air his scorched lungs sucked in was pure and mercifully cool, and ahead of them, on the far side of a large gravel courtyard, he identified the portico surrounding the king's private wing of the palace.

His wing.

The ragged party staggered across the open space, putting a safe distance between themselves and the burning building. By the goddess's mercy, no wind stirred the flames in their direction. A handful of men and women in servants' and guards' uniforms rushed past them with buckets and beaters to fight the fire.

The royal family was safe for now, but what of those behind the thwarted coup? Had any of them escaped?

Halnashead released Marten's hand and wrapped both his arms around Annasala. Leith tottered over to a stone bench and sank down, shaking her head in a dazed fashion. Her fist relaxed, allowing her elvish sword to fall to the ground with a hollow clang.

A male figure trod past Marten back towards the raging inferno, and he recognised Rustam Chalice, a craft master he'd only been vaguely aware of before today. He narrowed his eyes to study the lithe dancer. Clearly Master Chalice was injured. He held one arm clutched against his side, leaning over to protect either the arm, or more likely, his ribs. Dark hair plastered the man's head, and his shoulders slumped in despair.

"Risada," he called, pain cracking his voice, and Marten glanced quickly around. Lady Risada, slayer of the would-be usurper, was not present.

"Where is she? Where's Risada?" Marten turned towards Halnashead.

Chin resting on top of Annasala's head, Halnashead stared at the burning building, his eyes filled with anguish. "She was the other side of the roof beam that fell. She would have had to get out the far end of the hall."

None of them said what they were all thinking; how unlikely that was 'to have happened. Rustam Chalice collapsed to his knees.

"Rusty, son, help me with your sister," Halnashead implored.

Marten's head jerked round. Had his uncle just acknowledged the dance master as his son?

Rustam struggled back to his feet with the appearance of a man carrying a load far too heavy for his damaged body. He limped over to Halnashead's side, and it was then that Marten realised although Annasala was upright within the protective circle of her father's arms, she hung limply. He made a move to help, but Halnashead stopped him.

"See to Leith, will you?" His uncle frowned. "I assume she was drugged. Rusty?"

"Yes," confirmed Rustam. "Hestane, to block her magic. The bastard gave her an overdose, but I think the sword is dealing with that, otherwise she'd be dead by now."

Marten shuddered. In a kingdom that forbade magic on pain of death, he'd seen more than he'd ever anticipated in the last few days, some of it from the man he now realised was yet another relative, even if illegitimate. Marten's feelings swayed between outrage and gratitude—without Rustam's intervention they would all be dead by now.

With Annasala supported between them, Halnashead and Rustam moved awkwardly away, heading towards the princess's rooms. Obedient to his uncle, Marten offered a hand to Leith, but she shook her head.

"I'm not moving anywhere, Marten. What I need is the antidote Hal keeps locked away in his study."

"But I thought—"

"Yes, yes." Leith cut him off. She flicked her fingers towards her discarded sword. "It won't let me die, but I can *really* do without this beast of a headache for the next two days. Please, Marten, be kind to your aunt. I may not look old, but today I feel it."

Marten surveyed the deserted courtyard.

"If you aren't sure which bottle it is, bring them all. I'll know which one."

"It's not that, Aunt Leith; I don't like the idea of leaving you here. What if any of the traitors escaped the hall?"

"The only traitor that matters is dead. None of the others command magic. They aren't going to risk coming against this." She nudged the elvish sword with her foot.

"But—"

His aunt scowled. "I know you aren't used to running errands, Marten, but my head is pounding and it isn't going to get any better without that antidote. Please?"

"You're sure?"

"Go!"

Marten tugged his charred and tattered tunic into some semblance of straightness, before setting off towards his uncle's suite. He hesitated at every turn, checking corridors and doorways to make sure he was still alone. The solitude unnerved him.

He was the king. He was never alone.

Since ascending the throne at the age of fourteen—three whole years now—free will had taken a permanent leave of absence from his life. His days followed prescribed routines, with duties and meetings, book studies and sword craft, always surrounded by guards and advisors. This was the first time in his life he'd ever gone anywhere unaccompanied.

To add to his disquiet, the normally familiar corridors

proved disturbingly different. The tapestries that had once lined the walls were nowhere to be seen, and all the furniture was missing. Marten's boot steps echoed off the blank walls, sharp taps as he strode along. A mustiness tickled his smoke-irritated throat, reminiscent of the smell of a long-abandoned building.

His footsteps fell silent as he stepped onto one of the few remaining rugs, soiled with goddess-only-knew what. Marten had no wish to inspect the russet stains too closely. While there had been at least one traitor amongst the guardsmen, some of the men had been as near to friends as Marten allowed. Now, many of them were dead, and others missing. Sorting out this mess wasn't going to be a quick—or painless—affair.

Perhaps, though, I'll finally be allowed to make some decisions of my own. I value all my advisors, and Uncle Hal most of all, but I have to start ruling on my own at some point, and this might be a good—

The whisper of silk against the tender skin of Marten's neck gifted him just enough warning to get three fingers beneath the elegant noose before it tightened above the metal collar. He yanked against it, but to no avail.

"Don't fight it, little man," crooned a low voice beside his ear. "It's better this way. If you die now, you'll never grow into a perverted monster like your grandsire."

Despite a smoke-induced huskiness, the speaker was unequivocally female.

A woman! Surely, I can fight a woman?

But whoever she was, this woman held every advantage. Her slight body pressed against his back, so he could not see her. The silk scarf tightened further, forcing his knuckles against his throat even as a light cinnamon fragrance caressed his senses. His vision darkened and his legs trembled. Shame sapped his remaining strength—that the king should die by the hand of a woman.

Marten staggered backward, stepping on his attacker's foot. She yelped, and the pressure around Marten's neck eased enough for him to catch a breath. He seized the opportunity and stamped down hard, rewarded with a loud crack as he broke the woman's instep.

"Charin take you!" The croaked imprecation close beside his ear set a ringing in his head to join the swimming effect brought by the lack of air. Marten gathered his last shreds of strength and jabbed an elbow backward. It sank into soft flesh, eliciting a harsh grunt. He pressed his minute advantage, wrenching at the deceptively soft garrotte. His assailant clung on, yanking back in turn, pulling Marten off balance. He landed on one knee.

Uncle Hal, forgive me. I should have paid more attention to my self-defence training. Chel, sweet goddess, take me in your arms…

Blood pounded through his head, tapping out a beat that expanded to fill his awareness until it blocked out all else. He was dying, he knew it.

But why, then, did his heartrate not slow?

Realisation came at the same instant the suffocating pressure vanished—the rhythmic tapping wasn't his heart beating its last, it was the sound of bootsteps approaching along the very same bare flagstones he himself had trodden only moments before.

Marten fell to his hands and knees, gulping air. When he was able to look round, the would-be assassin was nowhere to be seen. Marten pushed himself to rise, unwilling to be found grovelling on the floor.

"Sire! Praise Chel, you're alive! Are you injured?" The masculine voice moved swiftly from jubilant to concerned, and Marten shook his head, setting off a coughing fit. He doubled over, gasping. The boots that hove into view were those of a guardsman, and relief flooded Marten. A hand hovered near his arm, the guard obviously uncertain whether to follow protocol, which forbade anyone from touching the king without his express permission. The frightened boy in Marten ached for the physical support, but the recently crowned king drew on an inner strength that was new to him, and he straightened, waving the man back.

"I'll survive. Too much smoke," he croaked, and coughed again. He was relieved to find he recognised the dark-haired young man. Not one of his personal guards, but one who'd stood by his door on many occasions; one he'd barely acknowledged, but familiar nonetheless.

"Did you pass anyone just now?" he managed to ask when he'd recovered his breath.

"No one, sire. At least, not in the royal apartments." The man glanced anxiously back along the corridor. "Beg pardon, sire, but did any of the rest of the royal family escape?"

"My uncle, Princess Annasala, and Queen Leith, are all very much alive."

"Praise Chel!"

"It'll take more than a pretender to wipe us out," Marten declared. His defiant words bolstered his confidence, and he assumed his customary regal posture. While his attacker had successfully avoided being seen leaving the scene, he would have spies seeking her identity before the day was done.

He beckoned. "Come with me, we have work to do, traitors to find and execute."

With the bitch who just tried to kill me top of my list.

As Marten resumed his interrupted journey with the comfort of a guardsman by his shoulder, he mulled over the mystery woman's few words. He comprehended them all too well for he, too, feared turning into his grandsire. For the most part, Marten considered King Belcastus's legendary carnal practices abhorrent.

If only he hadn't discovered the thrill that a little pain could add to a dalliance.

As he walked, Marten considered the girls he'd found pleasure with. Had they truly enjoyed those rough sessions, or had they merely told him so, because he was king? Was that the reason behind the woman's attack?

Marten tightened his jaw. He had no one he could discuss this with; he was too embarrassed. Perhaps it would be better if he abstained, but he knew he was too weak; before long the urge would turn from itch to demand, and he would acquiesce.

He determined to take greater care in future with his choice of partners; he had no desire to inflict his shameful appetites on anyone who did not share his tastes. He would also be vigilant, keeping his senses open for the distinctive cinnamon scent worn by the would-be assassin. Such a pity her voice had been roughened by the smoke, or she might be easier to identify. On the other hand, she'd be limping for a while, so that might help.

Mere thought of the encounter made him cough again, and he paused, leaning against the wall. He knew he should tell Halnashead—his uncle was, after all, his spymaster—but then he would have to admit he'd been stupid enough to walk the palace corridors alone in the aftermath of a coup. He should have waited with his aunt until guards came, and not acceded to her drug-befuddled plea.

Marten suspected the attempt on his life had been opportunistic. Before the woman had the chance to plan and execute another—assuming she had the temerity to try again—he was quite confidence his spies would find and deal with her. He was not going to embarrass himself by admitting to his uncle how close he'd come to dying at the hands of a woman. This was one security issue he would manage on his own.

There. My first solo decision. I pray it won't prove to be one I regret.

At the doors to Halnashead's suite, his new bodyguard stepped in front of him before he could enter.

"What are you—"

"Begging your pardon, my liege, but I should check inside first; make sure it's safe."

With a nod, Marten waved him on. *Damn, but I need to get my head around this. People are really trying to kill me.* He shuddered. The threat had always seemed so remote he'd not taken it seriously before.

The rooms had been ransacked, but proved empty of

intruders. It crossed Marten's mind there was always the possibility of lethal traps left behind, but if the usurper's plans had been concluded, most of the royal family would have been executed by now, making it unlikely anyone would have gone to the effort.

Crossing the reception room, Marten scowled at the wanton damage inflicted upon pieces of furniture that had been in his family for generations. He paused to pick up the remains of a mutilated portrait. Setting it on top of a listing cabinet with a shattered leg, he propped the broken bits of frame together until it stayed upright against the wall. He frowned at the image staring back at him—his own image, with a great knife slash diagonally across his painted face.

Perhaps someone did me a favour with this one, he considered as he held the canvas edges together. He inspected the slender visage with its aquiline nose above thin lips, close-set hazel eyes, and the unremarkable light brown hair that always kinked the wrong way on the left-hand side. Even the artist hadn't seen fit to correct that annoying detail.

I never cared for it, and I'm sure Uncle Hal will insist I sit for a new one.

He placed the offending picture face down on the unsteady cabinet. It promptly slithered off and crashed to the floor. Marten shrugged and turned his back on it, heading for Halnashead's office. He pushed the door open and scanned the chaos within. Had the bottle of antidote survived?

Behind him the guardsman cleared his throat, snagging Marten's attention.

"Would you like me to call a locksmith, sire?"

Marten fingered the heavy metal collar still clasped around his neck. "Yes, but please find someone else to do so—you are hereby promoted to the position of my personal guard. You are—?"

The man's face coloured as he snapped to attention. Sharp blue eyes stared out from a smooth face only a few years older than Marten's. "Davi, my liege," he answered. "Thank you, my liege."

Davi's dark eyebrows drew down as he peered at the offending collar. "I think an apothecary will be in order as well, sire. That's a fearful nasty mark it's made around your neck."

Marten agreed, and waved Davi towards the door. He lifted the collar slightly away from his neck to finger the sore skin beneath, and a grim smile raised the corners of his lips. The collar was the perfect explanation for the marks left by the silk scarf. No one but him—and the woman who'd attacked him—would ever know he'd nearly been strangled.

1. CHEL'S CASKET

Two years later…

Marten glanced over his shoulder as his boot heels click-clacked along the stone-flagged corridor. This was his cousin Risada's mansion, not his palace, and on Uncle Hal's instructions he'd left Davi to guard the outer door to this private passageway. His back felt exposed without his loyal guardsman one step behind him, and a shudder rippled down his spine as the phantom sensation of silk slid across his neck.

He rubbed a finger over the raised ridge of scar tissue everyone believed to be legacy of the metal collar used to hold him during the coup. Marten knew better. Perhaps the blistering beneath the hot metal had formed a blemish, but every time he studied his reflection, all he could see was the mark of the silken ligature that had so nearly ended his life.

Frustratingly, even after two years, Marten's personal spy network still hadn't uncovered the identity of the would-be strangler. With the kingdom's nobles all assembled here at the Second House for the funeral of Lord Iain Merschenko vas Domn, he was taking no chances. *She* might be amongst them.

Turning his attention to the reason for this visit, Marten's feet dragged. Lord Iain had been another of his cousins, brother of the remarkable Lady Risada who had survived the coup against all odds, albeit with a crippling injury to one arm. Since then, she'd married his Uncle Hal. Did that make her his aunt now? Or was she still his cousin? Or both? It was all too confusing.

Marten halted. The unguarded door at the end of the corridor was a novelty for a king unaccustomed to opening doors for himself. He laid one hand against the warm wood and paused. What awaited him the other side? Uncle Hal had called him to this meeting with no explanation, and that made Marten's stomach uneasy. Though his life was full of meetings, he was always provided with a brief beforehand, so he could be the well prepared and wise ruler he sought to be. This lack of information was *so* unlike Uncle Hal.

Mind you, since they'd arrived at House Domn, Halnashead had been distracted. And strangely relaxed. It was not like the head of royal security to be *relaxed*.

Marten squared his shoulders. He would learn nothing by standing like a rooted tree on the wrong side of the door. He lifted the latch and pushed.

The scent of burning sweetwood and wash of warm air surprised him. It was almost high summer, yet a fire crackled in the hearth of Domn's spacious main parlour. The bulky figure of Prince Halnashead sat before the flames in a large armchair, with his feet stretched towards the heat like an old man. Despite his greying hair and ever-expanding waistline, Marten had never thought of his uncle as old. He banished the notion before it took root; Halnashead would *never* be old.

As Marten stepped over the threshold, the lean young man seated beside Halnashead sprang to his feet in a fluid, sleek motion.

Rustam Chalice. Uncle Hal's secret bastard.

Marten hadn't expected to ever see Rustam again after the coup. For the crime of using magic—even if it had saved the kingdom—Rustam should have been executed, but Halnashead had created a loophole in the law and banished his son instead. After a two-year absence, Rustam was only here at the funeral courtesy of diplomatic status, representing the kingdom where he'd found sanctuary.

Marten snicked the door shut behind himself, and

acknowledged his uncle with a slight nod. He waved Rustam back to his seat. "I'm tired of ritual," he said. "Please, let it go, at least for today."

The lack of formalities now the death rites were complete was a novelty to Marten, and one he intended to make the most of before returning to the capital. A comfortable armchair near his uncle beckoned, but a familiar shape caught Marten's eye, and he sighed, knowing what hid beneath the blood-coloured cloth resting upon the small side table.

Will I never be rid of the thing for long?

He strode across the room, wending his way between an assortment of chairs and tables to confront the offending article. As ever, he wrestled with the conflicting sensations of the unholy attraction that tugged at his soul, and the bitter taste flooding his tongue. He grasped a handful of the concealing cloth, unnaturally warm between his fingers, and braced himself before tugging the fabric aside to reveal what lay beneath.

The ancient, battered box, with its faded paintwork and one charred end was unimpressive, even for a holy relic. What lay *inside* the disappointing receptacle, *that* was another matter. Even without lifting the lid, it called to Marten, seductive and sweet, offering the fulfilment of all his dreams: respect, autonomous power, adulation.

Temptation clawed at him, but with the strength of long practice, he resisted. Of course, he wanted those things, but not at the price the *thing* inside the box would levy.

If only he could dispose of it, his life would be simpler. But it was the king's lot to guard the box, and to keep others safe from the power imprisoned inside it. Chels Casket represented the goddess's seal of approval on the rule of Marten's House, but surely a locked vault somewhere would be safer than carting it across the kingdom?

"Uncle Hal, what are we to do with this? You say it's not safe to leave it behind when I travel, but I can't take it everywhere I go. Where can we put it that *will* be safe?"

Before Halnashead could answer, movement caught Marten's attention. Rustam Chalice was on his feet and approaching the table with stuttering steps, as if his body was controlled by another.

It is, Marten realised as Rustam's hand stretched towards the box. *That's probably exactly how I look whenever I come near the damned thing.*

"Rustam!" Halnashead's stern voice cracked through the air, halting his errant son. It was only then that Marten registered how near Rustam stood to him. The royal guards would never have allowed any but his closest family into such proximity. Marten's skin crawled. Undoubtedly Master Chalice could be as deadly with his hands as with his unholy magic.

Rustam's fingers stretched out to hover over the casket's curved lid, and Marten relaxed. There was absolutely no reason for Rustam to want him dead, but events of the last couple of years had eroded Marten's trust in his fellow nobles.

Not that Rustam's a noble; at least not in society's view. What must it be like, to know you are royal by birth, but never able to unveil that knowledge in the light of day?

"I'm sorry." Rustam shook his head. "I can't believe it survived." The man's fingertips all but brushed the surface of the casket. "May I?"

Halnashead glanced towards Marten, entreaty in his eye. The prince never did anything without a reason, and although Marten could only guess what that might be, the situation offered an opportunity to confirm beyond doubt that Rustam really was Halnashead's son.

Marten shrugged his acquiescence. "Why not? He has as much right as any of our Family."

The gratitude on his uncle's face astounded Marten before he realised how proud Halnashead was of his secret son. Here, in the seclusion of this parlour, and in the presence of his monarch, the prince could acknowledge Rustam, and the opening of Chel's Casket would seal that truth.

Marten watched as Rustam touched the box. His whole body jerked, and a shocked gasp burst from his lungs. Marten sympathised—he knew the sensation: like lightning running up your arm.

He also knew when it faded, as Rustam's face took on a determined cast and he lifted the box from the table, turning it around, studying the seam between lid and carcass. As if guided by an unseen hand, Rustam gripped top and bottom and twisted, separating the two halves.

So, there was the truth of it. Rustam was, without question, Halnashead's get. Marten studied his cousin, searching for a familial resemblance, but finding little. The man took after his mother's blood more closely than his father's. Although Marten had never met Rustam's mother, he knew her history; how she was one of the offspring of old King Belcastus's abhorrent breeding programme, daughter of an elf forced to mate with a human.

The very notion of his grandfather's twisted experiments thinned Marten's lips to a hard line.

He scowled, dismissing the sour thoughts. Beside him, Rustam placed the lid on the table and lowered the box to stare at the awful thing inside.

Marten could see into the casket too. The serpentine talisman's surface shimmered with shades of red and yellow that ran over, together, and through each other to create an illusion of movement.

How can such a beautiful thing be so evil?

Rustam's hand ventured inside the box. Again, his body had the appearance of being controlled by some outside influence. Marten's stomach tensed; at what point should he halt this encounter? He watched Rustam's fingers curl around the thing, and experienced twin pangs of envy and horror. He'd never had the courage to go that far; to actually *handle* the thing.

And then Rustam's hands snapped open. The box clattered to the table with the rejected talisman still inside. Marten snatched up the lid and slammed it down, shutting the malevolent object away from sight. Even so, he caught a glint of ruby, like a baleful, bloody eye winking at him, before the edges of the box sealed together.

What in Charin's hell was that?

Rustam's strangled croak proclaimed what Marten already knew. "That thing is *evil*."

Rustam sank to the edge of a chair, trembling.

Marten allowed himself a tight smile. *I'll take it as encouragement, that an experienced spy finds that* thing *as unsettling as I do.*

Halnashead patted Rustam's shoulder. "And now you know the truth, m'boy. That little trinket was placed within the casket to stop it from falling into the wrong hands. Our Family is its keeper."

Rustam screwed his face up. "So Chel's Favour is a lie?"

Marten felt the need to defend the goddess. "Not exactly. It was a priest of Chel who sealed it with the magic that prevents any but our bloodline from opening it. He apparently felt we were the only Family who could be trusted not to try to use it, which made us the most likely choice for a ruling House. Perhaps 'Chel's Choice' would have been a better title, but the 'Favour' label stuck."

"I'm surprised our esteemed grandsire didn't try," Rustam mused.

"I believe fear stopped him," said Halnashead, patting the air above the box, not quite touching it. "According to the lore passed down with the casket, the evil it contains cannot be controlled, even by the one who summons it. Pray Chel no one ever tries." He withdrew his hand. "Cover it up, Marten, and leave it here for now. No one will touch anything in this room without orders from Risada, and I'll consider a more permanent site for it before you return to Darshan."

Halnashead positioned himself in front of the fire, hands clasped behind his back. "And now, young sirs, to more immediate business."

Marten's heart sank; he knew exactly where this conversation was leading. He slouched into a nearby chair in the full knowledge he gave an impression of a sulky child.

They're grooming me to be the king they all want, but they don't seem to trust me to rule. I'm nearly twenty years old, for Chel's sake! What will they do if I refuse their counsel? I have my own ideas...

A daydream wandered across his vision, dressed in little more than tantalizing strips of silk and leather, revealing soft, feminine curves striped with weal marks from a triple lashed whip. Heat stirred in Marten's groin, warring with the self-disgust his arousal prompted.

Since that first clumsy, youthful grope in a dark store room when he'd discovered that inflicting pain excited him, he'd lived with the fear of developing his grandsire's depraved appetites. His dread had only deepened when he'd determined that without such stimulation, he remained impotent.

Why am I like this? Did I do something to offend you, Chel? Or is it a sick joke of Charin's?

He dragged his attention back into the room in time to hear Uncle Hal turn his conversation with Rustam to that most vexing of subjects.

"—so now I'm afraid I must add to your burdens," Halnashead said to Rustam, all the while glowering at Marten.

"Charin take your options," Marten muttered.

Halnashead narrowed his eyes. "Your Majesty knows my counsel. The matter of a queen becomes ever more urgent, and there are few suitable candidates available."

"But a child!" protested Marten, picturing a gawky adolescent with a baby face. *Not* what he had in mind for a bed partner. Come to that, the obvious reason for needing a queen was the production of an heir, and what was the likelihood a well-bred and genteelly-raised child would willingly embrace his fetish?

Halnashead quelled him with a look. "Princess Sabina may be only twelve, but by the time negotiations reach fruition she will be old enough."

Mustering his most potent protest, Marten ignored the age gap as an unviable excuse—men married children all the time. "But will the people accept her?" he asked, putting on his best 'concerned monarch' expression. "She's part elf."

Halnashead gestured towards his son. "Rusty is part elf. Would you know it by looking at him?"

"Well, no," Marten admitted.

Halnashead rubbed his hands together before the fire. "From what I hear, the princess looks no more elven than Rusty does, and such a marriage would give you stronger ties to Shiva as well as Kishtan, which may prove important to the future security of Tyr-en."

They had been over this topic more than once, and Halnashead was determined Sabina was the only suitable match. Marten grimaced; he had no valid arguments left, and he simply couldn't bring himself to tell his uncle the real reason for his reluctance.

Rustam leaned forward. "So, I'm taking messages and what—gifts?"

A pang of envy stabbed Marten. Life was so simple for someone like Rustam. The dancer spy could come and go as he pleased, not ruled by court etiquette, and always watched over by guards. He could make his own life choices, marry whomever he wanted. Marten was ruler of an entire kingdom, yet he had less freedom than a craft master.

It's not fair!

Marten inhaled slowly, banishing his childish pique. *Fair* was a concept for those without breeding, those without duty. It fell to him to find a way to make his marriage fruitful for the sake of his kingdom. His people deserved that much.

How, he did not know, but he *would* find a way.

A breath of air across his cheek announced the arrival of Uncle Hal's wife, Lady Risada. There had been many times when Marten's fantasies had worn Risada's beautiful face, but watching the former mate of his dreams waddle across the room with her protruding belly distending her brown mourning gown, his dream imploded. Pregnancy put her beyond his reach, even more so than marriage to his Uncle Hal.

Halnashead hurried to his wife's side and led her to her chair, where he fussed with the cushions like an old nursemaid. Marriage appeared to be having a very odd effect on the kingdom's spymaster, in Marten's opinion.

"Pardon me, m'dear," Halnashead said to Risada, "Marten and I have things to discuss, so if you will excuse us, we'll leave you to Rusty's company."

Halnashead kissed his wife's hand and then ushered Marten from the room. Just before the door closed behind them, Marten was sure he detected tension between Risada and Rustam, but Halnashead gave him no time to dwell on his observation.

"I've decided to remain here when you return to Darshan," said the prince as they walked. "There are no pressing issues on the horizon that require my personal attention, and I fancy this would be a good time for me to take a step into deeper shadow. Would you be comfortable with that?"

Marten stumbled. Was Uncle Hal suggesting what Marten *thought* he was suggesting? His stomach flip-flopped before a sense of calm stole over him. He stopped short of the door at the end of the passageway, drawing Halnashead to a halt.

"This is what I've trained for all my life, but do *you* think I'm ready?"

Halnashead placed a large hand on Marten's shoulder.

"Do you really think I would make the suggestion if I felt otherwise?"

Marten shook his head, emotion closing his throat.

His chief advisor finally believed him ready to rule alone. Now all he had to do was to prove to his uncle—and to himself—that he could do it.

2. DARSHAN

Music filtered through the crowded salon, blending with the rise and fall of conversation. A riot of contrasting perfumes mingled with the scent of warm oil rising from the richly polished wooden floorboards. The massed nobility of Tyr-en thronged the palace halls, resplendent in their finery, each vying to outdo their rivals like a flock of strutting glitterbirds.

Marten shifted his weight from one sore foot to the other.

Why is it I have to stand? I'm the king—surely, I can make my own rules? He smiled to himself. *Perhaps that should be my first decree; that I get to sit down between greeting guests.*

Marten had never hosted a function without Halnashead at his side. He knew exactly what to do, but still a tiny worm of doubt burrowed through his gut. What if he said the wrong thing? Or failed to remember details of each of his guests' Families? It was his job, as monarch and host, to have such information ready for polite conversation, and Marten aimed to deliver the best possible impression he could on his first solo engagement. If only his insecurity didn't tangle his tongue.

He drew a steadying breath which graced his senses with a mouth-watering blend of aromas wafting from the banquet hall. Saliva pooled beneath his tongue. He glanced around and, not finding any new guests in his immediate vicinity, decided it would be a good time to settle his unsteady stomach. He spun towards the enticing smells, startling Davi into motion, and took two steps before the next interruption arrived.

"Allow me to introduce my niece, sire."

Hurriedly manifesting an interested expression, Marten turned to greet the latest of the eligible noblewomen paraded before him this evening like fillies in an auction. Young and old, thin and fat, beautiful and, if not downright ugly, plain women gowned and jewelled to impress. Marten's memory felt stretched by the challenge of recalling all their names, and he considered how soon it might be acceptable for him to withdraw from this overwhelming bridal pageant his nobles had forced upon him.

The first few had engaged his interest, but then he'd reminded himself it was a pointless exercise. Even if his subjects did not yet know, Halnashead had already chosen his betrothed, and it only remained for a deal to be brokered with the Kishtanian royal family before he would be married to a part-elven child with magical abilities.

Marten suppressed a shudder. Magic was the contentious topic of the moment, with the Temple standing firmly in condemnation, while Halnashead, the kingdom's ever-practical chief of security, considered ways to legalise its use for the defence of the realm. Without the means to fight magic, Tyr-en was vulnerable. But did that justify a return to using a power that had destroyed their original culture?

Marten sighed, his breath caressing the latest hand presented for his kiss more heavily than he intended. Heat flared in his cheeks as he raised his face.

A pair of twinkling blue eyes met his gaze, and the mouth below them curved into an amused arc. Flustered, he returned the smile. "Pardon, my lady, I failed to catch your name."

The tiny, slender beauty, with a cascade of golden tresses worn unconventionally loose, smiled again and dipped a curtsey. Marten's eyes travelled involuntarily to her décolletage, and his cheeks burned even hotter.

"Betha Fontmaness, my liege."

"Ah, Herschel's widow, yes?"

"Indeed, sire."

A widow. That was a unique experience this evening. As he paid more attention, Marten realised this lady was alone;

no one had presented her as an offering. He considered her afresh.

She was older, though not as old as he expected a widow to be. Marten's lips twitched with a wry smile. Why should a widow be old? If this woman had been of a similar age as his own prospective bride when she was married to Herschel, then she was probably no more than a handful of years older than Marten himself.

"Is there anything I can do for you?" Marten found himself asking.

Lady Betha laughed; the tinkling sound of water splashing in a fountain. "Aside from find me another husband?" She shook her head. "No sire, there is not. But I will keep the offer on record, if you have no objection? There may come a day when I need it."

"You're sure? I'm certain I could find you a suitable match if you wish it."

A dark shadow crossed her face. "I'm certain, thank you all the same. I have no shortage of suitors."

Of course, she doesn't; she'll be a fine catch. Her House is a fairly minor one, but the lady herself? Breath-taking.

Betha's lavender fragrance filled his lungs, chasing the heat so recently warming his cheeks towards his nether regions. His tongue stuck to the roof of his mouth, and to avoid the necessity of prying it loose for idle chatter, he bent to kiss Betha's hand again before stepping away to indicate her time with him was at an end. She inclined her head graciously and swept away, the skirts of her azure gown swishing rhythmically with the sway of her mobile hips.

Don't get ideas, Marten admonished himself. The ghost of Betha's dainty hand, still rested against his palm. *A lady of that delicate constitution would never be robust enough to indulge my tastes.*

As if to reinforce that view, the first person Marten saw once he managed to drag his attention away from Betha's provocative motion, was Brother Padrus, his personal priest.

"My liege," the ancient brother creaked a shallow bow.

His frown was almost lost in the abundant wrinkles crimping his face. He cast a glance after the departing lady. "Remember, Chel sees all."

"I know, brother. I have you to remind me of that. Constantly."

The lines on Padrus's face creased into a mischievous smile. "And yet you struggle to learn the lesson, my liege."

A snort of amusement escaped Marten. "Perhaps that's because I focus more on Chel's delight in new life brought into the world, and less on the practicalities of how it is made. We all need practice."

Brother Padrus raised a skimpy eyebrow. "And you have an eye on a new training partner?" His face drew down into a serious cast. "Take care, sire. Even at my vast age, I can recall the hot blood of youth and the urges it brings, but your position makes you unique, and the consequences of your choices potentially far more serious than those of a simple man."

Marten inclined his head. "As, yet again, you remind me often."

"Perhaps, then, I am not the man for this position, as it seems my teaching methods are ineffectual."

The affection underlying the old man's words warmed Marten's heart. It was good to know someone without a political agenda was in his inner circle. But Padrus's next words dented that confidence.

"My liege, before you dismiss me for my undoubted incompetence, I have something serious I must discuss with you. Something *very* serious, and not for prying ears. Will you meet with me later, in your chambers?"

All warmth fled Marten's body. This could only mean trouble, and just when Marten was without his uncle to advise him.

He squared his shoulders. This what he'd been training his whole life for.

"Of course, Padrus. You know I always have time for you. Last bell before midnight?"

Padrus bowed his agreement and shuffled away. Marten regarded the ancient priest's retreating form with concern.

He's really starting to feel his age. How much longer will you loan him to me, Chel? Life without his kind wisdom will be hard.

As usual, the goddess held Her peace. It rankled that She would speak with a low-born priest like Padrus, and not with the king She entrusted to rule Her kingdom. Not to mention guard that thrice-damned box of Hers.

A pang of guilt stabbed Marten. Padrus might be low-born, but the old man's goodness made it unsurprising he was one of Chel's Blessed; those rare few even amongst the priesthood who had actually heard Her voice.

The pang transformed into a loud grumble, and with no other interruptions in his immediate vicinity, Marten willingly acquiesced to his stomach's demands. He followed the delicious smells escaping the banquet hall, keeping his eyes resolutely downcast, determined to make it to the table and eat something before facing any more of his subjects and their available female relatives.

A table laden with delicacies filled his vision. Succulent joints of meat, butter drenched vegetables, pastry wrapped delicacies, sauces and jellies, sweets and savouries, all tempted his palate, and he reached out a hand, undecided where to begin.

"Knew I'd find you here eventually."

Marten grimaced and withdrew his empty hand, but the smile that followed was genuine. "Aunt Leith, how lovely to see you. Have you been waiting long?"

The diminutive queen of Shiva chuckled. "Long enough. I've been watching the parade. They really are desperate, aren't they?"

"Who? The lords, or their various offerings?"

"Probably both. I suspect someone's sniffed out Hal's plan for your prospective spouse. Half of them won't approve, and the other half want the kudos of marrying into the royal family. They all think if they strike now, you might make a decision for yourself instead of waiting on Hal's arrangements. Too many of them think you're that naïve."

Marten's shoulders tightened. "You don't think I'm ready to make my own decisions?" His tone came out sharper than he intended.

"Are you?" Leith raised an eyebrow.

"Isn't that what you've all been preparing me for?"

Leith merely smiled, and reached past him for a pastry parcel, which she popped into her mouth. Marten's toes twitched inside his boot, threatening to start the old habit of toe-tapping his aunt had forbidden him. "Never show your impatience," she'd counselled. "Show no emotion you don't intend to be seen. You are the king; you are above such mundanities."

She's testing me. Fine. I can play that game too. At least I get to eat.

Marten inclined his head, and snared a drumstick dripping in a rich red sauce. He cupped his other hand beneath it to catch the drips.

"Sire, permit me," murmured a quiet, respectful voice at his elbow, and a woman's long-fingered hand proffered a polished silver bowl.

"Thank you, Sister Valaree," Marten acknowledged his aunt's moral guardian.

He knew Leith considered the constant presence of a priestess at her elbow everything from irritating to downright intrusive, depending on her disposition of the day, but the Temple deemed it wise, and Marten accepted their caution. Leith possessed the ability to wield magic, and she wasn't reticent about admitting it, even in a kingdom where magic users were still condemned to death. As a foreign diplomat, she was exempt from their judgement, but the Temple insisted she not be left unsupervised.

Valaree performed a respectful bow. She was a woman of rare stock; tall, with a rich copper tone to her skin, and hair the deep black of a moonless night, worn tonight in a neat coil atop her head. Her white priestess's robes set off her colouring to stunning effect, and Marten felt a stirring in his loins. He took the bowl from the priestess, allowing his fingers to linger over hers, and inhaled her unique scent: a mix of spices and incense. His heart beat faster.

A firm hand grasped Marten's elbow.

"Come, nephew, I fancy to dance."

Casting a regretful glance at Valaree—and the loaded banquet table—Marten put down his barely tasted morsel and permitted his aunt to lead him away. The music he had, until now, kept at a distance, swelled to replace the idle chatter filling the intervening halls. As the two royals stepped beneath the ornately carved wooden archway into the rebuilt Great Hall, Marten was dazzled by the swirling kaleidoscope of Tyr-en's nobility. Myriad coloured silk and satin, leather and linen formed their finery, with jewels glinting against fabric and skin, and twinkling in the intricate coiffures of the highborn ladies. The cacophony of colours swept past in a dizzying array almost as overwhelming as the melange of perfumes.

Memory flashed—a silken garrotte and the scent of cinnamon.

That fragrance! It's here, I can smell it!

"Shall we?"

Leith didn't wait for an answer. She spied an opening in the complex dance form and drew Marten into motion. His body responded automatically to the rhythm, following the patterns learned since childhood. He knew his skills fell far short of cousin Rustam's, but they were passable. Like sword fighting and diplomacy, dancing was another craft at which the king was expected to excel, and Marten made every effort to please his tutors.

His petite partner danced with verve, and yet she seemed distracted. As the dance form swung them past the grand archway through which they'd entered, Marten caught a glimpse of Sister Valaree, her white robes stark in their simplicity against the sumptuous apparel of the nobles. Leith spun him away, back into the centre of the crowded floor, and Marten understood her sudden desire to dance.

"You did this to get away from Valaree, didn't you?"

Leith snorted and rose on tiptoes to be heard. "That transparent, am I?" She shrugged and changed her hold. "I tire of her presence more every day. And besides, you were showing far too much interest in her. And not for her priestly guidance, I might add."

Heat pulsed up Marten's neck and he averted his eyes from his aunt's obvious amusement. Concentrating hard on his steps, he turned his partner this way and that, in an effort to distract her, but it appeared her mind had already moved on without his assistance. She tapped him on the shoulder.

"Come, let's get out of here."

Leith didn't wait for his consent. She linked their elbows and led him to the far end of the hall, to the huge double doors that gave out onto the grand courtyard. With their arms firmly entwined, Leith guided him out of the throng, into the blessedly cool, jasmine scented night air, and the relative privacy of the open space. Music spilled through the open doors behind them, muted to the extent they no longer needed to raise their voices to converse.

"It'll be some time before Valaree realises we're gone," said Leith. "Long enough to have a private conversation."

Marten sneezed, and sweat trickled down his cheek. Unease prickled his shoulders as he wiped a kerchief across his brow. Leith was an anachronism in a kingdom that outlawed magic, and her deliberate evasion of the Temple's representative placed him in an awkward position.

What would Brother Padrus say now? If she raises the subject of magic, should I refuse to listen?

"Marten, are you paying attention?" Leith turned to face him, hands on her hips.

"I'm listening," he said, hearing the sulk in his tone with annoyance. He was the king. How did his aunt manage to make him feel like an errant pageboy?

"Good. This is serious, Marten. There's trouble rumbling in the belly of the Temple, and I don't like the implications."

Marten's eyebrows lifted. This was not what he'd expected. He recalled his earlier meeting. "Brother Padrus asked to speak with me later this evening. What are the odds it's the same thing? He seemed worried, and that's unlike him."

"Ah, Padrus. He's a good man. More world-wise than certain of Chel's servants I could name. See what he has to say, and if he wants to discuss a different matter, then please raise my concerns with him. Rumours of a schism within the Temple are unprecedented in recent times, and call for speedy investigation."

A schism within the Temple? Marten shuddered. Hadn't he dealt with enough turbulence in the kingdom since the attempted coup? Divided loyalties, noble lines decimated, Families left without male leadership, unrest in the guilds. Things were finally settling down, and now this?

He raked one hand through his hair. "I will. And thank you for bringing it to my attention. If there is truth in it, it's extremely worrying, and I'm concerned I've not heard of it before. Do you have any details?"

Leith grimaced. "Sadly, no, just a rumour, and without Hal here, information is taking longer to filter through than it should. I understand his desire to stay with Risada until their child is born, but he should know by now there's never a quiet time for the kingdom's head of security."

Marten hackles rose. Despite Uncle Hal's assurances that he was ready to rule alone, Leith's words implied she believed otherwise. His spine snapped straight. "I have resources of my own. Not as well developed as Uncle Hal's, but I am not without ears in the kingdom."

"Apparently none inside the Temple."

Marten's jaw tightened. "Apparently not. How did *you* hear of it?"

Leith smiled with a predatory edge. "Valaree might be my watchdog, but such close surveillance can work both ways." She heaved a sigh. "Speaking of Valaree, I suppose we should be getting back before she comes looking. I would rather this meeting remained between the two of us."

"Of course, aunt." Marten took the Shivan queen's hand in his, and bent to kiss it. Panic slammed into him.

Cinnamon.

The warm fragrance rose from Leith's wrist. It was all Marten could do not to leap away and call for his guard.

Stupid, stupid, boy! Where's Davi when I need him?

In all likelihood Davi had been as hoodwinked by Leith's manoeuvres as Sister Valaree.

Marten's mind whirled, spinning in concert with the music drifting from the Great Hall. How could Leith be the assassin? When the attack happened, she'd been laid out on a bench, sleeping off the effects of the drug used to block her magic.

Hadn't she?

Marten knew he'd broken the assassin's foot, but although Leith hadn't limped in the days following the coup, perhaps she'd cured the injury with magic once he'd given her the antidote. Marten had no knowledge of what was possible with magic.

Goddess knew, Leith had motive. Her sister—Marten's mother—had been misused by her husband in his oft drunken state. Not the deliberate cruelty of old King Belcastus, but abuse nonetheless. Might Leith have decided to prune out the male line in favour of a fresh start? Cousin Annasala, for instance?

Is she mocking me? Has she sabotaged all my training? What should I do?

"Marten!" Leith snapped him back to the present. "What ails you? You've gone white as a priest's robes."

"That perfume," he blurted. "Do you always wear it?"

Leith scrunched her face up in confusion. "What's the matter? You don't like it? It's very popular at court, I can't believe you haven't encountered it before."

She didn't answer the question, he noticed, even as the ramifications of her statement slammed home. 'Very popular'. What an effective way for the assassin to misdirect his attention.

Did that exonerate Aunt Leith? Possibly. Probably. Marten all but groaned. He didn't know what to think.

His training, true or not, rose to the surface, offering the only solution he could accept.

"Sorry, Aunt Leith. I can't say I have, and I fear it disagrees with me. I must be on my guard when I next meet a lady wearing it." He forced a bright smile. "On the matter of your discontent with Valaree's close attendance, I have a proposal for you. All things considered, I believe now would be a good time for you to return to Shiva. Uncle Hal has confidence I can rule alone, and I think it would be better if there was no question of any outside influences on my decisions. You've been incredibly generous with your time and guidance, but your kingdom and your husband must be missing you by now."

Leith fanned one hand across her upper chest. "You're dismissing me?" Pride flared in the depths of her ruby eyes. "Perhaps Hal's decision wasn't so hasty after all. You're certain you want this?"

Guilt clawed at Marten even as he nodded. His little speech sounded so well considered, and Leith believed his reasoning, when in truth it was an excuse to get rid of her because he wasn't certain he could trust her.

His political tutors would be proud of him. Say one thing while meaning another entirely.

Their shoes crunched on the gravel as he led the way back towards the party, fretting about his decision. Had be made a wise choice? Now he would have no family to turn to for advice, and although he still had the noble council, how many of them genuinely had his best interests at heart?

With his aunt on his arm, he re-entered the ballroom. Sweat ran down his back; it was too late to retract his words now.

3. HUSBAND HUNT

Concealed behind a pair of gossiping ladies, Lady Betha Fontmaness surveyed the dancing throng. She caught a glimpse of King Marten flash past in the arms of his diminutive but formidable aunt, Queen Leith, the Shivan queen.

Such a sweet boy, thought Betha as she watched Marten's impeccable dance moves. *And he blushed so prettily.* The pink tinge that had climbed his neck when he held her hand had set off his sandy brown hair favourably.

Betha smiled indulgently. *Goddess, to be that young and innocent again. Was I ever that naïve? Probably. But such a long time ago.*

Passing the age of twenty-three last solstice had left Betha feeling old. In a short handful of years, she'd buried and avenged her brother, married and mourned a husband, helped foil a coup, and trained to become one of Halnashead's spies.

She scanned the heaving mass of prancing nobles, and spotted her first mission as a fully-fledged operative sneaking out of the hall, led by his aunt. Somehow both Marten and Queen Leith had managed to slip away from their respective guards, and on their own either one of them made an excellent target for assassination. Such a bold move in the game these days could not be discounted.

When Halnashead first sent orders that Betha should 'keep an eye' on the young king for him, she'd deliberated about how she was going to achieve that. But Marten had made it easy for her, throwing this unscheduled fest to celebrate the opening of the new Grand Hall, built over the ashes of the old. Even minor nobles had been invited, so here she was, fulfilling her employer's orders while enjoying the lavish hospitality on offer.

Uncomfortable with the two royals being unprotected, she slipped along the edge of the hall after them, marvelling as she went at how the new structure replicated the old building so accurately it caused cold shudders to ripple down her spine. The phantom smell of smoke filled her lungs, accompanied by a scorching vision of ravening flames and frantic, panicking nobles superimposed for a moment over the joyful throng. A sharp pain in her wrist recalled her tussle with one of the villains as she'd dragged the unconscious Lady Risada from the burning building. She'd barely begun Halnashead's training programme at that time, but she'd acquitted herself well that terrible day. Not only had she saved Risada, the heroine of the day, but by tossing the manacle keys through the flames, she'd also provided Rustam Chalice the means to free himself, and the royal family.

As far as she was aware, no one but Halnashead knew the part she'd played, but she was content to remain in the shadows. It was a familiar and comfortable position, and one of inestimable value to Halnashead and, by extension, the kingdom of Tyr-en.

Reaching the huge doors leading out into the courtyard, Betha caught sight of Marten and Queen Leith standing in the centre of the open space, deep in conversation. Torches lit their surrounds, preventing any threat from sneaking up unseen. Marten should be safe enough, alone with his aunt, yet his body language betrayed extreme anxiety. Had Leith imparted some unsettling news? Or had he sensed danger?

Unease quickened Betha's breathing. Should she remain hidden, or step into the light to offer a distraction?

"Ah, Betha, sweet one, you can't hide from me forever."

Betha jumped. She was so focussed on the pair in the courtyard, she'd been unaware of the man approaching her from behind.

Halnashead would be so *impressed,* she thought

sarcastically. *The spy he sets to watching over his nephew gets herself killed because she can't follow the most basic rules, and stay aware of what's going on around her.*

But the familiar voice reassured her she was not about to meet the goddess this day. The honeyed tone set her insides quivering, even before Ordell's distinctive masculine fragrance wrapped her senses. She wasn't deliberately avoiding her current beau, but the mission took priority, and she'd hoped he wouldn't find her before the king retired.

His warm hand cupped the back of her neck, and his lips grazed her exposed collar bone. Her thoughts scattered. She bit her lip and placed a hand on his, arresting its descent.

"There you are," she said as she spun to face him, blocking his view into the courtyard. "There are so many people here tonight it's no great surprise you didn't find me sooner."

The cool, jasmine-scented night air caressed her exposed back, eliciting a small tremor.

"You're cold." Ordell swept off his short velvet cloak and swung it around to drape her shoulders in one smooth movement. Betha smiled her thanks. She couldn't tell him it had nothing to do with the evening's temperature.

I wish Marten would come back in. He's too exposed out there.

Gravel crunched behind her, and a quick glance proved her prayer answered. When she turned back, she was even more relieved to see both the king's guardsman, Davi, and the priestess, Sister Valaree, approaching together around the edge of the dance floor. The pair had obviously realised their respective charges were no longer amid the swaying crowd, and come in search of them.

Their presence released Betha from her current surveillance, and she linked arms with Ordell, drawing him towards the dance floor.

"Come on, let's make up for lost time."

"My lady." Ordell bowed deeply before sweeping her into the steps of the complex dance. Betha relaxed into his arms, willingly relinquishing control. Ordell was a fabulous dancer. In fact, he was superb at many things, and good looking too, with his dark blonde hair and strong jaw. Betha leaned against his muscular chest and in response he tightened his grip, almost denying her the ability to breathe.

Of all the suitors she'd entertained since Herschel's death, Ordell was by far the best candidate. A second son, he was unlikely to inherit his family's lands, so marrying a widow with a small but secure estate was a good option for him.

In fact, they seemed perfect for each other.

If only he wasn't so gentle when we make love. He seems to think I'll break. Oh well, I suppose I'll educate him to my tastes eventually. It didn't take too long to train Herschel once I discovered what pleased me.

A pang of grief clutched her heart as she recalled her husband.

Herschel, dear Herschel. How scared I was, when they told me I was marrying an old man who had already buried two wives. Yet you were the perfect partner for me, your appetites matching mine, and sometimes I regret pushing you so hard, physically. But you died a happy man.

Memory tightened her grip on Ordell's arms. He drew his head back, raising an eyebrow in question.

"Would you like to retire?" His voice deepened to the edge of husky.

Betha flashed a coquettish smile at him, and allowed herself to be led from the hall. Her suite was on the first floor, and as they ascended the grand curved staircase, arm in arm, she took a brief glance back, reassured by the sight of Marten heading for the banquet hall with Davi two steps behind. Her duty was done for the night.

* * * * * *

"Have you considered my proposal?" asked Ordell as soon as the doors to the plush suite closed behind them. His etiquette was impeccable as he settled her in a comfortable chair and waved a servant with a wine pitcher over to fill the glass he held for her, but his demeanour spoke of impatience.

Have I? Betha considered. *He's so ideal, in so many ways. By far the best yet. Why am I delaying?*

Deep inside, Betha suspected her hesitancy was fuelled by her independent streak. She'd ruled her estate alone for more than two years now, and she'd not found it onerous. Rather, she enjoyed the challenges it brought. Was she really ready to give up that autonomy?

Tradition said she must. It was not a woman's role to head a Family, and whilst her labourers, and the craft guilds resident on her lands, had put up with the situation during the unprecedented aftermath of the coup, there was a limit to their forbearance. There was nothing they could do about it legally, but their discontent with the situation was becoming ever more obvious. They wanted her married, with a man in control and heirs on the way to secure their future.

Betha understood their position, and yet a spark of rebellion within her refused to be quenched. If she was capable of feats such as those she'd performed during the climax of the coup, why could she not rule her own House? If only they knew how capable she was.

But no. Her role was to remain secret, she accepted that, and so tradition must prevail. Hence the husband hunt.

"Betha, my sweet, are you dreaming, perhaps, of our wedding night?" Ordell leaned down until his words whispered only for her ears. "I can give you a preview now, if you like?"

Betha's skin tingled. "I'd like that." She ran a fingernail up his arm. "It might help me make up my mind."

He leaned in, nuzzling her neck. Betha prepared to yield. Perhaps it would be for the best, after all. Heat flushed through her, and she wriggled within his embrace.

"Ordell," she murmured, "the servants. They have orders to clear up."

His impatient huff gusted across her cheek. "Very well. But when *I* am lord, they'll do it in the morning." He straightened. "You! Get finished, quickly now."

Betha's maid and the manservant supplied with the suite scurried around, tidying the remnants of an earlier snack and several clothing changes. Ordell's fingers grazed the nape of Betha's neck, back and forth, back and forth, palpable impatience heating the air between them.

Distracted, Betha foresaw the impending collision a fraction too late to prevent it. In their hurry to complete their duties, her maid and the manservant collided. An entire decanter of ruby wine flew from the man's grasp, spraying Betha's azure gown and Ordell's white breeches, painting the couple with lurid splashes of red, as if they'd attended a bloodbath.

"Imbecile!"

Ordell's shriek of fury rocked Betha both physically and mentally. She put a placating hand to his chest. "It was an accident, Ordell. Clothes can be replaced."

The big man shrugged her off to grab the hapless servant by his collar. "You'll pay for this insult. I'll make sure you never work in the palace again. Or anywhere else, for that matter!"

With each word Ordell shook the man harder and harder until he lost his footing, and ended up dangling, suspended by his clothing. His face turned puce, and his mouth opened and closed soundlessly as his fingers scrabbled at Ordell's fists.

Betha surged to her feet, anger overtaking shock. "Ordell! Release him at once. It was an *accident*!"

Refusing to let go, Ordell's jaw tightened as he continued to raise the servant until the man teetered on tiptoe. "Don't concern yourself with one such as this, my sweet. These peasants need keeping in order, and once we're married, I'll remove that responsibility from your dainty shoulders."

"Put him down *now*!" Betha roared. She'd rarely had cause to use her prodigious lung capacity to such extent in recent years, but she still recalled the impact it had had on her husband's guard dogs when they ignored her quiet requests.

Like the dogs, Ordell responded instantly, dropping his victim. The gasping man gathered his feet beneath him and scurried out the door, closely followed by Betha's terrified maid.

Ordell rotated his shoulders and drew a deep breath before turning to face his prospective bride. "Betha, sweet one," he said, gently clasping her shoulders in his big hands. "You mustn't upset yourself so. Soon all this crushing responsibility will be mine to bear, and all you'll need worry about is taking care of your pretty face and your pretty gowns, and our children when they arrive. I swear it, you will never have to deal with servants again."

Betha stared at him with wide eyes. How could she have been so blind? Dismay swamped her. She'd almost made the most terrible mistake of her life, shackling herself to this bully. She shrugged his hands away. "If that was an example of the way you'd treat our staff and labourers, then you have absolutely no idea how to run an estate."

Ordell began to speak, but Betha held up an imperious hand, hoping he wouldn't notice how it trembled. "No," she said, "you've just proven you don't have the temperament I need in a husband." Her short-lived rush of anger gave way to bitter disappointment. "I think you should leave. Now."

Ordell gaped at her. "But—"

Betha shook her head. "No. No buts, Ordell. It won't work. I can't tell you how sorry that makes me, but better we know now than after we've announced a betrothal we have to cancel."

Ordell's posture deflated. He made one final attempt to reverse his fortunes. "But I love you, Betha, sweet one. Doesn't that mean anything to you?"

Tears leaked onto Betha's cheeks. "Don't. Just don't. Go now. *Please.*"

With slumped shoulders, Ordell dragged himself on heavy feet across the rich carpet. The double doors swung shut behind him with a painful finality.

Betha's chest constricted. *Did he truly love me?* A sob escaped her control. *I honestly believed he was the one. Stupid, stupid girl. How will I ever know if a man loves me for me, or just for my inheritance?*

She tottered the few steps back to her chair before her legs gave way. Tucking her knees up to her chin, she buried her face and allowed the tears to flow. Memories spun round and round of Ordell and his cultured wooing, his charming words of love, the breathless excitement his touch imparted.

His violent treatment of a servant not even in his employ, and his look of bewilderment at her disgust.

It was my only choice. I could never inflict such a man on those who look to me for support and guidance, as well as service and employment. Oh Chel, could you not have shown me his true nature sooner? Before I let him into my heart?

With a loud sob, Betha smothered the pain in her chest and straightened up. She scrubbed a sleeve across her wet cheeks. Weeping over a broken future would get her nowhere. She must begin again.

At least she was in a good place to search for a husband. Most of the eligible noblemen in the kingdom had been summoned to attend Marten's impromptu fest, and somewhere out there must be her ideal match. She simply hadn't encountered him yet.

In the meantime, she had Halnashead's commission to immerse herself in.

Marten was about to gain a new shadow.

4. PADRUS

As the penultimate chime before midnight faded away, a discreet knock on the outer door to Marten's chambers announced Brother Padrus's arrival. Marten signalled Davi to open the door, and the guardsman confirmed the priest was alone before permitting him to enter.

Marten ran a critical eye over his visitor's weary posture. "Wine, brother?" he asked. "Or something stronger?"

Padrus smiled. "Your Majesty is too kind. I fear the news I bring tonight warrants a stronger brew than we usually share. Brandy, perhaps?"

Marten nodded briskly before pouring generous measures of the spirit into two glasses. He'd already dismissed the servants, wanting no ears to overhear what passed between them this night. Davi would remain; anything that might threaten Marten was legitimately his bodyguard's province.

He placed the glass of amber liquid into Padrus's hand, misliking the tremors rocking the old man's grip.

"Come, sit," Marten invited, and led the way across the spacious receiving room and on into his private sitting room. To one side of the inner door they passed a broad, circular table on top of which squatted a rectangular shape draped in a deep red, heavy fabric. Marten studiously ignored the tiny jolt, like a pinprick, that stabbed him in the gut. Even shrouded by its insulating cover he could not escape the unholy impulse to open the box.

Magic.

Naming it, 'Chel's Casket', placed it squarely within the Temple's jurisdiction, but Marten felt uncomfortable with that label. Where did magic end and religion begin? He was honestly unsure.

Preoccupied with the impending birth of his child, Halnashead had forgotten to consider a safer place for the box before Marten returned to Darshan, and Marten was at a loss as to know what to do with it. Hence, it continued to sit in his rooms until his uncle's return.

Marten whispered a brief prayer to Chel for the safe delivery of his new cousin, before halting at a pair of upright chairs arranged beside a small table. Padrus waited until Marten sat down before lowering himself with a faint groan.

Marten frowned. "You really should see a healer."

"I am grateful for Your Majesty's concern, but my aches and pains are a welcome reminder of how much life Chel has blessed me with. And besides, even the best healers cannot treat old age." Padrus held his glass aloft, swirling its contents to release a fruity aroma. He inhaled appreciatively. "This, on the other hand, has a wonderful medicinal effect." He raised the glass in salute to the king before taking a sip. "Ahh, that's good, but I should convey my concerns before I partake of any more."

Marten took a fortifying swallow of his own drink, tracing the warmth and evolving aftertaste as it spread down his gullet. Some experiences should be savoured to the full, especially when they were soon to be soured by unwelcome news.

"Go on," he invited with reluctance. Padrus *never* asked for anything stronger than wine. How bad could this news be?

Padrus drew a heavy breath before continuing. "There have been too many minor miracles of late."

Marten frowned. "What do you mean? Surely any miracle is a blessing from Chel?"

"Indeed, that should be true, but I am not fully convinced these events all originate from the goddess."

Marten clamped a grip on his spiralling apprehension. He hoped he'd misunderstood Padrus's implication. "Please, explain."

Padrus stared at his drink in silence for a while, before

suddenly raising the glass and downing the contents in one gulp. Marten began to sweat.

"I am loath to draw such a grim conclusion," Padrus admitted, "but the nature of these so-called miracles, and the people who have performed them—I fear we may be witnessing the rebirth of the Cult of Charin."

Blood thumped through Marten's head, promising a massive headache. He joined Padrus in draining his glass. "I'd say I don't believe it, but with all that's happened these last few years we'd be stupid to discount the possibility. You can single out those responsible for these 'miracles'?"

Padrus sighed. "Mostly young acolytes—those easily led. But a few senior clerics also, and that frightens me more than I can express, my liege. I'd like to believe we'd left such hubris behind on the old continent and consigned the Cult of Charin to history. But time has dulled the tales of horror, and the lessons so rigidly enforced when our ancestors landed here. Magic has become the evil, not the men who practised it. That the Cult of Charin was behind many of the vilest atrocities seems to have gradually bled from the tales." He grimaced. "Or perhaps it has been deliberately expunged over generations. We may unwittingly have brought a handful of Charin's devotees with us on the ships. Now there's a highly disturbing notion we must force ourselves to consider."

Marten pushed to his feet and began to pace until Padrus's disapproving stare halted him. With reluctance, he returned to his seat.

"Your Majesty knows it is unwise to display such unsettled behaviour."

"I know, I know. But Uncle Hal does it all the time."

"Yet you are not your uncle; you are the king."

"As if I need reminding of that," Marten muttered, knowing Padrus's hearing was less than sharp. This time, however, he heard.

"Then I suggest you refrain from prompting the necessity, Your Majesty. You have granted me your friendship, but above all else you will always be my king, and it is my duty to advise you, even when it is something you would rather not hear."

Marten bowed his head, accepting the rebuke before returning to the worrisome subject. "What makes you think Charin's Cult is behind this? What's the nature of these miracles?"

"Small displays of power, for the most part. The destruction of an implement believed to have been *made* by a magic wielder. The incineration of a stone shrine built without Temple approval. An acolyte who can light a candle without touching the wick. None of the actions evil in intent, but witnesses report lightning jumping from the clerics' fingertips, disturbingly reminiscent of the preferred method of execution Charin's devotees used to employ."

"And no one else has made this connection?"

Padrus shook his head. "Few study the old texts, these days. Fewer still those who believe such powers might still exist. The Temple teaches that Chel guided us through the cleansing path of fire on the old continent to destroy the corrupt, and this bounteous new land is our reward. If that is true, then such wickedness should have been destroyed forever."

"A view you don't share."

Padrus spread his liver-spotted, tremulous hands. "I am but one man, sire. Perhaps you should consult with others to gain a more balanced view."

"I'd rather investigate further without alerting anyone to your suspicions, and I would be grateful for a list of those you believe to be involved. But for now, go and get some rest."

The elderly priest made two attempts to rise before Marten could bear to watch no longer. He stood up and put one arm beneath Padrus's, levering him upright.

Padrus creaked a shallow bow. "My thanks, sire, for your assistance, your ear, and your brandy. I pray we have many more such consultations over less distressing subjects. I shall bring you a preliminary list in the morning."

Marten scowled. "I have meetings all day, and I'd rather not have such sensitive information left unattended. Our regular session is scheduled for the following morning; let's keep to that and not give anyone cause to be suspicious by changing routine. In the meantime, I'll consider how we might proceed. My thanks to you, Padrus, for bringing this to my attention. Queen Leith has suspicions of her own, though I don't believe she'd reached the same conclusion as you. Yet."

Padrus raised a thin eyebrow. "Perhaps she might attend our meeting. If she has additional information it could prove useful."

"Unfortunately, Queen Leith will be on her way home by then, so we'll have to make do without her counsel." He nodded to Davi to open the door. "I'm sure we'll manage fine on our own."

5. WEIGHT OF RESPONSIBILITY

Marten rubbed his temples. Last night's headache lingered in a dull ache behind his left eye. What he truly wanted was to lie down and sleep until it quit. Instead, a whole day of unavoidable meetings stretched ahead, promising to fill his life with tedium, and the likelihood of a pounding head by nightfall.

If only Uncle Hal was around, he'd deal with some of it for me.

Marten gave himself a mental slap. He'd been coached for this his entire life. How would it look if he requested help now? He'd assured his aunt he was ready to cope alone, when he'd told her to leave, and she'd taken him at his word.

Queen Leith had departed early, successfully evading her Temple watchdog by riding out before the sun cleared the horizon. Sister Valaree's frantic search of the palace had amused Marten for a short while, before he'd relented and informed her of the Shivan queen's withdrawal. He suspected the cleric would pursue his aunt before long, and wished Leith a speedy journey. Sister Valaree might be agreeable to the eye, but Marten could well imagine how bothersome it would be to live under her constant surveillance.

Returning his attention to the matter before him, he stretched out each arm in turn to inspect the pinned up sleeves of his new tunic.

"Thank you Marganie, that looks much better." The willowy seamstress peered at him with her head cocked to one side. A row of pins sticking out of her pursed mouth prevented her from answering with more than a nod. Wisps of greying blonde hair escaped her knotted up tresses as her head bobbed, and Marten noticed for the first time how much

Marganie had aged in the past two years.

Like a lot of us. The coup didn't let many escape unscathed.

Marganie had been making his clothes for as long as he could recall. She was another of those constants in his life, like Uncle Hal, and Brother Padrus, that Marten was beginning to realise would not be around forever. The very idea was unsettling, and one he determined to ignore until he could no longer do so.

He glanced over his shoulder, hoping to catch a glimpse of Marganie's assistant, but the buxom blonde had withdrawn after delivering her armful of garments. Marten huffed with disappointment. As distractions went, the girl, Nonni, rated highly in his estimation. She possessed curves in all the best places, along with a talent for displaying tantalising glimpses of pale skin whenever boredom was about to overwhelm him.

Resigning himself to tedium, he shook both wrists. "Perhaps the cuffs a touch shorter?" he suggested.

Marganie removed the pins from her mouth. "This is formal attire, Your Majesty, not every day wear. You won't be riding or practicing swordplay in it. Longer cuffs are more elegant."

"Marganie, I bow to your expertise. Davi, do you have an equally formal outfit for me to wear today? Because if you do, I'll ask you to change it for something more comfortable."

Davi's muffled snort of laughter brought a smile to Marten's lips. Since his abrupt elevation to king's bodyguard, Davi had embraced the secondary aspect of his role with enthusiasm. Marten had not anticipated how adept his new guardsman would turn out to be as a valet. With flair and taste uncommon for a soldier, and a sunny disposition, Davi brought humour and warmth to Marten's life of unrelenting duty. His existence would have been duller if Davi had not been the one to find him in the palace corridors that terrible day.

Unbidden, Marten's fingers strayed to his neck to rub the

raised ridge of scar tissue. Sometimes, on the edge of sleep or daydream, his mind conjured the scent of cinnamon, jolting him to sweating wakefulness. In the early days, he'd seen the question in Davi's eyes whenever the momentary panic gripped him, but as time passed and he held his silence, he supposed his bodyguard had concluded it was recollection of the coup that sometimes rattled his composure.

If only he knew the truth. But no, I'm glad I never confided in anyone. She's not tried again. I guess it was just a random opportunity that slipped from her grasp. Too dangerous for another attempt.

The thought comforted him as Marganie stripped him of the unfinished outfit, and Davi replaced it with a well-worn familiar one. Marten barely noted the seamstress's exit as Davi tugged a velvet tunic over his head.

"Comfortable enough for you?"

"Thank you, yes. You always seem to know what I want even before I do."

"That's my job, sire."

"And you're very good at it. Just don't forget your main task is keeping me alive."

Davi placed a hand to his chest, a mock affronted expression widening his bright blue eyes. "As if I would! I have no wish to return to the ranks, sire, believe me."

Marten detected a slight edge to the jocular comment. "You didn't fit in? Why am I not surprised: you're far too well-versed in fashion and cuisine for the average soldier." He cocked his head. "Or is it something else? You have a secret you wish to confide in me?"

Davi lowered his gaze to the laces crisscrossing the front of Marten's jacket. He drew them tighter until they closed the opening almost up to his neck. "No sire." Davi shook his head, gaze fixed on Marten's scar. "Not unless you want to exchange confidences."

His final tug at the upper laces closed the collar, hiding the blemish from view.

"You want your king's secrets? What, you plan a new

career in espionage?"

Davi's grin was infectious. "Foiled! What gave me away, sire?"

"I have my spies, you know. Nothing escapes my notice." Marten became serious. "Speaking of which, I haven't heard from my man in Risada's House for a while. I'd like to know when my uncle might be thinking of returning—arrange a courier, will you?"

"Yes, sire, as soon as you are safely installed in the council chamber, I'll see to it."

Marten groaned. "Oh, how I hate council meetings. All my lords are such pompous wind bags."

Davi smothered another snort of laughter. "Be that as it may, you can't rule your kingdom without them. You know what your uncle would say."

"I know, I know. Keep them sweet and keep them in order. Listen to them but always check everything they say. Preferably have the knowledge before you go in there." He shook his head. "I'm trying, but my spy network will never rival Uncle Hal's."

"Nor should it, sire. That's why he's your spymaster."

Marten squared his shoulders. "Ah well, can't put it off any longer. How do I look?"

"Ready for anything they throw at you, sire. I'll always make sure of that."

On impulse, Marten clapped Davi on the shoulder. Etiquette demanded he refrain from touching and being touched by any but immediate family, but Davi had slipped into his affections like the brother he'd never had. Here, in the privacy of his own rooms, it felt good to disregard protocol.

"And I will always rely on that. Come on, time to be a soldier again."

With a quick grin and a bow, Davi donned his gear and strapped on his sword.

"Ready?"

"Ready."

Walking beside Marten, Davi's head swivelled constantly, sweeping the corridors for hazards both in front and behind as they traversed the private wing of the palace.

Marten squinted, plagued by the brightness slanting through the windows. His shoulders hunched, sending stabbing pains into his skull. He kept his face lowered, turning away from the cheery summer sunlight encroaching on his inescapably dreary day. He and Davi rounded the corner leading to the top of the king's private staircase. Marten blinked hard. A shaft of sunlight glistened strangely along one border of the brown speckled rug at the edge of the landing.

"Stop!" Marten's hand shot out to grab Davi by the shoulder. His bodyguard spun around, seeking the threat. Marten pointed. "It might be nothing but…"

"Stay here," Davi instructed, and bent to inspect the oddity. He drew his sword and, using the point, lifted the nearest corner. He stiffened.

"What is it?" Marten demanded.

Davi slid his weapon back into its sheath before grasping the rug with both hands. He slid it to one side, revealing the slick surface beneath. Marten ventured forward and wiped one finger across the shiny, treacherous boards. His heart thumped against his ribs.

"If I'd stepped on that…"

"You'd likely be at the bottom by now, possibly with your neck broken. No one else uses these stairs; this was meant for you."

Davi drew breath to call the guards from the hallway below, but Marten grabbed his arm. "No," he said, with a shake of his head for emphasis.

"But sire…"

Marten swallowed the rock lodged in his throat. "I won't have anyone else know about this."

"But—"

Davi paused, then his bewilderment sharpened. "This isn't the first time, is it?"

Unable to hide the truth any longer, Marten rubbed a finger around his neck. "No, but I won't discuss it here. Later. After this meeting."

Davi stared at him with a closed expression, but asked no more questions. His tight jaw was the only evidence of his frustration as he led the way around the treacherously greased floorboards, and on down the stairs. His eyes scanned each step for further danger.

Marten concentrated on descending the stairs safely, not quite trusting his shaking legs. Was it the same assassin? Or did someone else want him dead too? Perhaps a still undiscovered traitor from the time of the rebellion. His stomach churned.

How in Charin's hell do I find an anonymous assassin? If it is *the same woman, she's hidden successfully from my spies for over two years.*

He gritted his teeth.

I suppose now I'll have to tell Uncle Hal. I can just imagine how he's going to take that.

* * * * * * *

"This situation is intolerable!" Lord Edlund emphasised his disapproval with a meaty thump of his fist on the heavy oak table.

Marten winced. Right at that moment, he would have preferred to be almost anywhere but this council chamber filled with discontented, belligerent nobles. He had more important things to consider. When would the assassin strike next? What form would the attack take? How disappointed would Uncle Hal be in him, concealing such a monumental secret from his spymaster? The discussion at hand seemed so petty in comparison, yet it was his duty to moderate and address the concerns of his lords.

Lord Edlund continued to hold forth at high volume. "Craft masters thinking they can bargain for higher wages, labourers wanting a say in how our estates are run. Who do they think they are? I demand you allow us to *do* something about it!"

Bushy grey moustaches bristling with self-importance, the portly lord of the Seventh House glanced up and down the long oval council table, eliciting approving nods and murmurs from many of the gathered Family seniors. Marten gathered his thoughts, and waited until they'd finished their mutual ego-stroking. The open defiance written on so many faces at daring to question their sovereign, distracted him enough from his concerns it almost made him laugh out loud.

They'd never *dare such a challenge if Uncle Hal was here. Do they really think I can be pushed around so easily?*

Marten squared his shoulders. He'd survived an assassination attempt. Pushy, self-important lords were a minor inconvenience in comparison. "You. Demand." He enunciated quietly, allowing the full weight of his disapproval to bear on each word, dragging each syllable down like mud-sodden boots in a bog. Uncertainty flickered across several faces.

Lord Edlund was never quick to take a hint. "If your uncle was here, he'd advise you to listen to your elders." The man puffed his chest out, obviously expecting the support of his peers, then deflated when none appeared. "Your Majesty," he added belatedly.

Marten permitted the silence to stretch until the rustling of fabric evinced uneasy fidgeting. He rose to his feet. "Prince Halnashead is otherwise engaged, and my other former advisor, Queen Leith, has returned to her own land. They have both deemed me ready to assume sole responsibility for my kingdom. Do any of you disagree with their assessment?"

All along the table, heads wagged from side to side, even Lord Edlund's, though his high colour and grumpy expression suggested he would have favoured dissent if he'd had backing.

Satisfied, Marten sat back down. "Lord Edlund, your observations are in accord with what we have all seen growing since the coup. However, dealing with this situation is not as simple as flogging a few peasants and removing privileges. This is all a part of the changing structure of our society, and needs to be guided, not throttled."

A small, dark haired man, midway along the table stood up. "All that is true, Your Majesty, *if* we are to allow such perilous change." The quiet, reasonable tone of Lord Urien contrasted favourably with Lord Edlund's bluster, yet his words supported the other man's views.

"As those responsible for the coup have all been rooted out and dealt with, why can we not return to our former ways? Undoubtedly a few additional safeguards would be advisable, but I'm sure now we've seen magic at work we'll be able to identify it before it reaches such dangerous proportions again."

With a satisfied smile playing around the corners of his mouth, Lord Urien retook his seat.

Marten frowned. *Such false confidence! Why does he think we'd be any more able to recognise magic a second time around? The whole point is that skilful magic is so subtle no one can spot it.*

Unease crawled over Marten's skin. He rubbed his nose and sneezed. Glancing around the council chamber, he located a bouquet of flowers displayed inside one window. If he'd had any magic of his own, he would have obliterated the blooms with the heat of his glare.

Movement at the far end of the table caught his eye, and even as a second sneeze seized him, he made out the slight figure of Lady Betha Fontmaness striding towards the window embrasure. Deftly, she scooped the offending vase and its contents up, and carried them to the far door, where she handed them out to a startled guard. Without a word, she returned to her seat at the bottom of the table.

She met Marten's eye, more brazenly than he was accustomed to from a lady. His neck warmed, and he squashed the urge to return her smile. Instead, he acknowledged his thanks with the barest bob of his head.

Returning to the matter at hand, he settled his attention on

Lord Urien. "We cannot go backward. For centuries we have lived in ignorant isolation, certain the younger kingdoms were of no consequence to us. And yet they've not only thrived, but built their own societies, none of which conform to our laws or tenets. We relied on the mountains to guard our borders, but now we know that security is an illusion." He stared down the length of the table, once again catching Lady Betha's eye. The tiniest hint of a smile bolstered his confidence. "My Lords, we have no choice. Change has been forced upon us and we must turn our attentions forward."

In the midst of a wave of muttering that might have been either approval or dissent, Lord Urien rose again, and bowed crisply. "Your Majesty's conclusions have merit, but I would raise another concern at this juncture; one which may impact upon your undoubtedly wise plans."

Can I not deal with one thing at a time? Marten drew a deep, thankfully pollen-free, breath, and waved an open hand towards Urien. "Please, enlighten me."

Urien delayed a moment, raking his dark gaze over the assembled nobility, ensuring he had everybody's full attention before delivering his information. "It cannot have escaped the notice of anyone here that our population is neither large, nor growing. For too long we have made the assumption this was a result of people moving away from Tyr-en to form the other kingdoms. But I took it upon myself to task the Temple scholars with studying the situation, and their disturbing conclusion is that our lack of manpower results from insufficient births each year.

"To compound this issue amongst the nobility, with so many Family seniors killed during the coup, many Houses have been left in the hands of widows. While some," he inclined his head graciously towards Lady Betha, "have managed their estates with admirable efficiency, others are barely coping, and none—" he glanced again at Betha, this time with less approval, "—are producing heirs. Much of the unrest to which our esteemed fellow, Lord Edlund, refers, is surely a direct consequence of these two unsettling factors."

He raised a hand to forestall the rising cries of support. "The solution to this problem appears simple to me, sire. We must find suitable husbands for these women, to take a firm grip on the reins of their estates, and breed a new generation. This will quell the unrest brought about by such an abnormal state of affairs and mitigate the concern regarding the question of accepting magic into our society."

Marten's cheeks flamed. He wavered between outrage that Urien had dared co-opt Temple scholars for his own personal use, and consternation at their conclusion. Discussions in the past about lack of manpower had always centred around those leaving to join the younger kingdoms, not about birth rates. A shocking notion rocked him.

We never noticed because we consider such things the province of women, not worthy of our attention. A bitter taste coated his tongue. *I'm going to have to do something about this; something that's not going to make me popular with our unmarried ladies.*

He kept his gaze deliberately averted from Betha. While he knew she, at least, was actively seeking a husband, this new information demanded a rapid conclusion to that search, and he could well imagine Betha's dismay at the idea of the self-important boors gathered around this table decreeing whom she must marry. Marten determined if anyone was going to make that choice for her, it would be him.

Lord Edlund chose that moment to confirm his pomposity, targeting Betha as the only woman present.

"An excellent proposal, Urien. Nigh on half the Families have no male representative at this time, but we don't see their women here, trying to meddle in affairs beyond their competence."

Betha's gasp of outrage intruded into the uncomfortable hush that followed Edlund's speech.

Marten sat paralyzed for a moment. *How dare he? Betha has as much right to be here as any of them, and I wouldn't be at all surprised to find her estates run more efficiently than many of theirs.*

Praying Betha would forgive him, and determined to hold a private discussion with her as soon as it could be arranged, Marten rose to his feet. Silence spread outward as all eyes turned toward him. Suddenly he understood how a performer felt when they stepped onto a stage.

He smothered a moment of panic. *I can do this, Uncle Hal. I can do this.*

He thrust his chest out. "Your suggestion is noted, Urien," he began with a slight frown directed toward the slender lord. "In fact, I will take charge of this situation personally; you need trouble yourself no further."

He transferred his attention to Edlund. "I regret, my lord, that your experiences of women have been so poor, you feel it necessary to denigrate the intelligence of them all. I've noticed you don't bring your wife to court. Can it be you're worried she might say something to prove her wit?"

Smothered laughter rippled around the table. Edlund's face turned purple, and Marten held up a hand to head off the brewing outbreak.

"My lords, I thank you for bringing your concerns to my attention. Rest assured I shall give your suggestions my full and immediate consideration, and take what actions I deem appropriate. May Chel guide us all."

The formal blessing dissolved the council, forestalling any further comments, and Marten strode from the room with his eyes fixed on the escape offered by the door. As he passed Betha, deliberately not meeting her gaze, he could feel the heat of her angry glare rake him. His cheeks flushed again, and he walked faster.

Foregoing custom, he slammed the doors open with such force it startled the guards outside. Cool air washed over his face. Never had he been so glad to see Davi waiting to escort him to his suite where he could shut out politics and the spectre of all the women he was about to enrage.

There was, of course, still a difficult conversation awaiting him when he and his bodyguard were alone, but even that seemed preferable to facing Betha or one of her fellow widows with instruction on whom they were to marry.

With eyes downcast, alert for anything unusual beneath his feet, he stomped along the palace corridors. Each step jarred his aching head, adding to a mounting fury he made no effort to quell. Despite his best efforts and intentions, he suspected Lords Edlund and Urien of manipulating him, herding him down a path of their choosing. Were they working together? He couldn't be certain, but those two would bear closer scrutiny. Marten made a mental note to assign spies to watch them both.

The guards outside Marten's suite swung the double doors open in the nick of time for him to stride through without breaking pace. Davi followed him into the reception room and took up his position inside the door, reading his king's mood well enough to know now was not the time to raise the subject of their delayed conversation.

Marten ripped off his formal tunic and flung it on the floor. In the privacy of his rooms, with only Davi as witness, he let rip a growl of rage, and proceeded to vent his anger on a desk of unimportant papers. Heaps of scrolls and loose pages, writing implements and ornaments flew into the air as he swept an arm across the polished wooden surface. He slapped the flat of one hand down hard, in his mind's eye seeing not the unyielding table, but the rounded flesh of a woman's backside. One woman in particular filled his inner vision, but he quashed that image before it fully formed. Betha was so slender, she probably didn't have enough spare flesh to fill his palm, let alone his whole hand.

"Davi."

"Yes, sire."

"I wish to entertain one of my special friends tonight. Gemma, perhaps? Please convey my invitation."

"Yes, sire."

Marten scanned his bodyguard's face, but as ever detected no condemnation there. Davi well knew how Marten and his 'special friends' indulged their passions; there was no hiding such things from a man who shadowed the king's every movement. At first, Marten had been embarrassed. As a youth he'd had more freedom to keep his assignations secret. But once he'd ascended the throne, all that had changed, and Davi had proven to be the ideal guardian of this particular confidence; total discretion with not a flicker of disapproval. It occurred to Marten this might have bearing on the personal secret he suspected Davi of concealing, but so far, he was content to return the courtesy by not asking any questions.

After today's events, that might change.

As Davi reached for the door handle, Marten added, "Please also tell her I am feeling—energetic. If she would rather decline, then try Nonni instead."

With a short bow, Davi slipped out. Marten heard him issuing firm instructions to the door guard to not admit anyone until he returned, followed by the diminishing tread of his boots as he went to deliver his king's message.

Finally alone, Marten indulged in a bout of agitated pacing. The hidden defiance of his etiquette tutors sent a heady mix of guilt and satisfaction sweeping through him, bringing a dull throbbing to his temples. This Charin-benighted headache refused to submit, and he had other duties to attend to before he could meet with Gemma, or Nonni, or whoever Davi secured for his assignation that evening. Marten's fists clenched and unclenched, bringing the phantom sensation of a whip handle to his palm. His lips drew into a tight smile.

Even if he could not rid himself of his fears, or his headache, at least he would be able to distract himself sufficiently to ignore them for a while.

6. HEALING

Betha slammed her fists into the wall with such force, three knuckles split, leaving bloody smears on the pastel yellow paint.

The biting pain felt good. Clean. She punched the wall again.

"My lady! My lady, please stop," pleaded Quart, Betha's seneschal.

Betha ignored him and continued to pummel the wall. "How." Right punch. "Could he." Left punch. "Do that?" Right punch. "To me?" Left punch.

One of her fingers finally succumbed to the abuse, the long bone snapping with an audible *crack*. Betha huffed and glowered at the damaged digit, welcoming the sharp sting.

"Please, my lady, what has the wall done to offend you?" Quart stood beside her, wringing his hands together.

Betha smothered a small snort of almost hysterical laughter. Almost, but not quite. Despite her apparently frenzied actions, she was fully aware of what she was doing. With a final glare at the blood-stained wall, she turned her back on it and folded her fingers into a fist. Pain flashed along her nerves, jagged lightning forks of white-hot power.

Power only she could embrace.

With deliberation, she put that moment aside for a while, permitting the discomfort to build.

"I'm sorry, Quart, I'm vexed that the king has chosen to select my next husband for me. I suppose he thinks he's saving me from the council doing it. Which I suppose he is, but I don't have to like it. Why should any man choose who I marry?"

Quart raised his grey eyebrows. "My lady? Begging your pardon, but your first marriage was arranged by your grandfather. Surely this is not so different?"

Betha shook her head, snatching a gasp as the movement jarred her fractured finger. She spied blood dripping from her fists, and raised them. She jerked her chin at her shawl, hanging on the back of a settle. "Hand me that, would you, Quart. I don't want to make any more of a mess; it takes too much explaining. And I suppose it isn't, I simply expected as ruler of my own House to have some freedom of choice. Dammit! If it hadn't been for Urien, this wouldn't be happening."

She took the shawl from Quart and wrapped it around her hands, deliberately jostling the damaged limb. Her mouth stretched into a smile of anticipation as pain pulsed up her arm. "Give me a moment, and I'll explain, but I'd better do something about this before anyone comes in and sees. Perhaps you could wipe that wall down for me, please?"

Quart turned his full attention to removing all evidence of Betha's altercation with the wall while she slipped into her bedchamber and sat down at her dressing table. With her hands held above the wooden surface—so much easier to clean than a bedspread, or a rug—she unwrapped and inspected the split flesh of her knuckles, the swelling already starting to distend her fingers.

She couldn't recall when she'd last indulged in such a violent tantrum. It was as well Quart understood her. He wasn't entirely comfortable with the knowledge, but his loyalty to her Family secured his silence, and Betha took care to ensure he did not have to witness anything illegal first hand.

Of the royal court, only Prince Halnashead knew her secret, and he prized her talent for the unique gift it was. A spy with no fear of pain could be sent into situations where another might falter.

Thought of the prince brought her full circle, back to Marten and his assumption of responsibility for the unmarried ladies of the court. Betha's shoulders slumped at the prospect of having another husband foisted on her without any say in the matter.

At least Herschel became accommodating once we got to know each other. Perhaps the next one will be the same. She considered the candidates, many of whom she'd already dismissed from consideration. *Though I need to speak with Marten before he comes to any decisions; his offer at the ball sounded as though he'd be amenable to discussion.* She smiled. *Yes, that's the answer; ask for an audience as soon as may be. So, better get cleaned up.*

Spreading her bloody hands across the table top, Betha pressed her weight forward onto her palms. Throbbing discomfort greeted her action, and she focussed her mind on the tempo of the thumping pulse, drawing her consciousness inward, narrowing it down onto the source of the pain. She closed her eyes, the better to savour it, and her world became darkness lanced with sanguine flashes. Her heart raced in anticipation, and her skin tingled, growing hypersensitive, waiting, begging for sensation. The soft fabric of her dress felt too coarse where it slipped gently across her shoulders as she breathed.

Power gathered, stoking a heat born in her chest. Ripples of energy spread outward, vibrating through the layers of her body until her skin felt as flushed as if she'd stood naked all day beneath the midsummer sun. Sweat sprang from her pores, trickling down her back.

With the ease of long practice, she drew the excess heat from her surface and concentrated it into a writhing mass, like a miniature sun, held for an infinitesimal moment as she aimed it, and then unleashed it upon her injured hands.

Ecstasy cascaded along her nerves, washing away all traces of pain, transforming hurt into such pleasure it overwhelmed her mind and body, flooding her awareness, making her gasp for air like a lover in the throes of orgasm.

Remoulded by the power innate to her body, the broken bone knitted, lacerated knuckles smoothed over, swelling vanished. Her hands spasmed, nails clawing the table top as an almost unbearable bliss swept through her again and again. She clung to the sensation greedily, prolonging the rapture only her personal, private magic could bestow.

When eventually she could hold onto the fading echoes of euphoria no longer, and her lungs ceased to suck air like frantic bellows, she opened her eyes to inspect her slender, elegant hands. Using the already ruined shawl, she wiped the remainder of the blood from her unblemished skin, and flexed her fingers. Whole and good as ever.

And now, I suppose, I must make that appointment.

A knock on the door prompted her to resume normal life.

"Lady Betha? May I have a word?"

"I'll be with you in a moment."

Taking a cloth from the stand next to her dressing table, Betha dipped it in the bowl of cold water resting there. Coolness spread across her skin as she wiped the sweat from her brow, her neck, and her arms. She needed to bathe, and change her dress, but that would mean summoning her maid, who at this time of day would be assisting in the kitchen.

Slightly disgruntled at having to wear the soiled garment until help arrived, she grimaced, but lifted her chin and, with her composure back in place, returned to her salon to see what Quart wanted. Now her temper was sated, she recalled he'd arrived from her estates while she attended the council meeting, which meant he had brought important business requiring her personal attention. Nothing less would force him to leave her demesne while she was absent.

"My apologies for the delay, Quart. It must be something urgent to drag you all the way to the capital."

She knew how Quart hated to travel. He'd been Herschel's steward for many years before her marriage, and even then, his old bones had protested the jouncing and jolting of a long carriage ride.

"Master Lorndar is demanding you meet with him, my lady."

Betha's attention sharpened. "Lorndar? Why? That man

has been nothing but trouble since Herschel died. He would rather I'd been buried with my husband, than see a woman ruling the Family."

"Your ladyship sees truly. The blacksmith's guild members have no time for women, and Lorndar has dared to start questioning openly why you are still unmarried two full years after Lord Herschel returned to the goddess. Trouble spreads from him, my lady. That is why I felt this news should not wait."

"He'd get on well with Edlund and Urien," Betha muttered. "There is too much going on here, I can't just break away and travel home on the summons of a guild. Even if circumstances did not compel me to remain, to answer him in person with such haste would send the message that I am at his beck and call. That would be a dangerous precedent."

"My lady, I agree, but Lorndar can cause much trouble if you leave this to fester. I recommend you return as soon as you can, to forestall any further developments."

Betha chewed her bottom lip. *I can't leave Marten; Prince Halnashead's relying on me.*

"I won't be pushed into action by a guildsman," she said. "If he wants to speak with me, he can come here."

Quart's discomfort displayed in his shuffling feet and wringing hands. "My lady, I will relay your message, but I fear he will take it poorly."

"And what, exactly, can he do about it?" Betha placed a spread of long, elegant, undamaged fingers upon Quart's forearm, intending the touch as a comfort. The smallest tremor betrayed her seneschal's unease, and she withdrew her hand. Quart knew her magic was limited to her own body, unusable on anyone else, but even so, Tyr-en's cultural abhorrence for magic was deeply rooted in him.

"My lady, if the blacksmith's guild refuses to work for your estate, tools will fall into disrepair, and replacements will not be made available. The short-term impact would be negligible, but in the long term? Crops might go unplanted or unharvested, carriages become unusable, even the kitchens might fail."

Betha glowered. "Much though I hate to agree with him in any form, this is what Edlund was complaining about. Since when did a guild even consider refusing to work for a Family?"

But she expected no reply. She and Quart both knew the answer: since magic re-entered Tyr-en and threatened the livelihoods of many guilds. Since the royal family openly considered abolishing the death penalty for magic users, proposing a form of licensing instead.

Even though decisions had yet to be reached, the guilds felt at risk of becoming redundant; replaced by those capable of fashioning objects and materials from thin air.

Despite being perturbed by the concept of guilds challenging the nobility, Betha could understand their concerns. On the other hand, she staunchly supported Marten's view: magic had been openly demonstrated both for good and for evil during the coup—pretending either it didn't exist, or wasn't a threat, was no longer an option. Tyr-en could not go back to its old ways.

What the future shape of society might be, Betha had no idea.

She hoped that Marten did.

7. DISCOMFORT

Someone tried to kill me.

Despite Nonni's excellent talents distracting him throughout the night, once morning rolled around, and Marten was forced to confront the bright light of another summer's day, he could no longer ignore the latest attempt on his life.

Was it the same woman, or someone else?

Secure in his private sitting room, he cradled his still aching head in his hands and prayed to the goddess for relief.

As usual, She maintained her silence, and the drumming inside his head remained constant. Marten groaned as he pushed up onto his feet, preparing to endure another day of battling the misery that summer always visited upon him. While other folks enjoyed the sun and warmth, choosing to walk in the gardens and smell the flowers, Marten remained indoors, suffering his way through the symptoms delivered by the fair weather. His eyes itched, his nose itched. He sneezed so often, newcomers to the court stayed well back, apparently believing whatever plagued him might be catching.

Like the dark rings beneath his eyes, the headaches came and went, but after one night of blessed relief this one had returned with vigour.

I suppose I should be thankful, as without it I'd never have spotted the greased floor. I pray I'm as fortunate today, though if you wouldn't mind, Chel, I'd rather do without a repeat.

The parlour doors swung open, and overloud bootsteps— or so they seemed to Marten's delicate head—marched towards him: Davi, all brisk efficiency with none of his usual banter. Last evening's difficult conversation threatened to form a barrier between them.

Marten sighed. "Are you still annoyed I didn't tell you about that first attempt?"

Davi came to a smart halt two steps in front of him, and saluted. "Sire, if you choose to withhold critical information, that's your prerogative, but it puts me in a difficult position. How can I guard you effectively if I don't have all the facts?"

Marten glared at him. "Surely anticipating attempts on my life is part of your job. Am I mistaken?"

He winced inside. He hadn't meant to sound so sharp, but the prospect of losing Davi's respect rattled him. His bodyguard was the nearest thing he had to a friend, and he didn't want to sour that relationship.

Tight jawed, Davi shook his head. "No, sire, you are not. But I can do my job more efficiently if I know of pre-existing threats." He stared over the top of Marten's head, avoiding eye contact. "If you don't trust me with that information, perhaps I'm not the man for this job."

Being that bit shorter, Marten's eyeline came on a level with Davi's jutting chin, so he stepped backwards to draw the other man's regard. "Davi, I trust you, but when that first attempt happened, I didn't know you as I do now. I didn't know if I could trust *anyone*. We'd just survived a coup, and anybody might have been a traitor. As time passed and it didn't happen again, I assumed it'd been a chance attack and there wasn't going to be another, so it didn't seem worth bringing up. Can you see that?"

Davi's face lost some of its tautness. "I do, sire, but now there has been, anything you can tell me will make it easier to catch the perpetrator, assuming it's the same person. Even if it isn't, that'll give me a starting point."

"I had my spies investigate that first attempt. but they found nothing."

Davi's dark eyebrows lowered. "And you trust them?"

Marten permitted himself a half smile. "They've served me since I was a child, and they all remained loyal through the coup. Yes, I trust them, but they're few in number, and they don't have access to all levels of society, so they might have missed something."

"In that case, I'd like to start again," said Davi, warming to the subject. "May I see their reports?"

The tension knotting Marten's stomach eased. "You may, though you know I won't be revealing any identities, don't you?"

"Of course, sire. I'm a soldier; spies are not my department." Davi paused, then cleared his throat. "Before we go any further, if I may ask, are there any other confidences you would care to share with me?"

"I think not. The king must have a few secrets to call his own." Marten tilted his head. "I suspect you have a few of your own, Davi. Correct me if I'm wrong."

Davi flashed a slight grin. "Nothing that need concern you, my liege."

Marten's mood brightened. *Aha, a challenge! If he thinks he's going to hide anything once I set my spies to work, he has another think coming.* He paused his planning, even as he shrugged into the cloak Davi held out for him. *I wonder. Perhaps they know already, and I haven't asked the pertinent question.*

With Prince Halnashead absent from the capital, Marten's reliance on his own personal covert network was teaching him a lot about handling both spies and the information they unearthed. Asking the correct questions turned out to be a key ingredient.

Davi fastened Marten's cloak with an ornate gold filigree broach, and stepped back to give his king's appearance a critical appraisal.

"You'll do," he said. "I have one more question before we leave. I assume you've had your spies check the backgrounds of your—companions?"

Marten felt the tell-tale flush rise up his neck. After all this time, why did he still find it uncomfortable to talk about the ladies who shared his appetites? He covered his embarrassment by taking the lead towards the door.

"I have," he confirmed, "and they've turned up nothing. Absolutely nothing."

Marten was surprised to realise how angry and helpless that admission made him feel. Huffing in annoyance, he allowed Davi's longer legs to overtake him as they approached the door. On leaving his apartment, a pair of soldiers fell in behind them—one of the extra security measures Davi insisted upon after the previous day's assassination attempt. Marten's irritation level increased. He was accustomed to being accompanied everywhere he went, but the extra guards not only made him feel hemmed in, they also announced to the kingdom that something had changed; that their king no longer felt safe with only his bodyguard in attendance. Not a good message to broadcast while he was still establishing his competence to rule.

Marten's glower was snatched away by a sneeze, causing his temples to pound in protest. In an attempt to distract himself from his discomfort, he summoned memories of the previous evening's entertainment. Seamstress Marganie's assistant, the flirtatious blonde girl, Nonni, was possessed of very specific tastes. His mind's eye displayed her as she'd spent much of last night, hanging tangled in ropes, and secured to a metal frame angled against one wall.

But when the bound woman looked up, instead of the expected over-bright face paint leering hungrily at Marten, the features staring from beneath the golden tresses were elfin, with only the barest hint of makeup to emphasise the distress welling from the woman's azure eyes.

Betha Fontmaness.

Heat rushed to Marten's groin and he cursed beneath his breath. Betha occupied too much of his mind already, what with his guilt over assuming responsibility for her future, and apprehension about their scheduled meeting this afternoon. Must she also invade his dreams?

Not that he *wouldn't* like to have her trussed up that way, but—*stop it! That's never going to happen.*

He gritted his teeth, immediately regretting it when the thumping in his head redoubled, and his arousal slid from excitement to bitter ache. A violent double sneeze gripped him as Davi led the way out of doors, and Marten squinted in the brilliant sunlight, wishing that the short ride ahead was already over. The cool dimness of their destination—the lofty, echoing Temple—offered relief for the remainder of the morning, but they had to get there first.

Brother Padrus had requested their regular meeting be held on Temple grounds today, rather than inside the palace, and although this was not uncommon, the timing set Marten's nerves on edge. Had Padrus uncovered something dangerous while putting together his list of suspects? Perhaps news he considered too risky to impart within palace walls, which in turn implied a breach in royal security.

Queasiness added itself to Marten's discomforts.

His spirits revived somewhat as the party strode across the gravel courtyard and entered the stable compound. Tacked up horses stood ready for each of them, held by smartly-dressed grooms. The sun glistened off polished coats and harness, and the familiar tap-tap of horseshoes on cobbles wove a welcoming soundscape in the enclosed yard.

The wholesome aroma of horse roused Marten. He so rarely had time to ride these days, that any chance, even a short walk through the city streets, offered a few moments of escape from his duties. Not from being on show to the populace, but from being constrained to converse with all the many people who wanted something of him. Marten embraced his obligations as king, and would never contemplate shirking any aspect of his role, but those few stolen moments aboard an animal free from agenda or concept of class, were moments he cherished.

A proudly smiling lad presented Marten's horse at a mounting block. Goldcrown was every bit a mount fit for a king. From his gleaming chestnut coat and large, lustrous black eyes, to his prancing, polished hooves, the magnificent stallion's quality Kishtanian breeding shone for all to see.

While Tyr-en produced its own bloodstock, the neighbouring kingdom of Kishtan was without peer for breeding the best riding horses, both for pleasure, and for war. Prince Halnashead had selected the horse carefully, ensuring his nephew's stallion possessed a superb temperament, even in the company of the most coquettish of mares, and his training was second to none in all of Tyr-en.

Well, reflected Marten as he stepped up onto the mounting block, *probably not as well-trained as Rustam's horses, but none of my grooms have my cousin's innate talents. Unless there's another part-elf hiding somewhere in my stables.*

He patted the gleaming shoulder, and Goldcrown turned to nudge his pocket. Marten laughed and presented the horse with the requisite treat.

A commotion drew his attention. Marten was horrified to see a junior groom, wrestling with a skittish bay horse, raise a whip and slash it across the animal's haunches. It leapt forward, only to suffer a savage yank on the reins, causing it to half rear, jaws wide open in protest.

"Stop that at once! Get that man away from that horse. In fact, away from any horse in my stables." Shaking with anger, Marten noticed his hand obsessively stroking Goldcrown's neck, as if the stallion was the injured party.

The offending groom was hustled away, and the distressed horse led back to the stables. A replacement mount was hurriedly presented for the remaining guardsman, and the rest of the party mounted up. Goldcrown pranced proudly as his rider settled into his saddle, and Marten shook his head, dumbfounded at the way some people treated horses.

"Move that man to a job where he'll never handle animals again," he ordered when the embarrassed stable manager presented himself to the king.

"Your Majesty, of course, Your Majesty. I can't apologise enough that you had to witness such behaviour."

Marten reined Goldcrown to a brief halt. "You still have my full trust, Haskin," he spoke quietly to the stiff-backed man, "I'd rather have seen that and dealt with it, than think such abuse might happen where no one sees it."

Haskin bowed. "Thank you, sire, it won't happen again, you have my word."

As the royal party clattered out of the stable yard, Marten caught a quizzical glance from Davi. He followed his bodyguard's line of sight to where his gloved hand rested on the reins, and to the whip gripped between his fingers. Dismay jabbed him.

Goddess! Does he think I would strike a defenceless beast, because that's what excites me with a woman?

The very idea repelled him, though on an intellectual level he could understand Davi's concerns. He shook his head slightly and spoke so only Davi could hear. "I would *never* countenance raising a hand to anyone without their consent. You do understand that, don't you?"

The look of relief on Davi's face gave Marten pause. If even his closest confidant entertained doubts about his behaviour, was it any surprise the woman who'd tried to kill him believed him capable of such atrocities? With that disturbing notion teetering uneasily on the surface of his mind, Marten and his escort entered the wide, packed-earth streets of Darshan.

8. TEMPLE

The stifling smell of hot dust irritated Marten's sensitive nose, tickling it until he sneezed. He squinted against the glare bouncing off the cream-coloured stone of the nearby buildings—big, square constructions designed to house whole families and their retainers. This close to the palace squatted the oldest dwellings, erected by the original noble Families—those that had successfully clung to some portion of their riches on the ships escaping the Wizard Wars. Each house displayed the relative wealth of its builders, evident in sheer size. Walls blank of any embellishments spoke volumes of the utilitarian nature of the homes, almost small fortresses, recalling the war-like rivalry between Houses in the earliest days of the settlement.

Marten grimaced. If his ancestor hadn't fetched Chel's Casket across the sea, his Family would never have become rulers of the new land.

If only someone had dropped it overboard and let one of the sea monsters take it, I'm sure that would have secured its vile contents against all would-be users far better than I can guarantee.

He squared his shoulders. No point wishing for the impossible. Chel's Casket was his responsibility, his token of kingship, and his burden to bear for the safety of all his subjects, and he *would* rise to the task.

As his party left behind the old quarter, the dwellings grew smaller and more decorative. The houses of these minor lords sported colonnades, windows on the ground floor, even some gaily-coloured awnings in house colours of red and blue, green and white, orange and brown, draping limp in the windless air but offering shade to those walking the edges of the street.

Passing along the centre of the broad avenues, Marten paid little attention to the people making obeisance as he passed. He raised a hand and waved it back and forth with little conscious effort, and his mouth drew into a smile at intervals in much the same fashion. The vocal approbation of his subjects rose around him, and Goldcrown arched his proud neck, strutting along the hard-packed earth of Darshan's streets in the patent belief he was the one beloved of the public.

Their route brought them to a private entrance to the main Temple. The big gates swung closed behind Marten and his guards, excluding the tumult of the streets. Four priests, with brown tabards over their long white robes, held the horses while they dismounted, before leading the animals to individual stables constructed along the inside of the towering wall.

A further two priests offered the visitors water, both to drink and to wash the dust from their skin. The familiar ritual comforted Marten, giving him a moment to order his thoughts and bring his attention to the matter before him. He hoped Brother Padrus had been careful in drawing up his list of suspects. If the old man's conclusions were correct, and the Cult of Charin had, indeed, been raised again, anyone threatening their secrecy would be in grave danger.

The attendant priest, a tall, ascetic man vaguely familiar to Marten from previous visits, led the way into the Temple's outer chambers. The huge building housed not only the main hall of worship, but also the living accommodations of all the priests, priestesses, and acolytes, along with living and working areas, meeting rooms and classrooms. Once, it had been a grand hall standing in isolation, splendid to behold and awe-inspiring to the general populace. Now, thanks to all the added buildings and extensions growing outward from three of its four sides, it crowded the surrounding walls, leaving only the dominant front façade free from additions.

The royal family's private foyer, across which Marten now marched, opened into one side of the main devotional hall which offered free access to the general populace. As always, the lofty arched ceiling, from which depended numerous candelabras, each bearing hundreds of lit candles, brought Marten a sense of peace and goodwill; a closeness to the goddess he could not achieve elsewhere.

As was his habit, he paused at the base of the steps leading up to the plain altar before the twin-faced effigy, to bend his knee and give homage to the goddess. Chel's beautiful, carved face, stared down upon the offerings strewn across the altar surface, while that of her brother Charin faced the empty darkness behind. Wrapped in his own concerns, a sudden bout of sniffles by Marten's side caught the king by surprise. He glanced to his left to discover a peasant child kneeling on the ground and bowed over with obvious grief.

Marten put a consoling hand on the lad's shoulder. "Take comfort in Chel," he said, recalling how he had knelt in similar fashion after the loss of each of his parents. "Always remember your loved one is never truly gone, but returned to Chel's bosom until She delivers them to a new life."

The child, a young boy, Marten now saw, peered at him through tousled brown hair, the deep shadows of mourning painting dark hollows beneath his hazel eyes.

"Thank ye, sir. I knows my granfer is safe with Mistress Chel. I was there when he went, and his face were a picture, so it were, he were so happy."

"Then why the sadness?"

The lad shrugged. "'E 'ad a hard life, my granfer. I'm just prayin' to Chel to let 'im come back as a lord next time. You know, to 'ave an easier life."

Marten smiled to himself. If only the child knew what being a lord—or a king—entailed, perhaps he'd not wish such a fate upon his departed grandfather.

"I'm sure Chel will listen to your prayer," he said with a small pat to the boy's shoulder before rising to his feet. He turned to discover one of his guards frowning at the lad.

"You have something to say?" Marten enquired.

The guardsman flushed. "The child is disrespectful, sire. He doesn't even recognise you."

Marten's jaw tightened. Why was it that other people felt the need to be affronted on his behalf?

"Leave the child be. Why should he recognise me? I'm sure there are plenty of country folk who have no idea what I look like."

Glancing round, Marten found himself the subject of a wide-eyed stare worthy of a deer startled by a pack of hounds. He smiled down at the child.

"His duty to Chel and his grandfather are admirable," Marten declared, turning back at the guardsman. "I'm making it your personal responsibility to ensure this child and his family receive the appropriate provisions they need for a celebration fitting for their farewell to a beloved grandsire."

The guardsman bowed deeply. "Yes, Your Majesty."

Moving on, Marten and his entourage departed the hall of worship via a small side door which led to a selection of private meeting rooms. The tall priest showed them into the snug chamber where Marten had received instruction from Padrus since he was a small boy. The two guardsmen took up positions outside the door, with Davi inside. Marten settled onto a plain wooden chair to wait, unease nibbling at the edges of his mind again.

It was unlike Padrus to keep him waiting.

"By your leave, Your Majesty, I will bring Brother Padrus to you," said the tall priest.

"Thank you, Brother…?"

"Freskin, sire, Brother Freskin."

Marten waved a hand in dismissal and settled down to wait. Very soon, raised voices in the corridor outside brought him sharply to his feet. Brother Freskin re-entered and bowed deeply.

"Sire, I regret to inform you, Brother Padrus has left us to re-join the goddess."

Steely fingers wrapped around Marten's heart. He put a hand to the table beside him for support.

Padrus, gone! Padrus, who had been like a second father to him alongside Uncle Hal. A presence he could rely on to guide him through the maze of a king's life, to care for him and be a friend, no matter how difficult the decisions he must make. Padrus, who'd spoken with the goddess face to face; Marten's go-between with the divine.

How could he be gone?

Brother Freskin's face took on a comforting aspect. "He was old, sire, and beloved of Chel. We should rejoice She has taken him to Her bosom. The pains in his joints were becoming hard to bear; now he will suffer no more."

Marten nodded, unable to force words past the lump in his throat. All these things he knew, but the more his mind whirled round and round with memories of his final conversation with Padrus, the more the timing of the old priest's death sent waves of unease rolling over him.

Why didn't I cancel something and see him yesterday, as he wanted? Surely Chel would not have taken him at so inopportune a moment, just when he'd raised the possibility of Charin's Cult returning?

Another idea stabbed him, and he jerked upright. *What if it wasn't Chel who took him? What if I signed his death warrant, asking him for that list of names?*

Marten forced his mouth to form words. "I want to see him, now, before his body is moved."

Brother Freskin bowed again, though he hesitated, his feet scuffing the stone flags with a degree of reluctance as he led the way to the humble apartment Padrus had inhabited.

As they walked, Davi's gaze bored into Marten's back. Did Davi suspect danger, here, in the heart of the Temple precinct? Or did he, like Marten, harbour suspicions about the untimely death of the gentle priest?

Freskin drew aside the coarse, plain hanging that served as a door to the priest's chambers. Davi slipped in ahead of Marten, holding up a hand to prevent his king from entering until he was certain no threat existed. Following a swift check of the sparsely-furnished rooms, he beckoned Marten in.

Padrus sat in an upright, tall-backed chair before a writing desk, slumped over so his body hid whatever document he had been working on. The red devotional flame in the sconce set upon the wall above the desk had been extinguished. Marten shivered. He'd never visited Padrus's rooms, but he doubted that flame had ever been allowed to go out in all the long years the priest had resided there.

Davi pulled the door hanging from Freskin's hands and allowed it to drop between them, keeping the priest's prying eyes off the scene. Marten stood back as Davi leant over the corpse and gently eased the old man upright until his body rested against the chair back, head lolling to one side. The ancient, faded eyes, almost hidden in the relaxed fall of wrinkles wreathing the wizened face, stared emptily at the wall. Padrus's liver-spotted hands spread across a parchment ruined by a spill of ink, making the words illegible.

Marten's throat tightened again. *Chel, take care of him, he was a very special man.*

Marten's skin twitched beneath the sensation of gentle arms enfolding him. At last, the goddess chose to comfort him. Awe expanded through his chest, squeezing his lungs. All the many times She had ignored his pleas, why now?

It must be because of Padrus. He was Your beloved priest, one of Your Blessed.

Marten's tense shoulders relaxed as the illusory touch spread warmth through his cold, heavy body.

He wondered what Chel and Padrus had talked about. He'd never asked directly, although he knew the goddess had given the priest purpose when he was a young man.

Sadness tightened his chest as he watched Davi inspect the mortal remains of his old friend. Leaning in close, Davi used one hand to waft the air near Padrus's slackly open mouth towards himself. His nose wrinkled in disgust.

"It's as I feared, my liege. He was poisoned."

Chel's comforting warmth transformed into a molten surge of anger. Marten smothered the urge to roar aloud, to shout his intentions for the murderer in the hope they might hear, and quail at their assured fate. Instead, he compressed his roiling emotions into a ball of rage which he tucked behind his heart.

When he could bring himself to speak, his words came out strangely flat.

"It can't be a coincidence, considering what he was working on." Marten's gaze dropped to the ruined parchment. "Bring that. If there's anything we can decipher, even part of a name, it'll give us something to go on."

Tight lipped, Davi gently drew the parchment from beneath Padrus's limp hands. At least the priest's aged body showed no evidence of a painful death. Whoever had perpetrated the crime had had enough compassion to use a swift-acting poison, and that, if nothing else, might earn the culprit a quick death.

Marten turned away. The euphoria endowed by Chel's touch evaporated, leaving him empty.

"It's my fault," he muttered, not even aware he'd spoken out loud until Davi contradicted him.

"Don't go that route, Marten. It's not your fault, it's the fault of the bastards you asked him to name. Or it could be something else entirely, like someone trying to knock you off balance while they raise a challenge to your rule. We need to remain vigilant, but do *not* under any circumstances shoulder the blame—at best that will bring you heartache. At worst, it's a distraction from what's really important."

Head buzzing, Marten directed a small glare at his bodyguard—a man who against all protocol, had called him by his given name. A man he regarded as his only real friend.

"And what's that?"

"Staying alive, and staying in control."

Marten prowled the tiny room, clenching and unclenching his fists, while Davi conducted a more intensive search. He knew what Davi said was true, but his grief for the old priest threatened to undermine his resolve to stay strong.

Uncle Hal, I know I said I could cope without you, but that was before everything went wrong. I know you want to be there when your child is born, but I could really do with you here, now.

"Aha!" Davi pried a few brown threads from the roughened edge of Padrus's old desk. "Something that shouldn't be here. With this—" he waved the defaced parchment in one hand, and held the threads up in the other, "and this, we have a starting point."

Plans for sending a messenger to summon Tyr-en's Chief of Security back to the capital fled Marten's mind. They had clues. Perhaps Marten might yet prove to his uncle he was capable of ruling on his own.

9. HAL

Thirteen days later, at Domn

The warm summer air in Risada's parlour quivered with tension. Princess Annasala perched on the edge of a generously padded chair. Sister Valaree stood by her side.

Facing them, Risada occupied one end of a settle upholstered in fern green leather, and Rustam the other. An immense, floral-patterned, scarlet and emerald rug covered the floor between the opposing parties, like an empty battlefield anticipating first bloodshed. The spacious room reeked of disuse and anxiety.

"This is *my* father's body we are discussing." Annasala's brittle tone reflected the expression she wore.

"Hal was *my husband*," Risada snapped, "and father of my son. My *kidnapped* son. Of course, his body should be treated with the utmost respect, but I will not be traipsing all the way back to Darshan while my son is still missing. Hal would have understood."

Her last words came out slightly strangled. *Oh Hal, I miss you so much. I can't believe you won't fling that door open at any moment, and march in to talk some sense into this pair.*

Annasala's jaw tightened. Rustam slid along the settle and slipped a hand over Risada's. Her heart fluttered at that simple touch, and warmth spread across her icy skin. Valaree's gaze dropped to their joined hands. The priestess's mouth pursed in disapproval.

Risada bridled. "What? You can give Sala comfort, but I'm denied any?"

"It isn't that I begrudge you comfort, Lady Risada, it is the source of that comfort that troubles me."

Rustam's fingers tightened around her fist, but Risada chose to ignore his tacit warning. She'd seen first-hand how dangerous Valaree could be, but exasperation overruled caution. "Because he's a man, or because of *what* he is?"

Valaree frowned. "Both of those, and more. It is unseemly for any man to be touching you so soon after your widowing."

Anger drew a flush of heat to Risada's face. "Rusty is my *friend*, and the man who brought Hal's murderer to justice."

A sudden notion gave her pause. *Surely this would be the best time for Rusty to reveal his true relationship to Sala?* She glanced at Rustam, but he was staring at Annasala with an intensity that suggested perhaps he was considering exactly that.

"Even so," Valaree continued, "he's a magic user, and not to be trusted."

Livid, and empty of patience, Risada snatched her hand from beneath Rustam's, and surged to her feet. She winced, immediately regretting her thoughtless physical action. *How long will this take to heal,* she pondered as she put a hand to her abused abdomen. Five days had passed since the assassin had kicked her hard enough to bring on early labour. Five days since she'd given birth to a baby unready for life outside her womb. Five days since her child had been whisked away to Shiva to be healed by the magical properties of the Shivan air, and subsequently kidnapped.

Five days since Hal died.

She took five measured steps forward until she was within spitting distance of the priestess. "If it were not for magic, my son—Hal's son—would be dead. Would that please you, Sister Valaree?"

For once, Valaree appeared nonplussed. She glanced down at the plush rug beneath her feet before raising her face and shaking back her long, loose, midnight hair. Dark eyes met Risada's challenge with a carefully constructed expression of superior morality. "Such an outcome would not have brought me pleasure, Lady Risada, but it would have been the will of the goddess."

Rage tightened Risada's chest until each breath hurt. Words were never going to solve the differences between them, nor would acting on the urge to throttle the woman, though her fingers flexed and clawed with the desire to do exactly that.

Hal, you'd be so proud of me! Look how I've embraced your teaching—I finally understand that killing is not always the best answer.

She buried her twitching hands inside the capacious sleeves of her sepia mourning gown. Whether Sister Valaree did, or did not, approve of her relationship with Rusty was irrelevant. The woman wielded power over Annasala because the princess relied on her and trusted her. Risada did neither, but she acknowledged Annasala's dependence on the priestess who'd been her comfort and support through her difficult recovery following the coup. Now was not the time to challenge Annasala. Decisions needed to be made and, for now, they must find a way to cooperate.

The king's courier had been dispatched to inform Marten of his uncle's passing, but Hal must be buried, and soon. They'd staved off the immediate necessity by stripping the estate of every bottle and barrel of brandy that could be located, and placing the prince's remains inside a liquor-filled casket, rendered leak-proof by one of Domn's master vintners.

Risada recalled the one moment of levity she'd attempted to cut through the overpowering sadness, when she'd remarked that, "Hal would be pleased he's used up every bottle of brandy this House has to offer. We can truly say he's swimming in it."

Unfortunately, Annasala had taken umbrage and refused to discuss anything with Risada for a full day after that, and yet the prince's rites could not be put off indefinitely.

Not long enough for me to find our son, Risada acknowledged with a heavy heart. She sighed, squared her shoulders, and took a step back to meet Annasala's troubled gaze. "Sala, I have no wish to upset you further, but I will *not* abandon our son. Hal deserves the full rites according to his station, and that can only be performed in Darshan. You'll have to take him home without me."

Annasala's eyes widened. "Surely you're not planning on searching for your infant yourself? In your condition?"

"How could I trust this to anyone else? I'm his mother."

"*He* can do it," said Annasala, jerking her chin towards Rustam while keeping her eyes averted. "You know he can; it's what he does."

Risada heard Rustam's inhalation but got in first. "Rusty's in little better condition than I am. Or have you forgotten how grievously he was wounded?" She canted a glance towards Valaree, gauging the woman's potential reaction before adding, "It's only by the grace of Chel he's still with us."

As she knew Valaree would, the perceived insult to Chel enraged the priestess. Her mouth opened wide to protest and Risada stepped in close, staring the woman in the eye until she subsided. Even though Risada had accepted restraint as a valid course of action, Valaree didn't know that, and, courtesy of Annasala, the priestess was fully aware of Risada's former profession. The capable hands of a renowned assassin so close to her person were an exceedingly effective threat.

"Leave Sister Valaree alone, Risada. She's not the enemy."

"Oh? And who is?"

Annasala's shoulders slumped. "Just now, I honestly don't know." She rose to her feet and put a hand on Risada's arm. "I don't want us to be at odds, but too much has happened to ignore the dangers magic has brought into our lives. Rusty," she addressed Rustam over her shoulder, still refusing to look directly at him, "I've known you since I was a little girl, and you were always a loyal servant to my father, but this *thing*, you've embraced, it's *evil*. Can you not bring yourself to ask

Chel to purge it from you? I'm sure that would have pleased father; he always regarded you as the son he never had."

She really has no idea, does she? Risada thought with sadness, even as she fixed Rustam with a meaningful glare. There would never be a better time.

* * * * * * *

Rustam had done his best to stay out of things.

The current situation was something Risada and Annasala needed to resolve between themselves, and anything he said was sure to inflame the already delicate truce. He even managed to hold his tongue when Valaree riled Risada, though his hackles stood to attention, wary for any sign of the priestess manifesting the miraculous lightning he'd heard she could produce from her blunt fingertips.

Likewise, he held his breath as Risada faced up to Valaree, knowing full well how swiftly lethal the former assassin could be. He succeeded in remaining silent even when the impulse to explain to Annasala why he had a legitimate reason for his presence in the room almost overwhelmed him.

But Sala's assertion that Hal would have approved of him denying his birth right was more than he could stand. He'd spent much of the past few days wrestling with his conscience while he rested, recovering from his injuries. Did he have the right to tell Annasala the truth, when their father had forbidden it? When Hal was alive, Rustam would not have contemplated disobeying his father's directive, even though he believed it wrong to prolong Annasala's ignorance. Hal had promised he would tell her himself when the time was right.

Now, that time was never going to come for Hal. What purpose would it serve to keep the knowledge from her any longer? Her mental fragility concerned Rustam, but any delay would only serve to make the shock greater in the future.

He clasped his hands tightly together until two knuckles cracked. "Sala, there's something you should know."

His sister finally turned to face him. "Yes?"

Rustam studied Annasala. He was struck by how gaunt she appeared, youthful slimness given way to an angular figure. She no longer wore her abundant brown hair loose in the fashion of a girl, instead it was pulled back into a low coil at the nape of her neck, framing her oval face. Rustam winced as he traced each new crease on her brow, each furrow radiating from the corners of her eyes, each frown line that should not have been evident on a face as young as hers. Annasala wore the horrors she'd suffered at the hands of the pretender openly for all to see.

Grieved that he must now hurt her further, Rustam flexed his fingers into fists, drawing the courage to shatter any lingering illusions she might still hold about her father.

"Hal did have a son, Sala. He was my father."

All colour drained from the princess's skin. "I don't believe you," she whispered, shaking her head. "He would have told me."

Rustam ached to enfold her in his arms, but the moment was too fragile—any movement might send her bolting from the room, so he remained still, hoping his words might salve the great gash he'd just torn in her heart. "He was going to tell you, but he wanted to wait until you were stronger."

Rage boiled up, bringing high colour to Annasala's prominent cheekbones. "How long was he going to wait? Until I was an old maid? Oh, goddess help me, I believe you. Why else would he have treated you better than me? All that time I was recovering, when I needed him the most, he was with *you,* wasn't he?" Now venom rolled off her tongue. "Even his *bastard* was more important to him than his daughter!"

"No, no! That's not how it was," Rustam protested. "He was too ashamed to face you."

Incredulity warred with a hint of hope, both quickly consumed by Annasala's righteous fury. "That I can believe, too," she grated. "And when, precisely, did he tell you he was your sire?"

Rustam gulped, feeling once again like the naive pageboy Hal had always brought out in him. This wasn't going well. Somehow, he had to redeem things. "He didn't. I found out while we were in Shiva." He glanced at Valaree, knowing things were about to get worse, yet committed to the truth beyond recall. He flung an apologetic glance at Risada. "Risada told me."

"You *knew*?" Betrayal shook both Annasala's words and the accusing finger she pointed at Risada.

Risada shook her head. "Not before Shiva. Chel granted me a vision in one of the elves' sacred pools. I'd always believed Rusty was *my* father's bastard; *She* corrected me."

"Blasphemy!" Valaree cried.

Rustam could almost feel the lightning building around the priestess, like the oppressiveness that weights the air on the leading edge of a stormfront. "Calm down, everyone, please. There's no need to fling accusations." He spread his hands in entreaty. "If you'll let me explain?"

"Your Highness," Valaree said in a tightly controlled tone. "I recommend you do not listen to any more of these lies. Chel would never soil Herself by entering a heathen land like Shiva." She glared at Risada. "It must have been Charin, up to his usual mischief."

Annasala placed a restraining hold on Valaree's arm. "Sister Valaree, I understand your desire to protect me, but I need to hear this. Chel or Charin, I have no doubt what Risada saw revealed the truth. We can debate identity and motives later." She turned again to Rustam. "So, you truly didn't know before?"

"I didn't," he said, astonished she sounded so reasonable, and clutched the sliver of hope on offer. "And when I wanted to tell you, our father forbade me. He was determined to tell you himself, but he didn't feel he'd found the right time yet."

"And after he died? You couldn't bring yourself to tell me then?"

Rustam grimaced. "If you recall, I tried to speak with you, but you refused to see me."

The reasonable Annasala vanished, overtaken at shocking speed by an angry, accusatory version. "I'd rather not be speaking to you now, either. He's only *dead* because of you. If you'd *listened* to me, we wouldn't have ridden down on the camp at precisely that moment, we wouldn't have drawn the guards away from him, and he'd still be alive! But no, you ignored my warnings, and insisted on using *magic* to locate him." Her glare turned to outright hostility. "You used magic, and Chel punished you for it by taking the life of the very person you meant to save—*my father*. He might have been your sire, but he was *never* a father to you!"

Rustam clenched his fists. He wouldn't ever consider striking his sister, but at that moment he wanted to lash out, to hurt somebody. Anybody.

Because, with the exception of Chel's involvement, everything Annasala said was true. If he hadn't used magic to find the camp, if they hadn't drawn the guards away at that critical moment, Halnashead might not have died.

And Rustam had carried that guilt with him every day since.

What he *didn't* need was anyone pinning the blame on a divine response to the use of magic, but he knew his sister well enough by now to know he wouldn't convince her otherwise. "Have it your own way," he snapped, frustration carrying him past the edge of prudence. "Yes, it was my fault. Don't you think I know that? Don't you think I've regretted it every moment since it happened?" His volume rose with each admission, but he was beyond caring.

Annasala stumbled back, shock blanking her face. Silence stretched while she stared Rustam up and down though narrowed eyes, as if it pained her to look upon him. He wished he could take it all back, find another way to tell her, or a better time. Like he'd wished a thousand times over he could have done things differently and saved their father. But no matter how much magic he could wield—Chel knew, it was little enough—or how hard he prayed, time stubbornly refused to reverse.

Annasala gathered her skirts, swung around, and started for the door. Two steps short, she spun to face Rustam with her chin high and her face devoid of emotion.

"Rustam Chalice, it's time you returned to Kishtan. You came here under a diplomatic truce which will be honoured for as long as it takes you to reach the border. Don't come back. I'm revoking my father's conversion of your death sentence to exile. If you set foot in Tyr-en again, your life will be forfeit."

She swept from the room, Valaree bringing up the rear like a shepherd herding her flock of one. The door slammed behind them.

Rustam's body suddenly felt too heavy for his legs. He dropped back to the settle.

"Can she do that?" he asked.

Risada glared at the closed door. "I fear she can. Unless Marten over-rules her, she has royal prerogative."

Her next words were so quiet even Rustam's sharp, elven-enhanced hearing, barely heard them. "I can't believe she did that."

Rustam felt empty inside.

I've barely got used to the idea I'll be able to come home again. His eyes drank in every detail of the woman standing before him, like a hanged man gasping for his final breath. *I don't think I can bear to lose you again, Risada.*

Chel, what can I do?

10. CHIEF OF SECURITY

Shafts of sunlight pierced the clouds like celestial spears, bouncing off the burnished helmets of Princess Annasala's guard. Rustam watched from a first-floor window as the party escorting Prince Halnashead's body to Darshan dwindled into the distance.

He'd had no wish to intrude on Risada's grief, nor desire to raise Annasala's ire by his presence, so he'd stayed hidden away while Risada said her final goodbye to her husband, laying a jewelled necklace atop the sealed casket with instructions it should rest next to Hal's heart when he went to his grave.

Rustam had made his own silent farewell from a distance, his throat too tight for words. Only once the dust settled into the hoofprints and wagon wheel tracks did he venture downstairs and out into the fresh air. By the time he stepped through the doors, Risada was nowhere to be seen.

Rustam set off towards the stables.

The horse pastures began where the gardens ended, long stretches of railed paddocks laid out in serial ranks, each with two or three occupants calmly cropping the lush green grass. Rustam's feet carried him along the dirt track between two of the fields while his mind revolved round and round his dilemma.

Annasala had reinstated his death sentence. As a member of the royal family, that was her prerogative, and the only person who could gainsay her command was the king. But the king was in Darshan, and that's where Annasala was going, making access to Marten difficult.

Rustam's original intention had been to return to Kishtan,

and the position he'd carved out for himself in King Graylin's court. But so much had happened since he arrived here at Domn under that diplomatic flag, and for a while he'd been gifted a glimpse of Halnashead's plans for his future return to Tyr-en.

Plans that had died with the prince.

And yet nothing was ever simple. Risada and Halnashead's infant son was missing, and, like Hal's death, Rustam accepted blame for that too. If he'd been stronger, or quicker, or smarter, the child would never have been placed in jeopardy. It was his responsibility to rescue the innocent mite and return him to his mother.

He'd said nothing at the time, but he agreed with Annasala—Risada should not be setting off to recover the babe herself. She was too weakened by the traumatic birth, and by grief. Rustam was, obviously, the man for the task.

But returning to Tyr-en once he'd rescued the child would put him squarely in opposition to Annasala's dictate.

First, find the child. Then *worry about the death sentence.*

Light drops of warm rain pattered on the top of his head. He hunched his shoulders and strode faster. Domn's stables were located inside a light and airy barn, and as he dashed beneath the cover of the high roof, Rustam sniffed the air. A brief smile touched his lips as he smelled the mingled aromas of fresh straw and sweet meadow hay.

At this time of day only one horse stood inside. Fleetfoot, Rustam's bright bay Shivan stallion, dozed on his feet in the middle of the walkway, disdaining an actual stable. None of the stable lads would dream of trying to coax him into a loose box—he'd shown them how such an attempt would end within half a day of his arrival in the barn. Fortunately, as the season was so warm, the lad in question had dried out quickly after his dunking in the water trough.

Fleetfoot acknowledged Rustam's arrival with a shake of his neck, his long black mane swishing from side to side. Rustam patted his shoulder.

"It's good to see you resting, my friend. We've an

important task ahead."

He ran a hand along the stallion's muscular crest beneath the heavy fall of mane, marvelling as always at the softness of the horse's hair. Fleetfoot bent his neck around and blinked at Rustam.

"We have to recover Risada's baby. Actually, he's my half-brother, which might make it easier to find him if we can get close enough. I might be able to sense a blood-link like that." Rustam sighed. "I'm guessing the hardest part will be persuading Risada to stay behind. Ouch!" He leaned against the stallion's shoulder, pushing hard until the horse lifted the hoof he'd planted on Rustam's foot. "What was that for?"

Rustam hopped a few steps, before rubbing the top of his abused foot against the back of his other calf. He'd never held any illusions about the weight of the substantial animal even before being trodden on. "That's going to be one almighty bruise, thank you very much. What did I say to offend you?"

Fleetfoot arched his neck, lowering his head until he matched eyelines with Rustam. His expression revealed both dismay and disapproval. Rustam shook his head. "For someone who can't utter words, you have an amazing ability to express your opinions. You think Risada should come with us, don't you?" Fleetfoot bobbed his head down, once, twice.

"Do you have any idea how unwell she's been? It probably isn't safe for her to be riding yet, let alone going into the sort of country we need to scour."

Fleetfoot swung his head away, effectively turning his back on Rustam.

"Fine! I'll give her the option. I don't fancy having to ride a strange horse, and I have a strong suspicion you'd make me do that, wouldn't you?"

The bay stallion chewed thoughtfully, lowered his neck, and returned to his standing slumber.

I know when I'm beaten, Rustam acknowledged silently, jumping when Fleetfoot snorted. "What, even my thoughts aren't private anymore?" He slapped the horse hard on the shoulder, smirking slightly as Fleetfoot flinched.

Rustam beat a speedy retreat to avoid any further bruising the huge horse might choose to inflict. Having an intelligent Shivan warhorse had its disadvantages.

It had advantages too.

* * * * * *

Rustam had a good idea of where he might find Risada. He pushed open the door to the drawing room-turned-office Hal and she had shared, unsurprised to see her seated behind her late husband's large desk. What he hadn't anticipated were the tears sliding down her cheeks. The foreign show of emotion on a face so adept at hiding secrets stopped Rustam mid-stride.

Forcing himself back into motion, he hurried across the expanse of opulent rugs, dodging the scattering of elegant, tall-backed chairs. "Risada, are you unwell?"

Risada raised her wan face, made even paler by the unflattering sepia colour of her gown. Her elegant, deadly hands crumpled the piece of parchment she'd been reading.

"Did you know about this?" Her voice rose to a shrill peak.

Rustam halted uncertainly. "Did I know about what?"

Her fist waved the scrunched parchment beneath his nose, as if she somehow expected him to discern what was on it by its mere proximity. Her familiar floral perfume sent a wash of nostalgia over him, and he had to force himself to keep his mind in the moment.

"I'm sorry, I can't quite read it like that."

Risada's expression froze, before more tears welled from her eyes. Rustam's nostalgia sharpened to worry; Risada didn't readily lose control.

With a gulp, Risada regained some composure, and scrubbed the edge of a shawl across her wet cheeks. "It's a letter from Hal. To me. In the event of his death."

Two ice blue eyes pinned Rustam as effectively as the

spear that had impaled him six days earlier.

"Did he know he was going to die?" Risada demanded. "Did someone foresee it and warn him?" A single, defiant tear traced a track down the side of her nose before she dashed it away in irritation. "Did he *know*?"

Coldness filled Rustam's core. To know the time of your own death? He could imagine nothing worse, though he'd believed on more than one occasion—one very recently— that his time had come to re-join Chel. But Chel—and Charin—had both declared they had other intentions for him, yet to be revealed. And so, here he remained.

He shook his head firmly. "No, I don't believe so. You saw how happy he was, how much he was looking forward to the birth of his son. If he'd known—no." He paused to consider. "But he was chief of security, so the risk was always there, and Hal was *never* unprepared." Leaning forward, Rustam captured the long-fingered hand still randomly flourishing the crumpled letter. "What does it say?"

Risada composed herself. "He left me instructions, and a directive. He's charged me with becoming Tyr-en's new chief of security."

A swell of pride puffed Rustam's chest. "He's been grooming you for this ever since the coup. I could tell by the way he watched you, he had total confidence in you."

As do I, he agreed silently, before adding, "I can't think of anyone more qualified."

Risada's gaze dropped to the desk littered with sheets of parchment and half-written notes in Hal's neat handwriting. She snorted softly. "What if I don't want the responsibility?"

Rustam released her hand and straightened to attention. "My lady, you were born for this task. If you don't take it, the king will be left vulnerable. You are unmatched in experience on both sides of the game, and your entire life has been dedicated to upholding your family's honour. When you married the prince, you assumed the same obligation to the royal family. You cannot deny this duty."

Risada's shoulders grew stiffer as he spoke. The gaze she lifted to his face flashed anger and hurt.

"As if I would dream of—" Dismay melted into disbelief, swiftly followed by incredulity. "Oh, you fool! Did you really think I'd consider *not* taking the job, even for a heartbeat? Trying to guilt me into it? That's low, even for you."

Rustam kept his expression deadpan. "Well, the only person more qualified than you, would be me. And I *certainly* don't want it."

Risada's eyes rounded and developed a sparkle as she fought a losing battle with the smile tweaking the corners of her lips. "Then, sir, you are fortunate we would not consider you for the role. There is something rather unsuitable about a dancer boy having that much power, and I, for one…"

Risada gave up her struggle. She clamped one hand over her mouth and dissolved into soft giggles edged with a hint of hysteria. Rustam remained po-faced a few moments longer before he, too, succumbed. Reality would still be there, waiting to bite, soon enough, but in Rustam's opinion they'd earned a brief respite.

When, eventually, their chuckles died away, Risada reached across the table and squeezed Rustam's hand.

"Thank you, Rusty, I can't remember the last time I laughed. It would have been with your father, he had such a wonderful sense of humour." She withdrew her hand, dropping it into her lap. "I miss him so much."

Rustam hooked a chair leg with the toe of one boot and dragged it, screeching, across the polished wooden floor. Risada winced, distracted from her maudlin moment as Rustam intended. He plonked down on the chair with a huff.

"*You* might find it funny, but it's been a long time since anyone called me 'dancer boy'," he complained. "They certainly don't in Kishtan. There, I'm just 'that foreigner', or "Graylin's outlander envoy'." He ran his fingers through his hair. "And frankly, I think I have too many grey hairs to be called 'boy' anymore."

Risada snickered. "Despite all that's happened, at least your vanity's intact. If you can find more than a handful of grey hairs, I'll volunteer to work in the kitchens for a month."

"Please no—your household doesn't deserve that punishment! I capitulate; I've only found two so far."

Settling back into her husband's outsized chair, Risada studied Rustam. "Rusty, are you happy in Kishtan? It sounds like you're still a bit of an outsider."

Rustam shrugged. "I always will be. It was fortunate Graylin already knew who—and what—I am. It meant he could put me to work easily, and it hasn't been uninteresting at times."

"But?"

"But it isn't Tyr-en. This will always be my home, even if I can never live here again. Which, if Annasala has her way, will be the case."

Risada's brow lowered. "You leave Annasala to me. As the new chief of security, I can't promise to change things quickly, but I know Hal's long-term intention was to revoke your sentence and bring you home, and for me that plan still stands. It might take me a while, but I promise you, it *will* happen." Her expression cleared, replaced by something almost furtive. "I always thought you'd settle in Shiva. Didn't you have a thing going with that dryad? What was her name, Xindy?"

If Rustam hadn't known better, he'd have said Risada's tone was jealous.

Don't be ridiculous, man. She was happily married to my father. She obviously moved on from whatever it was we had, a long time ago.

"Xindaya," he corrected. "And it was never serious. She helped me understand a few things about myself, but it wasn't ever going anywhere. Last time I travelled through there I saw her in the distance, but she just waved, and disappeared into a tree."

"Literally, into a tree?"

"Oh yes. I don't think it's something I'll ever forget, having twigs rifling through my hair when only a second before, they were fingers."

Risada's smile took on a brittle cast, and Rustam hurried on, diverting away from talk of magical happenings. "It's about time we started planning our search strategy, don't you think?"

"You said 'our' search." Risada sounded suspicious. "Aren't you going to argue for me to stay here, like any other weak and pathetic woman?"

Rustam shook his head. "Wouldn't dream of it." He bent down to rub his instep. "At least, not since I had the notion vetoed by a certain stallion."

"Are you seriously telling me your horse has an opinion about my situation, and you're willing to listen to it?"

And we're back to magical happenings. Should have kept my big trap shut.

"Risada, I know you aren't a lover of all things Shivan, but believe me, when Fleetfoot has an opinion on something, I'd be a fool to ignore him." He wiggled his toes inside his boot. "With bruises to prove it."

Risada placed Hal's creased letter down and smoothed it out. Then she rose and walked around the vast desk until she stood next to Rustam. "At this moment, I don't care where the advice came from, I'm truly grateful for it. And yes, let's do some planning; the sooner we have some idea how we're going to proceed, the sooner we can start looking. I want my son back."

11. SHOCK

Two days later

Marten waited until the door lock clicked before permitting himself to relax. It was all well and good having a secret entrance to his office that only his spies had keys to, but after the most recent attempt on his life, his confidence in the safety of the arrangement stretched thin.

But how else do I keep their identities secret? It's not as if a maid or a stable boy would have permission to use the main door.

Marten shook his head. It was so much easier for Uncle Hal, whose rooms lurked deep inside his private wing, where no one might remark the comings and goings. Marten's office opened off the side of the palace's main public rooms, and the guards standing duty outside were there to ensure only legitimate petitioners crossed the threshold.

Returning his attention to the latest missive on his desk, Marten pinned one side down with his forearm and smoothed the curling parchment with his opposite hand. To his frustration, after fifteen days of investigation Padrus's murder was still unsolved.

At least he'd received some information on one of his other investigations.

He glanced up as the main doors swung open and Davi slipped in. His bodyguard raised an eyebrow as he read the king's expression.

"You have something?"

Marten nodded. "Only a nugget, and not about Padrus, but

I finally have confirmation that Lords Edlund and Urien are conniving together."

"That's worth knowing, and begs closer investigation before the next council meeting." Davi's dark eyebrows drew together. "I'm sorry to add to your concerns, but news has arrived of the death of the courier you sent to Domn."

Marten's heart sank. "How? He must have been returning with an answer from Uncle Hal by now—do we have it?"

"I'm afraid not, sire. It appears to have been a simple accident. He was found on the south road with his neck broken, probably from a fall. Unfortunately, his horse hasn't been located, so we don't have his document pouch. Should I send another courier to Domn?"

"Yes, please. I can't afford to trust that any accident is truly accidental without proof. Did the man have family?"

Davi shook his head. "No, sire, mercifully not."

Marten breathed easier. One less thing to worry about. "Was there anything else?"

"Not on the troubling side, sire. Unless you expect your upcoming meeting with the Lady Betha Fontmaness to be tricky?" Davi's eyes twinkled in response to Marten's groan. "What, you're about to be alone with a beautiful lady and you aren't pleased?"

"It would be a lot simpler if she was fat, dull and ugly," Marten grumbled. "I suppose there's no way to postpone it again? No," he interrupted himself, "I've already put her off for longer than I should have." He rose from his chair and drew himself to his full height. He ran his left hand through his hair, as ever trying in vain to tame the annoying kink folding the wrong way against his cheek. "Show the lady in."

Davi strode back across the open reception area, spacious enough to house a royal retinue if need be.

And theoretically sufficient distance for Davi to apprehend any threat that might get beyond the door guards. Goddess, but that latest attempt has me seeing assassins everywhere!

A vision in a flowing azure gown swept through the open

door and drifted across the expanse of empty stone flags. She seemed to glide, almost without touching the floor, utterly soundless in her passage. Unease crawled up Marten's back. Was she real, or a phantom? Without doubt she was silent enough to be an assassin.

Drawn by the gentle lavender perfume preceding his guest, Marten discovered himself the other side of his desk with no recollection of how he'd arrived there. Covering his confusion, he reached for Betha's hand and raised it to his lips. Her long, slender fingers felt cool against his suddenly sweaty palm.

"My Lady Betha, how delightful to see you again."

Her fingers slipped from his grasp, and Marten self-consciously wiped his palm on his tunic. He could feel the dreaded flush creeping up his neck.

Her musical voice soothed him, its quality as exquisite as her person. "Thank you for seeing me, Your Majesty. After your declaration at the council meeting, I find myself eager to discover who, precisely, you intend for me to marry."

Marten clasped his hands behind his back. *Straight to the point. Not normally what I expect from a woman, but this one's not normal. I mean… Dear Chel, save me from myself!*

As he had been taught, Marten paused a moment to gather himself. He ambled back around the desk to cover his discomposure, keeping the lady waiting until he'd settled into his ornately carved chair. Long ago he'd taken note of how his uncle preserved his comfort while seated for so long each day at his desk. Marten's chair, like Hal's, boasted plush cushions for both his back and his behind, and a firmer, shallow one, on which to rest his feet.

Once he was comfortable, he invited Betha to sit. Also in keeping with Halnashead's practices, the petitioner's chair had no such comforts, all the better to discourage lingering.

Lady Betha sat down with an abruptness that startled Marten. He winced. *That must have hurt. She can't have much padding over those seat bones of hers.* Heat flushed his cheeks. *Pull yourself together, man. Stop thinking about her body.*

He cleared his throat. "First of all, Lady Betha, I want to apologise for the way my lords treated you. You have as much right to attend council as they do, they simply aren't accustomed to dealing with women in that setting."

Betha's fair eyebrows lifted. "Your Majesty, you honour me with your apology. The rudeness of your lords is hardly your fault. I admit to having been taken aback when you volunteered to act on their concerns in person, but I'm sure that's preferable to delegating responsibility to them in so sensitive a matter."

Embarrassed by Betha's implicit approval, Marten studied his hands where they twined together in his lap. "Yes, well, Uncle Hal would give me a tongue lashing if I allowed those bullies the magnitude of authority they were obviously angling for."

Betha's gentle laughter lured Marten's gaze, and he smiled tentatively at his guest.

"Your uncle is a very wise man, as we all know."

"We are fortunate to have him," Marten agreed. "Though he has more than earned this current break from duty."

"Has there been any word? Surely the birth is due soon?"

"Quite soon, I believe. Uncle Hal is remarkably enthusiastic about becoming a parent again, considering his age."

He rifled through a stack of parchments on his desk, and drew out the one he sought. Caught up in his concerns about Padrus's murder, Marten had not given the matter as much thought as he'd have liked. He handed over a short list of names of the most obvious lords suitable for marrying into a minor House. "I freely admit, I haven't had the time to consider this fully. I'll happily give it further attention if you find none of these candidates suitable."

"Thank you, sire; I know you are a busy man." She placed the parchment on her lap and leaned forward to scan the list. Marten swallowed hard as the valley between her breasts caught his eye. He clasped his twitching fingers together, wondering how it would feel to glide his fingertips down her graceful neck, and bring his palms to rest on either side of that groove.

Forcing his attention back up to her face, he noticed how Betha's gaze lingered on one name on his list, causing her to suck her bottom lip. She blinked twice, three times, holding back moisture collecting in the corners of her eyes. Marten's fists tightened; what had the named man done to her?

"If none of them catch your fancy, please say so, Lady Betha. I have no intention of forcing you into an unsuitable match."

Betha's eyes glinted as she met his gaze. "You are generous, sire. Most would not be so considerate. I am only a woman, after all."

Marten allowed a soft snort of laughter. "I'll let you in on a secret; my life so far has proven to me that women are as strong as men in all but physicality, and even there, they can excel with swiftness and cunning." He shrugged. "I believe a man underestimates a woman at his peril."

Betha's smile flashed so fast he almost believed he'd imagined it. She cocked her head. "It seems there is more to our king than some might realise." Betha's cheeks brightened, and she clapped a hand over her mouth. "Sire, I am so sorry, please forgive my familiarity, it was totally inappropriate."

A genuine smile lifted Marten's face. After so long bestowing faux smiles upon tiresome courtiers, the real thing brought a warmth to his chest.

"My lady, please, I would rather you speak your mind honestly. I have enough sycophants around here already. My uncle would probably counsel me not to encourage such informality, but he isn't here."

Betha met his gaze with boldness. "Well then, perhaps I should wish for him to be delayed somewhat longer—"

They both jumped at the crash of the main double doors slamming open. Marten was halfway to his feet reaching for the knife at his belt before he identified the intruder as a member of his personal guard. The man hurried across the anteroom with Davi one step behind him.

The guardsman halted a couple of steps before the desk and bowed perfunctorily. "Your Majesty, please, you must come. It's Prince Halnashead."

Marten blinked. If Uncle Hal had returned, why the urgency?

Dear goddess, did the birth go amiss? Is Risada dead? Or the child? Was that the message my courier was bringing?

"Forgive me, Lady Betha, I must attend my uncle."

He hurried around his desk, only to find Betha standing in his path. Gripping her upper arms to move her aside, he noted distractedly how her physique felt more robust beneath his fingers than he'd expected, but he pushed the knowledge aside; there would be time to reflect later. The brief glint off something reflective—a jewel, perhaps—caught the corner of his eye, but vanished inside the folds of Betha's gown as she folded into a curtsey.

"Of course, my king."

With his guardsman leading the way, Marten hurried through the palace. Davi kept pace with them, but maintained a grim silence, adding to the palpable air of anxiety. To Marten's consternation, they headed towards the main entrance, not the private family wing.

As they stepped through the open doorway, the glaring mid-morning sun forced him to narrow his eyes. He peered, uncomprehending, at the static tableau filling the large courtyard.

Dusty horses and guardsmen surrounded a flatbed wagon upon which rested a man-sized casket. The animals stood with their heads lowered, blowing hard through reddened nostrils, and their riders' stony-faced expressions sent a shiver of dread down Marten's spine.

"Marten."

A hand alighted on his arm and he glanced aside in shock—no one but family would touch his person without invitation, and the voice was not Halnashead's.

"Sala?" He frowned at Halnashead's daughter before gesturing towards the wagons. A horse stamped a hoof, breaking the hush. "Where's Uncle Hal? Who...?"

"He's here, Marten," Annasala murmured, barely audible. "In the casket. He's dead. Murdered." Her voice broke on the final word.

The world receded from Marten, shrinking to an empty, sealed off bubble of space. He viewed the scene before him through a hazy curtain of shimmering light, and his ears rang with the buzzing of a swarm of bees.

How could Uncle Hal be dead? Sala must be wrong, it must be Risada, or their child, inside the casket, not Uncle Hal. Any moment now the prince would walk up to Marten and clasp him by the shoulders, look him in the eye and tell him what had really happened.

Marten shook his head. "I don't understand."

"Come, pay your respects, Marten. I'll explain later."

Numb, and feeling like he was watching actors play out a scene on stage, Marten allowed Annasala to lead him to the wagon. She lifted his hand and placed it against the sealed wooden casket. The wood beneath his palm was warm and smooth, displaying the strong grain of a throne tree. Marten's shoulders slumped.

"When?"

"Ten days ago. He was struck down by an assassin. Did the courier not reach you?"

Marten shook his head. "He had an accident. An assassin? Was he caught?"

Annasala's jaw tightened. "Yes. He's dead."

"How did he...?

"A knife to the heart. A knife created by *magic*. Marten, you must uphold the old laws; magic is *evil*. The Temple agrees; isn't that correct, Sister Valaree?"

Only then did Marten notice the striking priestess standing to one side of the wagon. Her white robes displayed the stains of long wear, and her face betrayed exhaustion, yet she stood tall, with her sharp chin raised, and anger sparkled in her eyes.

"Your Majesty." She bobbed her head. "It is true, your uncle was struck down by magic. The assassin was Tyrenese, but he employed a sorcerer to craft a blade from air after they'd been searched for weapons. The Temple backs Princess Annasala in her call for magic to remain outlawed. I pray you will heed our advice."

A lump the size of a small boulder settled in the pit of Marten's stomach.

Dear goddess, Uncle Hal, you can't leave me like this! I have absolutely no idea what I should do.

12. INTRIGUE

Betha tucked her dagger securely into the hidden sheath in the bodice of her gown, and mentally berated herself. Her clumsiness had almost revealed her secret to Marten. She had no doubt the king had glimpsed the weapon in her hand, but by good fortune it appeared he'd been too distracted for his brain to process what his eye had seen.

The startling interruption by the guard had triggered her training, slipping the blade smoothly into her fingers without conscious thought. She'd stood ready to defend her king, but when he darted around the desk and manhandled her out of his way, she'd frozen.

What were you thinking? Halnashead bade you keep an eye on him, yet the slightest touch of his hand had you all in a fluster. She gritted her teeth. *My tutors would crow; I know they don't believe anyone starting to train at my age can learn to be a successful spy, and I seem to be proving them correct.*

She sucked on her bottom lip, and then scowled, recalling how she'd revealed the self-same tell-tale when she encountered Ordell's name on Marten's list of proposed spouses, giving away her feelings to anyone who could read expressions. *Perhaps I'm never going to be any good at this spying game.*

Rubbing her hands over her arms where they still tingled from Marten's grip, she reconsidered her original opinion of the young king. He was considerably stronger than he appeared. A quick flick of her personal magic wiped away the nascent bruises, drawing a small hum of pleasure from her throat.

Perhaps my unguarded words were true, and there's more to our young king than meets the eye. Perhaps... No! He's the king, *not some lowly lord looking for some fun. There is the serious matter of a husband to acquire, I must focus on that.*

Taking several deep breaths to regain a state of calm, Betha became aware that a disturbing silence had fallen over the palace. She gathered her skirts, swept out of Marten's office past the rigid door guards, and halted the first maid she came upon.

"What's amiss?" she asked, alarmed by the tears streaking the girl's face.

"Beggin' your pardon, ma'am, but it's the prince: he's dead."

Betha's throat squeezed shut. She was vaguely aware of the maid slipping away, leaving her rooted like a petrified tree in the centre of the corridor.

It can't be true; how can he be dead?

She spurred herself to action, hurrying to the main palace entrance, weaving on shaking legs that she feared might fail her at any moment.

He can't be dead. Please Chel, please.

Tears blinded her. She dashed them away as she stumbled to a halt beside the grand double doors. She pressed one fist to her mouth. Leaning against the doorjamb for support, she stared down at an unremarkable wagon bearing an unmarked casket. Beside it stood the dejected king with his head bowed and one hand resting on the long wooden box. Prince Halnashead's daughter, Princess Annasala, hovered by his shoulder, venting her grief and fury in loud and vitriolic words condemning magic.

Betha shuddered and turned away. She staggered blindly back into the hushed depths of the palace.

Prince Halnashead was—had been—a kind man. He'd taken Betha's heartache at the loss of her husband and helped her channel it in a way that gave her life fresh purpose and fulfilment. Yes, he'd gained a valuable asset by transforming her into one of his spies, but he'd never made her feel she was merely a tool. He'd continued to show an interest in her personal needs long after she'd completed her training, filling the raw gap gouged by her father's early death. In many ways he'd become a father figure to her. Perhaps it had been his way of maintaining control of his operatives, but he'd always made Betha feel cared for, and she appreciated that consideration.

What will we do without you? You've guided us and kept us safe and we will all miss you so much.

Uncaring who saw, Betha sank to a stone bench intended for page boys waiting on their masters at court. She dropped her face into her hands and wept until her tears petered out.

What should I do now? Now you're gone, who should I report to? The carrion birds will be all too quick to dive in, full of their own agendas, willing to tear the kingdom apart in their efforts to gain influence over Marten. I can't just abandon him.

Betha rose and smoothed her gown. No matter how she ached inside, the game would not wait for her to recover. Unscrupulous lords would seize the moment and she must be ready to support Marten in any way she could. She owed that to Halnashead.

Allowing her training to take charge, Betha tagged onto the rear of a group of chattering noblewomen and mentally documented their conversations. In a kingdom where espionage was an integral part of life, Betha was repeatedly astonished by the loose tongues of so many of her peers.

Perhaps it was that they did not believe, as women, that their words would be taken seriously. Chel knew, to a large extent that was true.

The group she'd attached herself to, swept into the grand salon, making a direct line for another gaggle of ladies. Betha paused inside the entrance to survey the opulent hall. Rich drapes festooned the many deep windows, and bright silk tapestries lined the walls. The crowded parquet floorspace seethed with a mass of excited, lavishly dressed nobles, and a profusion of expensive perfumes assailed Betha's already queasy constitution. She clenched her teeth.

The court was abuzz with the shocking news, tongues busy, games forgotten on abandoned tables. Huddles of noblemen and women gathered in clusters according to their stations and affiliations, and Betha's trained memory captured mental pictures of those tell-tale groups. In more than one, Betha identified the common agenda with little effort; those who'd chafed at the prince's influence over the king as opposed to those who'd supported him. Here and there congregated small knots whose motivations were less clear. Adrift with no firm objective, Betha concluded her skills would be best put to use determining where those individuals' loyalties resided.

Who she'd report her findings to, she would consider later.

She drifted between clusters of nobles, sometimes adding a word or two, sometimes doing no more than listening from the fringe. Her standing as lady of a minor house was of little consequence to those of higher rank, placing her in an ideal position to listen but not be heard; the very quality Halnashead had prized her for. Few of the conversations were of any import, mostly shocked reactions and speculation about the possible consequences for the kingdom, and for individual houses, but one group drew Betha's interest.

Much though she wanted to keep her distance from the corpulent Lord Edlund, he was a strong contender for troublemaker. Betha loitered on the outskirts of the nearest collection of gossiping ladies and tuned out their nervous jabber. The deeper male voices were harder to isolate, but with Edlund's lack of capacity for volume restraint, his pronouncements cut through the general hubbub.

"Without Halnashead, the king will be in need of a new privy advisor. Urien, he already respects you; you are the obvious choice."

Lord Urien bowed his dark head. "It would be my honour

to serve his majesty in that capacity." He straightened up and considered each of the five lords around him. Although he was the shortest of the group by far, his presence commanded the regard of all. "In return for your endorsements I will, of course, keep favourable count."

Betha's jaw tightened. *Halnashead's not even buried yet, and they're vying for his position. It doesn't surprise me, but that in itself is a sad reflection of this court.*

Two more lords of major houses joined the huddle and were apprised of the group's intention to place Urien into the influential position of king's advisor. Betha shook her head minutely at the display of sycophantic support the proposal garnered.

She was about to wander away when Lords Edlund and Urien excused themselves and separated from their allies. With the flow and chatter of unsettled nobles as cover, Betha trailed them across the salon at a discreet distance. When they slipped into the open maw of a servant's corridor, she feared she might be about to lose them, but they stopped there, and she was able to slide into a booth on the other side of the wall. She couldn't see them, but once again, Edlund's thunderous volume provided her with half the conversation without strain, and she could pick out enough of Urien's words to keep up.

"What good fortune! I assume we have our benefactor to thank for this turn of events."

Betha's head jerked up. *Benefactor? Was there a darker side yet to Halnashead's death?*

"Hush Edlund, keep your voice down. Talking about *him* is dangerous, you know that. Leave it for the meeting tonight."

"Of course, so true. Ironic, isn't it? Chel's Temple hosting us. If only they knew."

"Yes, well, they don't. And it makes meeting with the clerics easier. I'm looking forward to hearing how their plans are coming along. Pity the king realised the old priest's death wasn't natural causes, but I'm sure it can be turned to our advantage."

Brother Padrus was murdered? Goddess! What else don't I know?

Betha could imagine what Halnashead would have said to her: *"It isn't your place to know everything; that's* my *job."*

But now Halnashead was gone, did anyone know how to gather all the threads? Did Marten?

Suddenly she knew who she must report to, though she dreaded admitting to the king she's been spying on him, even if it had been at his uncle's behest. He was such a sweet boy, too young and innocent for this burden. Too handsome...

Betha blinked. *Where did that come from?*

She averted her face as Lord Urien strode past her hiding place, and remained unmoving until Lord Edlund departed in the opposite direction a short while later. The conspirators were obviously doing their best to avoid being seen together except in the company of their peers.

Betha made one more circuit of the salon before concluding she'd identified the most crucial information that was likely to come her way. Now she had to work out how to let Marten know about the mysterious meeting scheduled for that night.

How would he take the news she'd been one of Halnashead's spies? An indigestible lump settled in her gullet as she contemplated telling him, and in particular admitting to her recent surveillance commission.

She had the sinking feeling he wasn't going to take it well at all.

13. BONES

Risada shifted position in her saddle. She'd done it so many times since they'd left Domn she'd lost count. Each change brought temporary relief to her aching abdomen and legs, sometimes for longer, sometimes shorter. But always in the end the dull pains returned to plague her. She huffed irritably, causing Rustam's head to swivel around. The look of sympathy and concern he tried to hide annoyed her even further.

"What?" She narrowed her eyes. "If you're going to say 'I told you so', get on with it and be done. I might remind you, you were in favour of my coming."

She felt almost remorseful as he ducked his gaze away from hers to stare ahead at the broad, wheel-scarred dirt track.

Almost, but not quite.

Of course, this journey wasn't a wise move for someone in her delicate physical condition, but her son was missing.

Hal's son.

How could she let anyone else lead the search for him?

The rolling grassland behind them had given way some time ago to rising paths threading between hillocks of ever-increasing loftiness. Risada had little memory of passing this way before, yet it had been no more than a double handful of days since she and Hal had travelled the very same trail, and even less since the dispirited party returned with the injured Rustam and Risada, and escorting Hal's body.

Risada drew another deep breath. Watching Rustam's shoulders twitch as he resisted the temptation to turn around again, fetched a wry smile to her lips.

They rode on in silence, taking frequent rest breaks that chafed Risada's patience, but which she accepted were wise. On the surface, Rustam appeared recovered from his injuries, but Risada noticed he slept more often, taking short naps each time they dismounted. They'd already taken six days to cover the distance the wagon train had done in five; appallingly slow progress for two people mounted on fresh horses.

Risada patted Greylegs' neck. The slow pace suited her trusty mount, fat and unfit as he was. Rustam had raised an eyebrow when she'd ordered Greylegs saddled, but this horse had carried her faithfully through trial and travail on the last danger-filled journey she'd undertaken with Rustam, and always kept her safe. There wasn't another horse she trusted half as much, and Rustam had given in quickly, though he'd made sure to pack ointments for rubs and galls. Risada had found some of them useful for her own skin, but so far hadn't needed to treat Greylegs at all.

Slowing Fleetfoot, Rustam waited for Risada to draw alongside. "I'm sorry we had to come this way, but there's no avoiding it."

Risada stared ahead, not trusting her voice. They ambled across the clearing which still exhibited signs of the abandoned encampment, avoiding the site where Hal's pavilion had stood. Neither of them wanted to get any closer to the spot where he'd died than they had to.

"It isn't far now. I just hope we can find some indication of which way Chayla went."

The simple sound of Chayla's name filled Risada with wrath. Murderous thoughts ran through her mind as she pictured the many ways she might kill the woman who had taken her baby. She ground her teeth together but held her tongue as Rustam led towards the site where he'd brought Hal's murderer to justice. And nearly lost his own life.

Would there still be evidence of the traitor's remains? Rustam had described Dench's demise in minute detail, his words and tone betraying his grim satisfaction at the grisly manner of the death, eaten alive by thousands of nippers. Risada wished she'd been there to witness it.

Knowing such brooding was futile, she turned her attention forward. In front of her rode the man she'd long adored, though she could never admit it to him. Feeling faintly guilty, as if she was being disloyal to her dead husband, she studied Rustam's graceful figure, the supple sway of his hips in the saddle, his proud posture, and his gentle hands on the reins.

Why did I not have the courage to leave with him when he was exiled? We could have married and lived together in Kishtan, perhaps had a child of our own by now. Why was I such a coward?

But she knew the answer. Duty had demanded she produce an heir for the Second Family once it became clear her brother would not live to do so. In the end, even that obligation had become complicated by her decision to marry Rustam's father, because until Marten produced an heir of his own, her son was the only living male member of the royal family, aside from the king.

And then there had been the issue of magic, legally licensed in Kishtan. Whilst Risada's magic phobia had lessened as a result of familiarity with Rusty's abilities, the prospect of living in a kingdom where magic was accepted as a part of everyday life was something she'd not wanted to face.

Coward, twice over...

"It's over here."

Riding side by side, Rustam and Risada crested an ascending crease of land and halted to survey the natural amphitheatre stretching before them. The level meadow was defined on their side by a grassy ridge arching in an elongated semi-circle, and on the far side by a corresponding curve of flat rock, backed by a jagged cliff face.

Rustam led the way down into the bowl, the horses' hooves silent on the springy turf. Approaching the centre, Rustam drew rein and halted, staring down with a grim expression at a few gnawed bones. Risada's pulse quickened.

"Is that…?"

Rustam nodded.

With her heart jumping erratically, Risada slithered down Greylegs' side, clinging onto her saddle, all the while wondering if her legs would hold her when she hit ground.

Mercifully, they did. She stood immobile for a moment, collecting herself. Tears sprang to her eyes, which she still found alarming after spending most of her life almost completely divorced from her emotions. Dashing the irritating droplets away, she pushed herself into motion and marched the few steps to the remains of Hal's murderer. She aimed a hefty kick, scattering the few bones not yet scavenged by local predators.

"I expected more."

Rustam's words beside her shoulder made her jump. She hadn't noticed him dismount.

"Nippers don't leave much," he said, placing a careful hand on her shoulder.

Risada allowed her head to drop forward, the better to disguise the slight blush she felt creeping across her cheeks. It was too late for her and Rustam, too much had happened in the intervening years, and yet she cherished the comfort of his touch. Remaining mute, she placed her hand over his.

Why? She flung the accusing word at the goddess. *Why did my life turn out this way? I'm tired of Your manipulations; I've played Your game and lost, even if it got You what You wanted. Isn't it time You left us alone?*

* * * * * * *

Rustam jumped when Risada's fingers curled over his. He'd intended the gesture as one of support, but suffered a disquieting flashback when their bare skin touched. The Risada of old would likely have removed his hand with a dagger, or at least threatened to do so. This new woman who stood beside him accepting his comfort was a conundrum. He didn't know what to expect from her.

His father had worked some sort of magic, turning Risada from the bitter, untrusting assassin into a passionate, caring woman he ached to hold in his arms, but knew he never would. It was obvious to him that Risada had loved his father deeply, and for that he was grateful. At least one of them had achieved some measure of happiness, even if all too brief.

Pushing the unsettling, chaotic emotions aside, Rustam focussed his mind on what to do next. They stood where Risada's child had been taken by Chayla. He had a vague memory of the event, but the overpowering agony of being impaled by a vicious spear overrode any details.

Assuming Chayla had seized her chance to escape from Tylocian captivity during the ensuing fracas, where would she have gone? Rustam scanned the rockface at the rear of the grassy enclosure. There were only two exits, one leading back into the Aeron mountain range where the Tylocians held sway, the other heading away, travelling along the base of the ridge into the Middle Mountains. Provided Chayla had not attempted to cross the mountain range—and who knew, for the woman was more than a little insane—she should have exited the foothills back into Tyr-en somewhere to the north-west of where they now stood.

But where?

"We won't find her by standing here," Risada observed.

"True. We should follow the trail and see if there's an obvious exit point."

Dissatisfied with the vagueness of their plan, Rustam nevertheless remounted and led the way. Fleetfoot hopped up onto the level rock platform with ease, and the clatter of Greylegs arrival reassured him Risada was close behind. He sent a swift prayer winging its way toward the goddess. *Please, Chel, let this route be wide enough for the horses; Risada won't manage on foot.* He eased his back by bending forward for a few steps. *Come to that, I'm not sure I would either!*

To his concern, they hadn't gone far before their knees

began to scrape along the high rock walls of the gulley, and they were forced to clamber back down from their saddles.

"Let's hope it doesn't get any narrower," he said as he stepped in front of Fleetfoot and gathered the reins in one hand, ready to lead.

Risada snorted. "Feels like we've been here before, although that time we were underground, and we only had a pack pony."

Memories flooded back, and Rustam smiled. "And a suspicious werecat. Don't forget him."

"As if I could! All those muscles on display, and an extreme reluctance to wear clothes. In the end, though, he turned into an excellent ally."

"He did that."

They continued in a companionable hush, broken only by the clatter of horseshoes on rock as the sun moved overhead and passed from their line of site. The temperature at the bottom of the narrow defile dropped enough for Rustam to pause to drag his jacket from where it was lashed to his saddle, and shrug into it. To his relief, not long after, the channel widened, spilling out onto a heavily forested hillside. The rocky footing gave way to a thick carpet of pine needles.

A small mountain creek crossed their path, the clear water bouncing over miniature rapids where it rushed downhill. Beyond the stream, the track split. One branch stretched away ahead of them while the other angled downward, dropping rapidly out of sight into the dense forest. An idea stirred in Rustam's mind.

He halted. "Decision time."

Risada's head swivelled between the two options. "It could be either. We have no idea where she's going." Her voice sounded strained. "If she's harmed him…"

Rustam attempted to reassure her. "Why would she? Chayla's nothing to gain by harming your son, and everything by keeping him safe. She's probably angling for a pardon. After all, her husband was the traitor, not her."

Risada treated him to a scathing look. "She knew exactly

what Ranjit was about, and did nothing. That makes her every bit as much a traitor as him. When we find her, I'm going to kill her."

That sounded like the Risada of old. "First," said Rustam, "we have to find her. Once we've recovered your babe, we can decide what to do with her."

Risada's eyebrows lifted. "What, you don't think she deserves to die? She kidnapped my son!"

"It wasn't quite like that, Risada. She may have taken him to safety. Goddess knows, there weren't any other options at the time."

"Rustam Chalice, are you *defending* the woman?"

He rubbed his chin. "I don't know about that. What I *do* know is, the simplest solution isn't always the best one."

"We'll agree to differ on that for now. The important thing is, how are we going to find her?"

"Well, I think we might need some help on that. I have an idea, but it's probably not one you want to witness."

Risada sighed. "Rusty, I think you'll find my prejudices have dwindled a fair bit since we last rode together. If you're going to perform magic, don't mind me, I'll cope."

It was Rustam's turn to raise his eyebrows. Without question, much had changed in his absence. "I have no idea if this will work," he said, "but it can't hurt to try."

14. DIRECTION

Risada watched Rustam drop his bay stallion's reins and walk a little way along the path to the edge of the bubbling mountain stream. He hopped nimbly onto a jutting boulder that parted the flow, and balanced there like a heroic statue bathed in the afternoon sunshine. Risada's throat tightened, and despite a pang of guilt, she couldn't help herself from admiring the figure he cut.

Forgive me, Hal, but your son is unfairly handsome.

She ran her right hand down the length of her distorted left arm. As ever, the legacy of her injury disgusted her. If only someone had been allowed to treat it at the time, she might not have been left mutilated, and unfit for the job that had been her life before the coup. She regarded Rustam with a tinge of jealousy. It was so unjust his facial scar only made him more desirable.

She gave herself a mental shake. *Stop feeling sorry for yourself. Even if I wasn't a useless cripple, I could never expect him to forgive me for choosing his father over him.*

Resolutely, Risada turned her back on the unattainable, and set about making the horses comfortable. She now appreciated the contentment such simple tasks could bring, long past her youthful disdain for manual work. So much had changed in the last few years, not least her opinion of herself. Oftentimes she liked herself better now; something Hal had encouraged.

But Hal's not here anymore.

Tears welled up. Her husband, her friend, gone.

Does this ever get easier?

A flash of light startled her. Greylegs snorted and pranced

a few steps, dragging her back up the track away from the stream.

"Woah, silly! There's nothing to get excited about."

I hope.

Untangling her hand from her reins, she admonished herself for wrapping them around her fist—something only a novice rider would do—and hoped Rustam hadn't noticed. She couldn't bear the prospect of his wordless rebuke. She knew it was a stupid thing to do, asking to get dragged and possibly far worse, but the skills of horsemanship didn't come naturally to her. She turned Greylegs back around and retraced the few steps to the riverbank. She was relieved to see Rustam's eyes were shut, so he hadn't witnessed her transgression.

Hovering in front of him, the source of Greylegs' anxiety became all too obvious: two miniature golden dragons, their tiny wings fluttering so fast as to be almost invisible.

Salamanders!

The last time he'd summoned elementals had earned him the death sentence, before Hal commuted it to exile.

The sentence Annasala now decreed reinstated.

How are we going to work our way around that one? We must find a way. I couldn't bear it if he's forced to leave Tyren again. I have to find a way to change Sala's mind.

She watched Rustam's cheeks puff out. Next moment the dragonets were tumbling through the air, blown away by his sharp exhalation. In quick succession, they blinked out of existence.

Rustam wriggled his shoulders and ran his fingers through his hair. He looked across the water towards Risada. "I have *no* idea if that worked, we'll have to wait and see."

Curious, and feeling safer now the elementals were gone, Risada approached the stream. "What did you do? Where did they go?"

Rustam hopped back onto the bank beside her before lowering himself to sit on a flat patch of ground. He peered up at her. She noted with concern the tightness around his eyes, the pinched look of his cheeks. She could only guess at the energy drain such magic demanded, and although he hid it well, she knew he wasn't fully recovered from his recent ordeal.

"I've never tried sending them anywhere specific before," he said. "I don't even know if it's possible, but I thought it worth a try. If they went where I suggested, then any mo—"

A loud *pop* spun Risada around. Her mind put together what Rustam had been about to say before her body acknowledged it was safe to relax from battle readiness.

"Hello, Nessa. Thank you for coming," said Rustam.

Risada felt her eyebrows disappearing upward as she inspected their visitor.

A short, split skirt revealed a pair of long, tanned legs. Criss-crossed thongs laced the girl's calves above open sandals. Around her waist and lower torso rested a girdle studded with cat's eye gemstones, and a collar of matching stones hugged her throat. All the jewels perfectly matched her unusual striped eyes—the mark of the legendary gemeyes.

Nessa smiled. "Your request came in such an unusual manner. How could I refuse?"

The last time they'd been together, Nessa had been gaunt to the point of starvation. Now, while still slender, her skin radiated a healthy glow, and her figure was sleekly muscular. Her hair continued to sport the striking silver stripe placed there by the goddess as a mark of Her favour, but where before Nessa's straight brown locks had flowed long and plentiful in the manner of a young girl, now they were cropped until they barely brushed her shoulders.

Quickly grasping the incongruities in Nessa's appearance in comparison to how she'd appeared a scant few days before, Risada asked, "How long has it been for you, Nessa? Does the time difference in your valley work randomly, like Shiva, or is it more predictable?"

Nessa shrugged. "I'm still working that out, Lady Risada. I *think* it's fairly constant in being faster than this world, but I haven't been there long enough yet to be sure, and the others are so vague about it. Once you've lived there for a while, that sort of thing ceases to matter."

"That's how it is for the elves," Rustam put in. "Remember how Elwaes struggled with the concept of time?"

"I do," Risada confirmed. "Nessa, you look well. Are you content in your new life?"

A shy smile reminded Risada how young Nessa really was, despite her air of self-confidence.

"I am, my lady, and I'm Cat now, not Nessa."

Of course, gemeyes are named for their jewels.

"Well and good then, Cat. Please call me Risada; we have no need for formalities between us."

"Thank you, Risada. It's an honour."

A tiny salamander flashed into existence beside Cat, and vanished again. "Yes, of course," she said, and Risada was under no illusions the words were for either her or Rustam.

Cat glanced from Rustam to Risada and back again. "You summoned a gemeye for a reason. How may I be of service?"

"My son…" Risada's throat tightened, stopping her words.

Cat's hands flew up to her face. "Of course! My lady—Risada—it was all my fault! I should have recovered him at the time. I should have followed Chayla, but she promised; she swore she would keep him safe when she took him. The look in her eyes—I believed her, and then…"

"And then you were too busy saving my life," cut in Rustam. "There was nothing you could have done, except leave me to die, and I'm extremely grateful you didn't."

"As are we all," Risada agreed, torn by the guilt she hid, placing Rustam's life ahead of her son's safety.

I should blame Nessa, but I don't. She wasn't choosing one life over the other. My son still lives, I know it. I would feel it if he didn't. Nessa—Cat—made the only choice she could, and now I have the chance to have both my son and Rusty in my life.

For the first time in a long while, Risada directed a plea to Chel. *Please help me discover a way to thwart Sala's decree. I couldn't bear it if Rusty's banished again after all Hal's plans to bring him home.* She acknowledged her own selfish desire, hoping the goddess would understand. I *want him to come home.*

"We need your help to locate the child," Rustam said to Cat. "You can do that, can't you?"

The gemeye bit her lip. "I think so. I'm still not supposed to use my powers outside of the valley, but when your message arrived, my tutors were intrigued enough to let me come." She raked her fingers through her short hair, and gave a brisk nod. "I'm going to take that as permission."

Decision made, she positioned herself obliquely to the dividing paths, and settled into the stillness of a hunting wildcat. Risada could barely discern the girl's breathing, and realised after a moment that she was trying to emulate the shallow respirations. She drew a deep lungful of pine-scented air and shook herself.

It won't help if I pass out. What does she see, I wonder? How does the world differ, viewed through the magical lens of her gemstones?

Everything around Risada seemed to pause. The wind soughing through the treetops dropped, the bubbling of the brook muted, and the sun remained constant, no clouds marring the steady brightness of the day.

Would Cat find her baby?

Cat's eyes appeared vacant, staring into the distance, fixed on something only she could see. The moment elongated until Risada wanted to scream.

Dear Chel, please—

A bright flash of argent light wrapped Cat's body and she cried out. Rustam bolted to his feet and caught the gemeye as she fell, easing her to the ground. Risada dropped to one knee beside her to see if she was conscious, but recoiled from the sightless stare of her eyes, entirely glazed with silver.

"What happened? Who was that?" Risada stood up and

stepped back, rocking from foot to foot in anxiety. That distinctive colour meant one of the deities had intervened.

But which one?

By tiny increments the metallic glitter faded from Cat's eyes. Once the brown stripes of her irises re-emerged, she stirred, endeavouring to untangle her limbs. A few moments later she reached up to grasp Rustam's proffered arm, allowing him to haul her back up to her feet. She blinked several times and knuckled streaming eyes.

"Goddess! That's never happened before." She squinted, obviously struggling to regain focus as she faced Risada. "I truly sorry, but I can't help you. Or at least, not as much as you'd hoped." She pointed towards the descending pathway. "Chayla took him that way, but beyond that I can't *see*. Either Chel or Charin blocked my *sight*."

"We noticed that," said Rustam. He caught Risada's gaze. "I didn't tell you before, but when I was first recovering, both Chel and Charin paid me a visit. They saw fit to inform me neither one of Them is finished with me yet." He glanced down. "I'm so sorry, it looks like your son is caught up in Their game."

Coldness enfolded Risada, despite the balmy day. *I should have known.* Anger replaced fear. *How* dare *You use us like toys? Are our lives worth so little?*

Her defiance of the deities bolstered her resolve to find her son, and to deal with the traitor, Chayla. It must surely be the god, Charin, trying to thwart their rescue attempts. He was always behind malicious actions such as the abduction of an innocent babe.

Chayla must be one of His creatures. All the more reason to kill her.

Risada put a foot into her stirrup and mounted Greylegs.

"Cat, thank you for giving us a direction. Rusty, hurry up. It's time we taught Them we aren't going to be Their playthings any longer. I've had enough of it!"

Risada swung Greylegs around and set him on the downhill path.

"Risada, wait!"

Rustam's call tugged at her. Huffing with impatience, she reined Greylegs back around in time to see Cat drop to the ground, cross-legged. Ready to burst with frustration, Risada rode back and dismounted. Her damaged stomach twinged in protest.

Damnit! I don't have time for this!

"She's exhausted," Rustam said, gesturing towards Cat. "You know magic steals energy. We haven't eaten recently either, and a short break isn't going to make any difference."

"How can we be sure?"

"We can't. But rushing off when you're exhausted and underfed isn't going to help either. Take a break, Risada. You know your body needs it."

Grumbling beneath her breath, Risada yielded. She might not like Rustam's logic, but couldn't deny the truth of it. She slipped the bridle off Greylegs and gave him a shove towards the scant grass growing along the stream bank. With a morose grunt, she lowered herself to the ground alongside Cat. The gemeye ducked her face away.

"I'm sorry, Risada, if only there was something more I could do, I would."

Guilt squeezed Risada. "Please don't think I blame you for any of this, Cat. If there is any blame to be laid, it sits squarely at the feet of Chel and Charin."

"I can agree with that," said Rustam as he folded his legs, sinking gracefully down beside the women. With a flourish, he spread a clean cloth on the ground and proceeded to lay out a small portion of their remaining stores.

Only Rusty could make sitting on the ground appear stylish.

Turning her face away to conceal her nascent smile, Risada caught Cat's eye. The knowing gleam there told of their mutual admiration for the dancer.

"Oh! I have something we can share." Cat removed a small vial from a loop of leather attached to her corset. She held it up and swirled the viscous peach-coloured content.

Risada eyed it with suspicion.

"What is it?"

Cat beamed. "Liquid energy."

Risada's skin crawled. "Magic?"

"No, not really. It's called *caris dew,* and while it does come from Shiva, its actually the nectar from a caris plant." She beamed. "As natural as honey, but five times as sweet!"

Saliva rushed from beneath Risada's tongue. She gagged. "Five times? That sounds nauseating."

"Fortunately, you don't need much to get the effect." Cat plucked the stopper from the bottle and offered it to Risada. "Here, try a sip."

Risada shuddered. "You first."

With a shrug, Cat tipped a couple of drops onto her tongue. She swallowed, licked her lips, and reached for the water flask Rustam presented.

"You know this stuff, don't you?" Risada accused.

"I had some the last time I visited Shiva," Rustam admitted, making a face. "I know exactly how it tastes. I also know how energising it is." He accepted the vial from Cat and did as she'd done, taking a couple of drops washed down with fresh water from the canteen he'd refilled in the mountain stream. "It's safe, Risada, it'll help you heal."

Despite her pounding heart, Risada took the bottle from Rustam. She rocked it gently, watching the thick fluid cling to the inside of the glass. *Magic.* Maybe not in a form most people would recognise, but if it came from Shiva, there would be magic bound up in it.

On the other hand, if it helped mend her weak and disappointingly slow-to-heal body, she'd be a fool not to partake.

She dribbled a few drops onto her tongue.

"Goddess! Hand me that water!"

Risada washed the cloying stickiness from her mouth, swallowing it resolutely when her body threatened to reject it.

"Ugh. Please don't ever ask me to do that again."

A horrifying notion burst into her mind.

"My baby! He'll be starving!" She scrambled to her feet and grabbed Greylegs' bridle. Mid-lunge towards her horse, she froze. Her voice came out a harsh whisper. "Suppose we're too late? Chayla can't feed him: it's not like she's a wet nurse."

"If Chayla knows what *caris dew* is," said Cat, "there was a bottle in his blankets. I brought it with him from Shiva in case he needed some when we returned to this world."

Risada experienced an uncharacteristic urge to hug the gemeye, but instead smiled her gratitude. "I'm sure Chayla will have had instructions on its use from Charin. He obviously has a plan that revolves around my baby, so He won't let him starve."

"We can't make the assumption that Charin's behind this, Risada," cautioned Rustam. "It could as easily be Chel."

"What would the goddess want with my child?"

"When has She ever shared Her plans?" he countered.

"Then let's catch up to Chayla and settle the question. Time we were on the move. Cat, you have my gratitude. Safe return to your comrades."

Not waiting for Rustam to finish clearing the uneaten rations, Risada set about bridling Greylegs. It was only after she'd swung up into the saddle with an agility she hadn't felt in a very long time, that she accepted the *caris dew* had done her some good. Revitalised, Risada set Greylegs into motion. The descending path was too steep for anything barring a careful jog, but a fierce purpose gripped Risada as every step carried her closer to her objective.

She had a child to rescue and a woman to kill. Sometimes the simple choices were the easiest to make.

15. COUSINS

Marten led the way across the antechamber of his private suite. The clacking of his boot heels on the bare boards echoed inside his hollow heart. He would never again hear Uncle Hal's distinctive tread march across the floor, or listen to the booming laughter that shook the prince's huge belly so hard it bounced his fancy belt buckle up and down.

The lighter steps of Halnashead's daughter, Annasala, and the priestess, Valaree, intruded on his sorrow, reminding him he was not alone in his grief.

Poor Sala. How must she feel?

Whatever emotion gripped her, his cousin hid it well. Her composure in the courtyard had been accomplished, a touch of brittleness in her movements the only hint of her carefully managed self-control.

She's had a few days to come to terms with it, Marten reflected, before the reality of their mutual loss knifed home again. *Uncle Hal, how will we cope without you?*

Pinpricks of magic distracted him, tingling along his muscles as he neared the doorway to his private sitting room. Marten attempted to avert his gaze, but as ever, failed. His eyes were drawn to the covered lump resting in the centre of the large circular table. In light of the means of his uncle's demise, the mere thought of magic made him feel ill.

Annasala's footsteps faltered. She'd felt it too.

"Is that…?"

Marten halted beside the hip high table. The thick, insulating scarlet fabric pooled over and around the box like spilled blood, and for the first time Marten questioned if that image might be prophetic. Why had the disquieting colour of the cloth never struck him before?

"Chel's Casket," he confirmed with reluctance. The awe on Annasala's face bothered him. Surely, she must know the truth of the box's malevolent contents?

Beside the princess, Valaree sank to her knees. Her expression of rapture perturbed Marten even further.

"May I?" Annasala requested, hand hovering above the crimson covering. With no reason beyond baseless misgivings, Marten dipped his head in consent.

Annasala pinched a fold of fabric between thumb and forefinger, and drew the cloth aside to reveal the battered old box. Marten swayed as the previously muted demand to be opened blasted through his mind.

His cousin's eyes gleamed. She lifted the box as though it was fragile, and ran a soft fingertip around the nearly invisible seam where lid met body. Grasping the two halves with such tenderness Marten felt sure she wouldn't be able to separate them, she confounded him by sliding them smoothly apart.

Magic cascaded over Marten like a waterfall. He struggled to breathe.

Replacing the now open box on the table top, Annasala dipped her hand inside.

Marten's fists curled. He'd been envious when Rustam had reached in to touch the talisman. This time his resentment cranked up to full-blown jealousy.

The box and its contents were *his* responsibility.

"Enough!" he snapped. "It stays inside the casket."

The set of Annasala's jaw gave him a moment of doubt. Would she relinquish it? He knew very well the strength of the object's compulsion.

Annasala's fingertips brushed the talisman, and to Marten's horror it appeared to writhe beneath her touch. The blood red eye—this time there was no mistaking; it *was* an eye—stared directly at him.

All the air sucked out of his lungs. The floor rippled beneath his feet, rocking him off balance.

With a sharp *crack*, a flash of silver light blinded him, and the air sizzled with the sharp scent of a lightning strike. Marten coughed, and when his vision returned, little by little, the casket squatted once more in the centre of the table with its lid firmly in place. He met Annasala's shocked gaze across the table.

"Blessed are we!" Valaree's pronouncement cut past the ringing in his ears. "Chel has favoured us with Her presence!"

Was that—?

Marten's moment of doubt fled as a feather's touch brushed his shoulders, as it had when Chel comforted him in the wake of Padrus's death. *She* had graced them with Her protection; that light had been Hers, not Charin's.

Valaree rose to her feet, one palm pressed against her chest. Awe sparkled in her eyes. "Your Majesty." She bowed deeply. "Your Family has guarded the casket for centuries, but She has chosen you, my king, to wield its power."

"That's a bit of a leap," he protested. "*She* shut it, I won't argue with that. But isn't it as likely She did so to remind us that while we *can* open it, we shouldn't? That thing in there—it's evil!"

Valaree shook her head. "Your Majesty, as an acolyte of the higher mysteries I can assure you the jewel is neither evil nor benevolent. What makes it one or the other depends upon which of the divine aspects wields it."

Marten tried digesting that idea, but the leaden sense of unease refused to be banished.

Valaree searched his face. "Sire, I can see you are uncertain, and perhaps it isn't my place to impart such knowledge. I will seek guidance from the Temple and request a senior cleric advise you."

"Cousin," Annasala spoke beside his elbow, and Marten started. He'd almost forgotten she was there. "You can trust Valaree. Her devotion to the goddess is absolute."

"I don't doubt that, Cousin Sala, but I find it hard to believe our Family has been wrong about that *thing* for generations, and in all that time the Temple has failed to enlighten us."

"Perhaps because what just happened, never happened before?" Annasala suggested.

She has a point, but why now? And why me?

Valaree bowed. "By your leave, sire, I should go to the Temple immediately and report this miracle."

Marten waved his hand in dismissal and the priestess hurried away.

Miracle? Was it really?

Padrus's warning of 'too many minor miracles' rang inside his head. How would the old priest have viewed this event?

Bringing Padrus to mind renewed the ache of loss, and Marten coughed to clear his scratchy throat. He leaned over the table and jerked the crimson cover back over the box, breathing with more ease as the awful compulsion dwindled.

How he wished he'd asked Padrus for advice about where he might place the damned thing—preferably somewhere deep and dark where he wouldn't have to come near it again—for safekeeping, rather than waiting for his uncle's suggestion upon his return. A return that now, would never happen.

Turning his back on the casket in disgust, Marten gestured Annasala into his sitting room. He glanced back at Davi and made a brief hand gesture to reassure his man everything was under control.

I hope, he thought as he followed his cousin into the well-appointed room and closed the door, shutting the cursed box outside.

How can I tell the difference between a miracle and magic? Please Chel, won't you explain?

Nothing. No whisper, no touch.

"I didn't imagine that, did I?"

Annasala shook her head. "No Marten, we all saw it."

"But what did it *mean*?" Marten's heart beat faster, just thinking about it.

Annasala perched on the edge of an elegant upright chair, and folded her hands primly in her lap. "I believe Chel saw fit to reconfirm our Family as guardians of the casket. Beyond that, I don't know. I think it would be best to wait for guidance from the Temple."

Uneasy from lack of answers, Marten marched over to the sideboard and raised the pitcher set there ready for him. He glanced towards his cousin. "Wine?"

Annasala raised one eyebrow. "Surely you have servants? You are king, after all."

Marten shrugged. "There are few spaces in my life for privacy. I choose to keep this room as one, even if it means serving myself." He tipped wine into two goblets. "It's hardly taxing."

Marten handed Annasala a cup. An awkward silence ensued, and he pondered how best to breach it. The spectre of Halnashead's death hung between them, almost eclipsed by their encounter with the goddess, and yet the harsh reality of losing someone they both loved and relied upon seemed somehow more significant in that moment.

Annasala sipped her wine before fixing Marten with a hawk's stare. "You must uphold the old laws, Marten. You do see that, don't you? Even if Chel had not blessed you with Her presence, you must realise magic is an evil we cannot allow back into Tyr-en."

Her words drew out a memory of Uncle Hal instructing him to do the exact opposite.

Marten, m'boy, recent events leave us with no choice: Tyr-en must accept the return of magic. We've tried suppressing it for four hundred years, but this coup proves that's no longer effective. We need to place it inside the law to establish control over it.

Marten's throat closed up. *I'm sorry, Uncle Hal, but magic killed you. I don't think I can follow your advice this time.*

How to handle the threat effectively; that was the new challenge. And if Charin's Cult had indeed been resurrected, things were likely to get nasty, and soon.

"I know father believed otherwise," said Annasala, misreading his silence. "But in my opinion, his death proves he was wrong. If you're still not sure, why don't you discuss it with Brother Padrus? He's always a good man for an unbiased view."

For the second time that day, a wave of grief swamped Marten. His eyes stung.

"I can't. Padrus was murdered yesterday."

"What?" Annasala's hands flew to her mouth. "How? Where?"

"He was poisoned. In his own rooms."

"Goddess!" Annasala leaped to her feet and began pacing. Marten concluded such restlessness must be a family trait. Either that, or both he and Annasala had caught the habit from Halnashead.

"Are you investigating?" she asked. "Is the Temple?"

"I am. I assume the Temple is too, but they don't share that sort of information with me." Marten allowed his annoyance at this state of affairs to leak into his tone.

"I'll speak with Valaree as soon as she returns. We should be working together on this." Annasala halted facing him. "Has the Temple allotted you a new spiritual advisor?"

Marten shook his head. "Not yet."

Annasala pursed her lips. "I'll ask Valaree to expedite the matter; this is no time for you to be without Temple guidance. Nor should you be without a civic advisor. I can't help but wonder about the timing of these events, that both your closest counsellors should be murdered within days of each other."

Marten's breath caught. Distracted by his grief, he hadn't yet considered that coincidence.

But I should have. Uncle Hal would be disappointed in me, but he'd have been proud of Sala; she's obviously inherited her father's powers for analysing information. I admit, I'm impressed.

He already held his cousin in high esteem. During the

coup she'd willingly forfeited her freedom for the good of the kingdom. Without her sacrifice, there would have been no rescue for any of them. Now it appeared she was as smart as she was brave.

Annasala set her empty goblet down decisively. "I have the perfect solution. *I* shall don the mantle of civic advisor in my father's stead."

"And I accept. I can think of no one worthier."

Oh, that's going to upset a few of my lords! I can imagine they're already vying for the position. Edlund's face will be a portrait when he hears it's been filled by a woman! And Sala being who she is, they won't be able to dispute her competence.

Rather looking forward to making that announcement, a sudden jolt of sorrow slammed the reality of the day's situation home again.

He's really gone. I still can't believe it.

Another question popped into Marten's head; something that the shock of Halnashead's death had completely dislodged.

"What of Risada?" His chest tightened. *Please don't say she's dead too.*

Annasala's lips stretched into a tight line. "My father's wife has gone to recover her child instead of returning for her husband's rites." She held up a hand when Marten attempted to speak. "She was injured by the assassin, and the child came too early. He should have died, but he was dispatched to Shiva to be saved. By *magic*." She grimaced. "Cousin, we are the last of our House. Until you produce an heir, that child is the only other male in our Family, and he's been tainted by magic before he's even off the breast."

Marten's throat constricted. While Uncle Hal was alive, the issue of a queen hadn't seemed urgent. Why, he'd argued with Uncle Hal about it the very last time they'd been together.

Had that really been their last conversation? Yes, it had. What must Uncle Hal have thought of him?

Why, in Charin's name, did he ever think I might be ready to rule without him?

"Marten, are you listening?"

Marten blinked. "Sorry, I'm still struggling to take it all in. I keep expecting Uncle Hal to march in and sort everything out."

Tears sheened Annasala's eyes. She reached across to Marten and rubbed a hand up and down his arm. "I know. I keep expecting the same. It's going to take a lot of getting used to."

Quiet settled over the pair of them, united in their grief. Marten placed one hand over Annasala's small fingers and wondered where his petite cousin found her well of strength. There was no question she'd suffered more than anyone should have to.

While he didn't like to raise the subject of Halnashead's plans for his marriage, under the circumstances, he felt he must. "Were you aware Uncle Hal had made overtures to Kishtan regarding a wife for me?"

"I travelled with that embassy, or weren't you aware? I strongly opposed the plan, but my father would not be swayed—he was convinced the benefits of an alliance outweighed the appalling idea of marrying you to a part elf. If any good can be made from this terrible situation, that must be it. The letters were never delivered, so we can dismiss the idea without risk of insult."

"They weren't delivered?" Marten wasn't certain whether he should be displeased or relieved.

Annasala wiped a hand over her eyes, and for the first time Marten noticed the puffiness of her pale cheeks.

"There's so much to tell you," she said, "I hardly know where to start."

Marten rose and returned to the sideboard. He poured them both a second generous measure of wine. He handed one to Annasala and returned to his seat. He had the feeling they were both going to need it. Annasala surprised him by draining her cup in a few quick gulps. She placed the empty goblet on a small side table and straightened her shoulders. Then she filled him in on the events that had led up to Halnashead's murder.

When she was finished, Marten closed his eyes and kneaded his temples. He could feel another headache coming on.

"That's a lot to take in. If anyone else had told me, I wouldn't believe it, but coming from you, I'm forced to accept it as truth.

Annasala blushed. "Thank you, Marten. That means a lot to me, and that's a good basis for our new relationship."

"I think so too, cousin, although I can't always guarantee to take your counsel without question."

"Nor should you. I pray you will find my advice sound, but you are the king; final decisions will always be yours." Annasala paused and chewed her lip for a moment before fixing him with a bold gaze. "Marten, did you know Rustam is my father's bastard?"

Ah, someone told her at last.

Marten swallowed a mouthful of wine. "I did, yes."

Annasala's face darkened. "Why is it that *everyone* knew but me?"

"It was your father's choice," said Marten carefully. "He forbade us from telling you."

"Shouldn't it have been *my* choice?"

How, exactly, would that have worked? Marten pondered, but chose a diplomatic shrug.

Annasala's fingers curled around the ends of her chair's armrests. Her knuckles turned white.

"Well, that's one bastard who will never be a threat to the succession; I've seen to that. Before we left Domn I rescinded my father's sentence and reinstated the original edict. His life will be forfeit should he dare show his face in this kingdom again."

Marten gaped. His astonishment that Annasala had taken such a decision upon herself without consulting him was mitigated by the fact that with Halnashead gone, Rusty would probably have no desire to return anyway.

I hope he has a better life in Kishtan, Marten thought, recalling how settled Rustam had seemed in his role as King Graylin's envoy.

Goddess knows, he's earned it.

16. THREAT

Dappled light filtered through the branches overhead, providing a respite from the bright afternoon sun. Rustam swayed from side to side in his saddle, absorbing the exaggerated swing of Fleetfoot's movement as his horse negotiated the steep downward incline. Thick pine needles crushed beneath the animal's hooves muffled the sound of their passage and gifted the air with a clean aromatic scent.

A facetious notion occurred to Rustam. *If there's anyone out here, they likely won't hear us coming, but they may well smell us before they see us.*

Alongside him, one of Greylegs' hind feet slipped. The horse executed an abrupt halt, jolting Risada forward onto his neck. She righted herself with a wince, followed by a quick scowl.

Rustam smothered his sigh.

"You do understand *caris dew* isn't a cure?" he said. "It provides an energy boost to speed healing. It's not an instant remedy."

The affronted glare his companion turned on him was almost worthy of the old Risada. "You think I wasn't listening?"

"I *think* you were hoping for a miracle. Was I wrong?"

"Hmph!" She patted Greylegs on the neck and urged him back into motion, sticking to the middle of the trail and forcing Rustam to follow in single file. "You have no idea how much you sound like your father," she shot over her shoulder.

"I do?" a sad, half smile tugged at the corners of Rustam's mouth as Fleetfoot ambled along behind the grey gelding. "I suppose I do. I'd all but forgotten how infuriatingly correct he always was."

"Oh, and don't forget modest. You share that trait too."

A companionable hush settled between them as they threaded their way through the tall, straight tree trunks. Lichen draped from many of the branches, and in some places long tendrils trailed so low the riders were forced to bend over their horse's necks to avoid entanglement. The bubbling of the spring diminished as their path diverged from the water course to head deeper into the forest. Rocky crags sprang up in spaces between trees, almost as it the mountain behind them refused to relinquish the land to the forest. The trail looped back and forth, skirting the rock formations, and Rustam's attention sharpened when he spied a bushy tail whisking into a crevice at the base of one crag.

He pushed Fleetfoot to draw level with Greylegs. "Did you see that?"

Risada nodded, her lips a tight line. Trusting his stallion's instincts for danger, Rustam centred himself and allowed his eyelids to drop.

"What are you doing?" Risada whispered.

"Bear with me a moment."

He'd expected wildlife, but what Rustam heard were human voices. On the farthest edge of his elf-sharp hearing range, they were too far away for him to distinguish words, but close enough to determine gender by their deep pitch. He raised a hand to signal a halt and continued to listen for several moments.

"Men," he told Risada. "At least four. Somewhere ahead of us."

"Coming towards us, or away?" she asked, her tone gaining a dispassionate, professional edge that threatened to raise too many difficult memories for Rustam in that moment. He banished them with equal professionalism.

"Neither. I'd guess they're taking a break, or maybe even setting up camp. We can probably go around them if we go that way." He indicated a faint trail leading around the far edge of the huge chunk of granite where they'd seen the tail disappear. Risada favoured it with a dubious glance.

"It might lead nowhere. Or into trouble." She transferred her regard to Rustam. Suddenly her face lit with a bright grin. "Let's do it!"

Without waiting for his reply, Risada nudged Greylegs down the path. Rustam fell in behind her, a sense of inevitability bringing a matching smile to his lips. Whenever he travelled anywhere with Risada, he was never going to be the one in charge.

The path skirted several of the rocky outcrops, delving into deep gulleys between them. Springy turf underfoot assured the quietness of their passage. Both riders scanned the rocks often, acutely aware of the potential for ambush, trapped in the narrow channels. Rustam did what he could to seek out any hint of life energy larger than the wildcat he'd identified as the owner of the elusive tail. Without dismounting, he couldn't achieve the secure connection to the soil he needed to spread his consciousness very far, but within limits, he felt they would likely avoid any undesired meeting.

After a while, it became clear they were heading back into the foothills, with ridges of rough stone angling away to their right-hand side. The third time they had to pick their way across rough scree deposits at the base of what was becoming undeniably a cliff face, Risada stopped.

"We need to head that way." She pointed downward, to their left, with a daunted expression shadowing her face. Rustam studied the impenetrable growth of tree trunks, too tightly spaced to permit the horses passage. They might have squeezed between on their feet, but with no guarantee they would get further in than a few lengths. In front of them, the pathway opened up into a deep valley.

"We'll have to go this way and cut back across when the trees open out."

"If they do." Risada huffed. "And in the meantime, we're getting further away from Chayla."

"There really wasn't any option, unless you wanted to risk finding out who those men were."

"Perhaps we should have taken a look. But we're here now; let's get on with it."

Rustam fell in behind her again. Once more, a feeling of familiarity struck him, following the confident assassin who never second-guessed herself. For a fleeting second Rustam speculated about who the men had been, and if they'd been a genuine threat or not, but he dismissed the question within the space of a hoof beat. They weren't going back, so onward was the only choice.

The valley gradually opened up into a wide vale. The land sloped sharply downward from the crag on their right to the dense forest several lengths below. The horses shuffled as they walked awkwardly, with their hooves on one side higher than on the other. Rustam's concern grew as he detected a slight limp in Greyleg's gait. The gelding wasn't fit enough for the uneven going.

"I think we should lead them," he suggested, a tiny knot of anxiety lodging in his stomach. His conscious mind knew Risada had changed, but on a deep level he still expected her derision.

"That makes sense," she said, dispelling his unfounded concern. They both slithered down their horses' shoulders on the uphill side, the opposite of their customary dismount. Taking the lead, Rustam chose a gentle angle downhill as well as forward to lessen the punishing tilt on the horses' limbs. As the sun sank lower, he was forced to cup one hand over his eyes to manage the glare, his whole attention consumed by scouting the best path ahead.

A wild yowl shocked the travellers to momentary immobility, followed rapidly by uneasy sideways jogging from both horses.

"Whoa, easy there."

Behind him, Risada murmured calming words to Greylegs even as the rising screech came again, echoing off the sheer rock wall to bounce around the valley. A dark shadow slunk from between the trees, the only point of brightness about it, the impressive display of sharp teeth in the snarling feline mouth.

A quick glance towards Risada reassured Rustam. On the journey so far, the former assassin hadn't displayed any obvious weapons about her person, but some habits were clearly never going to die. A tiny blowpipe had materialised from nowhere to rest against her lips.

The sleek black cat padded closer, glaring at them with bright emerald eyes. Like the tumblers in a lock dropping into alignment, Rustam's memory of another set of eyes that exact same hue slotted into place.

"Hold!" He raised both hands, palms facing outward. "We are no threat to you, or your *pahn*."

With another aggressive hiss, the huge feline raised itself on its hind legs, standing tall as a man. Taller. Rustam felt his eyebrows lift even as he reached behind himself to put a reassuring hand to Fleetfoot's shoulder. The stallion quivered beneath his fingers, muscles bunching ready to fight or flee.

"Shh, easy fella. This big guy isn't going to hurt anyone." He aimed an intense stare towards the posturing cat, forcing himself to ignore the claws flexing in and out of the massive paws. "Is he?"

Black fur rippled and smoothed to the silky texture of skin. Physical shape blurred as joints transformed and proportions altered. In little more than the space of a blink it was over, and a tall, black, naked man stood before them. His intense jade-coloured eyes glared at Rustam.

"Why should I not?" His words rumbled up from deep within his chest. "How isss it that you know of my *pahn*?"

Taking a quick glance to the side, Rustam noted Risada's eyeline firmly fixed on the upper portions of the werecat's muscular body. The blowpipe still rested against her lips, and that offered a modicum of comfort in the face of the powerful predator. He wasn't convinced Risada's dart would strike home fast enough in the event of a disagreement, so he determined to do his best not to allow things to reach that point.

"Of your personal *pahn*, nothing. But we've worked with your kind before."

The werecat tilted his head. "You tell the truth," he said, sounding puzzled. "Then you have no connection to thosssse who track me?"

Rustam peered at the treeline, half expecting a band of hunters to appear, even though he sensed no other large life forces within range. His awareness had expanded once his connection to the soil was not interrupted by a horse between him and the ground, although he was disappointed with himself for missing the werecat's approach.

Too busy thinking of other things, like how to get back on track. I hope one day these senses will work without me having to think about them.

"We do not," he confirmed. "Who are they? Do you know?"

"Tylocian renegadesss with no Clan."

Rustam's already tense shoulders tightened even further. To be outlawed by Tylocian society, brutal as it was, must be quite an achievement, and not in any good way.

He glanced towards Risada. "I think that justifies our detour."

She gave a single, grim nod, before voicing the question Rustam had been about to ask.

"Why are they hunting you, master werecat?"

The glower on the werecat's human face was only slightly less daunting than his earlier feline snarl. "A werecat's fur isss highly valued amongsst the clanss. One pelt will buy many months suppliesss."

Anger spiked Rustam. "They'd kill you for your skin? That's obscene, even for Tylocians."

"Consider us animalsss, they do. I thought to essscape them by descending into Tyr-enese landsss, but they have followed me where I believed they would not."

"I wondered about that," Risada mused. "I've never heard of a werecat sighting in Tyr-en. You'd cause apoplexy if someone saw you transform!"

A fleeting smile touched Rustam's lips. "Now there's a picture." He stared speculatively towards the forested slopes. "I wonder how far down they're willing to come." His focus returned to the majestic nude figure of the werecat, envious of the impressive muscle tone on display.

I've let myself get soft. Once this is all over, wherever I end up, I'm going to get fully fit again. He took a quick, sideways glance at Risada. *I know she will. It's strange to see the Lady of Domn in less than peak physical condition.* His eyes skittered over the slightly odd shape outlined against her left sleeve. *She's so strong, she'd never let even an impairment like that thwart her. Once she's back to fitness from this pregnancy, she'll be as perfectly lethal as ever. I only hope I'll be around to see it.*

The pall of Annasala's judgement hung over him like a personal cloud.

Later. We'll work it out later.

"Assuming they're following you, I suggest you go that way," Rustam twisted around to point back up the trail they'd come down. "That will let you skirt around them and head back into the mountains." He paused to send his perceptions spreading through the bedrock beneath his feet. After a moment he located the marauders on the very edge of his range. "They aren't close. We should all get moving if we want to keep it that way."

The werecat tilted his head, regarding Rustam with fresh appreciation. "Now I undersssstand. A hint of elf-smell hangss around you, yet you appear human. A trickle of elf-blood runs through your veinsss, yess?"

"It does," confirmed Rustam. "Enough to grant me some small measure of their abilities. I'm still learning how to apply them, but what I've said I am sure about."

With a feral grin that spread around sharpening teeth, their new acquaintance reverted to feline form and bounded away up the path leading back into the mountains.

"Well," said Risada, "that was interesting. I must be

getting accustomed to speaking with strange naked men. I don't even feel surprise any more."

"I'll remember that," Rustam muttered before recalling how sharp Risada's hearing was for a human. He cringed slightly at her small snicker.

Without further embarrassing himself, Rustam took the lead and set off down the valley. To his dismay, the forest and the cliff face began to draw together again, narrowing their path until they were in another tight channel, forcing a return to single file. Scrubby bushes tugged at their legs and snagged in their clothing. The only upside was that this track was more level beneath their feet and cushioned by moss. The horse's shoes maintained a precarious grip that kept them to a cautious pace, and Rustam prayed to Chel that the way ahead remained clear of rockfalls.

They rounded the base of a bluff with only the cry of an eagle for company, until the unmistakeable sound of a goat bleating nearby brought them to an abrupt halt. Rustam sent his consciousness into the ground, but it remained stubbornly blank.

He peered forward in the conventional manner, spotting a dark opening further down the hill. "I can see what looks like the entrance to a cave," he whispered.

The bleating came again and he cocked his head, listening, but heard nothing else. "It might be wild goats. Stay here with the horses, and I'll scout ahead."

Risada didn't waste breath arguing, though when Rustam glanced around for her approval, her rigid jaw made it clear she was not happy with the idea. A terse bob of her head was his only blessing.

Calling on his dancer's agility, Rustam tiptoed towards the cave mouth, stepping lightly over the ground, testing each step before trusting the stones beneath his feet not to roll and throw him off balance. A particularly thorny bush caught his hand, nicking a small snag in his skin. He licked the blood off, the salty tang reminding his stomach he hadn't eaten recently. The growl of complaint from his guts was loud enough to warn anybody within fifty paces, and Rustam groaned inside. He remained frozen in place for a count of twenty, but when no raging beast or menacing human emerged from the dark crevice ahead, he pushed forward again. The path turned from stony track to loose rocks as it led up to a raised terrace in front of the yawning hole in the rock wall.

Ten careful steps later, a sturdy chestnut nanny goat raised her head from behind a scrubby bush. She stared at Rustam with unblinking striped eyes while continuing to chew cud, unalarmed by his approach. A length of rope encircled her neck, with the other end looped around a rock pillar. A hint of wood smoke drifted from the dark cavity behind her.

Footsteps clicked on stone and a dishevelled figure strode out into the lingering daylight. The rags of a Tylocian woman's split skirt hung around skinny hips. Narrow shoulders barely supported a filthy blanket held pinned across her chest by an incongruently large emerald jewel. Tangled hair of indeterminate greasy grey draped limply around a face displaying undeniably fine bone structure. The woman turned an intense green gaze down upon Rustam, regarding him with an impatient air.

"What took you so long?" demanded Chayla. "I expected you days ago."

17. CHAYLA

"Is that you, Chayla? Where's my son?"

Rustam glanced around to see Risada storming towards him, the horses abandoned on the track behind her. A whisper of air lifted a few strands of hair on the back of his head and when he turned back to the rock platform, Chayla was nowhere to be seen.

Damn, but she can't have gone far.

He scrambled up onto the raised terrace, wondering in the back of his mind how they were going to get the horses up there. Showers of stones tumbled behind him and he didn't need to look round to know Risada had clambered up behind him. Before either of them could get any further, Chayla reappeared, this time cradling a fur-wrapped bundle against her meagre breast. A pair of small, chubby arms waved beneath her chin and her face lit with a brilliant smile.

"See here, my sweet," she murmured in a sing-song tone. "Your mama has found us at last. I don't know why it took her so long, but I daresay we'll forgive her, won't we?"

Risada choked something incomprehensible, and Rustam slipped a glance at her to ensure she wasn't asphyxiating. Her face radiated a delicate shade of puce, but she seemed to be breathing fine, so he assumed she was simply stunned by Chayla's bizarre speech and appearance. Without question, the gaunt and tattered woman standing before them bore little resemblance to the buxom, well-dressed Lady Chayla they'd known at court.

Not to mention she sounded crazy.

Perhaps she is. She was a captive far longer than Nessa. I hate to think what she went through.

"Don't you dare talk about forgiveness! You stole my baby; now hand him over," Risada demanded.

Chayla frowned at her. "What, no thanks? I saved your son from those monsters and you kept me waiting so long I questioned if you were coming at all." She stepped backward with a possessive frown. "Do you even know *how* to handle a baby?"

Rustam noted Risada's momentary hesitation. It appeared Chayla's words had struck like a dart through a chink in the assassin's guard.

"Hand him over so I can pay you back," Risada answered, her silken tone promising anything but reward.

Rustam felt the need to intervene before bloodshed occurred. "Ladies, we can discuss this in a civil manner. Chayla, we're here now, so you can return your charge to his mother." He narrowed his eyes at Risada. "Risada, Chayla's kept your son safe. There has to be some merit in her actions if you give her the chance to explain."

Risada scowled at him. "What merit could there be in stealing a baby?" Her hand twitched towards her waist, and without pausing to think, Rustam grabbed her forearm. He knew where she hid that tiny dagger.

"Let go," she grated. "I'm going to kill her."

"No," said Rustam, "you're not." He waved his free hand towards Chayla. "At least, not while she's holding your son."

"Then get her to put him down."

Rustam rolled his eyes. "Risada, be reasonable, you haven't seen him since he was born. At least let Chayla tell you how he's been, what she's been feeding him, that sort of thing."

Risada's arm relaxed beneath Rustam's fingers and he released her warily, though he kept an eye on her for any sudden movements.

"This is temporary," she said. "Just until I have the details."

"Well and good. She makes a fair point though: *do* you know how to handle a baby?"

Risada favoured him with a wounded look. "How hard can it be?"

He held his hands up. "No idea. Not my territory."

"Well then, leave it to the women here."

Risada stalked towards Chayla, who held her ground. Behind them, Rustam's lips curved into a smirk. He'd manoeuvred Risada into claiming kinship of sorts with Chayla, and she hadn't even noticed.

Risada reached a hand out towards her fur-swaddled son, but before completing the action, her head snapped around to pin Rustam with a glare. "And don't think I didn't notice what you just did."

Rustam didn't bother trying to smother his chortle. As long as Risada wasn't actively trying to kill Chayla, he was content, though he did wonder why he felt the urge to protect the woman. As the wife of one of the traitors, her life would likely be forfeit if she returned to Tyr-en. Perhaps it would be quicker and kinder to let Risada have her way.

Chayla met his gaze over Risada's head, and his answer came in a mercurial flash that lit her green eyes for a fleeting moment.

Chel!

Or Charin?

Rustam suppressed a groan. Once again, it appeared they were playing the deities' games.

Risada gave no indication of having seen the tell-tale glint, and Rustam heaved a sigh of relief. For the moment, at least, it would be easier on Risada if she didn't realise they were being manipulated.

"No, no, no! You have to support his head," Chayla instructed. "Like this."

Risada clasped the babe to her chest. A disapproving wail erupted from the bundle.

"Don't squeeze him so hard, you'll hurt him."

"He's *my* son," Risada snapped. "Don't tell me how to handle him."

The wailing increased in volume.

"You might have birthed him, but he doesn't know you. Here, let me soothe him."

Chayla reached to take the baby back. Risada lifted one arm to fend her off, clutching her son more tightly with the other. The furs began to slither through her grasp and she grabbed them with both hands.

"You nearly made me drop him, you stupid woman! Back off and keep your hands to yourself."

"I'm only trying to help!" Chayla protested. "He doesn't like to be held so tightly."

"Don't tell me what's best for my son!"

The ululating wails turned into lusty crying.

He has a good set of lungs on him, Rustam acknowledged with a wince.

"Ladies, can we take this into the cave, please? We know there are hunters in the forest, and we don't want to attract their attention, do we?"

Both women glowered at him for the interruption, but acknowledged his point by moving towards the dark crevice. Rustam pursed his lips and made a low whistle. The sound of approaching hooves clattering over the rocks made him both relieved and anxious at once. He had no doubts Fleetfoot could make the jump to the platform, but he wasn't so sure about Greylegs.

His worries proved unfounded when first Fleetfoot, and then Greylegs, hopped up the treacherous rocky slope without incident. The goat regarded the newcomers placidly, and as Rustam set about unsaddling the horses, he wondered where Chayla had acquired the beast.

Raised voices inside the cave drew his attention before he'd quite finished, and he slipped the bridle over Greyleg's head, turning the horse loose.

"Keep an eye on him, will you?" Rustam requested with a quick glance towards Fleetfoot. He wouldn't normally consider leaving a regular horse free to wander in such a perilous location, but he trusted the Shivan stallion to keep the gelding out of trouble.

He marched into the cave. "Please don't tell me you're still arguing?"

As his vision adjusted, he made out Risada sitting on the ground beside a small campfire, facing Chayla across the column of smoke rising towards a natural chimney overhead.

"She's feeding him goat's milk!"

Chayla rolled her eyes. "You have a problem with that? What do you think peasant women do when they can't afford a wet nurse?"

"But it comes from an *animal*!"

Chayla's laughter held a shrill edge as she shook her head. Her eyes fixed on a point behind Rustam's left shoulder.

"I know, I know," she said. "But she isn't making this easy, is she?"

Rustam glanced around. Who was Chayla addressing? There wasn't anyone there.

She really has cracked, hasn't she?

He shrugged. If all she did was talk to imaginary people, he could work with that. What he needed now was to not have the two women at each other's throats.

"Risada," he said, once more assuming the role of mediator. "Be reasonable. What else was she going to feed him on? It isn't as if she has any milk of her own to offer." He turned towards the other woman. "Speaking of which, Chayla, where did you find the goat?"

"Oh, I borrowed her from one of the farms down below. They probably think she was taken by a wildcat or a wolf."

"There are farms nearby?" Rustam's spirits lifted. They were close to civilisation after all.

"Yes, not far."

"Wonderful. Then as soon as we're rested, we can get back into Tyr-enese lands."

Even as he said the words, Annasala's edict flashed to the forefront of his mind. The look Risada darted his way told him she hadn't forgotten either.

"Rusty, we should think about this."

His heart swelled. Risada cared enough to be concerned

for him, even when the safety of her son was involved.

"We need to think about you two for now," he said. "We can worry about my situation when the time comes. Our first priority is to get you out of the borderlands and safely back onto Tyr-enese ground."

The baby's howls increased in volume yet further. Risada held her son at arms' length with an almost comical look of horror.

Mother she might be, but Chayla's correct; she doesn't have the touch yet.

"What's the matter with him?"

"Nothing," said Chayla. "He's a baby. They do this. He's probably hungry, or he needs changing."

Risada's nose wrinkled. "I suspect that's the problem." With obvious reluctance, she held him towards Chayla. "You do it."

"Oh no." Chayla's smile held a touch of vengeance. "I'll show you how, but he's your child. You were very clear about that."

Rustam watched with relief as Risada smothered her pride for the sake of her son. She pushed carefully back up to her feet, cradling the bawling infant with more care than her first attempt, and followed Chayla towards the rear of the shallow cave.

Don't suppose she ever saw herself doing that task, he mused. *Mind you, she's tough. Considering what we've been through, how hard can it be to change a baby's cloths? Or whatever it is Chayla's using.*

Rustam realised with surprise he was quite impressed with how resourceful Chayla had proven to be. He remembered her only as a rather vacuous, pleasure-obsessed wife of one of the arch traitors. He'd not had any cause to get close to her, back in his days of information gleaning. By the time they'd realised her husband was involved, the coup was already well underway.

The noisy yelling quietened down, becoming more of an intermittent gasping. The two women returned to the front of the cave with the child cradled once more in Chayla's arms. Risada's fingers curled and uncurled, and Rustam thought she might snatch the baby back, but he was clearly more content in Chayla's embrace than his mother's. Chayla rocked him back and forth, all the while crooning nonsense, and soon the snivelling sounds turned to cheery gurgles.

Rustam raised an eyebrow. "Where did you learn such skills, Chayla? To my knowledge you don't have children of your own."

Chayla gazed down at the babe with a tender smile. "I grew up in a small manor in the foothills. We only had one servant, and I had a younger sister. Mother died in childbirth, so I helped raise her." She peered at Risada through narrowed eyes. "That's how I know a goat is the best substitute for a wet nurse."

Risada's fists flexed. Rustam wasn't sure if she wanted to take her child back, or throttle Chayla. Or perhaps both.

Time for more deflection, I think.

"Why did Ranjit marry you?" he asked Chayla. "If your Family was as lowly as you say, it seems an unlikely match for someone of his ambitions."

For a fleeting moment, Chayla's dazzling smile overrode the abuse and neglect that had ravaged her features. "I was considered a great beauty, and Ranjit was a vain man. He *had* to have the most beautiful woman in the kingdom on his arm, no matter that my Family's status was far below those of other women he could have chosen." She shrugged. "It suited us both."

"Did it suit you when he joined the traitors?" The venom in Risada's tone snagged Chayla's undivided attention.

"He was my *husband*. What say did I have in the matter?"

For once, Risada seemed at a loss for barbed comments. Rustam decided another change of subject was in order.

"Did you name him yet?"

Risada stared blankly at him.

"The baby," he prompted. "Did you and Hal choose a name?"

Rustam's voice caught slightly as he named his father. *Damn, but I miss you, old man. You could be infuriating and obtuse and demanding, but you were always fair.* He cocked his head on one side. *Although telling me you were my father earlier would have made things easier.*

Risada shook her head. "We didn't talk about it. Hal was always aware our child was destined be heir to my House, not his. I suppose he was leaving it up to me." Her eyes squeezed shut and a single tear leaked onto her cheek. "Goddess help me, I wish he was here now."

"Me too," Rustam admitted.

"I'm sorry about Prince Halnashead," Chayla offered. "He was a good man."

"Don't you *dare* utter his name!" Risada spat at Chayla's feet. "But for you, he'd still be alive. It was only because those butchers presented you as a gift that he agreed to an audience."

"I had no choice! In fact, I've *never* had any choice. Would you condemn me for that?" Chayla stared into the darkness behind Risada. "She has no idea of fair, does she?"

It was Risada's turn to sweep the cave for whoever Chayla was talking to, and shake her head in puzzlement. An uncomfortable silence settled, punctuated by the baby's random chirrups.

"Give him back to me," said Risada, and it wasn't a request. Holding herself tall with admirable grace, Chayla complied. As soon as she surrendered the child, he began to grizzle.

"What's the matter with him?" Risada sounded exasperated. "He's *my* son; doesn't he know that? Why does he prefer to be held by you?"

Chayla leaned forward to stroke the fuzz of dark hair on the baby's head. "How should he know?" she asked reasonably. "This is the first time you've held him."

Rustam watched in fascination as the former assassin's lower lip quivered. That a tiny bundle of humanity should so affect the woman who'd killed more people than days the child had lived seemed preposterous, and yet the evidence was clear.

"But I carried him inside me, I felt his first movements. I *talked* to him. He's *my* son; Hal's son."

Her head jerked up and her expression cleared. "That's it! Hal's son. His name is Halson."

Rustam smiled. "Perfect," he said. "Absolutely perfect."

A sharp snort outside snagged Rustam's attention. He hurried out into the fading evening light to scan the trail in either direction. Nothing. And yet Fleetfoot's uneasy rocking from one hoof to another confirmed something was amiss.

Rustam centred himself—it came more quickly now, just a single deep breath—and delved down into the mountainside beneath his feet.

There! Somewhere directly ahead amongst the dense trees, a knot of life energy moving towards them. Rustam couldn't distinguish individuals to get a clear count, nor was he quite sure if they were human or animal, but either way, avoiding a confrontation seemed the safest option.

He touched Fleetfoot's quivering shoulder. "Take Greylegs, wait for us further down the path." He pointed along the track leading towards Tyr-en.

With direction for his pent-up anxiety, the bay stallion whipped around, flattened his ears to his head, and nipped the grey gelding on the rear. The smaller horse squealed a protest but obediently trotted away down the trail. Fleetfoot bounced up and down behind him, shaking his long mane in frustration at the gelding's steady pace.

Rustam cracked a grim smile as the two horses vanished around a bluff further down the path. He gathered their bridles and carried them into the cave.

Both women faced him, questions clear on their faces.

"Company coming," he warned. "Put the fire out and keep quiet."

"Who?" Risada asked as she gathered blankets with her free hand and dragged them towards the rear of the crevice. Chayla kicked dirt over the fire, smothering the flames.

"Don't know, but I'd rather not find out," Rustam said over his shoulder as he went back outside to retrieve the goat. He plucked the knot of her tether loose from the pillar Chayla had fastened her to, and led her into the darkness. Nobody spoke further. The three of them pressed themselves back into the darkest corner of the recess, and waited.

Bootsteps on the rock outside confirmed the species of their unwanted visitors. Low male voices exchanged chatter too thick with accent to discern clear words, but obvious enough to identify them as Tylocian.

A single set of boots trod hesitantly towards them. Rustam understood the caution—caves such as this might hide any number of dangerous occupants.

Such as three people, two of whom were trained killers.

However, with a baby to protect, Rustam had no desire to engage in any fighting. He slipped the rope from around the goat's neck and pressed one hand to the back of her head. Inside his mind, he painted a vivid picture of a snarling wildcat, and with a quick prayer for forgiveness, thrust the image at the goat.

With a startled bleat, the nanny shot out of the cave.

"Charin's balls!" The approaching Tylocian shot backward to avoid the fleeing animal, and Rustam smirked. Probably the first thing the man knew about his 'attacker' were those horizontal barred eyes coming at him from the dark.

"Ha! Biltack shit his pants!"

The sound of a scuffle outside mixed with curses and insults.

"Catch it, you useless crud-lovers! That's tonight's supper!"

Rustam felt bad for the goat, but she'd fulfilled her purpose. He fervently hoped she'd escape. The foul-mouthed yelling receded in pursuit of the unfortunate animal.

Just in time, thought Rustam, as Halson began to grizzle.

"Try to keep it down," he warned. "We don't know how far away they'll get."

"*You* try," Risada snapped. "Babies don't listen to reason."

"Here, let me," Chayla offered, holding out her hands.

"You think I can't do this, don't you?"

Rustam spun to face the bickering women but he was too late; backing away from Chayla, Risada tightened her grip on her son. A vigorous shriek of protest rang out, followed by determined wailing. Rustam cringed, hoping the Tylocians were making too much noise in their goat hunt to notice.

"So," announced a heavy masculine voice from outside the cave, and a bulky body blocked a portion of the remaining light filtering in from outside. "What do we have here?"

Risada's sharp inhalation matched Rustam's. Neither would ever forget that hateful voice. Rustam knew that for Risada, it would be forever summon the pain of her crippled arm.

For himself, more recent memories sprang up. A fight to the death on the hillside fronting a Tylocian fortress. Rustam's victory had made him merciful, leaving his opponent unconscious, not dead.

A mistake he was now going to pay for.

"Well, well," said Hext-al. "See what offal can be found lurking when you know where to look."

18. SPY

Daylight filtered in through the diaphanous window hangings, and Marten groaned. The previous day's events crashed over him, shocking him awake. He threw the bed covers off, wishing he could crawl back beneath them and hide from his responsibilities.

Not something a king could ever do.

He sat up and raked his fingers through his hair. No matter how often he reminded himself of his status, it never made coming to terms with it any easier. So many things to attend to piled up before him in an ever-increasing heap. Without doubt, problems bred problems.

Arranging Uncle Hal's rites. Meeting with his nobles to advise them of Annasala's new position as King's Counsellor. Dealing with those affronted by that announcement. Greeting the new spiritual advisor the Temple was sending over. Oh, and rescheduling the audience Lady Betha had applied for last evening.

He was puzzled by that last one. Considering the dreadful events of the day, the timing of Betha's request struck him as downright odd. From what he'd seen of the lady so far, he would have expected her to have more empathy, and be willing to grant him the space to grieve, before expecting him to face mundane matters like selecting a new husband for her.

He'd refused her petition, of course, instead smothering his sorrows with a vigorous evening's diversion, facilitated by the ever enthusiastic Nonni.

Marten rolled his shoulders before forcing himself to his feet. No matter how he wished it, the day would not wait for him. Funny how people believed kings had power over everything. He probably had as little control over his own life as most servants, and less than many.

He dipped a cloth in the ewer on the sideboard and splashed cold water on his face. A memory from last evening heated his neck and he dipped the cloth again, not bothering to wring it out this time before applying it to his skin. Water dribbled down his back. He shuddered as he tried to squash the image in his mind, but it refused to be vanquished.

Nonni, wrists shackled to the bedframe, writhing beneath the caress of his whip. But when she opened her eyes, it wasn't Nonni's face he saw, but Betha's, staring back at him with passion darkening her gaze.

Dammit! What is it about her? She's a widow; a respectable older woman. Why does she invade my dreams?

With an irritable grunt, Marten dragged a tunic over his head before calling for Davi. When his bodyguard entered to help him dress, Marten submitted with poor grace. He knew he was being prickly, but he couldn't seem to stop himself.

"Sire! If you tug any harder at that collar, you'll rip it off. You aren't due for another fitting with Marganie for at least half a season; what you have now needs to last!"

"Don't fuss, Davi. I don't have the patience for it today."

Davi's head dipped. "I'm sorry sire, I hoped some levity might help."

Marten shut his eyes for an instant, once again wishing the world might leave him alone. "It's not your fault, Davi. This isn't going to be an easy day."

"Indeed, sire."

* * * * * * *

Marten quickly regretted choosing to meet with his new spiritual advisor in the comfort of his snug private office, rather than the larger public workroom. The withering glance had informed him of the priest's disdain for luxuries, as did the manner in which the man perched on the very edge of the plush, padded armchair.

Brother Freskin cleared his scrawny throat for the fifth time, the raspy sound chafing Marten's already abraded nerves.

The day, as expected, was proving difficult, and where before Marten had been able to rely on Brother Padrus for support, it was abundantly clear to him that Brother Freskin favoured a more formal approach. Perhaps things would change as they grew to know one another better, but Marten couldn't help wishing Padrus was still with him.

"I know Chel didn't actually speak, but there's no doubt her light touched me. Shouldn't I feel different, somehow?" he asked Freskin.

The priest's mouth stretched into a patronising smile. "Not necessarily, sire. That Chel chose to intervene in your situation does not imply either endorsement, or disapproval, of you as a person. The reasons behind Her actions may be beyond our comprehension; the weave of Her tapestry is complex."

Marten controlled his irritation. "And yet I must consider Her intentions. Without being vainglorious, I'm not just any man: I am the king, and warder of Her Casket. Surely that makes it more likely this event had some significance?"

"That may be, sire, and the Temple Council has been convened to discuss it."

Marten drew three measured breaths before replying. "Brother Freskin, I know you are new to this position, so I will forgive your oversight this once. In future, please give me such information at the start of our meetings, and not later."

Freskin stiffened. "Yes, sire. Yet I feel constrained to remind you that the Temple answers to the goddess, not to any man, king or not."

"We both serve Chel, brother. Can we not find a way to work more closely together? Quite apart from this incident, it would help me to know if you've uncovered anything about Padrus's murder."

Freskin relented a little at mention of his fellow priest. "Your Majesty, I will convey your request to the council."

"Thank you."

Determined to stay positive, Marten chose to accept that offer as a forward step, both in his seedling relationship with Freskin, and in the potential for a closer accord with the Temple. He added a prayer for good measure.

Chel, I'd appreciate your input, whether it comes directly from you, or via the Temple. Please.

"Brother Freskin, thank you for your attendance and I look forward to the council's reply, but I'm afraid that's all I have time for today."

Looking somewhat put out by his dismissal, Freskin nevertheless rose and bowed, his whip-thin body bending like a reed in a spring storm. Marten held his expression of patience until the door closed behind the priest.

"Well, that's going to be a joyful relationship," he muttered to himself. He would have been happier if the Temple had sent him almost anyone but Freskin. He knew with dismal conviction that every time Freskin attended him, the unwelcome memory of Padrus's corpse would resurface.

I wonder if I can request a replacement. Or find an even more important position to promote Freskin to.

He grimaced. Before Padrus's death, he'd been considering discussing his tricky personal life with the old priest. As the pressure increased on him to marry, Marten knew he needed wise counsel. Padrus had known of Marten's dalliances, but not the details of exactly how he and his partners indulged themselves, and now Marten had dithered too long thinking about how he might broach the topic.

Even the fear he might turn into a monster like his grandfather wasn't powerful enough for him to consider bringing it up with his new priest. As he'd done on so many occasions already, he buried the notion deep inside for another day.

Davi slipped through the door and marched up to his desk. "My liege, Lady Betha is outside."

"What *does* the woman want?"

Marten's protest burst out louder than he intended and he winced. "Do you think she heard?"

Davi shook his head. "The doors are soundproof, sire. Shall I send her away?"

"No, I might as well see her," Marten replied, tugging at his overtight collar again. "It seems she isn't going to give up until I do."

"Sire."

Marten tried to compose himself, but his vision from the previous night, of Betha's features superimposed over Nonni's, flashed across his mind's eye, making him squirm.

"The Lady Betha Fontmaness," announced Davi.

He stood as his graceful caller glided across the parquet flooring. Her pale blue, fitted, day gown emphasised how her body tapered from her bust down to her slender ankles, and Marten had to lick dry lips before he could coax his voice to life. "Lady Betha," he said, keeping his tone glacial.

Marten settled back into his chair, inviting Betha to take the seat opposite only after a pointed delay. A faint blush coloured her cheeks, and a twinge of remorse pricked him.

Then he recalled how much of his day had been spent arranging his uncle's rites, and righteous annoyance reasserted itself.

"How may I help you, my lady? As you must be aware, I have pressing matters to deal with concerning my uncle's death that prevent me from addressing your situation at this time."

"Forgive me, sire, but it's your uncle I must speak with you about."

Marten stiffened. "How so?"

Betha's gaze dropped to her clasped hands, white-knuckled in her lap. A rush of impatience swept through Marten. "Well?"

Betha raised her head, defensiveness radiating from her rigid posture. "I was one of his spies," she stated simply.

Her eyes searched his face, but he knew she would have

no trouble reading his shock. He couldn't hide it, despite his training.

Delicate, genteel Betha, a spy? Ludicrous!

And yet it would be so like Uncle Hal to employ the least likely person for such a position.

"Goddess help me, I believe you. Is *that* why you were so determined to speak to me? You have some intelligence about his death?"

Betha shook her head. "Not about his death, sire, that came as a terrible shock. He was such a kind man, I can't believe he's gone."

Marten's annoyance with Betha for intruding on his difficult day evaporated. Halnashead's death had evidently affected her life too. He coughed, trying to dislodge the lump that had inexplicably grown behind his tongue.

"So why the urgency? I assume you have something to report, and you've brought it to me now your master's gone."

Marten spotted a glistening tear forming in the corner of one of Betha's eyes. She blinked it away.

"You see truly, sire. I overheard a conversation yesterday, after—" She paused, and cleared her throat. "After the prince's cortège arrived. I believe it was urgent, but when you wouldn't see me last night, I tried to follow it up. I failed."

Betha's gaze dropped once more to her lap where her fingers twisted together. The urge to comfort her almost drove Marten from his chair, but he resisted. If Betha was one of his uncle's spies, she would be accustomed to a professional approach.

"From now on you'll report to me," he said firmly, pushing back unreasonable feelings of guilt. He couldn't have known she wanted to bring him clandestine information.

He knew what his uncle would have counselled, under the circumstances: "*If you missed it, worrying about what might have been only wastes time. Get on, and deal with what you have before you now.*"

"I'll ensure you have immediate access in future," he said. "Now, tell me what you overheard."

"It was Lords Urien and Edlund. They were discussing who should take over as your privy advisor, and they saw Prince Halnashead's death as an opportunity rather than a tragedy."

Anger laced her words, which Marten's emotions echoed. How dare they view Uncle Hal's death in that vein? Sudden eagerness consumed him as he anticipated informing his arrogant lords that the position they craved was already filled. By a woman.

"They also mentioned a benefactor," Betha continued. "I got the impression they thought he might have had something to do with the prince's death."

"Did they name him?"

Betha's eye's slid away from his. "No, but they sounded scared. They talked of a meeting with clerics in the Temple that evening to discuss it further." She shifted uncomfortably on her chair. "I tried to follow them, but I only got as far as the public chambers. The doorways into the inner precincts are too well guarded."

Marten grimaced. "I'm very aware of that. It makes me wonder what the Temple has to hide. From what you say, I'm correct to be suspicious."

"Oh, and they said it was a pity you'd realised Brother Padrus was murdered." Her teeth grazed her bottom lip. "I'm sorry, sire; I know he was your friend."

Marten cleared his throat. "He was. Thank you for your kind words. I can only assume from that comment they are involved in his death."

He considered his freshly employed spy. An idea tickled at his mind.

"Lady Betha, I have a commission for you. If you're willing to undertake a risky task?"

She answered without hesitation. "Of course, sire. It's what Prince Halnashead had me trained for. He chose me because I'm good at getting people to trust me."

I wonder if that includes me? Marten shifted on his cushions. *Is that why she haunts my dreams?*

Pushing the unsettling notion to one side for later consideration, Marten mapped out the start of a plan. "I want you to get close to Lord Urien. He's arrogant enough to believe a mere woman has no position beyond that of wife or mother, so he won't suspect you. Go to him, beg forgiveness for your presumption in attending the last council meeting. Ask him to take charge of your affairs."

A spark of indignation lit Betha's eyes, only to be quashed the next moment. She bobbed her head, a vacuous expression layered over her face.

"I can do that, sire, I'll go to him as soon as I leave here." Her tone was placid, but her eagerness to please shone through.

"While you're cosying up to Urien, I also want you to be my eyes and ears within the court. None of my other spies have your social standing so they can't get close to the noble ladies the way you can."

"Am I seeking anything in particular amongst the ladies?"

"Yes. Any whispers, any hints that an assassin lurks amongst them."

Betha's eyes widened. "An assassin, sire? Are you seeking to employ one?"

Marten considered his answer. Should he tell her the truth? Her obvious eagerness to please swayed him. That, and anticipation of seeing her on a more frequent basis.

"Not to employ one, no. To root out the one who keeps trying to kill me."

Betha's hands twisted in her lap, and her already wide eyes bulged even further. "Sire! When? How?" She bit her lip, hard. "I should have known."

Marten frowned. "Why should you have known? No one knows, except my bodyguard. Even Uncle Hal didn't."

"But I should have," Betha said stubbornly.

Marten tried to separate the fleeting expressions chasing one another across Betha's face. Guilt and remorse mixed with embarrassment. Marten recognised there was something going on here he should understand.

"Go on, please," he invited, endeavouring to sound dispassionate.

Betha glanced down, avoiding eye contact.

"Sire, when the court returned from Domn, and Prince Halnashead elected to remain with his wife, he instructed me to watch over you, and report any issues to him. What could be more noteworthy than an assassination attempt?" She bit her bottom lip. "I fear I am not up to the tasks you have set me. Such a failure proves I am unfit to be a player. I should retire to my manor and await the husband you choose for me."

Marten suddenly felt very, very tired. *Uncle Hal never did trust me to manage on my own, did he? Could he not have been honest, instead of setting a woman to watch me?*

Disappointment lent a sharp edge to his reply.

"You will stay. I have need of your services, and you will carry out your assignments to the best of your abilities. No excuses, no self-pity. Now go. Find me an assassin and ingratiate yourself with that bastard Urien."

Betha stood. She drew herself up tall and donned a blank expression. "I shall, sire," she confirmed, before departing with her customary grace.

As she approached the exit, the heavy door swung open to admit Annasala. Betha stepped aside and acknowledged the princess with a dignified curtsey.

Blocked from indulging in his own self-pity by his cousin's arrival, Marten had to content himself with slamming the heels of his fists down onto the mercifully robust armrests of his chair.

Annasala cocked her head. "Something you'd like to share, cousin?"

She didn't wait for an answer but twisted around to take in a last glimpse of Betha's light blue gown sweeping through the open door before it swung shut.

"Or perhaps someone?"

"Lady Betha was delivering her condolences," Marten said quickly. Annasala's implication made him break out in a sweat.

"Of course she was," agreed his cousin, a flash of calculation brightening her gaze. "She's a widow, isn't she?"

"She is," Marten confirmed, but hurried on to quash Annasala's train of thought. "I'm considering suitable husbands for her. We can't have yet another House without male leadership."

Annasala treated him to a disgusted glance. "Are you saying a woman isn't capable of ruling their own lands?"

Marten groaned inwardly. *I really must think before opening my mouth.*

"Not at all, cousin. But the political situation is unstable enough I have to limit changes that impact on general life. Having women in charge of their own Houses is a step too far at this time."

"As is legalising magic," Annasala said, doggedly returning to her pet subject, but her next words knocked Marten completely off balance.

"Have you considered marrying Betha yourself?"

"What?"

"She's eligible, she's young enough, and she's Tyr-enese through and through, so no danger of being tainted with magic." Annasala's brow drew down. "Mind you, she was married for a couple of years without producing children. The likelihood is that was Herschel's lack, as neither of his previous wives quickened either."

She stared straight into Marten's startled eyes.

"You should sleep with her and find out if she's fertile. If she gets pregnant, then we can arrange a swift marriage." A satisfied smile overtook her face. "There. I knew you needed someone to organise your life for you, I just didn't realise it would be so easy."

19. SUBTERFUGE

Betha strode through the palace corridors to her own rooms, not pausing to think. Once inside the empty suite, she slumped back against the door and closed her eyes.

The king was being stalked by an assassin! How could she have missed that?

Admittedly, she was only able to keep watch over him when he was in public, and presumably the attempts on his life were made while he was in his private chambers.

But even so!

The only thing that mitigated her failure was Marten's assertion that Halnashead hadn't known either. Whether such critical information had, in truth, remained concealed from the kingdom's spymaster, they would never know for sure, and Betha speculated if that had been behind her watching brief, at least in part.

She was under no illusions about her efficacy as a spy; her tutors had made it quite clear her skills and reactions would never match those of operatives recruited in childhood. It was only Halnashead's belief in her that had sustained her through the tough, compressed training designed specifically for her, the trainee starting too late in life. Betha's talents lay in her easy way with people, her ability to gain their trust, and to lubricate their tongues.

She aimed to put those talents to work immediately, now she had Marten's patronage.

She tipped her head back against the door. Without doubt she'd earned Marten's curt dismissal, but in reality, the interview had been far less awkward than she'd feared. News of her role in Halnashead's spy network hadn't wrong-footed the king for more than a moment, and while no doubt the revelation that she'd spied on him had been hurtful, he'd not let it distract him.

She'd even tested his mettle with her offer to retire to her allotted role as a lord's dutiful wife, and he'd handled that option with impressive positivity, forcing her to reassess her initial opinion of his maturity.

She pictured the king's long face, reminiscent of a boisterous puppy she'd raised while married to Herschel. The endearing kink in his hair that he was always trying to smooth out brought a smile to her lips.

Stop it! He's so obviously a romantic; he'd be horrified if he knew my tastes.

Pushing away from the door, Betha strode to her bedchamber. Time to get started.

She pulled aside the drapes concealing the selection of gowns she'd brought to court. What would be appropriate to project an air of submission to the odious Lord Urien? The black? No, too severe. The azure that was her favourite? She dithered, but rejected that too as insufficiently modest. In the end she settled on a moss green dress with a higher neckline than she favoured, and a straight cut skirt. It was what she opted for when inspecting her estates; comfortable, unprovocative, and practical.

Dressing awkwardly without the help of a maid, she thanked Chel for the simplicity of the un-fussy dress's drawstring fastenings. Perhaps she should avail herself of Marganie's skills when the palace seamstress was not occupied making or altering the royal family's garments. With only Marten and Annasala in Darshan, there should be a bit of spare time for the woman to exchange a few of the excess buttons on Betha's gowns for laces. Being able to change without the need to summon her maid from her secondary work in the kitchens appealed to Betha.

Selecting a matching pair of shoes, Betha took a moment to appraise her appearance. Should she wear her hair up? Or loose, as she preferred?

Bearing in mind the current fashion for updos, she took a moment to separate her thick locks into three bunches, which she plaited and arranged into coiled loops. She fastened them on the crown of her head with a fan-shaped clasp.

Urien would see a subservient woman, complying with the social mores of her class. A woman to be used by a man as decoration, and as wife and mother to his children.

Satisfied, Betha moved to the next stage of her preparation. She sat on a comfortable chair in a dark corner of her boudoir and closed her eyes. A few deep inhalations reaching all the way to her belly brought physical and mental relaxation. Using a technique she'd learned during her training, she pictured a thick-skinned bubble surrounding her body to form a barrier between herself and her surroundings. She delved into her psyche, seeking those aspects that were inappropriate to her planned persona.

Self-confidence. Self-worth. Sense of humour. A prickly temper. Her belief that women were intellectual equals with men.

As she located each unsuitable component, she drew it out, and endowed it with substance and colour, making it easier to grasp. One at a time, she pushed the undesirable elements through the one-way barrier, placing them outside her mental bubble.

As she consciously discarded each fragment, her mien transformed until she became the type of woman the authentic Betha would either despise or pity.

A very different Betha rose to her feet. A tiny, puckered frown formed a V-shape between her downcast eyes. Her shoulders hunched ever so slightly forward, and she moved towards the door with tiny, mincing steps.

Pulling the door to the outer hallway open, Betha slipped out of her suite. She hugged the shadows at the sides of the corridor as she set off to debase herself before Lord Urien.

* * * * * *

Betha sat alone in Lord Urien's reception area. In a deferential tone, she'd politely asked the guardsman outside the suite if she might gain an audience with his lord. She'd stood outside the blank door long enough to start to worry, before the man returned and ushered her into the unremarkable square reception room. He indicated she should take a seat, before resuming his post outside in the corridor.

Since then, she'd waited. The sixth and seventh bells of the evening had come and gone, and still no summons into Lord Urien's presence. She refused to speculate how much longer he intended to keep her tarrying, remaining immobile on her hard, upright chair with her hands folded primly in her lap.

Betha studied the room. Clean straight lines and sharp angles dominated. No fussy returns or embellishments on any of the woodwork. The sole exhibit on the mantle above an empty fireplace was a rectangular vase placed dead centre, its black and grey glaze matching the room's paintwork.

There was no evidence of a woman's touch anywhere: no flowers, no scented garlands, no splashes of colour to relieve the austere monochrome theme. Betha could not ever recall Urien bringing his wife to court. By all accounts, she never left their estate in the south-east. She'd certainly had no hand in the decoration of Lord Urien's palace suite.

Having requested an audience, and been granted one, she couldn't leave without offering offence. The faint aroma of cooked meat provided one possible reason for the prolonged delay.

Another explanation seemed rather more probable: Urien had chosen to assert his social position, deigning to see the lowly lady of an inconsequential House only when *he* was ready, and not a moment sooner.

Quashing her impatience, Betha used the time to reimagine the bubble she'd constructed around herself. She mentally reinforced the barrier before rehearsing the speech she'd prepared.

When the door to the inner chamber finally opened, her heart sank.

"Well, well. Look what we have here." Lord Edlund's blustering tone made her cringe. The obnoxious lord's bulging waistline appeared through the doorway ahead of the rest of him. Betha caught a brief glimpse of Lord Urien's smug smile before Edlund's bulk blocked her view.

"Are you lost, Lady Betha?" Edlund sneered. "This isn't the king's chambers you know."

Betha rose from her chair, keeping her gaze trained on the floor. "Forgive me, my lords, but I am where I mean to be."

Edlund snorted and drew breath to reply, but Urien cut in from behind him.

"Let the girl enter, Ed; I'm intrigued to hear what she has to say."

Huffing in annoyance, Edlund spun on his heel and re-entered the main parlour of Urien's suite.

Girl.

That was what Urien thought of her. In accord with the character she'd created, Betha accepted the belittlement and followed Edlund.

With her eyes downcast, Betha was unable to study the room as she would have liked, but the layout of most of the palace suites was similar, and she fervently hoped she would not be in need of an emergency exit. The door opposite almost certainly led into Urien's dressing room, with his bedroom beyond. The one on her left was probably the servants' access; her best goal if the meeting went dangerously awry. The door through which she'd entered, guarded on the outside by Urien's man, would be her second choice, but not one she would favour unless there was no alternative.

Edlund led the way to a group of chairs arranged around a table bearing the remnants of a small feast. Two almost empty goblets stood amongst the clutter, the deep red dregs explaining his somewhat flushed complexion and the rapidity with which he tottered forward and crashed onto his chair.

Betha held her breath, wondering if the bow-legged armchair would collapse beneath the assault, but with a creak of protest, it survived.

Urien acknowledged Betha with a short nod, but did not invite her to sit.

"So, my dear, how may I help you?" Urien's silken vowels sounded far more threatening than Edlund's bluster.

Betha composed herself.

"My lord, I wish to apologise for my presumption. I should never have attended the council meeting, I realise that now."

A brief silence ensued, forcing Betha to flick her eyes upward to check the men's reactions. Edlund focussed on quaffing the remnants of his wine. Urien's expression beneath his dark brows, was unreadable.

"Go on."

Betha returned her gaze to the floor. "Forgive me, my lord. I have been without a husband's guidance for too long, and your directive regarding the unmarried ladies of the court came as a welcome relief to me. Of course, the king has taken it upon himself to choose our new spouses, but I wanted to thank you in person for your proposal."

Betha winced inside. *Perhaps proposal was not the best word, under the circumstances.*

"I hope that is not too forward of me," she added.

Edlund's inebriated titter confirmed how much he'd drunk already that evening. A quick glance at Urien revealed a predator's smile bending his thin lips.

"My dear," he purred, "I would not hold such forwardness against you in light of your apology. Your misjudgement is understandable, considering how long you have been left in your lamentable state of widowhood. Do tell, is the king making progress with the situation?"

Betha accepted Urien's words as approval. She felt her cheeks warm.

"You are gracious, my lord. The king has produced a provisional list of candidates, though he expressed his wish to study the matter more fully before making a decision. Naturally, the tragic loss of his uncle will divert him for the time being."

"Of course, such a tragedy," Urien agreed.

Edlund waved his cup in the air. "Here's to a dead prince."

Urien scowled at him.

"What? I'm toasting his memory. You did the same earlier."

With a shake of his head, Urien returned his attention to Betha. "We all feel the king's loss keenly. Prince Halnashead was a wise counsellor, and Marten will be the poorer for his absence." He tapped his thumb against his chin. "I suppose it's unavoidable the mourning period will prolong your woeful situation, but I wonder…"

Urien rose and took a single step towards Betha before his right knee buckled. He swore, forced to put one hand to the table for balance. Sweat sprang to his brow, and a vein on his forehead stood out. With a grunt, he reached for a small glass bottle nestling in the centre of the table amongst the condiments, and tipped five dark red drops from it into the remnants of his wine. He drained his cup.

Interesting. I wonder what ails him, and what that remedy might be.

Replacing both cup and bottle on the table, Urien straightened and resumed his approach. Betha's nails bit into her palms. At close quarters, Urien's lean, compact frame proved far more intimidating than Edlund's fleshy bulk.

Urien limped past to stand at her back, and Betha battled the urge to shiver. His hand brushed her bare neck, one fingertip tracing the arch from ear to shoulder. When it halted, a finger-width beyond her collar bone, Betha thanked the goddess she'd chosen to wear a modestly cut dress.

"I believe I have an idea," Urien mused. "Betha, dear girl, you wish to make amends for your presumption at the council meeting? And you desire the leadership of a man to remove such a burden from your pretty shoulders?"

Betha gulped. She dipped her head, not trusting her voice.

"Good." Urien returned to his seat, already moving with more ease. "I believe I will introduce you to some friends of mine. We have a meeting arranged for tomorrow night. You are available?"

Betha wondered why he asked the question at all, when he obviously expected an affirmative.

"Of course, my lord. I am extremely grateful for your concern."

"Yes, well, it would be unkind to ignore your plight. My guard will fetch you at the eighth bell."

"Thank you, my lord," said Betha, although Urien's attention had already moved away from her as he reached for his empty cup.

"More wine!" Edlund thundered. A servant bearing a pitcher scurried through the door to Betha's left.

"My lord?" Betha breathed.

Urien's gaze snapped back to her, irritation plain in his frown. She waited until he gave a curt nod.

"Where will this meeting be held? How formally should I dress?"

"We shall be leaving the palace, so a cloak over regular court attire would be appropriate."

Edlund disagreed. "Wear something more revealing, girl. What good is a woman if a man can't admire what's on offer?"

Betha gritted her teeth. Thank the goddess Edlund was already married—the idea of his meaty paws touching her made her flesh crawl. She bowed her head and hastened from the room, pursued by Edlund's lewd laughter.

* * * * * * *

Betha scurried back to her own suite, unable to put distance between herself and Edlund fast enough. She slid through the outer door to her chambers, barely pushing it open far enough for her slender body to fit through. Once inside, she slammed the door shut and leaned back against it as if she might hold the memory of his disgusting laughter at bay.

Eyes closed, she popped her protective bubble and concentrated on taking deep breaths until she regained some control.

A knock on the door at her back launched her half way across the room. She placed a hand over her hammering heart.

Don't be ridiculous; it won't be him.

"Enter," she called once she'd composed herself.

Her seneschal, Quart, stepped in, and Betha's tight chest relaxed.

"It's late, Quart, what brings you here?"

Her words came out sharper than she intended, and the old man's apologetic expression made her feel guilty. Quart only ever had the best intentions.

"Forgive the intrusion, my lady, but I felt you should know immediately. I've had word from your estate: Master Lorndar is on his way here."

Betha scowled. A visit from the head of the Blacksmith's Guild was an irritation she could do without at this moment. Lorndar was always trouble.

"On his way here? Did he not receive my message?"

Quart wrung his hands together. "I fear he did, my lady. I believe he's decided not to wait upon your undetermined return."

"Surely his concerns cannot be *that* pressing? Neither he nor his guildmembers have suffered any inconvenience or lack of work since my husband's death."

Quart shrugged thin shoulders. "Perhaps the men of his guild have put pressure on him to do something about the situation? I suppose we shall know when he arrives."

"I suppose we shall." Betha raised a smile she did not feel inside. "Until then, thank you for your diligent service, Quart. You do know how much I appreciate you, don't you?"

Blushing like a young maid, Quart mumbled something that sounded like thanks, and backed out of the door.

Alone again, Betha reached up to rip off the clasp holding the coils of her hair. She untangled her locks from the braids and shook them free. Her neck and shoulders relaxed.

In many ways, the meeting with Urien had gone far better than she'd expected. If Chel had smiled upon her performance, then the friends Urien was taking her to meet may well be those the king was interested in.

Her mind slid back to the other person who would undoubtedly be accompanying them: Edlund. The illusory sensation of slimy fingers trailing across her skin made Betha shudder.

At least the king should be pleased with her. She realised with a jolt of surprise that at some time in the past season, pleasing Marten had become important to her.

If only she didn't have a husband to find, a lecher to avoid, and a guild master to appease, life would be so much simpler.

20. OBEDIENCE

Betha clutched her cloak tightly around her neck and pulled her hood further forward. It helped her avoid eye contact with either of her travelling companions.

She swayed and bounced with the carriage's motion, her muscles coiled so tight she was certain she'd be exhausted by the end of the journey. She kept her knees pressed together, not wishing to repeat the uncomfortable moment early on when her thigh had brushed Edlund's. Taking that accidental touch as an invitation, he'd put his fat hand on her knee until Urien glared at him.

Betha had never imagined she'd be grateful to Urien for anything, but she was extremely thankful for his tacit control over Edlund. She might have felt more comfortable with another woman present, but she'd not been offered the option to bring a companion, and as a widow her virtue was no longer a commodity society deemed in need of protection. To stave off her anxious queasiness, she concentrated on keeping her breathing steady.

If only she could ignore the vigorous masculine scent saturating the enclosed space.

The carriage horses trotted along steadily for an hour or more, adding to Betha's apprehension. Urien had implied they would be visiting somewhere within the city, but they'd left the capital behind some time ago. Betha had peeked past the window drapes a couple of times before the sun set, and had a vague idea of the direction they were travelling, but no way to tell where they were with any precision. They'd crossed a bridge over swift running water once—the timbre of the wheels changed audibly as they went from hard-packed earth to stone, and back again, with the rushing of the watercourse loud enough to penetrate the body of the carriage—which would narrow things down somewhat, but not a great deal.

The carriage took a long arc to the left, and the horses slowed to a walk, then halted. When the door swung open, Betha took a deep gulp of the fresh air blasted in by a brisk breeze.

Urien and Edlund alighted first, leaving Betha to be handed out by a liveried coachman. Staring up at the unfamiliar blocky building outlined by flaring lanterns, her stomach churned. She had no idea where she was.

You knew the risks when you took on the job, she chastised herself. *Remember why you're doing this. For Marten.*

She followed the two lords through the forbidding iron-braced double doors. Inside, a square vestibule contained evidence of a substantial number of people. Garments hung from every peg, and Betha was relieved to see a number of ladies' cloaks, though it appeared men outnumbered women by at least two to one.

Urien and Edlund shed their top coats and Betha followed suit, hanging her dark blue cloak over a brown one.

"Come, my dear."

To her surprise, Urien extended an arm, inviting her to take it. Edlund scowled.

Feeling uncomfortable, but gaining confidence from Urien's urbanity, Betha complied. Urien led her along a dim corridor and through another doorway. It took a moment to process the sight that greeted her, but when she had, her strides faltered. She tensed, but Urien tightened his grip on her arm so she could not break free without an undignified struggle.

She knew such places existed but had never expected to stand in one.

The opulent furnishings and hangings teetered over into gaudy. A pair of fiddle-playing minstrels wandered the room, their eyes averted from the couples and threesomes lounging on couches set around low tables heaped with food. Jugs and goblets littered the surfaces and the floor, and the overpowering aroma of strong wine thickened the air.

The women Betha had hoped might offer her refuge from unwanted male company would clearly be doing no such thing. Gowns designed to reveal rather than preserve modesty brought heat to Betha's ears. Activities she'd been raised to believe should remain private between couples, were on public display with no bashfulness on the part of the participants, even where a woman entertained more than one man.

Betha took a step back, but Urien's grip remained firm.

"Now, now, my dear, you agreed to my guidance, did you not?"

"My lord," Betha said, unable to control the tremor that shook her voice. "I am seeking a husband, yet you bring me to a bordello. I have said I will willingly submit to your advice, but I will not debase myself so."

Urien's quiet smile vexed her.

"My dear, have I asked you to participate? I believe not." He shook his head. "No, I have something else altogether in mind for you."

Hardly reassuring, Betha thought, but in her submissive guise, she bowed her head and allowed Urien to lead her around the edge of the revel towards another set of doors. She glanced back to see Edlund wrapped in the embrace of a young, slender brunette wearing only a flimsy divided skirt riding low on her hips. Edlund seized the girl's bare breasts in his pudgy hands and Betha averted her eyes, feeling sick.

Urien pushed open the left-hand door of an intricately carved pair. Betha swallowed bile as she focussed on the scenes of debauchery, torture, and war, jutting from every wooden panel. The repellent images boasted the work of a master craftsman, leaving no element, no detail, to the imagination, imparting a hideous life to the sculpted figures that writhed in perpetual torment.

Urien led between the doors, his grip of Betha's arm

giving her no choice but to accompany him. She crowded closer rather than risk touching the ghastly things.

Beyond, broad steps led down to a large oval floorspace. At the far end, a throne of elaborately etched wood dominated a raised dais. Its tall, incised back and curling armrests proclaimed it the work of the same artisan who'd created the foul entrance.

The dais overlooked what appeared to be an altar. The waist high rectangular block of stone had a heavy metal ring inset into each corner, and a deep red cloth covered its centre. Betha noted the sanguine colour, and allowed her surface persona to react with a shudder while her rational self scanned the room for exits.

There were none, save the one through which they'd entered.

"The others will join us soon," Urien announced in a perfectly normal tone. Betha jumped as he detached her arm from his. "Don't fret, my dear, there's nothing to fear."

Oh, really?

Urien descended the steps. He'd almost reached the bottom when his untrustworthy knee gave way and he fell.

Betha dithered, neither of her personalities sure how to respond.

With a grunt, Urien levered himself onto the bottom step. "Fetch wine," he ordered through gritted teeth.

Grateful for the direction, Betha fled back to the bordello and grabbed a full goblet from a table.

"Hey!" someone protested, but she nimbly avoided the hands clutching at her skirts and slithered back between the repulsive doors. She hurried down the steps and stooped to offer Urien the goblet, but he shook his head.

"Put it down." He pointed to the step above him. Reaching inside his tunic, he extracted a bottle like the one Betha had seen the previous night. He tipped a drop of dark red liquid from the bottle into the cup, and swore in annoyance when no more trickled out. He shook the bottle hard and a grudging droplet plopped into the wine. Urien swirled the contents before drinking. Standing beside him, Betha noted a pungent odour, but couldn't identify it.

"Falling down already, Urien?" The booming voice announced Edlund's arrival. Betha glanced up to see he'd mislaid his companion.

"Didn't know you'd had that much to drink!"

"Help me up, Ed, and don't be so stupid."

The insult bypassed Edlund, who strode down the steps and heaved Urien to his feet as if the awkward situation was an everyday occurrence.

Perhaps it is, thought Betha. *Definitely a weakness to bring to Marten's attention.*

Locking away the information for her report, Betha hurriedly sidestepped out of the path of two men who'd entered in Edlund's wake. Behind them, a trickle of new faces appeared through the doors, fast becoming a steady stream. Betha was shocked to see several priests mixing with the nobles, along with some dusky skinned foreigners draped in the distinctive brightly-patterned robes and turbans of Rylondese merchants. Visitors from the neighbouring kingdom had become a more frequent sight since the king opened trade negotiations, but now Betha questioned what else they might have brought with them in addition to legitimate goods.

Urien leaned heavily on Edlund's support as his friend helped him up onto the dais. The two lords took up positions either side of the throne-like chair.

Betha fingers twined together. Who would take the commanding seat? Was she about to discover the identity of the mysterious 'benefactor'?

As the gathering settled, Betha worked her way back up the steps until she could press her back against the cool wall. She scanned the crowd, committing to memory any faces she recognised.

Men. They were all men. Aside from her, no women had entered the hall.

The men took up positions on the tiered steps following

no particular ranking Betha could decipher, but with no jockeying for position she guessed they had allotted spots. They all ignored her, keeping their attention on the dais, which suited her fine.

A hush fell, until someone called out: "Will the Master join us tonight?"

All eyes turned towards Urien. He shifted his weight and could not hide his wince of pain. Schooling his face to a blank mask, he shook his head.

"His presence will not grace our gathering tonight, but we have an important interview to conduct, nonetheless. I trust you have been well entertained while you waited?"

Bawdy comments and gestures coloured the air.

"Then we shall proceed. You have all heard my proposal?"

Murmurs indicated both approval and dissent.

Urien frowned. "Whilst there are risks, they are minimal and should remain untraceable. If this does not work, all we lose is time."

"Do we even know your plan is viable?" came a challenge from the crowd.

Urien leant his head to one side. "An excellent question. Shall we find out?"

Approval hummed through the throng, and to Betha's horror all heads swivelled in her direction. She shrank back against the wall, but when Urien beckoned, she raised her chin, and complied. This was why she had come.

Betha descended the steps to the sunken floor with her eyes downcast like a good, biddable woman, her disgust at the vulgar calls and suggestions smothered beneath the carefully constructed layers of her surface persona. Drawing to a halt in the centre of the open floor space, she bowed her head and clasped her hands demurely.

Male voices blended into an animalistic roar. Stamping feet heightened the noise level and shook the floor. Urien stepped gingerly down from the dais.

The silence was instantaneous, shocking Betha as much as

the clamour. She stifled a gasp.

Urien stalked towards her with no more than the barest hint of an uneven step to mar the ominous aura preceding him. He halted so close Betha could smell the wine on his breath.

"Don't concern yourself with these boors, my dear," he soothed. "Not one of them will touch you, I guarantee it."

Betha's fingers curled into tight fists.

"Now," said Urien reasonably, "you offered your obedience to me, did you not?"

Not exactly, Betha wanted to clarify, but now was not the time to argue details.

"Yes," she whispered, and Urien's mouth stretched into a savage smile.

"You see?" He declared to his audience, pivoting to face them all in turn. Returning his focus to Betha, he smiled again. "A question, my dear. I believe the king looks upon you with favour, does he not?"

Betha didn't need to answer: the blush that rose to her face was there for all to see.

Urien's gaze swept his rapt audience, a sense of building anticipation thrumming in the air. He beckoned to a slender, ginger-haired priest who descended the steps. The cleric's wispy attempt at a moustache proclaimed his youth, although he appeared confident, even arrogant with his erect posture. Betha wanted to feel comforted by the presence of a priest, but his demeanour failed to inspire confidence.

He took up a position to Urien's left, and about two lengths away. His cold eyes roved over Betha with an impersonal air that chilled even the self-assured spy hiding beneath the surface veneer.

Urien returned his dark gaze to Betha. "I have a suggestion for you, my dear, that I believe will be to your liking. But first, we must assess your obedience. Take off your clothes."

Betha gaped at him. Urien's affable expression transformed in an instant to a glower.

"Do it," he hissed.

Betha glanced up. All around her loomed a sea of leering male faces. The single exit was hidden behind a wall of bodies she had no hope of breaching. There would be no escape.

So, this was what Urien had in mind: humiliate her before enough people to cow her spirit, while demonstrating to his audience that he had total control of his victim. Betha recognised the technique, accepting she would have to play along, although a tiny fragment of doubt plagued her. What made Urien so certain such a spectacle enforced in private would be effective? Eye-witnesses alone lacked the authority required for such dominance.

Setting an obvious tremor in her muscles, she licked dry lips and reached awkwardly behind herself to undo buttons and laces. No one spoke, but the syncopated rhythm of heavy breathing left no doubt as to the crowd's arousal. She dared raise a tearful gaze toward Urien in entreaty, but beheld no compassion there. Fumbling, she slipped her arms from the short sleeves, clutching the bodice tightly against her chest.

"Please?" she whispered.

"Obedience, my dear; you promised me your obedience."

Still puzzling over Urien's plans, Betha made a show of reluctance as she slid the dress down her torso. She cringed beneath the cries of encouragement. In response to Urien's stern gaze, she pushed the garment over her slim hips until the weight of the fabric dragged it down to settle in a heap around her feet. She crossed her arms over her chest, hugging her plain under-shift.

"Good," Urien said. "Now the rest."

Betha squeezed out some tears, grateful for the endless practice her spy master had commanded. Her hands felt as though they belonged to someone else as they slipped the narrow straps off her shoulders and allowed the lightweight fabric to slither down her body to join the dress on the floor. She clutched her arms across her bare breasts, tucking her hands into her armpits.

"That's better. Only one more piece to go."

At this final indignity, Betha's carefully suppressed temper threatened to flare. She hugged herself tighter and squeezed her eyes shut, happy for the moment to let her audience believe her too appalled to submit.

In her fleeting haven of darkness, she forced herself to remember why she was in this predicament in the first place.

She'd failed Halnashead. She'd promised herself she wouldn't fail Marten. He *had* to know what Urien and Edlund were up to, and it appeared whatever they were mixed up in was a lot worse than simple political manoeuvrings. She *must* stick to the plan.

Keeping one arm firmly in place, she slipped the other hand haltingly down her naked skin until the texture beneath her fingers changed to fabric. Clumsily, with one hand, she loosened the drawstring and let her last item of underclothing fall. She snagged it artfully for a moment between quaking knees before allowing it to drop. She opened her eyes.

A glow of satisfaction lit Urien's face. "You see? Obedience."

A voice called out from the crowd. "But does she look as good close up? The king won't be interested in sullied goods."

"Bring that light closer," Urien ordered.

To Betha's horror, Edlund stepped forward brandishing a candelabra. He came so close she could smell his distinctive sour odour even over the general reek of excitement. If he touched her, she wasn't certain she'd be able to control her reactions, yet she had no idea what she might do. Her small dagger lay buried amid the clothing pooled around her feet.

Following Urien's instructions, Edlund held the candles high. Betha flinched as Urien's fingers trailed across her naked back, her shoulders, her flat buttocks. His touch felt strangely impersonal, as if he inspected a horse he was considering for purchase.

"Not a blemish to be seen," he pronounced. His tone was quizzical, and he added quietly, "Considering Herschel's reputation, little short of a miracle."

Coruscating light flared on the edge of Betha's vision. She jumped, and her head snapped around.

A column of bright, insubstantial coils of light curled between the moving hands of the arrogant young priest. Betha gawped as he sculpted the incandescent beams with quick, stroking actions, compressing here, dividing there, until a coherent shape began to form. A human shape. A female shape.

Her shape, with its boyishly narrow hips and comparatively broad shoulders—a figure she'd disguised with cleverly shaped gowns and petticoats, until the modern vogue for fitted fashions had taken the court by storm. Naked, like this, there was no hiding anything.

In short order, a life-size, nude effigy of Betha solidified, apparently carved from marble. Even the clothing heaped around her ankles was reproduced in exquisite detail.

Urien strode over to admire the extraordinary work of art, and with a jolt of fury Betha comprehended how he meant to enforce her obedience. Such a scandalous statue displayed in public would be enough to ruin any chance she had of finding a suitable husband.

How the priest had created the figure raised another very worrying question. Had a member of the clergy just performed magic? Or did the status of the practitioner render it a miracle?

Whatever the answer, such a blatant use of power was another critical piece of information she needed to bring back to Marten.

Urien transferred his attention from the statue to the life model. "Your obedience pleases us," he said, with a gloating smile. "Now, my dear, we expect you to follow our next instructions precisely." He pivoted, making a show of admiring Betha's cool, white likeness before continuing. "You do wish to continue pleasing us, don't you?"

Betha jerked her head in a fractional nod.

"You will seduce the king. Your goal will be to get

pregnant, and then marry him. Are you capable of this?"

Shock stole Betha's inner composure. "You w-w-w-want me to w-what?"

"Is your hearing deficient?"

Urien's rapt audience howled with amusement and Betha's skin grew furnace hot.

"N-no, but I d-don't understand."

"Halnashead planned on marrying Marten to a half-breed elf girl." Urien tutted. "An appalling notion. No, the prince's death affords us the opportunity to prevent such a terrible mistake. Yet the king must be wed for there to be a legitimate heir—something dangerously lacking at present."

"Oh."

Are they nothing more than a bunch of perverts playing politics after all?

She glanced furtively at the empty throne. No, there was definitely more to this than nobles vying for status.

"Can you do that?"

"I can try," Betha whispered.

Apparently satisfied, Urien waved an arm towards her heaped clothing.

"Make yourself presentable, girl," he commanded.

Betha hunched over as she pulled up her clothing. Acutely aware of the men watching, she fumbled every string, lace and button. When she was finished, several buttonholes remained empty and her gown hung lopsided, but she didn't care. That simple layer of fabric between her and their lascivious scrutiny lent her cowed surface persona some small measure of comfort.

Urien offered her his arm. As they made their way up the steps towards the exit, she wasn't entirely certain which of them supported the other. Given a choice, she'd have taken advantage of Urien's unsteadiness and pushed him back down in the hope he might break his skinny neck.

But getting back to the king with her knowledge intact was of far greater importance. She might have to go through with the charade of seducing him until they'd uncovered the identity of the real mastermind behind this plot, but one thing was very clear to her: if she were to succeed in producing a healthy male heir, Marten would not live to see his child grow up.

21. REVENGE

Rustam gagged. The drug, hestane, tasted of rotting vegetables seasoned with furniture oil.

He spat the vile liquid from his mouth as fast as it was poured in, but when Hext-al punched him in the stomach, he folded over, gasping. Fingers tangled in his hair, dragging his head back, and he had no choice but to swallow.

"There, that should be enough." Hext-al sounded satisfied.

Rustam's legs sagged. He slumped back against the rough rock wall and slithered down to the accompaniment of ripping fabric. His back would have plenty of bruises by the next morning—if he lived to see another sunrise.

One of Hext-al's men grabbed his wrists and bound them with coarse rope. When released, they dropped boneless into Rustam's lap. He struggled to keep his head upright, but his neck seemed unable to hold the weight of his skull and it lolled sideways, scraping his cheek against stone.

At least he didn't feel any pain. He no longer felt anything.

A screech of rage cut through his torpor, and with a huge effort he focussed his eyes enough to watch one of the rogues wrestle the blanket-wrapped baby out of Risada's arms. Halson added his wails to his mother's curses.

Utterly helpless, Rustam watched Risada endure a ruthless body search. It appeared Hext-al had a good memory, going straight to all the places in her clothing she customarily concealed her knives and blow pipes. The haul was impressive; far greater than Rustam expected.

"Satisfied now?" Risada spat at Hext-al's feet. He backhanded her across the face, knocking her to the ground.

Stay down. Don't antagonise him.

Almost as if she'd heard Rustam's silent plea, Risada remained sprawled on the rock ledge outside the cave. Her breath came in shallow gasps, and Rustam prayed the rough handling hadn't reopened any of her barely healed internal injuries.

Chayla submitted passively to the same treatment. The tatters she wore could hardly have hidden any weapons of note, but the Tylocian brutes made the most of their fun, ripping what little of her clothing had survived so far until Chayla was forced to knot bits together to prevent the rags slipping off her spare frame.

Watching the resigned way Chayla handled her humiliation, Rustam came to the sickening realisation the woman was accustomed to such treatment.

"Shall I get rid of this?" The Tylocian holding Halson ambled towards the edge of the rock platform.

"No!" Risada shrieked. She rolled out of the way of Hext-al's kick with an agility that astonished Rustam and ignited a flare of hope. Was she more recovered than she was letting on?

"No," echoed Hext-al. "Bring it here, let me see."

He took Halson with a surprising degree of care.

"So, this is the child Keavok claimed as his own. *He* has no use for a son anymore, but I do."

Hext-al lofted the squalling infant above his head. "Hai lads, lookie here! Old Hext-al has his-self a son, and a son makes me a legitimate contender for Clan Leader." A fierce smile carved through his dense beard. "We can take a Clan House for ourselves, no more begging for scraps, no more freezing our nuts off. We'll feast and whore again, and be mighty lords of our own clan!"

Hext-al's ragtag group of cronies cheered and stamped their feet, drowning out the wails of the distressed baby.

Hext-al beckoned to Chayla. "Here woman, take my son and tend him."

Chayla backed up a step, shaking her head. She pointed

down at Risada. "She's the mother, she'll take better care of him."

"Oh no," said Hext-al with a vicious smile. "I have other things planned for her."

With obvious reluctance, Chayla accepted the wailing bundle. She rocked him and crooned to him, and in short order Halson quieted.

"Better," Hext-al declared. "And now, a feast!"

Two of his henchmen dragged the unfortunate goat up onto the rock platform, and Hext-al produced a long-bladed knife. Rustam's heart went out to the hapless creature.

Chayla marched over to the goat, placing herself between the animal and the astonished Tylocians.

"Out of the way, woman."

"No," said Chayla firmly.

"Move!" Hext-al roared and raised a hand to push her aside.

Chayla planted her feet. "Not if you want a healthy son. This goat is the only means of feeding him."

Taken by surprise, Hext-al hesitated. He stared at Chayla, then at the goat. And then at the child in her arms. He lowered the knife.

Muttering erupted behind him. Eight hungry Tylocian outlaws were in no mood to relinquish the hearty meal they'd expended energy capturing.

Hext-al swung around, snarling. "The boy must eat. Do any of you have the tits to feed him? No? Then find something else to eat. Make use of what's left of the day and catch something."

The muttering escalated, but Hext-al either didn't notice or didn't care; having dismissed his followers, his attention was all focussed on Rustam and Risada. He squatted down and tilted his head on one side, matching the limp angle of Rustam's.

"I knew this day would come." He glanced across at Risada, still lying curled on the ground where she'd evaded his boot. "I prayed to Chel and Charin and they answered me.

You two lost me my clan, and you—" his gaze snapped back to Rustam "—got me kicked out of another. Now's time I get my revenge."

Nausea crawled up Rustam's throat. Hext-al read the twitching muscles around his jaw.

"Oh no, you ain't getting away that easy. No overdose for you; just enough to block that foul magic of yours so's you can watch, but not interfere."

The fuzzy sensation on Rustam's tongue warned him of returning sensation, but he'd seen hestane at work before, and held out no hope of regaining any useful control over his body before Hext-al was done with whatever it was he had planned. Rustam worked his jaw and swallowed, forcing his lips and tongue to form words.

"I spared your life," he managed to grind out.

Hext-al thrust his face so close to Rustam's, the stench of rotten teeth made him gag.

"You condemned me!" Hext-al hawked and spat. "You knew Prashax would throw me out, so you left me for the hunters instead of finishing me off yourself. Coward!"

He lunged to his feet and grabbed a fistful of Risada's hair. She squeaked a protest as he hauled her to her feet.

"Me, I'm not gon' make the same mistake. You're gonna die, but not until you've watched me take her apart, bit by pretty bit."

The same knife he'd intended to use to slaughter the goat flashed in the last rays of the setting sun, and Rustam's throat closed as it pierced Risada's left sleeve.

He breathed easier when Hext-al sliced open the fabric to expose Risada's distorted arm.

"Did you like the little gift I left you with?" the bully asked, poking the puffy skin with ragged, filthy fingernails. "Mellis poison does such interesting things to flesh." He dragged the tip of the long dagger down the scar from shoulder to elbow, pressing hard enough to leave a thin line of scarlet in its wake. "Might be interesting to see what happens second time around."

Hext-al grinned, staring at Risada's clenched jaw, and Rustam ground his teeth together. It was the only movement he could manage.

"Mind, I don't think you'll be around long enough for us to find out. Pity, but there it is. Now, which do you wanna lose first: fingers or toes?"

He released Risada's hair and made a grab for her left hand. She snatched it away, her reflexes catching Hext-al by surprise.

"You wanna play? Good, it'll make this all the more fun."

He lunged at her again. Risada twisted deftly away. Titters from behind him alerted Hext-al to his audience. His men had ignored his instructions to go hunting again when entertainment was on offer. His face darkened.

He slashed at Risada with the knife, but she bent like a sapling in a gale, swaying backward. The knife passed through empty space.

Louder laughter spurred Hext-al, but with a visible effort he maintained a grip on his temper and began weaving the knife from side to side, herding Risada backward towards the rockface.

"You want this to take longer? I know plenty ways to keep you alive until you beg for the end."

Rustam's gaze tracked Risada. His fingers twitched; she was running out of space.

Hext-al lunged again, the tip of his blade aimed at Risada's shoulder. This time she closed to meet him.

In a move almost too fast for Rustam's sluggish eyes to follow, Risada spun in past the knife, and grabbed Hext-al's wrist. She twisted beneath his arm, keeping hold of the wrist, and came back up with his elbow forced upward at an acute angle. The joint popped. Hext-al roared and the knife fell from his nerveless fingers.

Continuing in one fluid motion, Risada's left leg swept his ankles from beneath him and the big man crashed to the ground, facing Rustam.

Still fighting despite his pain, Hext-al threw his weight

back against Risada's shins, aiming to topple her off balance. She gave his dislocated elbow a savage twist as she straddled him and slammed her heel backward into his midriff. He grunted loudly.

Rustam had a satisfying view of Hext-al's bulging eyes, and his heart swelled with fierce pride. Risada bent over the vanquished thug to scoop up the knife, squeezing her heel back harder against his liver.

"No one takes my son from me," she hissed into Hext-al's ear. "No one."

A hot, red spray splattered across Rustam's face, and the metallic stink of blood assured him his senses were returning. Feebly, Hext-al's fingers explored the gaping wound across his throat. His bewildered eyes met Rustam's.

Rustam found he could move his lips enough to form a complete sentence.

"You never did learn that lesson, did you? I was never the dangerous one."

22. PAYMENT

It was done. Risada had finally exacted payment for the injury that had ruined her career.

She wiped the long blade on Hext-al's breeches, satisfaction mingling with apprehension. Killing one bully was simple. Dealing with his eight followers would not be. She glanced at Rustam, relieved to see the return of some expression to his slack face. But it would be morning before he would be able to fight, and they didn't have that long.

She discounted Chayla. Maybe the woman had some hidden combat skills, but given her history, it was unlikely. And besides, she was holding Halson.

Risada grudgingly admitted that Chayla had shown backbone, standing up to Hext-al over the goat. Perhaps Rustam had been correct, and the circumstances surrounding Halson's abduction had not been as straightforward as she'd chosen to believe. Perhaps Chayla didn't deserve to die.

In fact, it appeared Chayla had suffered greatly by not dying in the aftermath of the coup. The fate of a captive woman in a Tylocian clan house was not one Risada wished to contemplate.

Straightening up, Risada winced. Her body remembered all her training, all the moves, but her muscles were out of shape and her gut still ached from Halson's violent birth.

"Come closer." She beckoned to Chayla. She couldn't protect more than one position, and Rustam wouldn't be moving anywhere soon.

Chayla scuttled out of the cave and slid behind Risada, taking up a position next to Rustam. So far, the Tylocians hadn't made any move towards them, ignoring them while hotly debating what to do next.

Silence fell. Eight scrawny ruffians turned towards them and raised their weapons.

"Wait!"

The command inherent to a high-born noble rang in Risada's tone. The outlaws hesitated.

"We are valuable," she said. "All of us. King Marten will pay a substantial ransom if you return us unharmed."

Her speech caused another brief huddle before a new leader emerged. Taller than the others by a handspan, this one wielded a wicked-looking curved sword.

"How d'ya suggest we collect? Walk into the palace an' demand money?" He spat over his shoulder. "You're too much trouble."

Staying in a tight group, the eight men edged forward. Risada swept the long knife she'd liberated from Hext-al right and left, and they baulked. Her lips thinned into a grim smile; at least they were wary of her. That gave her some small chance.

She grimaced. Eight on one, and that one unfit and hurting. She might delay the inevitable, but she wasn't going to win.

Chel, if you still have use for us, now would be the time to show it.

The tall man urged his companions forward. Leading from the rear, Risada noted. A wise coward. Not a predictable opponent.

The front man lunged at her with a rusty sword whilst the one on the right flank raised a pole with a knife strapped to its end, aiming it at Rustam. Risada whirled around and spun past the sword, which crashed into the rockface and snapped in half. She grabbed the makeshift spear with both hands, using her momentum to pull the bearer off balance. He tumbled against the man next to him, causing a knock-on effect along the pack. By the time they sorted themselves out, Risada was back in place, in front of her helpless companions. She now brandished the improvised spear in addition to Hext-al's knife.

So far, so good.

The bandits regrouped. Another muffled conversation produced a new approach. Three men edged away to the right, two to the left. Those in the centre advanced more slowly than the flankers. They worked with more cooperation than Risada had expected from such lowlifes. Apparently being forced to depend on each other for survival outside Tylocian society had bonded them into a more coherent fighting force than she'd bargained on. Her muscles bunched.

The scuff of shuffling boots was suddenly silenced by a rising caterwaul. The outlaws spun to face the new threat.

An imposing figure sprang onto the front edge of the stone platform. Tall and solid, his dusky bare skin blended with the lengthening evening shadows, but the intense gleam of his emerald gaze drew attention to his face, and his fearsome, pointed teeth. The mouth stretched around those teeth, curved into an indulgent smile as his eyes followed a dark shape slipping along the edge of the rockface behind the bandits.

The figure lunged from the gloom, revealing a snarling black panther. The three men furthest to the right fell beneath its attack. Two men died quickly. The third succeeded in raising a weapon, but the panther's huge maw closed on his arm and tore it from its socket with a slurping, sucking sound. Screaming hysterically as he bled out, the man toppled sideways to lie across his compatriots' bodies.

The remaining five bandits closed into a ring with their backs to each other. Their feet shuffled nervously, raising a cloud of dust around their ankles. They brandished a motley assortment of weapons, but the hopeless expressions etched on their pinched faces proclaimed they foresaw their ultimate fates.

"We can go now," offered their tall leader. "We don't want no trouble, we never meant to hurt no one, that was all *him*." He pointed towards the hefty body of Hext-al, sprawled at Risada's feet.

"Really?"

The nude man prowled towards them, and Risada recognised the werecat they'd met earlier. He cocked his head, regarding the terrified bandits with a predatory grin.

"You didn't intend to kill me for my ssskin? You were only chasing me for ssport. Yesss?"

"Yes! Just for the chase." The bandit leader's head bobbed up and down so hard Risada wondered if it rattled his brain. Assuming there was anything inside there to rattle.

"We don't know nothing about no skin."

"Really," repeated the werecat, before his body melted into his feline form.

Risada flinched. Magic would never sit easily with her, despite her acquired tolerance.

Avoiding the flashing blades of the five with clear disdain, the two werecats circled their prey. Risada considered joining them, but they exuded such confidence she decided to conserve her energy, just in case.

Taking his newly assumed responsibility as gang leader seriously, the tall man attempted to rouse his fellows.

"It's five against two, lads. Let's take 'em! You two, that un; we'll take this un."

Giving them no time to argue, he dashed forward, obviously expecting obedience. The man on his right joined him a split second later, and one of those behind him swung a short sword at the slightly smaller panther. Of the remaining two men, one remained stationary, enfeebled by fear. The other seized his chance and ran.

The more petite cat—a female, Risada noticed—dealt with her single attacker by sweeping sinuously past his wild blade and hamstringing him with a paw full of vicious claws. The man's legs folded, severed tendons dangling from gaping red holes behind his knees. His cries turned to bloody gurgles as his throat tore out in the grip of the cat's teeth. She then used his body as a launching stage to spring onto the shoulders of the dithering, terrified one, tumbling him over and onto the ground. When she padded away, all that remained was a tangled mess of raw flesh.

The assassin in Risada admired the cat's swift and efficient kills. She could only hope this werecat would be as cordial as her partner, but to be on the safe side she sidled over to where Hext-al had stashed her weapons, and palmed a blow pipe. She would not be permitting either of the big cats anywhere near her son. Or the still incapacitated Rustam.

Not realising their compatriots had fallen, the tall man and his accomplice traded feints with the larger werecat. Neither spared any attention for their rear.

The male cat bounced around in front of them, avoiding their weapons with an insouciance verging on teasing. His female companion's immobility was interrupted only by the tip of her switching tail.

The two men began to tire, making less frequent thrusts and swings with their blades, rewarding the cats' patience.

Working with uncanny harmony, the feline pair brought the standoff to a swift and grisly end. The female attacked from the rear with an ear-splitting yowl. Taken by surprise, the bandits half turned to meet her, exposing their backs to the male.

Risada took a grim satisfaction in the outlaws' ending. Her personal grudge had been with Hext-al, not his followers, but as soon as they'd threatened her son, they'd become her enemies.

When the cats were done, they sat in the midst of their carnage for a while, licking the gore from their paws. Risada crouched down beside Rustam. The abattoir stench at that level was sickening, and she wished she had the strength to move him.

"How are you feeling?"

He grunted. "A mite better for seein' those two turn up." His words were slurred, but clear enough. True to his threat, Hext-al hadn't administered an overdose; Rustam was recovering.

He narrowed his eyes, peering at her shoulder. "Wha' 'bout you?"

His anxious gaze reminded Risada of Hext-al's assault on

her damaged arm. She glanced at the thin red line tracing the original scar. "This? I'm fine."

"But—poison?"

"Oh, yes, undoubtedly. But I knew where this journey was taking us; the antidote's in my saddle bag. Leith made me promise never to go anywhere near Tyloc again without carrying it. As soon as we're cleaned up here, I'll get it, never fear. Mellis isn't fast acting, thank the goddess."

The look of relief on Rustam's face warmed her heart. She turned back to see the male werecat approaching in human form. Of the female, there was no sign, but screams rang out from the valley below, in the direction the one surviving bandit had fled.

The male halted at a comfortable distance and bowed, his action as courtly as any lord's, despite his nakedness.

"My thanksss for your directionss earlier," he said. "They enabled me to evade the hunterss and re-join my *pahn*. We decided it wass time for a hunt of our own."

"A fortuitous meeting for us all, then," responded Risada, choking slightly on the last word as a particularly agonized shriek ripped through the still evening air.

The werecat's savage grin was just visible in the twilight.

"My mate," he explained. "She likesss to play with her food."

Revulsion crawled through Risada's guts. "You *eat* human flesh?"

She immediately regretted her impulsive words. *Don't provoke him, we aren't safe yet.*

The werecat might have read her mind. Or perhaps her expression. If his eyes were as sharp in the dark as a house cat's, then probably the latter.

"You have nothing to fear from usss. We do not cusstomarily hunt humanss. Contrary to what ssome believe, we are not animalsss. But thesse vermin? They rejected the right to be called human the moment they chose to hunt my kind. And we live by the goddess'sss graccce—what would be the point of leaving good meat to rot?"

"He ha' a point," Rustam observed.

Risada's stomach tightened, but she couldn't raise an argument, so she held her tongue.

Just then, the female werecat returned. She sprang onto the rock platform, transforming fully before her two human feet touched the ground. As black as her partner, and with green eyes to match, she appeared far wilder, with lustrous ebony hair cascading to her waist and long fingers that flexed as though they still sported claws. She could have passed for human, but for the neat rows of teats extending down her torso in parallel lines beneath her full breasts.

She slunk across the open space with lethal efficiency. A slight musk scent tickled Risada's nose and she pinched it to keep from sneezing.

"You have our gratitude for your intervention," Risada said, keeping a weather eye on the female. "I'm very happy we could be of mutual assistance."

Neither of the werecats answered, and Risada questioned if she should be offering something more in return for the undoubtedly large contribution the cats had made to their safety. Then she marked their attention, riveted to one side of her. She risked a hasty glance.

Chayla, cradling Halson in her arms, stood pinned by their matching emerald stares.

Risada's hackles rose. Were the werecats a threat to her son? Could she fight them alone? Her brain started sifting tactics. She'd studied their techniques while they dealt with the bandits, but those men had been weak, stupid, and predictable. She was sure the cats would have other strategies for more challenging opponents. Her biggest advantage lay in her blowpipe, though she doubted she could incapacitate both in the same manner.

Without warning, both werecats dropped to one knee. The movement was so swift, it blurred Risada's vision. So much for her chances of reacting fast enough to best even one of them. She stared at the two dark, bowed heads.

"Lady." The single word rumbled up from the depths of

the male's capacious chest. Risada glanced over her shoulder, eyes narrowed. Chayla was plain Chayla. An emaciated, beaten-down wreck of a woman dressed in tatters. What else did the werecats see?

"Your actions bring honour to your *pahn*," Chayla said, the surrounding rock formations imparting a sonorous depth to her voice. "May your prey be plentiful and your hunt swift."

A trickle of icy sweat slithered between Risada's shoulder blades. Where had Chayla learned such ritual words?

The two werecats bowed deeper before rising. Without further speech, they set about the grisly task of dragging the bodies away. Disturbing the mangled corpses released a sickening melange of odours, and various bodily fluids left dark trails across the rock. When Halson began to cry anew, Risada snapped at Chayla.

"Take him back inside; I don't want him to see this."

Irrational, she acknowledged. Halson was far too young for any of this to warp his memories, but still she yearned to protect him from such ugliness. While profoundly unsettled by the werecat's attitude towards Chayla, Risada had no intention of leaving the still helpless Rustam alone, so her only choice lay in trusting Chayla with her son. For now, at least. She stared at Chayla's back as the woman obediently carried the baby away from the scene of the massacre.

They would talk about what happened later.

By the time Risada returned her attention to the rock platform, it was over. Aside from the gory reminders trickling across the uneven surface, no evidence lingered that a band of outlaws had met its end there. The werecats were gone with not even a hint of a sound to indicate in which direction they'd taken their prizes.

A loud rumble of thunder cracked the silence, and rain as soft as tears pattered onto the rock. Risada hunkered down beside Rustam and prepared to get wet. She didn't have the strength to drag him into the cave, and after the heat of the day and her recent exertions, she found she didn't mind the coolness the rain offered.

In short order it washed away the dust, the blood, and the charnel stench, replacing it with the freshness of a new start. The shower ended as abruptly as it had begun, leaving in its wake a mist that rose from their clothes, and from the summer-warmed rock.

Risada's arm began to itch.

"It's about time I took that antidote. Where did you send the horses?"

Rustam stirred and a different warmth filled her—he really was going to recover. The fear that had almost paralysed her when Hext-al forced Rusty to drink hestane evaporated with the last of the moisture.

"Gi' me a mo'ent."

She watched his lips work, his tongue darting out to moisten them. Her nails bit into her palms as she restrained herself from leaning over to cover his enticing mouth with hers.

Next moment, a shrill whistle jetted from between his teeth, and Risada relaxed back to her seat on the ground beside him. Already she could hear the sound of hoofbeats approaching. In short order, Greylegs popped up onto the platform with Fleetfoot nipping at his heels. The older horse gave a little squeal and a hop with his rear end in protest.

"Thank you, Fleetfoot, you can leave him alone now."

The bay stallion shook his neck, long mane flipping from side to side, before he ambled over to sniff at Rustam's boot. When Risada approached Greylegs, he rubbed his forehead against her shoulder, jostling her newly injured arm.

"Ouch!" She swatted him lightly on the chest. "You might have picked the other side."

He dropped his head and turned it away from her. She laughed, and patted his neck. "You're getting to be as good at human expressions as he is," she said, twitching her chin towards Fleetfoot. She leant close to whisper in the grey's ear. "Not that I mind, but don't tell him that."

She caught Rustam's eye, and her cheeks warmed, stoked

by the amusement twinkling there. When had she started talking to horses? Not long ago, she'd have been mortified by such foolishness.

Rummaging in her saddle bag for the bottle of antidote, Risada smiled to herself. She realised she no longer cared what anyone else—aside from Rusty—thought of her behaviour.

How liberating!

23. SEDUCTION

Marten marvelled at how perfectly Betha's slender-boned hand fitted his palm. He interlinked his fingers with hers, and took a quick peek at her as they strolled together through the packed salon. A besotted smile took control of his face and Betha's cheeks pinked in reply.

Games forgotten, gossip temporarily suspended, the buzz of conversation muted as the assembled nobles scrutinised their king and his new lady. They were accustomed to seeing Marten alone, but for his faithful bodyguard, and this fresh departure enthralled them.

The riotous blend of colours worn by the nobles painted the airy hall with the likeness of a formal garden, but thankfully without the pollen to irritate Marten's eyes and nose. A rich blend of perfumes and wines competed with the underlying aroma of ondal oil rising from the warm, polished wooden floorboards. Wending their way between the many gaming tables and tapestry frames surrounded by clusters of chairs and stools, Marten and Betha paused here and there to exchange pleasantries. When they moved on, the crowd parted before them, and then closed behind, as though the king and his lady moved within a private bubble of space no one else might breach.

Marten revelled in the attention, yet a void persisted beneath his heart. If only this courtship could be real.

When Betha had first brought Urien's plans before him, he'd been outraged. And yet, on reflection, he'd decided the best option would be to play along. Cousin Sala had suggested the same match, so the deception hadn't caused any raised eyebrows there.

They'd orchestrated a few meetings in public before appearing as a couple, and now, a double handful of days later, Marten couldn't think of anyone he'd rather woo.

On the other hand, the pretence was proving a strain. At night he slept little, consumed by fantasies of Betha in place of Nonni, the girl he was currently seeing rather more often than usual in an effort to keep himself sane.

"Might I say, sire, how pleasant it is to see you with such an agreeable companion."

Lord Urien's comment, accompanied by Betha's sudden death grip cutting off the blood supply to his fist, jolted Marten out of his daydream. The wiry lord was such a sycophant. Marten felt nauseous, knowing what Urien planned. He also had a fair idea something unpleasant had happened to Betha when she'd been taken by Urien to that meeting, but she wasn't sharing details of her ordeal, only of the plot she'd uncovered.

Marten stared Urien up and down. What made someone so outwardly successful crave yet more power? The man must have no idea of the realities of ruling, seeing only the power, not the constant effort needed to keep the kingdom running. Marten would have laughed in his face if he hadn't needed to play his part in Urien's little charade until they discovered who this mysterious 'benefactor' might be.

Marten inclined his head with a gracious smile. "Indeed, Lady Betha is most agreeable." He patted Betha's white-knuckled hand. "And I have you, Urien, to thank for bringing her to my attention."

Urien paled, stoking Marten's enjoyment of the moment. He held his tongue for a moment longer, making Urien sweat.

When he could bear the silence no longer, Urien asked, "I'm afraid I don't recall, my king. Did I introduce you?"

With a beaming smile, Marten shook his head. "No, it was the council meeting. If you hadn't made such a point of Lady Betha's presence, I might not have noticed her, and missed my opportunity with such a rare gem."

Urien blinked a drop of sweat from his eyes. "Delighted to have been of service, Your Majesty."

Marten scanned the huddle behind Urien. Lord Edlund lurked there, of course, his florid complexion announcing how far he'd indulged already this evening, plus five others, all with empty smiles on their lips. Each bowed in turn as Marten's gaze touched them, and he noted their faces for later comparison to the list Betha had given him of those in attendance when Urien recruited her.

Inclining his head, he drew Betha forward, abandoning the traitors to their empty scheming.

* * * * * * *

Davi's conspiratorial wink drew a faux scowl to Marten's face. Allowing Betha to precede him into his apartment, the king flicked his fingers in dismissal of his impudent bodyguard. With a quick grin, Davi swung the door shut.

That man lacks the respect due his monarch, but he'll get his comeuppance soon enough, thought Marten smugly. One of his spies had uncovered Davi's closely guarded secret, and Marten anticipated with relish the moment he would drop it into conversation.

In the meantime, he was finally alone with the woman of his dreams.

His good mood evaporated.

She stood like an exotic flowering plant in the middle of his functional sitting room; a brightly coloured blossom too fragile to survive long without tender care. In the midst of clusters of low tables and chairs, and groupings of more informal couches in muted shades, she appeared ready to wilt.

"You shouldn't mock Lord Urien like that!" she protested, voice brittle with anxiety.

In an effort to regain his good humour, Marten indulged himself, recalling how he'd toyed with Urien's unease. "But it was so rewarding," he said. "The bastard can't exactly say anything in public, can he?"

"He can't, but Marten, please don't underestimate him; he's dangerous."

Marten beamed. "That sounds like you're genuinely worried about me."

"Of course, I am. You're my king!"

"Is that the only reason?" Marten permitted disappointment to seep into his words.

Betha's lips curved into a coy smile. "Whatever do you mean, Your Majesty?"

Marten gestured towards a dark blue sofa, the perfect size for two. "I had entertained the hope you might see me as more than just your king. I am also a man."

Taking his proffered hand, Betha allowed him to lead her towards his seating choice. She shook out her skirts, claiming rather more than half the breadth as she settled. She patted the meagre space remaining. "Be assured, sire, I am aware of that. My eyesight has never been called into question."

Excitement raced through Marten as he folded himself into the intimate spot by her side. Inhaling Betha's lavender perfume, he found his eyes drawn to the graceful arch of her neck and on, downward, to the deep valley of her cleavage.

What am I doing? Even if she is kindly disposed toward me, this can only end in disaster. I could never be the gentle lover she deserves.

Betha's cool fingers closed over his. "I've been aware of it from the moment we met."

Heat pooled in Marten's groin. He shifted position ever so slightly, but Betha smiled knowingly.

Take control, man! This is a terrible idea.

Gently, Marten disengaged his fingers. Guilt consumed him as Betha's face fell, but he forced himself to continue.

"Well, madam, we have achieved our goal. Every noble in the palace, and likely many outside by now, knows we are together tonight. Urien believes his plan is about to be consummated, and all we need do to convince him, is remain here for the night. Even my cousin will be pleased, though I didn't seek to deceive her intentionally." He squeezed Betha's hand to soften his withdrawal before rising to his feet. "Please, take the bedroom; I'll sleep out here. The bed is more suitable for a lady."

Betha's brows drew together to form a slight frown, hinting at disappointment. "As you wish, sire, though I fear I do not sleep well alone."

Marten's heart jolted against his ribs. "My lady—Betha— when I agreed to this plan it was not my intention to force you to fulfil Urien's demands."

Her azure gaze trapped him. "Do I appear reluctant? Or am I, perhaps, reaching too far above my station? Lord Urien thought not. Nor, I believe, does your cousin. Is it that you wish our professional relationship to remain uncompromised? *That* I would understand, as no lady wishes to feel undesired."

"Damn it! Of course, I *want* you. I just don't think it's wise."

Her gaze fell away. "Perhaps so. I suspect we both have expectations, and I doubt either of us wants to be disappointed."

Stung, Marten defended himself. "It's *you* I don't want to disappoint."

Betha raised an eyebrow. "So, you'd rather avoid finding out, than take the risk? Funny, I didn't believe you lacking in confid—"

His lips crushed hers before she completed her sentence. Her surprised squeak sent a thrill down Marten's spine.

To his delight, Betha rose to meet him, tangling her fingers in his hair, and pressing her body hard against him. Marten's hands cupped her buttocks and he realised he'd been mistaken: they filled his palms to perfection.

Betha grabbed one of his fists and transferred it to her breast. Marten's heart rate rose another notch—he was accustomed to being the proactive one, but Betha clearly knew what she wanted. His hand slipped beneath the edge of her gown, sliding across her silky flesh. A hard nipple jutted against his fingers and he grasped it, rolling and stroking. She moaned into his mouth as their tongues twined together. Spurred on, Marten's fingers tightened, crushing Betha's breast. She yelped.

Marten yanked his hand free and jumped back. "I'm sorry! I'm so sorry! I never meant to hurt you!"

Panting, Betha's lust-darkened glare flayed him. "Then you'd be a serious disappointment."

"I don't—"

"Understand? *That's* what's holding you back?" She tugged at the laces holding her bodice tight. "I'll make this very plain: I *like* it that way!"

Marten gaped; how had he been so wrong? Surely an ethereal beauty like Betha wasn't made to endure the rough games that aroused him, and yet the hunger in her eyes stole his breath.

"Are you sure? You really mean it?" Marten cursed himself for sounding timid, but he had to be absolutely certain. He would never forgive himself if Betha had misunderstood.

Her highly improper leer convinced him.

Still doubtful, unwilling to believe his good fortune, Marten made one last attempt to see if he could scare her off. Grasping her hand again, he guided her through his respectable bed chamber, and halted before the tapestry concealing the door to his hidden den.

"If anything you see shocks you, or makes you want to leave, please, please speak out. I want you to know I would never do anything without your permission."

Betha put one hand flat against her chest and her words carried the breathlessness of anticipation. "Please, show me."

Marten pushed the hanging aside to allow her to enter his most private domain. Gentle candlelight flickered across the shelves of tools, the frames and chains, the array of whips, the neatly organised restraints. Hesitating in the doorway, Marten waited for Betha to flee.

Instead, she let go his hand and strolled around the

spacious room. She trailed her slender fingers over a rack of wrist and ankle shackles, before turning her attention to the leather cuffs dangling on chains from the ceiling. Her thumbs flicked the buckles, creating chiming, metallic music.

Moving on, she unerringly selected Marten's favourite whip from a shelf. She flicked the long lashes over her shoulder before dragging the five leather thongs slowly—oh, so slowly—up her body. As the knotted tips splayed out across her buttocks, Marten's groin throbbed. He suppressed a groan and Betha favoured him with an impish grin.

"Of all the places to find the answer to my prayers, I never dreamed it would be here. Or with you, my king. There can be no doubt: Chel has made us for each other!"

She grabbed his arm and dragged him the rest of the way into the room.

24. AFTERMATH

Lying prone on a warm, thick rug, on the floor in the centre of Marten's inner sanctum, Betha stretched, luxuriating in the languor born of an extended night of passion. The whip stripes across her back and buttocks stung as she moved, setting her pulse racing. She was still astounded by the marvellous turn in fortune that had brought her and Marten together. Surely, it must be the will of the goddess.

Reclining beside her, Marten blinked heavy eyes. Betha rolled onto her side and stroked a hand along his naked flank. She smiled. The young king possessed some stamina, but she was certain she could improve his staying power if he gave her the chance.

Would he? Betha pondered potential complications. She was certain she'd more than fulfilled Marten's hopes for a partner fully committed to his very particular tastes, but was that what he wanted? Or, indeed, needed? Would he take the risk on it compromising their professional relationship?

What if she conceived? Urien was dangerous now, but with the production of a royal child, he would become lethal.

And what of Princess Annasala? She'd suggested Marten take the same course, but with the hope of a fruitful marriage at the end. Did Marten want that?

The conflicting possibilities overwhelmed her, and she groaned.

Marten's eyes snapped into focus.

"Are you sore? Was it too much? I knew this wasn't a good idea."

She seized his hands, and kissed his knuckles. "Marten, it was a *wonderful* idea. You have no idea how I've despaired of finding a partner with your imagination. My husband was a good study, but he was elderly, and new ideas didn't come easily to him."

Marten puffed out his cheeks. "Well at least I don't have too much to live up to."

Betha smiled again and touched his cheek, wincing as she reached out. Concern clouded his face.

"We should put some salve on those marks; I keep some here for the girls."

His face reddened as he realised his admission. Betha was quick to reassure him.

"You don't gain skills like that without practice. Of course, you have other girls here. I'm under no illusion you've been sitting idly, waiting for me to come along."

That puppy dog smile she found so endearing lit Marten's face. "I'm trying to come to terms with my good fortune," he admitted. "I keep thinking I'll wake up any moment and find this was just another dream."

Betha chortled. "*Another* dream? So, I'm inhabiting your fantasies, am I, sire?" She raised a mock frown. "I hope I lived up to your expectations?"

Marten grinned. "More than. How could you not?" His finger traced the wheal marks across her breasts and his expression grew serious. "I do need one thing from you though: complete honesty. I would despise myself forever if I forced you into something you weren't comfortable with." He met her gaze with a fierce intensity. "Will you promise me that?"

"Of course, sire."

It was clear to Betha he had more to say, but whatever it was, he obviously found the subject difficult, so she waited for him to unburden himself.

He sat up and hugged his knees to his chest. "Since I discovered this—" he waved one hand at the implements lining the walls, "—I've lived with the fear I'm cursed. Chel or Charin, I don't know which, but why would any normal person need such things to, well, you know?" His shoulders drooped. "The prospect of turning into my grandsire terrifies me."

Betha rolled up onto her knees and grasped him by the shoulders. She gave him a tiny shake. "Marten, you are *not* your grandsire. You could *never* be like him. That the very idea scares you, guarantees you won't take that wrong turn."

His chin lifted defiantly. "But a king shouldn't be scared."

Betha traced his jaw, prickly now with a night's growth. "Are you not also a man? I seem to recall you pointing that out to me last evening."

"What did I do to deserve you?" He planted a kiss on her palm.

"I believe I asked the same question of the goddess, not half a day gone. Marten, don't you see? Chel has truly made us for each other. This is what I desire, and you need have no guilt when you're with me."

He frowned slightly. "But why? Explain to me why you enjoy pain. I know you aren't unique—the other girls do too—but that doesn't mean I understand it."

It was Betha's turn to pause, considering. Should she tell him? She'd shared her secret with so few people; it was safer that way.

Her hesitation brought a flash of panic to Marten's face. Betha clutched his hands before he could pull away. "No, no! I'm not about to destroy your illusions—I really *do* enjoy it." She made a lingering scan of the room. "All of it. But you need to know the whole story."

"Don't scare me like that again. As your king, I command it. Now, please explain."

Setting his hands free, Betha folded her legs beneath her. "I can't tell you what the other girls feel," she said with a shrug. "I can only tell you how it works for me."

Marten dipped his head in encouragement.

"It began when I was a child. I fell off a wall in our garden, and broke my leg." She winced. "It was a bad break; the ends of the bones were sticking out through the skin, and I couldn't move for the pain. My brother found me, but because I wasn't supposed to be out there alone, I begged him not to call for help. I don't know what I thought he could do; I was only thinking of the scolding I knew I'd earned."

She spotted her hand unconsciously smoothing the flawless skin over the old injury site. "My brother was always a practical boy. He went off to find sticks to make a splint, making me promise to lie still until he came back." She shrugged. "I tried so hard, but it hurt too much. I wanted to scream, but I knew if I did, one of my grandparents would come and find me. So instead I tried to straighten it out while wishing as hard as I could for the stupid accident to have never happened." She darted a glance at Marten to find she had an enraptured audience.

"That must have been grim for you. Go on."

"That's when the miracle happened. It was like a spark inside me catching fire. I don't know what it was—is—but this heat, this power, raced through my body and out along my leg. It pulled my leg straight, drawing the bones back through the hole they'd made and the ends fitted together as if they'd never been broken. Exactly as I wished." She shrugged. "Perhaps I'd prayed without realising it—I was only small at the time, and not very aware of the goddess. Who knows? But by the time my brother returned, there was no sign of any injury and I was standing up, bouncing on my feet. And you know the best thing? I felt *amazing*! My body felt super light, almost like I could fly, and I was buzzing with energy. Happy. Ridiculously happy in fact. I couldn't stop smiling. Well, not until my brother gave me a good shaking, anyway."

Noticing Marten's brow had gained a sharp 'v' between his eyes, she hurried on. "That's when he told me about our mother. She died when I was very little, but no one talked about how she died. When I heard the truth, I finally understood. I have what is known as 'the family curse', and it's what killed my mother. Not everyone in our family gets it, and apparently my grandparents were hoping if they kept quiet, it might miss me. But it didn't."

Marten's frown deepened. "How did she die?"

"Turns out this curse is addictive. The bigger the injury, the greater the bliss when you heal yourself. The more you use it, the more pain stops being pain, and becomes anticipation for what you know is to come. My mother harmed herself over and over for the sheer thrill of fixing herself. One day she went too far." Betha shivered, recalling the day she'd nearly done the same. Fortunately for her, her brother had been there to prevent her mistake from becoming fatal. "Either you let it take control of you, or you learn to control it. I learned."

She focussed on Marten's sceptical expression.

"It's probably best if I show you," she said, reaching across to give his hands a squeeze for reassurance. Her stomach clenched when his bunched fists didn't relax, and she withdrew her hands awkwardly.

"Whip marks don't take much effort to heal. It'll only take a moment." Aware she was blathering, she bit her lip and fell silent.

With the ease of long practice, Betha condensed her awareness. The scent of wax and the flickering candlelight raised delicious memories of their night's endeavours, and despite her concern about Marten's reaction, anticipation blossomed.

If only she could share the experience with him.

For such superficial injuries Betha had no need to delve too deeply into her well of healing energy. Even so, the blast of pleasure thrilled her to her core, and the wash of euphoria tipped her over into an unexpected orgasm. She cried out with delight, oblivious to everything around her.

When the shuddering pleasure waned, and she opened her eyes, alarm snatched away the aftermath. Marten was on his feet beside the door, wrapped in a soft robe covering him from neck to feet. Suddenly very aware of her nakedness, Betha drew her knees up to her chin and wrapped her arms around them. Even when stripped before Urien's lecherous supporters, she'd not felt so vulnerable.

"Sire?"

Marten's hollow gaze deprived her of hope. She shouldn't have told him the truth.

He swallowed twice before finding his voice. "You're a *magic* user!"

Tears pricked at the backs of Betha's eyes. "I wouldn't have shown you if I'd known it would offend you." His face grew hard and she hurried on. "You asked me to be honest. Would you condemn me for doing so?"

Marten shook his head, but the horror remained. "I should have you executed. Do you have any idea what sort of position you've put me in?"

"But I'm not even sure it *is* magic! It doesn't work on anyone else; it could as easily be a gift from the goddess, an answer to that childhood prayer."

"No," said Marten. "If this had been a gift from Chel, you would have felt the urge to join the priesthood. Have you?"

He's offering a way out, Betha realised, but she'd promised him complete honesty. If she lied now, she'd despise herself forever.

She closed her eyes. "No, sire. I haven't."

Silence stretched. She knew he was still there; she could hear his ragged breathing. When she opened her eyes again, he regarded her like a stranger. Hope wilted inside her, like a fragile blossom scorched by the sun.

"Get out," he ordered, words chopped into tiny chunks. "You will continue to serve me, but you will not use your foul magic. Not ever. Is that clear?"

With heavy limbs, Betha struggled up off the floor. She drew on her discarded clothes.

"Did my uncle know?" asked Marten.

"Yes. He considered a spy who isn't intimidated by threat of pain to be a huge asset."

She observed Marten shift uncomfortably at her revelation, but if he wished to continue using her clandestinely, he should know the advantage he was throwing away.

For her part, none of that mattered. The man standing so stiff and hostile before her had claimed her heart.

And broken it, all in one night. Nothing mattered anymore.

25. CONSEQUENCES

Bright mid-morning sun brought a cheery warmth to the palace corridors totally at odds with Betha's heartache. Keeping to the pretence Marten had ordered, she smiled in response to the greetings of the promenading nobles, but her skin prickled beneath the knowing glances scoring her back. Nobody missed the fact she was still dressed in the same gown she'd worn last night.

"Excellent work, my dear."

Urien's oily voice slicked over her skin. She clenched and released her fists before composing herself to respond.

"My lord. Thank you, my lord." She inclined her head respectfully, and Urien beamed.

"Keep it up," he instructed before moving away.

Betha blew softly between parted lips. She hadn't noticed she'd been holding her breath. Her skin rippled beneath her gown in a veiled shudder as she resumed the journey to her suite. She was desperate for a bath. At this time of day, she would have to draw it herself, but she felt so soiled it would be worth the effort.

Turning the last corner, she missed a step. Her seneschal, Quart, paced anxiously back and forth outside her doors.

"Trouble?" she asked as he came to attention.

The old man's face looked more haggard than usual. He bowed. "My lady. I trust not, but you must be the judge of that. Master Lorndar is here."

Betha balled her fists. A difficult meeting was the very last thing she needed. "Here? Or on his way?"

Quart flicked his eyes towards the apartment doors, hanging ajar.

"Here, my lady. And impatient as ever, though he furnished no warning of his arrival."

How rude! Betha let out a frustrated sigh. The Master Blacksmith was a misogynist and a boor. It was her poor luck his craft house stood on her land, making him her problem.

Though she was tempted to send him away, such a course of action offered only a temporary reprieve. Dealing with him now would permit her to dispose of both of today's unpleasant events—assuming no more reared up—before she shut out the world and wallowed in self-pity.

She smoothed her rumpled gown as best she could, ignoring Quart's sideways glance.

"Let's get this over with," she said softly, gesturing for Quart to open the door. She swept into the receiving room, putting on her best haughty posture, and was gratified when Lorndar jerked upright onto his feet. She frowned. The squat blacksmith had been sitting, uninvited, on her favourite chair. She stared pointedly for long enough to make him flush.

Quite an achievement, considering how red those cheeks are already. And I don't believe that's all down to standing over a forge every day, either.

Indeed, the smell of cheap wine confirmed her guess as she stepped past him to settle with great deliberation onto the high-backed chair she usually eschewed. It lent the impression of authority, but damn, it was uncomfortable. Resigning herself, she invited Lorndar to resume his seat.

"Master Lorndar. I have been expecting your arrival for a very long time. I trust nothing went amiss on your journey?"

With a deliberate glance towards the wine jug on the sideboard, Lorndar gathered his manners.

"Not at all, my lady. I used the journey to visit other craft houses along the way, and to meet with my fellow masters. Many of them joined me on my journey here."

Uneasy about what he might be cooking up, Betha permitted herself the small satisfaction of not offering him a drink.

"And the purpose of this journey?"

Lorndar's jaw tightened at her lack of civility. "I am here as a courtesy to you, Lady Betha, as mistress of the family my craft house is beholden to, to inform you we, the craft masters of Tyr-en, are here to bring a petition before the king."

He paused to see what effect his words would have, but Betha called his bluff, doing no more than raising her eyebrows.

He gave a small huff. Or he could have been clearing his throat. At this point, offending him was the least of Betha's concerns. Her longed-for bath was clamouring for her attendance, and although she doubted the stains clinging to her, both inside and out, could ever be washed away, perhaps they could be drowned.

"We," said Lorndar, sweeping his arm in an expansive gesture, "believe the time has come for the crown to recognise crafts as an entity separate from the noble Houses. In short, we want representation on the council, and autonomy over our own negotiations and trade agreements."

Betha's jaw dropped before she could prevent it, and Lorndar's gratified smirk did nothing to improve her mood.

As if Marten doesn't have enough problems to deal with at the moment. The council members will have apoplexy!

Snapping her teeth together with an audible click, Betha stood up.

"I doubt the king will be able to see you for some time, Master Lorndar. Your timing is inopportune, but I will convey your request to him."

Accepting his dismissal with a self-satisfaction that riled Betha yet further, the master smith rose to his feet. An overpowering bouquet of inferior wine and hot metal rolled off him.

"No need, Lady Betha, we have already requested an audience. Good day, my lady."

He swaggered from the room, leaving Betha once again open mouthed. How dare he bypass correct protocol? Commoners, even craft masters, did not approach the king without the permission of their liege lord.

But that was exactly the problem. No rules existed for their duty to a liege *lady*, and Lorndar had neatly thrust that very point down her throat.

Charin take him! I have more important problems. Like heating enough water for this bath.

Betha strode to her bedchamber and spun around. She caught a glimpse of Quart entering the outer chamber with a worried frown on his brow, but she could not face him. Not yet.

She slammed the door.

Alone at last, tears spilled down her face. Undoubtedly Quart would expect her to indulge in a bout of self-harming to offset the anger generated by Lorndar's slight. Under normal circumstances, her broken heart would have driven her to that dark place too.

But Marten had not only shredded her happiness, he had also banned her from her customary release.

She could yield to the urge here, in her own rooms, in total privacy, and he would never know she'd defied him. Her fists bunched, nails cutting into her palms. Anticipation sizzled.

Plopping down onto a vanity stool, she slid open a drawer to one side of her mirror. Reaching in, her fingers curled around the ribbed, comforting hilt of a small dagger. Withdrawing it, she held it up, studying the glint of candlelight off the polished blade. Such promise rested in her palm: a swift cut, a neat stab, a long, drawn out slice. Ecstasy, so tantalizingly close, bound up in such a tiny action.

An action Marten would never know she'd executed, when her self-healing talent—was it really magic? —would render her wounded skin as unblemished as that of a new born.

She bit her lip.

She would know.

When she'd promised Marten complete honesty, she'd

bound herself to that pledge, no matter their fledgling relationship had foundered mere moments later. Whatever his reasons, whatever motivation lay beneath his condemnation of her ability, she would no more break that trust than she would betray her king in any other way.

In disgust, she threw the dagger back into the drawer and slid it shut.

Opened it again. Reached in. Withdrew her hand. Reached again.

And finally thrust the drawer closed with such force the entire unit rocked back, crashing against the wall and spilling the jewellery and cosmetics from its surface.

Betha rose and stomped over to light a fire for heating water, leaving the debris on the floor where it had fallen.

26. DISTRACTION

The bitter taste on Marten's tongue trickled down his gullet, settling as an indigestible lump in the pit of his stomach.

He'd dared to believe for one brief, bright moment, that his curse was not a curse after all. That Chel had crafted him with a purpose: to complement the perfect mate She had fashioned for him.

And look how that had turned out.

Squeezing his eyes shut, he strove to banish Betha's persistent presence from his mind, but she refused to abandon him. Her sweet scent, her silky skin, her eagerness for his style of ardour, her soft cries of passion as they'd fulfilled each other's dreams. These, along with the heart-wrenching image of her beautiful, bewildered face when he'd dismissed her, saturated his mind and his senses even when he sought to expel them.

His disillusionment and frustration boiled over into undirected rage. Marten doubted he'd ever know which aspect of the deity—Chel or Charin—was responsible for his unenviable disposition, providing no clear target for his anger, so he chose to hold them both accountable. After all, if it was, as seemed likely, one of Charin's viler pranks, why had Chel not chosen to intervene?

I will no longer be a toy for You to manipulate; I choose to be my own man. I embrace this cursed appetite You've inflicted upon me, and I refuse to be embarrassed any longer by something I did not choose, yet is an integral part of me.

He squared his shoulders and raised his chin to permit Davi to fasten the high collar of his tunic. Squinting in the bright light streaming through the large windows into his dressing room, he set his mouth in a defiant, tight-lipped smile.

If that ruins your plans, it pleases me no end.

A glow of power swelled inside his chest, reward for his defiance.

"A little higher, if you please, sire." Davi's bland request plucked Marten from his mental tirade, and reminded him of why he valued his bodyguard so highly. Davi had taken one look at the king's thunderous expression, and refrained from his usual banter, asking no questions and offering nothing more than practical observations on his master's attire for the day.

A day which held the blessed promise of much needed distraction.

Marten had considered wilfully ignoring the mountain of paperwork waiting for him in his office, in favour of catching up on one of his missed combat training sessions. But in the end, he'd not had to make that choice.

"Did Freskin's messenger give no reason to support his request?"

"None, sire. Brother Freskin merely invites you to call upon him at your earliest convenience."

It irked Marten that even the king could be summoned by a priest, but under the circumstances, he had no reason to delay.

He shut his eyes for a moment, tired of fighting the glare intruding through the window. The instant his lids closed, Betha's face floated across his inner vision, bringing a tingle to his skin.

The warmth of her flesh beneath his palms. Her delighted gasp as the lash of his whip painted delicate stripes across her back, like a calligraphy brush caressing vellum.

His body jerked, eyes snapped open.

"Sire?"

He shook his head. "It's nothing," he muttered, anger surging again.

Nothing. How can she be nothing? She's everything I ever

wanted, and she proved my curse isn't the obstacle I believed. But how dare *she put me in such an impossible position? She knows my hold on Tyr-en is precarious—after the way Uncle Hal died, I can't risk condoning magic, even in secret. That's exactly how we got into the mess that birthed my bastard uncle and brought his accursed coup down on us. She should have known better; she's an intelligent woman, for Chel's sake!*

Curbing his desire to smash something, Marten twisted away from Davi's ministrations and snatched up his riding gloves.

"Let's go," he snapped, eager for some physical activity to dull his mind.

And his heart.

* * * * * * *

Goldcrest nuzzled Marten's pocket, seeking the treat his master always provided at the end of a ride.

"Take good care of him," he instructed as he handed his reins to the waiting priest. The golden stallion swept the treat from his palm and walked away, chewing contentedly. Marten tipped his head back, overawed as usual by the height and majesty of the Temple building. Even the royal palace suffered in comparison.

The serenity Marten had gained on the ride, in the uncomplicated company of his faithful horse, drained out through the soles of his boots.

The Temple serves the crown. How is it I'm always made to feel small here?

That same impression consumed him every time he visited; had done so ever since he was a small child, delivered to the brothers for his first lessons. Lessons that included accepting his position as monarch was at the goddess's decree, not man's.

As he passed into the shadow of the arched entryway, Marten shivered, then squared his shoulders. He might feel intimidated by the Temple, but he'd be damned if he'd show it.

"Thank you for coming so swiftly, Your Majesty."

Marten's eyes adjusted to the cool gloom of the lofty public chamber. That Brother Freskin greeted him here, instead of awaiting him in the chamber reserved for the king's visits, was unexpected. Even more unexpected was the priest's companion.

Sister Valaree bowed in greeting, but her tight expression filled Marten with unease. What was this meeting he'd been asked to attend? Had the Temple council reached some disagreeable conclusion about the episode with the casket? Or had they somehow discerned his improprietous behaviour with women? Perhaps they disapprove of his relationship with Betha. Given the reason he'd dismissed her from his bed, while deciding to retain her services as a spy—now *that* would make for a challenging conversation.

As Marten strode past Valaree, the scent of spices and incense curled around him. Where once he'd found the combination intoxicating, now it repelled him. No matter how striking the raven-haired priestess, her appeal would never come within ten leagues of Betha's.

Marten puzzled how it was he'd ever been aroused by Valaree, with her pious attitudes, and her apparent indifference to men. In fact, now he considered it further, Valaree's devotion to Annasala bordered on obsession. Was there more to that attachment than first appeared?

"Please, come this way," Freskin invited.

Marten dragged his attention back from that unsettling notion. He was about to protest that he knew the way well, when it dawned on him the priest was leading in a direction he'd never been taken before. A quick glance aside at Davi met with raised eyebrows as they headed deeper into the Temple complex. Marten scanned the corridors, finding them unremarkable to the extent he doubted he'd find his way back out again without a guide. A tiny frisson ran down his spine. He should be completely safe here, inside Chel's Temple, but in light of suspicions about the resurrection of Charin's Cult, he wasn't as confident as he'd have liked.

"In here, sire."

Freskin opened a heavy door. A door with bolts on the outside.

Marten baulked. "Before I enter, tell me what's going on."

Freskin inclined his head with a show of patience. "Of course, sire. Within, you will find the individual responsible for the death of Brother Padrus."

Marten stiffened. The whirling kaleidoscope of unrelated concerns fled his mind.

Padrus's killer!

Davi stepped past him. "Me first," he stated, daring the priest to disagree with him.

"Of course," Freskin said. "I can assure you, there is no danger. He is restrained."

"Nevertheless," Davi ground out, "I am the one responsible for the king's safety. You would do well to remember that."

Freskin made another small bow, but Marten caught a glint of something in the priest's eye. Annoyance perhaps? It appeared he'd planned a surprise for his king, and didn't take well to having it appropriated.

Davi's inspection left Marten standing outside the cell with the two clerics. He kept his gaze downcast, drawing on all his many wonderful memories of Padrus, unwilling to waste the few brief seconds remaining before he must bring that chapter of his life to an end. All too soon, Davi opened the door and beckoned him in.

Inside, the cell appeared no different to the small rooms the many priests and priestesses resident in the temple called home. A cot, a prayer stand and stool, and a small table and chair. The only remarkable thing was the chain fastened to a heavy ring set into the floor. Its other end terminated in a metal cuff around the prisoner's ankle.

Marten studied the unremarkable assassin. Mid height, middling build, mid brown hair brushing his shoulders. Even his tunic and leggings were of average cut, in unembellished brown cloth. His features held nothing of note to snag in the memory, and Marten was certain even if he'd seen the man before, he wouldn't have remembered him. The perfect player.

"Why?"

Not the most original question, but it popped out before Marten he could prevent it. The assassin cocked his head.

"Because I was paid," returned the predictable answer. The most memorable thing about the assassin was his rough voice, and the accent that proclaimed his origin as Rylond, the merchant kingdom. Marten frowned.

"By whom? You betray your affiliation by your words, but why would Rylond wish the death of a gentle priest—one of Chel's Blessed?"

The man glanced past Marten to where the clerics stood beside the door. Entreaty? Or accusation?

"If you think I know the why, or the who, then you are a fool."

Davi's hand snapped out, rendering a sharp slap across the assassin's face. "Show more respect for the king," he growled.

Expanded whites gleamed around brown irises. "The king?" His eyes flickered towards the clerics. "You brought him here?"

An undertone threaded his words. Surprise? Or fear? Marten's jaw tightened. The assassin would do well to fear him, for Marten's presence betokened only one end.

Or was it something else? Suddenly Marten wanted to question the prisoner without the clerics in attendance. He waved a hand in dismissal.

"Leave us. I wish to speak with him alone."

"But, sire—"

Marten spun on his heel. "You vouched for my safety. Are you uncertain now?"

Freskin shook his head. "No, sire, but it is not proper for you to be alone with a known criminal."

Marten's temper bubbled. "According to who? Do not presume to tell me what I can or cannot do."

Bowing low, Freskin and Valaree retreated with obvious reluctance. Still uncomfortable with being on the wrong side of a door with such heavy bolts, Marten motioned for Davi to follow them. His faithful bodyguard vacated the room without protest.

Marten stepped forward. The prisoner shrank back against the wall. At this close proximity, Marten noted the pinched look on the man's face, and the yellow of a fading bruise above the still fresh imprint of Davi's hand. A pungent odour caused Marten to wrinkle his nose: foreign spices mixed with fear.

"We're alone. Tell me who ordered this murder."

The man's jaw tightened. Marten slammed an open hand against the wall beside his head. He flinched.

"Understand this: Padrus was my *friend*. Not just my priest; my *friend*. He was a holy man; one of Chel's Blessed, and you *killed* him! How do you think that will place you when you stand before Chel?"

A bead of sweat trickled down the man's hairline. Marten leaned in.

"And believe me," he whispered into the assassin's ear, "it won't be long before you find out." Taking a step back, he locked gazes with the man. "You might lessen the consequences if you tell me what I want to know."

"Nothing can help me now. You have *no idea* who you're up against!"

Marten frowned. "You do realise you won't be leaving this room? Whoever it is, they can't get to you now. I can make this quick, or we can take our time. It's up to you."

Tears spun away from the man's face as his head wagged, and Marten realised with shock they were tears of laughter. Bitter laughter to be sure, but laughter nonetheless.

"You are as naïve as I was led to believe." His face grew serious again. "Enjoy it while you can, young king. Oh, to be so innocent once more."

Stung, Marten raised a fist, but lowered it again.

I am not *a barbarian, no matter what You want me to think of myself,* he railed at the deity.

"I haven't been innocent since the day my mother was murdered," he said. "And if you think fairness is a sign of naiveté, you merely proclaim your ignorance. On the other hand, don't mistake my sense of decency for mercy. I *will* discover who paid you, and I'll deal with them as they deserve, I'm simply offering you a deal that speeds up the inevitable for us both."

The first signs of genuine emotion flitted across the assassin's face. Fear, yes. And desperation. Marten wondered how the man had been recruited to his task: had he not known where it would lead?

"If I tell you, you'll do it now?"

Was the entreaty real? The fear most certainly was. The man's fists bunched, arms rigid. Marten measured the distance between them, and the length of the chain. He reversed another step.

The prisoner darted a glance towards the closed door. "Don't leave me to *them*. I've seen how *they* do it."

Marten held his neutral expression. He had no idea what the man was talking about; the Temple did not perform executions. Or did they? What did anyone outside of the priesthood really know about what went on inside this behemoth of a building?

Another mystery to unravel on a different day.

"You have my word. Now, tell me."

"I can't tell you his name; I never heard it. I *can* tell you he's a priest, but not of this Temple."

"What then: a Rylondese priest?"

The man shook his head. "No, you don't understand. The Temples are all connected; what one does, another knows and condones. This man is a priest, but not from any Temple you know."

Marten could feel his patience slipping away, running like juice from an overripe fruit crushed between his fingers.

"If you don't know his name, at least give me a description; something tangible I can hunt."

The assassin's expression became guarded. He shook his head again. "I cannot. I never saw his true face."

"What in Charin's Hell does that mean?" Marten yelled in frustration.

The man shrugged. "I have nothing more to offer you. If you're as smart as you think you are, you'll work it out for yourself. Stay angry, my lord king; it may lead you along the true path."

Lips pressed together, no matter what Marten threatened, the prisoner refused to say anything more. Willing to take the man's advice and remain angry, Marten strode to the door and yanked it open. Davi, who'd been standing with his back against it, jumped forward and spun round. The priest, the priestess, and Marten's bodyguard all regarded him in silent question.

"Get in here," Marten ordered. "Davi, it's time."

Wearing a grim expression, Davi marched back into the cell with the clerics trailing behind. Marten didn't care whether they witnessed this or not, but he wouldn't have them interfering.

"When we saw Padrus's death had been quick, I promised I would do the same for his murderer."

Davi seized the man's hair, yanked his head back, and slit his throat in one swift action. Blood jetted out, spattering the cleric's white robes. Valaree let out a tiny squeak and stumbled backward. Freskin swung round in fury.

"He was the Temple's prisoner! We have our own way of dealing with criminals like him."

Marten was only too glad to continue sustaining the anger the assassin had urged; it melded with the thumping of his speeding heart, and the short, shallow breaths that were all he could seem to draw in that moment.

"Don't tell me this wasn't my right: his crime was against my personal priest. That made it a crime against *me*." Marten glared at Freskin, daring the priest to argue, but he backed down with a grudging bow.

Marten returned his attention to the dying man. His twitching body sprawled across Davi's boots, gulping and choking as the still pumping blood filled his lungs. Plainly no longer conscious, it was still a gruesome thing to watch.

Marten had witnessed death before, during the coup, but never at his command. He clapped a hand over his mouth, grateful he'd not eaten that morning.

Chel forgive me; I just killed someone. He can't be fixed—he's never going to stand up again, never draw another breath or speak another word. Did I really have that right?

He gritted his teeth. *I am the king; that gives me the right.*

Still, doubts assailed him.

I know it had to be done, but did I allow my temper to sway me? Should we have taken him to the palace to interrogate?

The gurgles began to die down, and Davi shifted the carcass off the toe of his blood-drenched boot. A scarlet pool spread across the floor, tiny runnels of the stuff travelling along the grooves between the stone flags like scarlet worms. The malodorous stink of loosening bowels rose from the body to mingle with the coppery smell of the exsanguination.

"Time to leave, sire."

Marten nodded, not trusting his voice. He followed Davi from the cell without a backward glance. Valaree scuttled past him, but before Marten could raise an objection, he remembered they needed her guidance to leave the Temple.

That she was also keeping them from straying into other areas of the building did not escape his notice, but at that moment all he could think of was getting outside into fresh air. The curdling brew of fresh blood mixed with devotional incense turned his stomach. He fought not to embarrass himself, and when they finally reached the atrium, he almost ran past the priestess to get out into clean daylight.

He drew several deep breaths, and when he turned back, Valaree was gone. Only Davi stood there, concern clear on his face.

"Are you well, sire?" he asked quietly. "That was something you should not have had to witness."

Marten allowed a wan smile. "It was something I needed to do. For Padrus." He raked a set of fingers through his hair. "I'm afraid his fears have been borne out; the assassin claimed he was hired by a priest, but not of the Temple. That has to mean a priest of Charin, don't you think?"

Davi grimaced, but bit off his answer as a pair of priests hurried past them. A flurry of activity outside the stables delivered their horses in short order, and Marten swung into his saddle with huge relief. Somehow, things never seemed so dire when he was aboard Goldcrest.

However, with the Temple diminishing behind them, and Davi chewing his lip in an agitated manner but not speaking, Marten's thoughts fled back to the assassin's gruesome death. He'd ordered executions before, in the early days following the coup, but this was the first he'd witnessed. Had he made the best choice? He couldn't have shown compassion to Padrus's murderer, but might there have been a better death? An image of the shuddering body with its head flopping to one side, and blood cascading from the slashed neck, filled his mind.

Stop it! You know it had to be done. Dead is dead, and it was quicker than many.

He gave himself a mental shake. Goldcrest shifted uneasily beneath him, and he realised his unsettled emotions were distressing his horse.

"Sorry, boy. Not your problem." He patted the gleaming shoulder. The stallion heaved a deep sigh and settled back to his previous amble.

Marten wished it was as easy for him to relax.

Everything led back to Charin's Cult. Padrus's murder, Urien's plot to supplant him, possibly even the extended unrest amongst both nobles and commoners, challenging his reign at every turn since the coup. Could the recent assassination attempt be yet another symptom? Marten still felt certain the first attack had been an opportunistic seizure of extraordinary circumstances, but the recent one?

How far had the Cult's tendrils infiltrated?

Deliberately, Marten roused his anger again, this time with clear direction. It was time to go on the offensive, to cut out the canker before this beautiful continent they'd claimed fell victim to the cultists' evil magic, to suffer the destruction visited on humanity's last homeland.

Marten was not willing to let history repeat.

Grudgingly, he forced himself to confront the option he'd striven to avoid: his most valuable tool to infiltrate the Cult would undoubtedly be Betha. She was already in a position of trust with Urien, and that seemed the most promising snag in the weave to pick away at and unravel. Which meant he would have to work closely with Betha, despite last night's debacle.

Goldcrest pranced beneath him, and Marten relaxed his death-grip on the reins. He removed one hand, shook it to release the tension, and scratched the agitated stallion on the withers.

Yesterday, the prospect of continuing to work closely with Betha would have thrilled him. Now, he felt so conflicted he couldn't even contemplate how to start untangling the jumbled threads of his emotions.

No matter. He would work out his own issues for the good of the kingdom. He drew himself up taller and rode on, towards whatever the deities saw fit to throw at him next.

27. FEVER

"Why does he cry so much?"

Risada fiddled with the frayed blanket swaddling Halson, attempting to tuck its ragged ends more tightly around him. She frowned down at Chayla, who trudged along the grass beside Greylegs, the goat's lead rope held loosely in her hand. Even though the baby might have been safer with Chayla than where he was, lodged between Risada and the pommel of her saddle, she refused to consider handing him over.

"You keep disturbing him. He's probably overtired," Chayla answered, and Risada yearned to slap the woman for sounding so reasonable. She'd always assumed motherhood would be a stroll in the garden for someone who'd lived a life as challenging as hers, so why did she not have any of the instincts Chayla seemed to possess in abundance?

Risada glanced over her shoulder at the rolling hills behind them, dull green mounds beneath a haze of light cloud. As soon as Rustam had declared himself fit to ride, they'd abandoned the cave and descended into the southern reaches of Tyr-en. A day out from the foothills, they'd bypassed Risada's estate at Domn, half a day to the east of their route to the capital. Stopping at Domn had been tempting, but quite apart from the desire to pay her respects at her husband's grave in Darshan, Risada felt a pressing need to present Hal's son to the king as soon as possible. Much though the situation displeased her, until Marten had a child of his own, Halson was next in line to the throne.

So far, they'd kept to fields and tracks, where the first signs of autumn tinged the foliage with gold, and the fresh smell of ploughed fields was muted by recent rainfall. In deliberately avoiding the outlying farms and manors, Risada acknowledged she was allowing paranoia to rule her path, but since the coup, she couldn't bring herself to trust anyone outside her immediate circle.

At their current speed, Darshan now lay no more than two days' ride ahead, and her arguments and pleas for Rustam to turn back before anyone saw him rang with increasing desperation. Why was he so stubborn? The fool had a death sentence hanging over him, and yet he refused to believe Annasala would enforce her decree.

Risada frowned at Rustam's back. He rode in front of her, tall and straight on his blood bay Shivan stallion, hips swinging supply with the sway of the horse's walk, as if they danced together. Risada's joints ached just watching. In fact, her whole body complained, her previous injuries exacerbated by her fight with Hext-al. She was only six years Rustam' senior, but watching his lithe body made her feel old.

Halson grizzled again. Risada's fingers twitched; there must be something she could do for her son.

"We should stop," she said. "I think he's hungry."

Rustam wheeled Fleetfoot around. He stood up in his stirrups and scanned the surrounding hills and arable fields.

"It all looks clear," he declared before dismounting. "No water that I can see, but we've enough in our canteens to brew tea."

He slipped Fleetfoot's bridle over his ears and gave the horse a slap on the rump. The stallion raised a playful heel towards him, before ambling off to graze.

"Here, I'll take him." Rustam held his arms up to take the baby while Risada slithered ungracefully down Greyleg's side.

"Thank you," she said, as he handed Halson back. "Rusty, please, I need you to reconsider."

Rustam unbuckled Greyleg's bridle, and the gelding fell to eating alongside Fleetfoot. The goat joined them.

"I know what you're going to say, but save your breath: I'm going with you and that's an end to it. There could be more bandits or wild animals out here, even traitors who'd be thrilled to find the heir to the throne unguarded. I'm not leaving you."

"You're stubborn to the point of stupidity! What happens when we get there, and Sala has you executed? Don't think I'll forgive you for bringing that on yourself!"

"She won't do it—she's my sister."

Risada huffed. "This is your *life* we're talking about. You can't rely on a relationship Sala would rather didn't exist. She's pretty messed up, if you hadn't noticed, and she has Valaree whispering in her ear; I wouldn't trust that woman any more than I would a troll at a picnic. Remember what I told you about her? This is a priestess who does magic, and calls it the power of the goddess."

Chayla's amused cackle spun Risada around.

"What are you laughing at, crazy woman?"

Staring at the bush the nanny goat was browsing, Chayla tilted her head on one side, ignoring Risada in favour of the twiggy plant.

"They don't understand, do they. Should I explain?"

Risada stoppered her annoyance, knowing it would get her nowhere. She'd tried quizzing Chayla about the identity of her invisible companion, and about the werecat's strange deference, while they'd waited for Rustam to recover, but nothing the woman said made any sort of sense.

"She truly is crazy, isn't she?" Risada glanced at Rustam for confirmation. He raised his eyebrows.

"Perhaps she can see something we can't? I know how you feel about magic, Risada, but I can assure you there's a lot more out here than you know, and not all of it wants to be seen."

Risada shuddered. Halson began to cry in earnest. Exasperated, Risada grabbed hold of the other woman's shoulder, and gave it a quick shake.

"Chayla! Make yourself useful: that nanny won't milk

herself."

Blinking like an owl, Chayla wandered over to Greylegs, still muttering to her invisible companion. She rummaged in the horse's saddle bags for the precious elven bottle that had originally contained *caris dew,* sent with Halson when he was returned from Shiva. Now, with a teat Chayla had fashioned from a waxy flower, it served as a means of feeding him the goat's milk.

Risada squeezed her eyes shut. She didn't trust Chayla, and yet the deranged woman was the only one who could soothe Halson when he became fractious. It irked Risada to the verge of homicide, yet for the sake of her son, she stayed her hand.

"Let me hold him," Chayla offered once she'd filled the bottle.

"No." Risada couldn't help herself from clutching her baby tighter. Predictably, his wails escalated to howls.

Chayla's mouth pursed. "I can't feed him like that."

"Just give it to me," Risada ground out from between gritted teeth. Chayla handed the bottle over, but no matter how Risada presented it, Halson turned his face away, refusing the teat.

"Why will he take it from you, but not from me?"

Chayla ignored her, peering closely at the tightly swaddled baby. She laid the back of her hand to his forehead. "He's too hot," she declared.

"How can he be too hot? It isn't that warm today," Risada protested.

Chayla extended her hands as if she was about to lift the baby away from Risada. Tears sprang to Risada's eyes as Halson wriggled, appearing to reject her for the other woman's embrace.

And then his body stiffened.

His eyes rolled back, showing only the gleaming whites, and foam bubbled from between his lips.

"What's happening?" Risada's heart raced. "Chayla, what's wrong with him?"

"Strip him," Chayla ordered. "I told you he was too hot!"

Helplessness overwhelmed Risada, and she thrust the rigid baby towards Chayla. "I don't know what to do. Help him, please!"

Chayla shook her head. "He's best with his mother." She yanked the blanket away from the tiny, stiff body, exposing flushed skin and shaking fists. Foam continued to froth from his mouth. "Turn him on his side so he doesn't swallow it."

Tears slipped down Risada's cheeks. "What is it? He can't die! *Do* something!" She knew her demand was irrational, but she didn't care. How could her baby, that she'd only just found, be dying?

Chayla shook her head. "He's not dying, Risada, he has a fever. Fevers cause convulsions."

"You're certain? How do you know?"

Chayla's haggard features softened with compassion. Risada was unsure if it was for her, or the baby. Either way, gratitude welled inside her. Had Chayla not been here, she would have *no* idea what to think, or do.

"I've seen this before. We must nurse him through the fever, but Chel willing, it won't happen again."

In her arms, Halson's little body relaxed, turning gradually pliable once more. He blinked sleepy eyes up at her, and Risada bent over to kiss his head.

"Is that it? Is it over?"

"Provided the fever breaks, yes," Chayla confirmed.

Risada glanced up through the sparkle of tears on her eyelashes.

"Thank you," she said humbly, before turning to Rustam. He stood off to one side, like a kitchen maid at a tournament, shifting his weight from one foot to the other.

"We need shelter. Any ideas?"

Rustam stared at an angle to the headland they'd been following. Hedgerows stretched in both directions, and also at angles to where they stood, loosely enclosing ploughed fields and grassy pastures for as far as they could see. He pointed east, to where a knoll rose in the distance, topped by a distinctive formation of throne trees.

"If I'm correct about exactly where we are, there's a House of Chel less than half a day's ride beyond that hill. Will that do?"

Risada bit her lip. "It'll take us off route, but if that's the closest shelter…?"

"It's the nearest I can think of." Rustam threw a troubled glance at Halson before scooping up the horses' bridles. "Let's get going. I've a fair idea of where it is, but I might have to ride a few sweeps before I find it. The sooner we get started, the better."

Risada stood in silent agreement while Rustam readied the horses. In her mind's eye she replayed over and over, her tiny, defenceless baby, rigid and shaking, like a victim of a poison she'd once used, back when being the perfect assassin was all that consumed her.

Please Chel, don't take him from me. If you do that, all the lessons I learned from Hal about how to be more than just an emissary of death, will have been pointless. Help me, please, to become the woman he believed I could be. For that, I need my baby.

28. SECRETS AND DECISIONS

Seated on his well-padded throne in the small public audience hall, Marten caught his attention straying towards the woman standing off to one side, rather than keeping it where it should be, on Craft Master Lorndar.

Marten studied Betha's face, how she frowned at Lorndar, the creases on her brow marring her customary radiance. Even her gown reflected her sombre mood—a lacklustre emerald fabric with a mere handful of sparkling crystals to lift it beyond dowdy.

Marten ached to hold her, to soothe away the pain only he knew was eating her up inside. The skin on his palms tingled, recalling the silky-smooth texture of her body, and he shifted on his cushion, uncomfortably aware of how tight his breeches had become.

He jerked his head up and down, as if he'd been listening to every word the master smith had uttered. Public audiences did not usually afford such radical suggestions, and Marten fully intended to give this one the attention it deserved. No matter that Lorndar was a very annoying man, his solution offered a way forward for Tyr-en's stagnant cultural situation.

"I'll bring your request before the council, Master Lorndar," he promised. "Though I fear many will dismiss such a proposal without consideration. What you are asking for is unprecedented: a reform of our culture's entire structure."

"Yet one that is long overdue, in the view of the craft houses," stated Lorndar. "We are asking for no more than our skills to be recognised as tradeable commodities. The freedom to earn our own livelihoods will bring drive and innovation to our crafts; something our current situation fails to inspire. Your Majesty, we are falling behind the other kingdoms. Soon we will become an anachronism in the land our ancestors founded."

The delegation of craft masters arranged behind the smith nodded and murmured in agreement. Marten counted most of the important crafts amongst them: potters, weavers, tanners, leather workers, dyers, silversmiths, carpenters and masons. If they banded together and refused to work, the kingdom would stutter to a standstill.

That might prove to be the leverage Marten needed to convince the lords of the major houses to embrace this daring proposal.

"Master Lorndar, I can assure you this matter will take the highest priority at my next council meeting. In the meanwhile, I hope you have obtained suitable lodgings in the city while you await an answer?"

Lorndar bowed. "We have, Your Majesty. The innkeepers of Darshan support our undertaking." The man's mouth quirked into a self-satisfied smirk. "They have made us very welcome."

Vexed by the master smith's overweening attitude, Marten rose to his feet, indicating an end to the audience.

"I will overlook your breach of etiquette, Master Lorndar. This time. Before we speak again, I would remind you in future to follow correct protocol, and have your request delivered by your liege lady." He brushed imaginary dust off his sleeve. "Lady Betha has my confidence, and my ear. You would do well to remember that."

Lorndar's brow lowered over reddening cheeks. Marten bit the inside of his cheek, pre-empting the smile twitching his lips. He glanced towards Betha, then quickly away. What did it matter to him, if she was grateful or not?

Gathering his dignity around him, Marten marched from the hall without a backward glance. Davi fell in behind him, while a pair of guards preceded him along the halls. He directed them to take a somewhat circuitous route to his rooms to avoid the more populated regions of the palace. Being forced to keep up the pretence of a relationship with Betha pained him, and the less he mingled with inquisitive nobles, the better.

He also had no wish to be delayed for his appearance at the afternoon's festivities: the end of summer tournament.

"Will you be watching, this year, sire, or contending?" Davi asked as he followed Marten into his dressing room.

Marten rolled his shoulders. "I think I'll fight."

Davi set about laying out leathers and light armour while Marten paced back and forth. Of late, combat training had been less regular than he would have liked, but the tournament had arrived at the perfect moment for him to work off his pent-up aggression. Davi held out a light undershirt. "You'll have to hold still for a moment, sire."

"What, you can't keep up with me?"

"If you wish to appear dressed by an incompetent stable lad, then I dare say so."

Marten snorted. "Fine, you win." He stopped in front of the full-length mirror, and studied Davi's reflection as his bodyguard-come-valet deftly stripped him and layered on his sparring gear. In the two years Davi had served him, the man had changed little. Perhaps his girth was a fraction thicker. Could that be the result of contentment?

"Have you ever considered marriage, Davi?"

Davi's fingers never faltered, fastening a vambrace around his left arm, although his forehead puckered.

"I haven't, sire. It's not for the likes of me."

"But I must, whether I wish it or not." Marten held out his other arm. "It must be less complicated when you can make your own choices."

"I thought you'd decided to make your own decision on the matter?"

The spectral sensation of an exquisite female form, moulding against his side, heated Marten's groin. He cleared his throat.

"If only it was that simple." He dropped his arms to his sides, curling his fists beneath the intricately embossed vambraces. "Davi, have you never loved someone you know you shouldn't?"

He caught Davi's shocked expression in the mirror, and cursed himself for his blunder. This wasn't how he'd meant to let Davi know he'd discovered the other man's secret. He'd intended to tease him, to draw out a confession with playful jibes, not smack him bluntly over the head with the knowledge furnished by a spy.

Time to confess.

"I didn't mean it like that. Davi, I don't care who you love, it's not a problem to me. Chel knows, the way I am, I've no grounds to judge how others love."

Davi's fingers twitched. "What are you suggesting, sire?"

"I know."

Panic flitted across Davi's features before he regained control. "You know what, exactly? Sire."

"That your love is a man." Marten stared at the rug beneath his feet. "I had one of my spies follow you." He glanced up in time to see Davi's jaw tighten.

"I'm sorry," Marten said simply. If he'd fouled the one relationship in his life that was free from complications, he had no one but himself to blame.

For a long moment, Davi held his silence. Then he resumed adding the finishing touches to Marten's outfit.

"I should be angry, I suppose, sire. If it was anyone else, I would be. But you aren't just anyone, and I accept that. For all you knew, I might have been the one plotting your assassination so, in a warped sort of way, I'm proud of you. Information is what keeps you safe, so you have nothing to apologise for."

Marten met his eye in the mirror, knowing the potential danger in this revelation for Davi. The Temple's stance on such matters was not lenient. "Your attitude goes beyond duty, Davi. You have my admiration, and my thanks. I'd hate to lose your friendship."

"Thank you, sire, that means a lot. And it truly doesn't bother you?"

"Not one bit. I meant what I said. Oh, I know the Temple forbids such a thing, but I doubt they'd look favourably on my tastes either."

"It isn't quite the same, sire. Without wishing to sound crass, your liaisons have the potential to produce offspring, and that's at the core of their decree against my kind." He shrugged. "Perhaps they see truly."

"I refuse to believe that, Davi. We should all feel free to be who we are made to be, otherwise why would Chel create us that way?"

Marten froze. How long had he battled with this very plight? How often had he railed against the deities for making him the way he was? What, and when, had this new attitude emerged?

Betha. Somehow, even though she'd torn his heart in two, she'd healed him. He recalled his rant at the deity, in the aftermath of that one, glorious, night of passion with a partner who genuinely desired him exactly the way he was.

'I will no longer be a toy for You to manipulate; I choose to be my own man. I embrace this cursed appetite You've inflicted upon me, and I refuse to be embarrassed any longer by something I did not choose, yet is an integral part of me.'

His chest swelled. For the first time in his adult life, he consciously accepted who, and what, he was. From this day forward, he would not be ashamed of—or fear—his nature.

Betha, I am forever in your debt. If only things had worked out in our favour—perhaps you will always be my one true love, though we can never be together.

Attempting to swallow the bitterness coating his tongue, Marten cleared his throat. Fighting in the tourney beckoned; the ideal distraction.

He clapped Davi on the shoulder, startling him.

"Never be ashamed of who you are, Davi. I understand your need to keep this secret, especially when I'm dragging you into the Temple so often, but I assure you, my lips are sealed."

Davi blinked, then bowed his head. "Thank you, sire. It was never my intention to deceive you, it simply wasn't an issue of import."

"Good. We'll say no more on the subject unless you choose to raise it again. If ever you have the need, I *will* listen."

Davi bobbed his head, before standing back to inspect his handiwork. "All ready, my king."

Marten studied his reflection, from the leather hood compressing his unruly brown hair, to the toes of his supple boots. He settled a hand on the hilt of his sword. "Then lead on, my good man. I have bouts to contend."

Leaving his rooms with a jauntier step than he'd had in a good long while, Marten's mind strayed back to Betha. She would be there, watching, sitting in the place of honour beside his empty throne while he fought. He made a silent vow to win today, not just one bout, but the entire tourney. There would be no marriage, but he wanted to make her proud of him, all the same.

Without her accursed magic, he'd have permitted the love coiling through him to expand, to take over his soul.

If only that was possible.

29. TOURNAMENT

The overpowering stink of hot leather and sweaty men forced Betha to cover her nose with a handkerchief. She'd never sat this close to the arena before, nor did she wish to ever again. At least, as she wouldn't be marrying the king—even if the assembled nobles didn't know that yet—her absence from future events would not be remarkable.

She concentrated on drawing shallow breaths, aware of those around her misinterpreting her distaste for excitement. Beside her in the wooden stand, beneath the purple and white striped awning, Lady Tyldra, daughter of the Seventh House, squealed with delight and clutched Betha's hand.

"He's so handsome! Don't you think, Lady Betha?" she gushed. Then her head snapped around with huge, round eyes, and an 'O' on her lips. "Forgive me! Of course, the king is just as handsome. But Lord Urien…"

Betha flashed a tight smile and patted Tyldra's hand, before placing it firmly back into the girl's lap.

"It's fine, Tyldra. I understand."

Betha returned her gaze to the spectacle below. Down on the dirt floor, Marten faced his final opponent of the day, Lord Urien. With a lazy insouciance, Urien twirled his dull-edged practice sword before tossing it to the ground at Marten's feet.

Urien's voice carried easily to the stunned and suddenly silent crowd. "Boys' games, my king. How about we raise the stakes?" A page ran over to hand him a weapon belt with a finely tooled scabbard. The sword Urien drew glittered along its honed edge.

Marten raised his eyebrows. "I know you're skilled at

bluffing, Urien. I didn't realise that extended to reckless risk-taking."

Urien passed the finely crafted sword from hand to hand, weaving it back and forth with a studied expression on his face. He shrugged. "I enjoy a genuine challenge, Your Majesty. But if you'd rather not accept…?"

Betha stifled a gasp, one hand clapped over her nose and mouth. Surely Marten would not be so irresponsible? And yet, how could he refuse and not lose face?

"Very well," replied the king, and a leaden weight settled in Betha's stomach. "Three strikes, blood drawn. Yes?"

Urien's smile held an edge of satisfaction. "Perfect, sire. Shall we begin?"

A steward scurried to fetch Marten's sword, and then the combatants squared off across the hard-packed earth. Urien grinned, dancing lightly on the balls of his feet, his knee showing no sign of the instability Betha had seen before. The wiry, elegant lord had fought like a demon all afternoon, consigning one challenger after another to the ranks of the vanquished.

Betha's regard darted from Marten, to Urien, and back again. They had both won again and again, reducing the contenders until only the two of them remained. Who was the stronger? Before today, and secure in her knowledge of Urien's vulnerability, Betha had dismissed tales of Urien's martial prowess as sycophantic boasting on the part of his toadies. Now, with her heart in her throat, she had cause to doubt her assumptions.

The gong sounded to indicate the start of the final bout. Marten wove his blade back and forth as he sidled towards Urien's left flank. Urien sauntered away, maintaining his distance. Almost as if the fight had been pre-choreographed, the two men feinted and danced, testing, but neither finding an opening. The crowd became restless, calling for the real battle to commence.

Marten lunged. Urien struck with the speed of a snake, slipping his blade past the king's guard, and nicking his cheek. Marten spun away, but a dribble of bright blood trickled down his face. Urien's lips stretched into a wolfish smile.

The crowd roared its approval, even the king's supporters. The tournament showcased a display of skill, and both sides would applaud the winner, whoever it was.

First mark to Urien.

Betha pressed her hands into her lap, hiding them within a fold of her skirts where no one would be able to see her white knuckles. Why did men always have to fight to prove themselves? If it was strategy they wanted to test, there were many complex parlour contests that could prove their mettle. But no, they always had to do it in the crudest of ways. Ways that held the risk of serious injury, even when fought in the normal fashion, with dulled practice blades.

Anger stirred inside Betha. Marten ought to know better. He was fully aware of Urien's plotting, so why did he risk facing the scheming lord, flaunting temptation before him. What would Urien do if he found Marten at his mercy? Would he stay his hand, holding to his clandestine plot? Or might he decide not to wait? Killing the king would cause havoc, but perhaps Urien already had a contingency plan to take over, even without first securing a male heir of the royal bloodline.

Why did men have to be so stupid!

Tyldra jostled Betha's elbow. Decorum abandoned, the girl bounced in her seat, and Betha revised her thinking: it wasn't only men who were stupid. Tyldra was the sole heir to her House, but akin to other noble girls raised with no more training or ambition beyond securing a prestigious marriage, her mind was limited by convention.

Aren't I doing the same? Betha censured herself. What right did she have to disdain Tyldra's lack of aspiration when she, herself, had arrived in the capital with no more in mind than securing a suitable husband? That she sought a partner, rather than a man to take charge of her affairs, hardly elevated her to the moral high ground.

Tyldra's large but beautifully manicured fingers gripped Betha's elbow. "Ooh, he's so *fast*! Did you see that, Betha? King Marten's going to need a new tactic. Rushing Urien isn't going to work."

"I'm sure he'll find one, Tyldra. This isn't exactly his first fight."

"I know, but Urien fights *every* year; he has so much more experience. Obviously, it would be lovely if the king won, but I fear he's met his match today."

Tasting bile on her tongue, Betha swallowed. She would not disgrace either herself, or by extension, the king, who had positioned her in the most desirable seat of the day. On the other hand, the notion of vomiting all over Tyldra's stylish, pale rose dress offered a certain satisfaction.

The clash of weapons jerked her attention back to the unfolding spectacle. She flinched as Marten and Urien wrestled at close quarters, each trying to bring their swords to a usable position. Marten had a slight edge, being taller and heavier, but Urien displayed incredible speed, jumping back out of range before Marten could touch him.

Why, oh why, did the sly schemer not show any sign of lameness? Had that fall in the hideous meeting house been some twisted show he'd put on for Betha's sake? Feeding her a falsehood to take back to Marten, perhaps as a test of her loyalty?

And what must Marten think of her information now? Assuming he walked away from this contest, he was bound to take her to task for leading him to believe Urien was a cripple.

Without warning, Marten sprinted forward. His leading foot seemed to slip, and he fell onto his side, drawing a stifled cry from Betha, and indeed, from all those around her too. Her wide eyes followed the king as he slid at speed towards Urien, with one leg outstretched. Marten's foot connected with his opponent's shin and toppled him off balance before Betha's panicked mind recognised that the whole manoeuvre had been deliberate.

Marten's blade slashed upward, biting into Urien's wrist. If the fight had been for earnest, it would have removed Urien's sword hand.

The crowd's howl deafened Betha. Second strike to the king.

If he survives this, I might want to kill him myself for taking the risk!

By the grin on Marten's face, he was enjoying himself. What must Betha say, to make him consider Urien a genuine threat?

But the next strike went to Urien, with a darting slash that cut through the leather above Marten's right vambrace, exposing a shallow cut to the king's elbow. Marten's smile vanished.

At last! Will he take Urien seriously now?

The combatants fell to circling, each warier of the other. Urien only needed one more strike to win; the king, two.

Another flurry of sword strokes rang out in quick succession, reminding Betha of the clanging of the blacksmith's forge—a building she must pass every time she left her manor house.

Where was Lorndar? The master smith would surely be one to enjoy such a show, with the chance that someone might beat the king. Betha frowned as she searched the crowd, but Lorndar was nowhere to be seen. Nor were any of the craft masters. A feeling of unease prickled up her back. What were they up to now?

A united gasp drew her attention back to the arena. In the corner of her eye, she caught Tyldra's hands fly up to cover her face.

Urien backed away from Marten, limping. A flash of pale skin streaked with red showed through a long rent in his leggings above one ankle.

Whoever scored the next strike would be declared the winner.

Marten plunged in, clearly intent on exploiting the damage he'd inflicted. Urien paused until the last moment, before spinning away beneath Marten's sword arm with no sign of impairment. The speed of his fluid movement was awe-inspiring.

Betha flinched. Urien was playing with Marten! The injury hadn't slowed him one bit. Did he intend to kill the king?

Betha longed to stand up, to scream a warning, to send the guards down to arrest Urien. But why should they listen to her? She was only a woman. She had no authority, nor would any man take her alarm seriously.

And if she was wrong, and Urien didn't intend murder, Marten would never forgive her for the distraction, or for making a fool of herself. While the populace still believed she was his favoured lady, and a likely candidate for queen, he would expect her to comport herself with dignity and restraint.

Shaking, she compelled herself to sit still and say nothing.

She felt like she was dying inside.

Marten swung his sword and when Urien slipped inside his reach, jabbed at him with his other hand. Betha gasped. Marten's left hand held a dagger, hidden until now.

"That's cheating!" Tyldra protested.

Betha leaned back in her chair, a fraction of her anxiety uncoiling. "Tyldra, my dear, this isn't about rules, remember? It's about who wins."

Urien backed away with a nod of respect, but with the gesture still incomplete, spun around, his sword aimed beneath Marten's arm. With a sharp exhalation, Marten arched his spine backward, and Urien's blade flashed through empty space. A grim expression settled on the king's face, as if he'd finally realised Urien meant to do more than just win the tournament. Not permitting that insight to make him hesitate, Marten sprang forward again, pressing an attack reliant on his longer reach over Urien's speed. The smaller man ducked and twisted, passing beneath Marten's raised arm, his blade whirling so fast it became a blur.

For a fraction of a second—a second that stretched beyond

natural time—Urien's upturned face caught Betha's eye. A bright flash of silver intensified his gaze, stopping Betha's lungs.

What was *that?* A trick of the light? A warning from the deity?

She squeaked an unheard protest as Urien's sword descended towards the king's exposed left flank.

And then Urien stumbled to one knee. Marten completed the turn that had been both his undoing, and was, now, his victory. His sword came to rest against Urien's neck. The older man held his position, for all the world as if he was kneeling in homage at his sovereign's feet.

The crowd surged to their feet, their roar of approval drowning Betha's relieved sob. Beside her, Tyldra's lips described a moue of disappointment. Betha could not restrain herself.

"Better luck choosing a winner next time," she called out, leaning close to Tyldra's ear.

Her pride in Marten's success pumped her chest up, though a tiny talon of doubt threatened to rip her bubble to shreds. She doubted anyone else had seen what she'd witnessed, and she had no way of knowing how to interpret it.

Had the goddess stayed Urien's hand? Or for some nefarious reason, had Charin? Had the experience caused him to stumble? Or had Urien decided to allow the king to win?

Which begged the question: did Marten know what had happened?

30. PINS AND NEEDLES

"You told me he was a cripple!"

Marten's glare went unnoticed as Betha studied the rug beneath her dainty green slippers.

"I'm sorry, my king. I suspect he might have played me, but it seemed so real, at the time." She peered up through a waterfall of blonde tresses. "His knee did betray him though, in the end."

Marten harrumphed. He wasn't angry with Betha, although he refrained from informing her of that. His rage was all for himself, for being so gullible. Urien's mastery of the game bit home—on his cheek, and on his elbow, where his skin had parted beneath his skilful opponent's blade.

"He let me win."

Betha's gaze flashed up to meet his. Her awareness of the truth lurked in the depths of her bright blue eyes. So, he wasn't the only one to have recognised Urien's staged defeat.

"Did anyone *not* notice?" Marten allowed disgust to drip from his voice.

"Sire, I think most attributed it to luck, not to a deliberate move."

"Even so, they all think Urien should have won. That'll teach me not to fight him on a whim."

Betha's clasped hands tightened, knuckles blanching. "Please, sire, don't fight him again."

"Rest assured, it's not high on my agenda. I *would* like to know how real this impediment of his is, though. You mentioned a drug he takes to keep the pain at bay—obviously today with great success. I want to know what it is."

Betha dropped her face again. "I will do my best to find

out, my king."

He flicked a hand in dismissal, all the time wanting to do the complete opposite. He wanted to stroke her face, to soothe away the hurt his words and actions had etched there. To feel her warmth pressed against him.

He hardened his heart. No good would come of relenting.

He watched his rejected mate retreat across his sitting room, the droop of her shoulders cutting into him more deeply than Urien's sword. It took all his willpower to refrain from calling out, to stop her and tell her he didn't care about her magic, that he loved her regardless.

His chest grew so tight it hurt.

"Sire?" Davi's voice at his side distracted him, and when he glanced back, Betha was gone.

"I know, I know. Marganie's waiting."

Deflated, Marten trudged after Davi to his dressing room where they found Seamstress Marganie sorting through a pile of garments. A quick scan of the room revealed she was alone.

"No assistant today, Marganie?" Marten asked.

Not glancing up from her task, Marganie shook her head. "I haven't seen the feckless girl in days." She squinted up at him from the corner of an eye. "She's probably been beguiled by an unscrupulous man."

Sweat broke out on Marten's palms. Surely, Nonni wouldn't have revealed the intimacy she shared with him to a woman old enough to be her mother? Would she?

To cover his discomfort, Marten fingered the top item of clothing on the listing stack. He sighed.

"Really? All of these?"

"If you wish to continue being the best dressed monarch in the Five Kingdoms," Marganie admonished, waving him to the centre of the room, and the small pedestal upon which she expected him to stand. With a groan, he complied.

Davi duly stripped him and redressed him in a lavish outfit of white leather, with golden embellishments.

"This looks like a wedding outfit," said Marten

suspiciously. Marganie's pin-filled mouth smiled, though she didn't lose focus on her work, adjusting the length of the tunic's hem.

"I think people are getting hopeful," Davi observed, though Marten caught the sympathy in his tone. He glanced at Marganie, but she didn't seem to have noticed.

"Well, it might be a while yet."

Plucking the final pin from her mouth, Marganie chuckled. "Then I'll have plenty of time to make alterations, praise Chel. I swear you're still growing."

"I'm nearly twenty, shouldn't I have stopped by now?"

"You're ready to start filling out, sire," said Davi. "From here on, it's all about *not* growing any more, especially around the waistline!"

"Says you, old man!"

Davi patted his midriff. "Goes to prove I'm no longer a skinny youth. Not that I'm implying anything," he added with a wink.

"Men!" Marganie muttered under her breath. "Now the next, if you please." She pointed to the heap of clothing still to be fitted.

Dutifully, Davi removed the white ensemble, and replaced it with an outfit more to Marten's taste: utilitarian, unfussy, and plain brown.

"What's this one for?" he asked.

"Hunting, sire," Davi offered. "So when you fall off that brute of a horse, the mud won't show, and no one will be any the wiser about your close acquaintance with the ground."

Marten couldn't help but snicker. Once again, he sent a prayer to Chel, thanking her for placing Davi in his path that fateful day of the coup. Soldier and valet, he might be, but he always knew how to raise Marten's spirits, even when he was being impudent.

Marten posed patiently while Marganie pinned, cut, and adjusted numerous outfits, leaving his mind free to ponder the rest of the day. He had business to attend to, spies to debrief, council members to influence. He'd given Lorndar's application much consideration throughout the long night when sleep had eluded him. His body had been exhausted, but his thoughts were relentless, and although he could foresee all manner of objections from his parochial council members, he was determined to gain as much support for the proposal as he could muster.

The final decision, of course, was his alone. But going against a majority of his closest advisors would cause more strife than he had stamina to cope with, in amongst everything else going on in the kingdom at this time. Convincing even a few of them to his way of thinking might begin a wave of change, Chel willing.

Finally, Marganie packed away her tools and gathered those clothes destined for alterations. Davi began hanging up the finished items.

"Ouch!"

Davi swore, and shook a drop of blood from his finger. He stuck the injured digit into his mouth and sucked on it. Marganie looked mortified.

"I'm so sorry, I must have left a pin in."

Davi shook out the folds of the offending velvet cloak.

"Not a pin; a needle. Here." He extracted the slender, sharp object and proffered it to the seamstress. She took it with care, threading it into a scrap of fabric which she placed into her workbox.

"I'm so sorry," she said again, almost distraught.

"It's only a nick," Davi reassured her, before escorting her to the door. When she was gone, Marten raised an eyebrow and waved a hand towards the pile of clothing.

"Should we hunt the rest of these for such deadly weapons?"

Davi laughed. "I'm pretty sure I'll survive, sire. Now, you have a meeting scheduled with Brother Freskin next, do you not?"

Marten rolled his eyes. "Ah yes; the highlight of my day."

31. HOUSE OF CHEL

"I'm sorry, my lady." The skinny, grey-robed sister of Chel peered from beneath her puckered brow. "Your son's fever—it isn't coming down. We've tried everything."

Rustam watched the blood drain from Risada's already pale face. She leaned more heavily against the rough wooden refectory table, her customary proud posture sagging as if the weight of the sturdy building above pressed her towards the stone flagged floor.

"There must be something else you can try?" The tremor in her voice broke Rustam's resolve. He dared put an arm around her shoulders.

At first, she stiffened, and for a fleeting moment Rustam tensed, recalling how dangerous touching her could be. But then she relaxed and allowed herself to lean against him.

It felt—good.

"Is there *anything* else?" he asked. "Anyone with—" he paused, considering how to couch the question. "—a healing gift?"

The sister narrowed her eyes at him. "You mean magic?"

Rustam nodded.

"We are in Tyr-en, my lord. Magic is forbidden." Her lips thinned. "Are you testing us?"

"Do you think I would risk my child's life for a *test*?" Risada's tone held an edge as sharp as any of her assassin's knives.

"No, no, my lady. I'm sorry, of course not. For now, all we can do is keep him cool, and pray for his recovery."

Risada's shoulders drooped. "I believed coming here would be the answer, but we should have continued.

Someone in Darshan would know what to do."

Rustam stroked her bedraggled tresses, inhaling the freshness of rain-washed hair. "If these sisters don't have an answer, I doubt anyone this side of the mountains will. It would have taken us a couple of days to reach Darshan. At least here, he's out of the weather, which must give him the best chance. Don't you agree, sister?"

The woman's head bobbed up and down in accord. "Assuredly so, my lord, my lady. A sick babe, as small as he is, would have very little chance exposed to the elements. Here, Chel's will may stand sway, but out there…"

Without finishing that uncomfortable thread, the sister retreated through the nearest curtain-draped doorway, leaving Rustam and Risada alone in the low-ceilinged, snug refectory.

Not long after their arrival, two of the sisters had spirited Chayla away with exclamations about her dishevelled condition. While she had yet to reappear, the absence of her crazy behaviour was a relief to Rustam, as he knew it must be to Risada.

He reached for a goblet standing on the long trestle table, and handed it to Risada. The spiced wine scented the air, almost masking the meaty smell of mutton left over from the lunch their arrival had interrupted.

"Rusty, I don't know what I'll do, if…" Risada's voice wobbled, and Rustam hugged her tighter.

"Trust in Chel. I can't believe she'd let anything happen to your son, or to you. Not after everything we've been through."

Risada patted his hand before pushing away from him. "Thank you, Rusty. I truly hope that's so." She put the untouched goblet down. "I need to be with him. Come on."

Following the direction the sister had taken, they entered a long hall, with a huge fireplace central to one wall. With the weather still too warm to need a fire, the grate held fresh flowers, red and yellow and orange. The stone walls sported thick, colourful tapestries depicting scenes of Chel's blessings: weddings, births, and cheery images of rosy-cheeked children playing in the fields.

"Which way?"

Rustam pointed. "There. I can *feel* him."

Risada stopped so abruptly, he cannoned into her. "What do you mean? What can you feel? *Goddess!* Rusty, we're in Tyr-en now; you have to stop using magic!"

"It's not exactly something I can turn off."

He regretted his words as soon as they'd left his mouth. Risada had enough to deal with, without him adding to her problems. Perhaps he should simply have agreed with her.

She spun round to face him.

"This is why you can't come back to Darshan, don't you see? You absolutely *cannot* rely on Sala to retract her sentence, and the way magic drips from you at every turn, there's a good chance we won't get that far before someone takes it upon themselves to deal with you on her behalf. *Please* be sensible. Go back to Kishtan before anyone realises you're here."

"I'm sorry, Risada, but I can't do that. Believe me, I know how capable you are at taking care of yourself, but it isn't only you, this time. Halson might be your son, but he's also my half-brother, in case that point has escaped your notice. I'm going to see both of you all the way to Darshan, and that's an end to it."

And I'm not leaving your side, he vowed. *I should never have left you before. I was too wrapped up in being a martyr, convincing myself I was doing the best thing for you. I lost my chance with you, but I won't abandon you again.*

Risada all but stamped her foot, and Rustam couldn't help but grin at the image of the fearsome assassin, Dart, acting like a child.

"If they had horses here so I could send for an escort, I'd have them force you back over that border, whether you liked it or not!"

"Then it's as well for me they don't."

Risada shivered. Rustam longed to take her in his arms

again, but she shook her head. "Don't. Just, don't. Why do you have to be so noble? If something happens to you—"

"My lady!" The angular sister from before stood framed in the doorway at the base of a stair. Her hands twisted together, bony knuckles stark white.

"Oh, goddess!" Risada whispered, before shoving past the woman and bolting up the stairs. Rustam followed, bounding up two steps at a time. He caught the wisp end of Risada's blue tunic vanishing into a side room, and skidded to a stop before he overshot.

Risada bent over a cot, beside which hovered another, older, Sister of Chel. When Rustam crept close enough to see, he gritted his teeth. Halson's body shook with the strength of his seizure, his tiny limbs sticking out stiffly, like a petrified starfish.

But he wasn't dead. At least, not yet. Rustam's heart ached for both mother and son.

Risada uttered such a wail, Rustam's hands twitched towards his ears. Certainly, the entire House of Chel must have heard.

The sister who'd summoned them made to slip past him, but Rustam snagged her arm.

"Is there *nothing* you can do?"

The woman's face crumpled as she stared at the distraught mother.

"I assure you, we've tried everything. All we can do, is pray."

"Let me in." The soft request came from behind Rustam, and when he didn't move, Chayla pushed him hard enough, he staggered aside.

"It's time now, isn't it?" the crazy woman said, tilting her head at an empty chair.

"Chayla!" Rustam caught a handful of Chayla's grey dress. The sisters had loaned her one of their garments, he noticed, to replace her rags. "Chayla, not now!"

Chayla's head snapped around, and Rustam recoiled. There, shining in the depths of Chayla's green eyes, sparked a shard of silver.

"What—?"

"Let me go to him," Chayla said. The presence of the deity vibrated through Rustam's whole body, and his hands fell away, palms tingling.

Was this what the werecats had seen?

Chayla walked calmly over to the crib, and reached for the baby.

"Leave him alone!" Risada batted Chayla's hands away, her usual slick coordination absent. Chayla gently grasped Risada's wrists, and pushed them back against her chest.

"Peace."

With tears of defeat streaking her cheeks, Risada stumbled back a couple of steps. The attending sister's eyebrows drew together, before shooting up and vanishing into her hairline when Chayla met her gaze.

"Lady," she breathed, and backed away.

Chayla scooped Halson up, and laid one fingertip to his brow. A ribbon of quicksilver flowed down her hand, bathing the child in an ardent glow. Rustam's fists clenched, and he heard Risada gasp as she finally recognised the significance of what was unfolding before her.

Halson's ugly red colouring faded to a lustrous shade of pearl. Chayla bent, and kissed the top of his head. The small body relaxed, and a heartening cooing bubbled from his lips. Chayla wiped away the remains of creamy foam from the corner of his mouth, and stroked his cheek. He made a grab for her finger, tiny fists waving with intent.

Chayla smiled, radiating warmth and comfort to fill the room. The two sisters fell to their knees. Risada choked back her fearful tears, crying anew with relief. She held out her arms, but did not demand. Chayla kissed Halson once more, and then placed him into his mother's care.

"Thank you, thank you," Risada mumbled into her baby's blankets as she pressed his happy, wriggling body close to her face.

"I only ever meant to help him," said Chayla. Rustam saw

her eyes had returned to their customary shade of emerald.

"It's a miracle!" the older sister announced. "Why have you hidden your rank from us, lady? You are one of the Blessed! Surely, you are a priestess?"

Chayla's attention returned to the empty chair. "I should?" She shrugged. "If you say so."

Rustam found his gratitude for Halson's improvement compromised by Chayla's continued irrational behaviour. His frustration leaked out.

"What makes *this*—" he waved a hand at the child, "—a miracle, and not magic?"

The older, plumper, sister, glared at him in outrage. "Apart from the blessed outcome, for which we have been praying since your arrival, this woman, your companion, is hiding her status as a priestess. Either that, or her calling has been appallingly missed. You saw the presence of the deity in her, did you not?"

"I did," Rustam agreed. "And yet she is definitely not a priestess."

Chayla stepped between them. "But I should have been," she said. "Have you never wondered, Rusty, why I was named for the goddess? My mother was a priestess, and I was destined for the Temple until she died in childbed. I had to remain at home to raise my younger sister. Then Ranjit came along with a marriage proposal my father could not ignore, and my mother's intentions for me were laid aside."

"There. You see?" The older sister bowed to Chayla. "My sister in Chel, no matter where your life has taken you until now, you must go from here to the Temple, and become what you were intended to be." She regarded Rustam with fierce eyes. "This *was* a miracle. Magic is an evil done by those outside of the Temple."

Nettled, Rustam was unwilling to back down.

"And if Chayla hadn't had this background? If she wasn't to join the Temple? What then? Would you call this *miracle* an act of evil?"

"How could saving my child possibly be evil?" Risada

demanded.

"My lady, I cannot answer that, as it isn't what's happened. Chel has blessed you with this miracle. I urge you to be thankful without question."

Rustam bit back his temper in deference to where they were, and to the welcome outcome, magic or miracle.

But the event triggered an unsettling chain of conjecture regarding the future of Tyr-en.

Risada had related the story of the alarming destructive power manifested by Sister Valaree, back before Halnashead had been killed. Prior to that, Rustam had never heard a report of any cleric displaying such abilities.

At least, not since the Crossing. Back on the old continent, such things went hand-in-glove with the terrors of the Wizard Wars.

So, when had such talents re-emerged within the Temple community? Or had they always been present, but purposely hidden? On the surface, the Temple on this continent was devoted to Chel alone. But beneath? No one denied that the deity wore two faces. What if a portion of the clergy had chosen to serve the malevolent aspect, Charin?

Rustam's heartrate sped up. If he recalled his history lessons correctly, it had been the servants of Charin, along with some of the wizards, who'd abused their powers at the expense of innocents, sparking the devastating war that ripped their old society apart and unleashed hideous, evil creatures from the pits of hell.

Rustam shuddered, contemplating the awful possibility that such corruptions hadn't all been left behind, as they'd always assumed, when their ancestors crossed the deadly ocean. They may, unwittingly, have brought the seeds of atrocity with them.

Did Marten know? Or was the king kept deliberately ignorant by those members of the clergy who knew the truth?

Rustam gritted his teeth. He wouldn't burden Risada with his wild speculations, but it was urgent he speak with Marten. Until Halson was safe, and Risada could spare attention for the job Halnashead had bequeathed her, the king was without a spy master. Rustam considered, as Hal's eldest son, it was his duty to assume the mantle on a temporary basis.

Provided Annasala could be dissuaded from executing him before he could gain an audience with the king.

"How soon can we get back on the road?" he asked.

Risada frowned at him. "I nearly lost my baby today, and you want to rush on? We'll wait a while to ensure this recovery isn't short lived."

"She's still not convinced, is she?" Chayla asked the empty chair.

In the light of events, Rustam speculated if it was Chel Herself that Chayla was seeing, although he didn't feel the goddess's presence as he had on other occasions when She'd chosen to intervene in his life.

Reluctant to explain his sudden hurry, Rustam quashed his impatience. "Of course. I'm sure that's wise. We don't have far to go now, anyway."

Risada narrowed her eyes at him, proving she hadn't lost her edge, even so soon after the emotional battering she'd endured. "I think we need to talk, don't we?"

With her son cradled loosely in her arms as if scared he'd break, or fit again, she padded towards Rustam. With a glance over her shoulder at the other occupants of the room, she announced, "You have my gratitude, sisters, but we need some privacy, please."

The two daughters of Chel raised eyebrows at each other, but quit the room without complaint, taking Chayla with them. When they were alone, Risada jerked her head towards the far wall, and Rustam followed her, as far away from the doorway as they could get.

"Spill," Risada ordered in a quiet, but firm, voice.

Rustam sighed. Why had he thought he could keep something so important from Risada? He laid out his apprehensions succinctly.

Risada bit her lip. "I concur. Valaree's abilities worry me a great deal, and if she isn't the only one…"

"The magic ban's driven this underground, and that it's sanctioned by at least part of the Temple—we're in deep trouble," Rustam concluded.

"We should leave as soon as possible," Risada echoed Rustam's earlier suggestion. She placed a cool hand on his, and stared him in the eye. "I implore you, Rusty, please go back to Kishtan—it isn't too late. I can take this to Marten. Hal gave me this job and I won't shirk my duty, no matter what."

Basking in the welcome feel of her skin against his, a warm glow suffused Rustam. Taking care not to trap the assassin's hand, he laid his other hand on top of hers. "Believe me, I appreciate what you're trying to do for me, but I left you once before, and I won't do it again."

To his utmost astonishment, tears welled in her eyes. She shook her head, sending sparkling drops flying. "You fool! You had no choice—it was me who abandoned you! I was too cowardly to break from convention and follow you into exile, and your father—Chel bless him—was as near as I could come to you, and still keep my old life."

Rustam became aware of his jaws gaping. He shut them with an audible click.

Risada pulled her hand free from his and scrubbed her cheek. "I made my choices. I can't unmake them, but if you'll let me, I can keep you safe. No one need know you're in the kingdom. You can make it back across the border and live out your life in safety."

"Without you." His words emerged strangely flat. "I don't want that. I want to be with you. If that's only for a couple more days, until we reach Darshan, I'd count that more worthwhile than decades apart. I'm coming with you."

Risada's shining eyes widened, but she accepted his declaration without further argument, gifting him with a flash of a smile and an unexpected kiss on the cheek.

She turned toward the door before he could react, and Rustam just made out her quiet words.

"I don't deserve you. I never did."

32. CHAOS

Marten stared in consternation at the chaos within the Temple compound. The customary calm and order that had prevailed on every visit of his entire life until this moment, had been supplanted by alarming disarray. Overturned wheelbarrows and hay lay strewn around the courtyard, buckets and tools abandoned in random places. No one came to collect the royal party's horses, no water offered, nor, indeed, any form of welcome.

"Ho! What's happened here?" Davi tried to catch the attention of a priest who scuttled across the open space with his white robes hoisted above his knees for safety at the unorthodox speed of his gait. Inexplicably, the man ignored them and continued on around the corner of the main building.

Davi gestured their escort to close ranks around the king. "We should leave, sire. For safety. We can find out what's amiss later."

"Your Majesty!" A female voice called from the Temple building.

Marten peered through a floating cloud of dust. "Sister Valaree! What's going on?"

Valaree strode across the scuffed dirt, her white robe streaked with grime, and what appeared to be blood. Stands of her raven hair clung to her face in inky stripes, and short spikes stuck out at random angles all over her head, like displaced feathers on a dead bird.

Marten's guards moved to intercept her, but he waved them back.

"What's happened here?" he asked.

"Rebellion, sire. A faction has split away from the main Temple."

Marten's eyebrows shot up. "With bloodshed?"

Valaree glanced down, a grimace quickly hidden. "Sire, Brother Freskin can explain better than I."

"And where *is* the good brother?" Davi asked.

Valaree waved a hand towards the cavernous royal portico, the once welcoming dimness now a threatening gloom, hiding who knew what.

"Regrettably, Brother Freskin was injured, else he'd greet you himself. It's quite safe inside now, I guarantee it. The perpetrators are all gone."

"How can you be sure?" Davi questioned. "Looks like you were caught you by surprise. What makes you think you know who they all are?"

"Davi," Marten said quietly. "I need to hear details. Standing out here isn't going to achieve that."

He dismounted, forcing his guards to follow suit. Davi scowled, but quit his saddle and, with a few brief instructions, split the four guards so that two remained to handle the horses, holding them ready for a hasty retreat, while the other two fell in behind Marten.

"Sire, I don't recommend this."

"Nevertheless, I want to speak with Brother Freskin. That was the original purpose of this visit, was it not?"

Biting off a retort, Davi bowed his head obediently, and waved Valaree into the lead. He followed close behind her, with Marten sandwiched between him and the two rear guards.

They passed into the royal foyer and discovered, as Valaree had promised, the interior of the Temple to be serene, although displaced tables, scattered candles, and torn hangings, attested to the struggle that had taken place before their arrival. Acolytes bent to their tasks, cleaning up, and Marten was comforted to see a group of twelve clerics kneeling before Chel's altar in prayer.

Even Davi relaxed at that sight.

He thinks I'm being stubborn without good cause, but this sounds horribly like the very schism Padrus feared, and I must know what happened as soon as I can. This may be a critical point for the whole of Tyr-en, not just for the Temple.

Valaree led with measured steps across the public worship areas, and past a pair of grim-faced Temple guards, into the labyrinth of corridors housing the priests' cells. As before, Marten attempted to memorise the turns, but again failed to identify any landmarks to help, and gave up.

Stopping outside an unremarkable brown door, in an unremarkable passageway, Valaree rapped her knuckles on the plain wood above a latch, before opening it and standing back to permit Davi to enter ahead of the king.

Brother Freskin sat on a bed, one leg restrained by splints and bandages.

Marten eyebrows shot up. "What *happened?*"

"Your Majesty!" Freskin inclined his head with as much respect as his seated position allowed. "Please, forgive my indisposition."

Marten waved the priest's apology aside. "Unnecessary, brother. I wouldn't disturb you, but I need to understand. Sister Valaree says you've suffered a rebellion? What, precisely, does that mean, and what do you think might be the wider implications for the kingdom?"

"Indeed, sire. The Temple has suffered a divisive split in opinion, such as hasn't occurred since its inception on this continent. If I may speak freely?" His eyes flicked towards Davi.

"Yes, yes," Marten confirmed. "Davi has my complete trust."

Freskin shifted uncomfortably, and Marten reflected how he'd never expected to see the self-assured priest so disturbed.

"I believe Brother Padrus brought to your attention a spate of minor miracles?"

"He did." Marten's stomach churned. This conversation was running headlong in the direction he'd feared it would.

"What, perhaps, you don't realise, is that in recent times the Temple has taken in increasing numbers of acolytes blessed with the ability to channel the deity's gifts."

Worse and worse.

"What sort of numbers?"

"Two or three per season, where in the past, the appearance of one every few years would be cause for celebration."

Marten licked his lips, recalling a discussion he'd had with his uncle about the persistence of magical abilities in the population, despite all attempts to wipe it out. "And how are you certain these acolytes are genuinely goddess-touched, and not magic users entering the Temple to hide their powers?"

Freskin's scandalised expression bordered on comical. "Your Majesty! No one can hide the truth of their nature from the goddess! She would surely strike down any false supplicant."

Marten could not help but ask. "And has She?"

"No, Your Majesty. But here is the point where this situation becomes less than clear: we are discussing powers of the deity, not of the goddess alone."

Marten's legs suddenly grew weak. "Charin?"

Freskin nodded, his face grim. "And this is the situation that erupted today. Several young priests and acolytes banded together and attempted to seize control of the relics. Fortunately, they did not succeed."

Marten knew he appeared perplexed, when Freskin hurried on.

"The Temple guards a small number of artefacts from the old continent, carried across the ocean by our founding clerics. In unwise custody, they could be extremely dangerous."

The world receded, became indistinct, and Freskin's voice a blur. A raging pulse hammered inside Marten's head, and he bit his lip to regain control.

"You," he said, cutting off whatever further words Freskin

had intended, "have kept a secret of this magnitude from your rulers, this entire time? For *centuries*?" Anger boiled away whatever reverence he'd held for the priesthood. "This could be interpreted as treason!"

He spun on his heel, taking a step towards the door, but Valaree blocked his path.

"Move," Davi growled.

Valaree lowered her eyes, but remained immobile. "Sire," she said, "I'm sorry, but you need to hear the rest."

Marten swung back to the incapacitated priest on the bed. "Tell your aide to get out of my way."

"Your Majesty, with all due respect, Sister Valaree is correct; you need to know the full details of what happened here, so you may deal with the situation effectively."

Marten glimpsed Davi's sword half out of its scabbard.

What are we doing? This is Chel's Temple.

With gritted teeth, he reined in his temper.

"Fine," he ground out. "Tell me."

Davi's sword slipped home, and the anxiety level in the room dropped a notch. Freskin shifted his weight on the bed and gasped, clutching at his leg.

Marten struggled to hold onto his righteous anger in the face of the priest's suffering, but stayed his tongue while Freskin composed himself. When the colour had returned to his face, the priest continued.

"Once again, Your Majesty, my apologies. If you would care to sit, I will elaborate."

Davi picked up the single chair in the priest's cell, and placed it at the foot of the bed, taking up position between Marten and the door, where Valaree lingered.

No comforts here, Marten mused as he settled his behind on the hard wood, without benefit of a cushion.

"You are king," Freskin began, and Marten readied himself for a lecture. "But as you have been taught since childhood, your family was chosen to rule by Chel's divine blessing, and by her priesthood. The casket in your possession, which only a member of your family can open, is the seal by which you remain in power over the Families. The Temple, however, answers to Chel, and only to secular law where it does not contradict the deity's canon. As such, our guardianship of the higher mysteries, which include the relics, is not knowledge we are obliged to share with you."

While Marten's temper smouldered, Freskin paused to take a sip of water from a plain wooden cup.

"Your Majesty, what happened here today—the violence, the greed, the very disregard for others—I fear we are seeing the rebirth of Charin's Cult."

Marten jaw tightened. "That was Padrus's fear, and I believe it's what got him killed."

Freskin closed his eyes for a second, pain etched on his face. Was that for Padrus? Or his injury?

"Sire, the Temple Council discussed your recent experience with Chel's Casket, and judged it to be a sign the goddess has chosen you. For what, we were not certain, but I now believe it must be to deal with this very situation."

Marten didn't feel special, or chosen, or ready to deal with a cult that espoused violence and intimidation as a means of rule, backed by the powers of a god.

"How?"

Freskin caught and held his gaze with a desperate intensity. "You must open the casket, and use the talisman it contains. Only *that* will be strong enough to overcome such evil."

Marten felt sick. He recalled the *thing* inside the box, how it had glared at him, and the corruptness that emanated from it.

"I have always been told its power is uncontrollable," he protested. "That's why it was sealed in the box, and why it shouldn't ever be released."

"Indeed," Freskin agreed. "That has been the truth—until now. But Chel has placed Her blessing upon you. With Her patronage, *you* will be able to control it, and use it to eradicate those who threaten your kingdom."

"I mislike the sound of that—surely these people are still

servants of the Temple? Albeit in service to the god, not the goddess, but in the end, they are both aspects of the same deity."

To his shock, Freskin smiled; a sad quirk bending his lips. "My king, you see truly, but by their actions these renegades are serving no one but themselves, and Charin is liable to watch from the shadows and do nothing more than be amused by the havoc they will wreak."

Unwilling to contemplate Freskin's horrific suggestion, Marten balked. "Surely they can't be *that* dangerous? What sort of powers do they wield?"

"Perhaps, a demonstration?"

"What do you mean?"

Freskin beckoned Valaree to his side.

"Your Majesty, may I present one of the Blessed. Sister Valaree is a conduit for the goddess."

Marten stiffened. He'd known Valaree for years now, and she'd never shown any sign of being more than a devoted priestess. For Chel's sake, he'd fancied the woman! How could she be one of Chel's Blessed—those special individuals, like Padrus, who were revered and spoken of in hushed tones? He'd never heard anyone speak of Valaree that way.

He looked the woman up and down as she stood at Freskin's bedside, dressed in her soiled white robe, and detected a deepening of her complexion from its natural russet tone towards a burgundy blush. Ebony locks curled around her face, escaped from her disarrayed bun, and dirt smudged her chin.

Surely not.

"Sister Valaree," said Freskin. "The king must understand what danger he faces. Please, show him."

Davi stepped in front of Marten. "Is this wise? How dangerous *is* she?"

Freskin waved a hand dismissively. "Sister Valaree is no threat to you, guardsman, or to the king. I believe a display would be the simplest way forward."

Tight lipped, Marten gestured his assent. Davi remained standing in front of him.

Freskin pointed at a wooden bowl on the small table positioned between the bed and the door.

Valaree raised a hand. A silver glow crackled between her fingers.

"I can't *see*," Marten complained.

"Then you can't get injured," Davi replied.

Valaree stretched her fingers wide. A silver-white firebolt shot from her palm. With a thunderous *crack*, the bowl exploded into a hundred fragments.

Marten jumped so hard, his feet left the floor. The sharp tang of a lightning strike coated the back of his throat.

"Ouch!" Davi rubbed his hands together, smearing a droplet of blood where a sliver of wood had nicked his skin. "I thought you said we were safe?"

"My apology, guardsman," said Freskin. "I didn't expect you to stand so close."

Cold sweat trickled between Marten's shoulder blades. He narrowed his eyes at Valaree, before glaring at Freskin. "That looked like magic to me."

"Sire! Valaree is a priestess! If a commoner displayed such an ability, it would be magic, but what you have witnessed is sanctioned by the goddess herself!"

"Are you saying, brother, that the only difference between magic and miracle, is who performs it?"

"Not at all, sire. The Blessed channel the deity's powers, while magic springs from the vile practitioner's soul."

Not at all satisfied by Freskin's explanation, Marten refrained from dispute. While his Temple education urged him to accept the priest's words, his heart wished it to be otherwise.

"Your Majesty, I would not expect any man, even a king, to comprehend the full complexity of Chel's divine tapestry, I can only advise you to heed my words: today's radicals are not magic users, but they *are* backed by the god, which is far more fearsome. We need Chel's aid to deal with them, and

She has endorsed your use of the talisman contained within the casket. Please, for all our sakes, embrace Her permission and act swiftly."

Marten inclined his head. "You have given me a great deal to consider, brother. I will leave you to your rest now, and I assure you, I will reach a decision without delay."

"May Chel guide you, my liege. This may be the most important choice of your reign."

* * * * * * *

Marten nudged Goldcrest forward to ride alongside Davi. He squinted in the dust raised by the hooves of the two guardsmen preceding them. The horses in the rear escort snorted repeatedly. While the south of the kingdom had seen plentiful rainfall of late, the gentle showers over the city had failed to clear the air with any efficiency, and the stale smell of a spent summer lingered.

Marten sneezed, and wiped watering eyes. The oppressive atmosphere sent his mind scurrying back inside the fresh coolness of the Temple building, but the potentially catastrophic situation there left him feeling divorced from reality. In an attempt to rebalance himself, he turned to triviality.

"Brother Freskin's never going to let me forget I'm only ruler because the Temple lets me be, is he? Mind you, he was pretty stoic about his broken leg, and he seemed genuinely concerned about me as well as the kingdom. For some strange reason, I find myself warming to the dry old stick."

Realising he was chattering to himself, he spoke directly to his distracted bodyguard.

"What do you think, Davi?"

"About which part, my king? That we have a dangerous bunch of renegade priests with god-given powers loose somewhere in the city, or that the Temple thinks you should open a box that for centuries we've been told should never be opened?"

The snicker that Davi's facetious answer brought to Marten's lips was short lived. "That's about the size of it, isn't it? Which do I worry about first?"

Davi shrugged, his head swivelling as he scanned the unusually populated streets. "I would think that depends on which confronts you first. At this moment, I'm rather more concerned about the size of these crowds."

Blinking grit from his eyes, Marten took stock. The last time he'd seen a throng like this had been when he walked behind Uncle Hal's cortège, through the narrow streets of the lower city. Halnashead had been a popular man, and many had turned out to show respect.

But why were these people on the streets now? The only thing different about today was the Temple uprising, and that had, apparently, been contained to the Temple grounds.

Goldcrest arched his neck and stepped higher. People stopped and stared, and Marten heard his name above the general hubbub, but another sprang more loudly from a number of lips.

"Lorndar. Lorndar."

More took up the chant, until the master smith's name drowned out all else. At Davi's order, Marten's escort crowded closer, their hands hovering in readiness beside sword hilts.

"Peace!" Marten reined Goldcrest to a halt, dropped his reins, and stood up in his stirrups, brandishing his arms above his head. The surprise tactic sent a shock of quiet surging through the crowd. For a brief moment, all became still.

A single figure took a step forward. Davi tensed, but Marten caught his arm before he could draw his weapon.

"Your Majesty," the lone individual—a baker, by his flour-spattered smock—bowed low, and Davi's arm relaxed beneath Marten's grip. Marten let go, and indicated the man should continue.

"Beg pardon, Your Majesty, we's not meanin' no disrespect, sire, but we's heard tell of Master Lorndar's proposal, and we's wonderin' what your answer might be?"

Marten cocked his head. That explained Lorndar's absence from yesterday's tourney: he and his followers must have been canvassing support in the city.

He cast an eye over the crowd, noting expressions ranging from hopeful, to defensive. Some turned away from his gaze; others met it with a boldness that surprised him. It seemed Lorndar's revolutionary idea had been embraced with verve by many of the common folk.

And why not? Even I think it's a good idea. All I have to do is convince a bunch of hidebound lords it's time for a radical change to their comfortable way of life.

His trained voice carried easily over the hushed throng. "As I informed Master Lorndar, I will be discussing his suggestions with my council at our next meeting, which is only a few days hence. He will have his answer then."

A wave of muttering rippled across the crowd. The bold spokesman jerked his chin up.

"We knows how most of the lords feel, Your Majesty. Does Master Lorndar have your support, is what we's wonderin'?"

Marten raised his eyebrows, and the impudent fellow deflated.

"This is a subject for the council, not for the streets. Be content to wait for an answer."

The front escort rider urged his horse forward. "Make way for the king!"

Heads dutifully bowed, the throng parted to permit the riders to pass, and when Marten glanced back, he saw the crowd had broken into small knots of animated discussion.

"Master Lorndar has a lot of support," Davi observed, and Marten glanced at him, surprised by the edge in his bodyguard's tone.

"You think there could be unrest?"

"If things don't go the way they hope? Possibly, yes. Attitudes amongst the common folk have never fully settled back to the way they were before the coup." Davi scowled. "The Bastard might have been a magic-wielding dwarf that no one wanted as king, but he showed there *could* be change. Once that idea escaped, there's no putting it back in the box."

"Unlike some," said Marten, "I won't try to suppress it, or ignore it, or any other thing most of the older lords would like to do with it. Uncle Hal recognised the need for change; I just think he was heading down the wrong path by trying to integrate magic into society. If we implement Lorndar's suggestion, the people will have goals to strive for, for personal gain, and what better motivation could there be? We don't need magic; we need innovation and trade."

"You're going to say yes to Lorndar, then? Whatever blockages the council tries to put in your way?"

"I believe I am," Marten affirmed. "I won't do it without consulting them first, but as you say, change has overtaken us, and we can't rein it back in. Much better to embrace it and direct it where *we* want it to go, rather than risk another coup."

"It's a bold move, sire, but a good one, if you don't mind me saying so."

As they rounded the corner of a white-painted building, Davi glanced back at the lingering crowd. "It's a pity they don't know yet."

33. BENEFACTOR

"Betha, my dear, you have something to report?" Urien's satisfied smile reminded Betha of a house cat about to eat a mouse. At least Edlund was not present to undress her with his eyes.

She glanced around Urien's sitting room, searching for any sign of his medicine bottle.

"My Lord Urien, I felt, perhaps you should know—"

"Yes, yes." Impatience made Urien's fingers restless. "Spit it out, girl."

Betha plunged on. "The king believes you allowed him to win. At the tournament. He's suspicious."

"Of you?" Urien asked, eyes narrowed. Betha shook her head hurriedly.

"No, my lord, not of me. Of you."

Urien's shoulders relaxed. "Ah. I have no issue with earning his mistrust; I would consider him a fool if not. Now tell me, my dear, how goes your mission? I trust your assignations have been fruitful?"

Heat filled Betha's cheeks. "My lord, it is far too soon to say."

"I meant, you are continuing to sleep with him, yes?"

"Oh! Yes, my lord. As you instructed."

"Good." He beckoned to a servant. "Your presence here is fortuitous. I am about to leave for another meeting with my colleagues—a meeting I wish you to attend."

Oh goddess, not another one!

Betha smoothed the folds of her gown. "My lord, I would be honoured, but I have come woefully unprepared. I am neither dressed for such an occasion, nor do I have a travelling cloak with me."

"You may borrow one of mine. And as to the other, what you are wearing is quite acceptable."

Betha glanced down at herself. She was glad she'd donned the drab emerald gown she'd worn to the public audience, when she'd deliberately dressed down to convey her disapproval of Lorndar's behaviour. It wasn't quite as dowdy as the one she'd worn last time Urien took her to a 'meeting', but it would have to do. She shrugged into the dark grey cloak a servant held out for her. What would this meeting entail? They couldn't very well embarrass her more than last time, and Urien's plans kept her safe from other men. As he seemed to be in charge, she felt reasonably secure.

Still scanning the room for the glass medicine bottle, she was disappointed not to locate it. Perhaps, instead, she would finally answer the question she'd been unable to last time: the identity of the mysterious 'benefactor'. That would please Marten.

Betha's eyes stung, and she squeezed them shut for a moment. Marten had been so cold towards her this morning. Did he really blame her for misleading him regarding Urien's disability? His words suggested not, but his manner? She cleared her scratchy throat and scrubbed her eyes. It didn't matter how he felt towards her, she would never forgive herself for driving the wedge between them. She shouldn't have shown him her healing ability, though how could she have explained away the speed with which her blemishes would vanish?

And besides, omission was another form of deceit, and she'd committed herself to total honesty at his request—a thing she'd done gladly.

Oh Chel, why is life so complicated?

"Ready?"

Not trusting her voice, Betha nodded. Urien turned his back and marched from the room with Betha trailing obediently behind.

* * * * * *

Without the horrors of sharing the carriage with Lord Edlund, Betha found the trip much less stressful than the previous one. Late summer sun brought a golden glow to the air, and a certain warmth, necessitating open windows to prevent the passengers from being stifled. Staring out, Betha traced their route, matching up the sounds she'd stored in her memory from the last, dark trip, with physical reference points. From the bridge they crossed, she was able to identify the rushing river as the majestic Kresset, which ran clear from the Middle Mountains, passing to the east of Darshan, and finally out to sea, bisecting the kingdom neatly in two. Their destination, she realised, lay not far off the road that led, eventually, to the abandoned manor of Rees-Charlay, cursed birthplace of the abortive coup.

Betha nurtured the hope that, should the need arise, she might now be able to find her own way back to Darshan.

Urien held his peace the entire journey, for much of which he appeared to be sleeping. When the carriage swung onto the semi-circular drive fronting the squat meeting house, his eyes snapped open, and Betha recoiled from the strange glint in their depths, reminiscent of the flash she'd seen from across the tournament arena.

Urien climbed out of the carriage first, displaying none of the stiffness she'd expected from someone who had fought a dozen bouts the day before. Was this the result of his medication too?

When they entered the antechamber, Betha noticed an absence of feminine cloaks hanging on the pegs; only the dark, heavy mantles worn by noblemen. It was no surprise then, to find the bordello dim and quiet, with small groups of men standing around the edges, sipping ruby wine. The stale smell of sweat, mixed with the fruity aroma, turned Betha's stomach. Even so, she breathed faster, unable to quell her disquiet.

She'd prepared herself mentally for her meeting with Urien in the same manner as before, but where her surface personality portrayed a certain dullness, the real Betha beneath remarked details that fetched a cold sweat to her brow. Around her, the attendees conversed in quick, edgy voices, and their brisk gestures vibrated with energy. Up close, a powerful stink of masculine excitement mingled with the acrid scent of fear to override the lingering odour of wine and sex.

Approaching the hideous doors, a spike of anxiety stabbed Betha: a pair of armed guards stood one to either side. There would be no exit before whatever was to take place today was complete.

The guards swung the double doors open, and an unexpected wash of warmth and light spilled out. Urien led the way in.

Betha blinked, dazzled by the glare of a hundred candles grouped in banks around the perimeter, on stands staggered down the broad steps, and up high, set on tall, metal frames surrounding the stone altar. Light glinted off the metal rings set into each corner of the imposing block of stone, and Betha's heart lurched when she saw the bare top exposed, the blood red cloth that had covered it last time no longer in place. Great gouges in the freshly visible surface made it appear as though a monstrous beast had dragged huge claws across it, before belching fire to leave smoky residue embedded in the depths of the grooves. Other scorch marks added to the impression, elevating Betha's heart rate further.

Urien beckoned her to follow. He marched with self-assured strides down the broad stairs; so unlike his ungainly tumble the last time. Betha fancied she saw a small tremor in his knee one step before he reached ground level and indeed, he halted, plunged a hand into a deep pocket in his slate grey tunic, and extracted the very bottle Betha sought.

Urien took a small sip, stoppered the bottle again and re-stowed it in the depths of his clothing. Betha bit her lip: how was she ever going to get her hands on it?

The rustle of footsteps announced an influx of men into the hall. With a glance over her shoulder, Betha estimated fifty or sixty—enough to raise the temperature in the airless space significantly. She began to sweat, not all of it due to the heat.

Leaving her at the bottom of the stairs, Urien skirted the altar, and stepped up onto the dais. He faced his audience, allowing himself a long, slow inspection. The scowl on his features did not bode well.

Finally, his attention halted on a group of white-robed priests.

"Which of you was responsible for the riot in the Temple?" Urien's tone was tight with anger.

A riot in the Temple? It was the first Betha had heard of it. She managed not to react visibly, but her mind swam. That such a thing might occur! She felt the firm foundations of her world tilting.

The accused priests shifted uncomfortably beneath Urien's glare, sneaking glances at each other, but none admitted involvement. After a silence heavy with suspense, an older cleric dared speak.

"My lord, none of us here had any part in it. We were as surprised as you. That the renegades intended to steal one or more of the relics is clear, but what they intended to do with them afterwards, no one knows."

"Then find out!" Urien thundered. "We have our own plans for those artefacts; I will not have anyone pre-empting us."

"Yes, my lord," murmured the priests, en masse.

Urien stalked across the dais, and halted before the carved wooden throne. An eager voice from deep in the crowd called out the same question as the last time Betha had been present.

"Will the Master be joining us?"

Betha's fists tightened. The answer that time had been negative; would it be different today?

"He will," confirmed Urien in a pitch markedly deeper than normal. Or perhaps it was the acoustics of the low-ceilinged room.

At last! Now she would glean the information Marten

needed.

"About time," muttered a familiar, loathsome voice behind her, and Betha flinched as Edlund pushed rudely past. He lingered a moment too long, one hand on the small of her back. As it slid lower, she moved aside.

"Don't think you're beyond me," he whispered into her ear, his hot breath making her cringe. "You won't have his protection forever."

With a quick squeeze of her buttock, and a smug smile, Edlund continued on to join Urien on the dais.

Nor will you, Betha thought, fingering the small dagger in the hidden sheath sewn into her bodice. Taking advantage of being ignored for the moment, she worked her way back up through the crowd until she came to rest with her back to the wall, in the darkest spot she could find between candle stands. The rapt attention of all the men remained fixed on Urien, lending her the illusion that she was unobserved. As the only woman in the room, she doubted that was true, but it brought some small measure of comfort as the nervous anticipation in the room heightened.

Silence spread like a blanket drawn over the gathering. Expectant faces stared at Urien where he posed on the dais, before the ornate throne. His eyes gleamed, and a silver sheen spread over them like oil across water. Betha stifled a gasp. This time there was no mistaking the mark of the deity.

Urien's compact body began to grow, lengthening and widening, until he towered over Edlund, who stood, unintimidated, beside him. The lustrous sheen crept outward from Urien's eyes, sliding over his skin, coating his dark hair. His face vanished beneath a pearlescent glow, which continued to expand until it encased his entire body, leaving nothing visible of the man Betha knew.

A pristine face, beautiful beyond nature, emerged from the coruscating radiance. A physical body of divine proportions, emphasised by a figure-hugging white tunic, solidified, until a glowing creature, so exquisite it hurt the mind to look upon it for long, stood before the congregation.

He lowered Himself onto the throne, which creaked beneath His weight.

Betha's heart pounded against her ribcage, fighting for space in her chest with the air frozen in her lungs. She cowered back against the wall, leaning on it for the support her legs no longer provided.

Charin! The benefactor was the god Himself!

He surveyed His followers with a slow sweep of His argent eyes, and Betha hid behind the tall man in front of her.

"My faithful servants." Charin's words rolled around the chamber like distant thunder caught between mountain ridges. Betha whimpered and covered her ears, but the cadence of His words resonated in her bones.

"I come today to endorse your undertaking, and to mete out just punishment for a presumptuous act contrary to my objectives."

Raucous cheers beat against Betha's covered ears, but that was preferable to feeling the god's speech invade her body. She dropped her ineffectual hands.

Who was to be punished? Her gaze darted back and forth, seeking anyone in the crowd who looked guilty, but all she saw was a sea of fanatical supporters, their faces bright with fervour, tinged with an edge of fear as they beheld their god incarnate.

The terrible possibility that *she* might be the guilty party slammed into Betha like being run over by a herd of wild horses. Was this why Urien had brought her here today? Panic gripped her, and she tried to force strength into her limp legs, ready to run.

But even if the outer door had not been guarded, where could she run that might evade a god?

"Bring her in," ordered Charin in His terrible voice.

Betha slid down the wall, her legs failing her utterly.

But when nobody made a move towards her, it registered gradually in her fear-frozen mind that the silent throng was regarding the doorway with avid attention.

She pushed herself upright on trembling limbs.

THE PRINCE'S PROTÉGÉ

The loathsome doors swung open, and the two guards entered. Held firmly between them, a young woman stumbled dazedly, barely able to remain on her bare feet. The rags of a diaphanous cream gown did nothing to hide her buxom figure, or the slight swell of her belly. The remains of once-bright face paint streaked her cheeks, scored through by tear tracks beneath her large, doe-like brown eyes. Lank hair, probably blonde, hung in knotted clumps to her shoulders, where someone had hacked the rest away.

Betha's hand lifted, then fell back down. She ached to hold the stranger in her arms, to lie to her, to tell her that all would soon be well, but she could only watch in mute horror as the girl was dragged down the steps and hoisted onto the altar.

Golden manacles cuffed around the prisoner's wrists and ankles were secured to the rings at each corner until she lay, spread-eagled, on the gashed stone. She made a feeble attempt to raise her head and look at the shimmering figure on the throne, before subsiding into what Betha hoped was a drugged stupor.

Charin rose from His seat. "This *woman*," He said, and Betha's skin crawled beneath the contempt in that single word. "This common drab, has dared to permit the king's seed to quicken in her belly. I will not tolerate this abomination!"

The god raised his hands, and power crackled around them. Betha watched in horror as the girl's chest rose and fell in swift, shallow pants. Could it be the drug prevented her from reacting, while not dulling her understanding? To be trapped so inside your own body—a nightmare beyond imagining.

Firebolts shot from Charin's open palms, slamming into the girl's chest and belly. Her body jerked wildly, lit up with the brightness of a lightning strike. Incandescence played over her writhing form in jagged spikes, travelling along her limbs and sparking off the metal rings holding her in place. Smoke rose from her smouldering hair and clothes, and her

285

mouth gaped wide in an agonized silent scream.

Betha clapped her hands over her eyes, unable to watch. Around her, she could sense the tense thrill gripping the crowd. What could make men cruel enough to enjoy such a sickening spectacle?

The stench of cooking meat was Betha's undoing. She doubled over and heaved, spewing her last meal across her shoes. Slipping down to a crouch, she wrapped her arms around her knees and hugged them tight as the awful illumination died away, and silence spread across the chamber. Betha could not bring herself to rise again, to see the mangled husk her imagination pictured atop the altar.

Charin's last speech made her suspect the hapless victim had been the girl Marten had been seeing before her, and she wondered if the king knew he'd sired a child.

A child who had just been murdered, along with its mother, by the malicious half of the deity. What would Marten feel? Should she even tell him? What good would that do?

In that instant, Betha knew she intended to get out of this hellhole with her information intact. She forced herself to rise once more.

Sight of the blackened corpse, still with tendrils of smoke rising from it, made her retch again. She wiped sour-tasting bits from her tongue, desperately wishing for water to wash her mouth clean. The god's voice thrummed in her veins, but she was no longer listening to the words. She began working her way towards the door, staying low, hiding behind the men on the highest tier. Perhaps the guards had stayed inside the chamber while Charin indulged his pique. Perhaps she might, yet, sneak out unnoticed.

The rear view of a familiar figure forced her to halt.

Ordell! Her rejected suitor stood amongst the ranks of the god's devotees. If he spotted her, her life would be over. Of all the men here, he alone knew she was not the subservient, cowed lady she'd pretended to be. He'd experienced her wrath when she'd thrown him out of her rooms, and cut off their intended betrothal. Her counterfeit persona would never convince him. Either she'd been very fortunate he hadn't attended the last meeting Urien had brought her to, or he was a recent recruit. Either way, she mustn't let him see her.

Charin's hateful voice destroyed her slender hope.

"And now I wish to view the vessel chosen to bear the means of Our ascendency. Bring her forth."

Two guards appeared beside Betha. With a sinking feeling, she realised she'd never stood a chance; they must have been keeping track of her position the entire time.

Without touching her, they gestured for her to precede them down the steps, towards the ghastly altar. Defiance was all the armour she had left, so she squared her shoulders, drew herself erect, and descended with quiet dignity.

"But—"

Ordell's honeyed tones rang out as he recognised the cult's chosen child-bearer. She strode on, ignoring him. Perhaps Charin would ignore him too.

But Ordell was not content to remain unheeded.

"If this is the woman you've selected, you've made a grave mistake. I know of none less humble or submissive. If you believe that's what you have in her, you've been gravely misled."

Charin raked his eyes over Betha. Ice spread beneath her skin, and her legs ceased to work.

The god turned his terrible gaze on Ordell. "You dare dispute our servant's choice?"

Betha could hear the tremor in Ordell's answer, but he stuck to his opinion with more courage than she'd have given him credit for.

"Master, I must. This woman and I were to be married, but when I justifiably chastised one of her servants, she annulled the arrangement. She's a foul-mouthed bitch with airs far above her station. Whatever she's led you to believe, it's all lies."

Charin lowered Himself once more to His throne, placing one elbow on the carven armrest, and rubbing His chin with

His fingers in a disturbingly human fashion. He regarded Betha with interest.

"Your deceit is well played, woman—I admire your audacity. So, I assume the king knows of our plans?"

Still frozen in place, Betha could not answer, but that didn't seem to bother the god.

"No matter, his part in this charade is nearing its end. Already, you harbour the fruits of his seed."

Held immobile as she was, Betha felt all her muscles go rigid. What was Charin saying? That she was pregnant? It had been only two days since she'd lain with Marten; it wasn't possible for anyone to tell this soon.

But this isn't anyone. This is the god.

"What should we do with her?" Edlund asked. If anything, the sensation of his lecherous stare was worse than Charin's regard.

"Keep her here. This is a delicate time and I grow impatient; too many times my plans have been diverted from their course. Until this child is born, there is no certainty."

Edlund's face fell, and the tightness in Betha's chest eased a little. At least, for the moment, she had the god's protection.

The guards grabbed her arms, holding her upright when the feeling returned to her limbs in hot pin pricks. They supported her—not gently, but at least without excessive force—up the steps, with Edlund following behind. As she passed Ordell, he spat on her.

Such hate! Yes, she'd dashed his hopes for a comfortable and influential marriage, but she didn't deserve such an extreme reaction. She had the horrible feeling that her actions had brought him here, to Charin's embrace.

A clatter behind caught everybody's attention. The guards paused, allowing her to glance back. Charin/Urien was on one knee before the throne, and it didn't appear to be intentional. Urien's true figure was readily visible within the silver sheath of the god, which stuttered and shrank in random places. Charin's beautiful face twisted with rage before fading to an amorphous glow, which flickered a few times, and then blinked out.

Edlund swore, before dashing back down the steps to haul his unfortunate friend back to his feet.

"You didn't take enough, did you?" he chided.

Urien's hand dove into his pocket and withdrew the glass bottle, but even from half way up the steps, Betha could see it was empty. With a scowl, Urien threw it against the altar, where it smashed into myriad glittering shards.

"Today's business is concluded," he announced in a volume once more his own, and the gathered men bowed, no one questioning the god's abrupt departure.

Edlund and Urien ascended the steps, Edlund sticking close enough by Urien's side he could catch his friend should his knee fail again. Betha seized on the significance of what she'd witnessed.

Charin can't use Urien as a channel when he's in pain. That drug is the key!

Marten could use that against Charin: find a way to keep Urien from the drug, and he would be just a man, and a man with a crippling disability, not the fighting machine he'd become at the tournament, when he must have relied heavily on the potion.

But the knowledge was useless to Marten unless she could escape.

They entered the bordello. The guards guided her towards a small doorway at the rear of the building. Edlund sidled close.

"I'm going to enjoy breaking you, girl. I may not be able to touch your body—yet—but we have so much to look forward to."

A waft of fresh air swept into the room from the main entrance, along with a man dressed in courier's clothing. Edlund halted, one hand clutching Betha's upper arm, forcing her guards to halt. The courier glanced around until he spied Urien.

"My lord, I bring news from the south."

Urien's impatient glare hastened him on.

"The Lady Risada has been spotted, riding towards Darshan. She has the baby with her."

Urien's face broke into a huge grin.

"Perfect!" He swung around to face Betha. "We no longer need wait for Marten's get to grow; Halnashead's will do just as well. Perhaps Risada will turn out to be more pliable than you, and she has no husband to interfere."

Good luck with that, Betha thought, even as the potential implications struck her. Edlund caught on almost as quickly.

"Then we don't need her after all?"

Urien tilted his head, considering.

"We should keep her as a backup. Infants are so fragile; if something happens to Halnashead's child, we will still have the bloodlines we require."

Edlund visibly deflated. Urien walked over and patted him on the shoulder.

"Patience, Ed. Keep her body healthy and unsullied; you can have it later. The anticipation will only make the end sweeter."

"And her mind?"

Betha shuddered at Urien's smile.

"Break it. She made a fool out of me, and I need real obedience this time. Go, do what you do best."

34. TALISMAN

The hush blanketing Marten's reception room bore an air of anxious breath-holding, rather than a restful peace. The king stroked his bristly chin—this morning's shave seemed so very long ago—while he glowered at the circular table bearing Chel's Casket, hidden beneath its insulating carmine cloth. With all that had transpired, Marten still hadn't taken time to consider a safer location for the artefact beyond his well-guarded suite.

What would Uncle Hal have advised?

Marten cleared his scratchy throat. He remembered how excited he'd been, when Uncle Hal had told him he was ready to take the reins of the kingdom alone. Now, he'd do anything to have his uncle back, and lean on his decisive confidence once more.

The *thing* in the casket was, without doubt, magical. Did that make it something Uncle Hal would have suggested he accept? Family history, not to mention the certainty he'd felt about its evil nature, cautioned against such a course of action. Surely when Uncle Hal had proposed limited tolerance of magic as vital to defending the kingdom, he wouldn't have included the contents of the casket? Yet the Temple's senior clerics were instructing him to use it.

If he opened the casket, and it was the wrong thing to do, would the goddess stop him, the way She'd stopped Annasala? Did he dare try? Was the threat to the kingdom *really* enough for him to take such a monumental risk?

The Temple seemed to believe so.

Marten had been raised to respect the clerics, and to rely on their guidance and advice. He had no clear grounds to ignore them now.

His hand crept towards the edge of the crimson cloth. Blood rushed inside his ears, pounding in harmony with the compulsion the thing exerted. A dull throb in his veins sharpened to pinpricks, repeatedly jabbing against his skin from the inside out. His entire body crawled with the sensation, as if tiny beetles nibbled away at his flesh and the only way to stop it was to open the box.

When he was younger, still a child, its siren call had been sweet, offering fulfilment and power. The older he grew, and the longer he resisted its call, the sharper its claws became.

He gritted his teeth, and grasped the heavy fabric between one finger and thumb, reluctant to touch more of it than he must. With a sharp jerk, he swept it aside to expose the battered, charred casket beneath. His palms grew clammy.

"Stop!"

His nerveless fingers dropped the cloth, which fell to the floor beside him to lie like a pool of blood. He stared at Davi with wide eyes.

"Forgive me, sire, I know I'm overstepping boundaries here, but are you *sure* you want to do this?"

Marten ran his tongue around the dry cave of his mouth. After two attempts, he found his voice. "No, Davi, I'm not sure at all, but what else can I do? I need to know."

His bodyguard pursed his lips, and when Marten marked the pinching around the man's eyes, in conjunction with the tension in his body, he realised Davi was as scared as he was.

There was something else too.

"Davi, are you well?"

Davi's crooked grin relieved some of the strain on his face, although it accentuated its pallor.

"I reckon I ate something that didn't agree with me, sire. Thank you for your concern, but don't try to change the subject. Wouldn't it be better to wait and see if this Temple upheaval develops into anything serious?"

Marten glanced at the casket, trying to ignore the insistent prickles of magic. He shrugged. "I could do that, but suppose it escalates quickly? I don't know how long it will take me to master the thing inside there, assuming I even can."

"I'm sure Chel will guide you, sire, but I wouldn't be doing my job if I didn't question why you're doing this. You know I will always be your man, whatever you decide. Always."

Marten laid a hand on Davi's forearm. "Duly noted, my friend. Now go, take care of yourself—you look half dead."

With a token bow, Davi turned and marched from the room, leaving Marten alone once more with the sinister box. He wiped his hand on his tunic. It wasn't that warm an evening, and yet Davi was sweating. Worry? Or was he sicker than he was letting on?

Marten pushed his concerns aside. He would deal with them later. At this precise moment the box, and its malevolent contents, required his full attention.

He studied the artefact. The rectangular body with its domed lid would fit comfortably between his adult hands, with the blunt tips of his long fingers almost touching. Peeling and faded paintwork recalled a day when the box had been on display, venerated by previous generations as a holy relic, a gift from the goddess to Marten's family. Few knew what lay within.

One end bore severe charring from the conflagration that had reduced the Great Hall to scraps of blackened wood. And yet, somehow, the casket had survived. Was it protected by magic? Magic kept it sealed—the magic of the goddess—so, presumably Chel had protected it from the fire with some purpose in mind.

The Temple believed Chel intended for Marten to use it.

Marten reached across the table and snatched up the casket. His hands lingered, doubt still deterring him.

What if the thing inside transformed him into a tyrant, like his grandfather? Marten had lived with that fear his entire life. Only recently had he begun to gain confidence in being his own man. What if his old fears were justified?

On the other hand, he hadn't remarked any evidence of

deteriorating behaviour on his part as he'd matured, so perhaps he had no cause to be paranoid about his less-than-admirable heritage. Just because his father had been a drunk, and his grandfather a violent bully, why should he become either? Perhaps if he could handle the artefact and remain immune to its evil, it would prove he had the moral strength to become the wise and fair ruler he wanted to be.

His grip tightened. With a twist, the two halves of the box separated. He placed them both on the table and stared at the *thing* inside. It lay coiled like a snake about to strike. Metallic reds and greens shimmered in waves along its ridged surface, making it hard to discern if it moved, or not. A faint smell, like burning incense, slithered down Marten's throat.

Beads of sweat oozed onto his forehead. Sucking in a quick breath for courage, he reached into the casket and curled his fingers around the talisman. He lifted it out of the box. It felt heavy in his hand—far heavier than it should, for its size. And unexpectedly warm.

Raising it to eye level, he turned it over, studying the patterns that rippled across the strange substance. A tiny pinprick of ruby snared his attention, and his throat closed as he met the glaring eye.

With a curse, Marten tried to drop the thing back into the box, but it was stuck to his hand.

No, it was *clinging* there, tiny claws piercing his skin as he sought with rising panic to shake it loose. He grabbed a knife from his belt and attempted to pry it away, but it clutched even tighter, little droplets of blood forming around each needle-sharp talon.

"Help me!" Marten hollered. His cry shrilled through the empty chamber, yet bounced back as though it hit an invisible wall. No help came.

A miniature tongue darted out of the lizard-thing's mouth, lapping at his blood. A tail unfurled from where it had lain hidden, coiled around the creature, to arch above its head like a scorpion. And like a scorpion, it struck, the barbed point slashing through Marten's sleeve, half way between wrist and elbow.

He screamed as the white-hot tip lanced his skin and burrowed into his forearm. The creature's metallic body pulsed in time with the blood pumping through his arteries, and lethargy spread outward from the invading spike.

Marten's mind filled with images of bloody war; of helpless victims crushed beneath an onslaught of obscene, twisted creatures, straight from Charin's hell. Victims fell in charred and gory heaps, limbs torn off, eyes gouged out, entrails scattered like tangled ropes on an abandoned ship. The air shimmered with their mortal screams, and yet to Marten's horror, he felt only exultation, wallowing in the pain and trauma that flooded through him, thirsty for more.

Heat caressed his back, soft as a lover, terrifying as an assassin. He could not, *would* not, look round to see what he could sense easing into being behind him with a whisper of scales and the stench of molten metal. Unseen wings fanned scorching air around him, searing his lungs.

Summoning what strength remained to him, Marten raised his knife and stabbed at the *thing* cleaving to his hand, but the blade bounced off the articulated carapace.

There was only one thing left he could think of to try.

Marten drove his knife into his own arm, slicing after the metallic lance worming its way into his body. The sharp pain cleared his head, forcing the terrible images to recede. Moaning in anguish, he screwed up his face and jabbed hard. The knife point slid beneath the awful appendage, and he levered it back up and out of the gory hole in his flesh.

He dropped the knife and grabbed the lashing tail behind its spiked tip before it could strike again. He smashed the thing against the table, but its body was so hard he only jarred his shoulder and the agonising mess of his injured arm. He clung on to the menacing tail, but fear leached his remaining strength, and he knew his grip would fail soon.

Chel forgive me, I must be as wicked as my forebears after all. I never meant to free this horror. Please Chel, save my people!

Tears welled onto his cheeks only to evaporate in the blistering heat. He squeezed his eyes shut, and black dots danced against the ferocious light invading his eyelids. He prepared for the fiery death he'd cheated two years before.

A crack of thunder smote his ears and a flash of silver ice cascaded over his burning skin. He drew a lungful of blessedly chill air, and shivered. The slithering sounds behind him ceased, and a fragrant balm soothed his nasal passages. When he ventured to open his eyes, all around him was dark.

Had the fierce light blinded him?

But no, a silver glow rose to bathe him, as if he stood beneath the radiance of the two moons on a midsummer's night. He blinked, trying to make sense of the absence of any distinct shapes. The scent of flowers filled his lungs, and yet he did not sneeze.

"My son, your request pleases me."

The silken words whispered across his ears, and Marten's skin crawled. Surely this was magic? Or, no! It could not be...

"Chel?" he asked, voice small in the immensity of shining nothingness. He would have fallen to his knees, but his body was unresponsive, frozen in place, as if embedded in the very weave of the goddess's fabric. The words of the priesthood murmured across the chaotic background of his mind, speaking of Chel's fabled tapestry.

And of Charin's icy realm. Suspicion flared.

"Or Charin?" he accused. This time his question emerged stronger, echoing around the argent space. Eddies of grey and white rippled around him, and he shut his eyes, nauseous, but it made no difference; lids closed or open, he saw the same.

"I am both, and yet I am one," replied the deity in a strange dual tone, harmonious and grating at the same time. As the odd tonality faded away, so too, did both the strange paralysis and the glowing light. Throbbing pain drew Marten's awareness back to his injured arm, and he gasped as he tried to flex his fingers.

Goddess! What a mess.

But even as he inspected the ghastly wound, a pearlescent web spread across the gaping hole. Marten felt his eyes bulge as the strands of light drew the ragged edges of abraded flesh together. Agony flared as a slick line of silver traced ice along the length of the laceration, sealing the skin, but in its wake came blissful numbness.

When the light faded, nothing remained but a faint scar.

"You must make your own judgement based on actions, not words."

The hairs on the back of Marten's neck rose to attention. "Chel? Is that truly you?"

A shining mist gathered before him, coalescing at a leisurely pace into a face more beautiful than any statue of the goddess he'd ever seen. Trembling, Marten lowered his gaze, but illusory fingers cupped his chin to raise his head. He dared look upon the deity through slitted eyes, but even as he watched, the awesome beauty blurred, and transformed into features he knew well.

"Uncle Hal?"

Halnashead beamed that comfortable smile that had always brought warmth to Marten's belly. When he spoke, there was no mistaking the booming depth of the prince's voice.

"You've made an old man proud, m'boy. I always knew you'd have the courage my brother lacked. Siring you was the only good thing he ever did."

Bewildered, Marten shook his head. Surely, he must be delirious. He was talking to his dead uncle.

But it felt so *real.*

And when he glanced at his arm, the silvery line of a long-healed scar bore testimony to the evening's ongoing bizarre events.

"How, Uncle Hal? How are you here? You're *dead.*"

Halnashead's brow furrowed. "Did you not learn your lessons? I'm certain I employed competent priests to educate you." The frown softened. "Or perhaps your mind is still addled from what that creature showed you?"

"What *was* that?" Marten shuddered. He had no wish to recall the frightful images that had paraded through his head, but as much as he wished it, he couldn't unsee them.

Halnashead's expression turned grim. "Memories, m'boy. Memories of that foul demon, from the Wizard Wars. Back on the old continent. That *thing* you nearly raised tonight was there, and it hungers to repeat its atrocities."

Marten's fingernails bit into his palms. He'd been that close to releasing a *demon*?

"Marten? Marten! Listen to me, dammit, boy."

He blinked, and refocussed on his uncle's spectral visage.

"The important thing is, you didn't. You rejected it. You have no idea how special that makes you, how strong. It gives us hope our design may yet prevail."

Mistrust surged again. Marten licked his lips. "You said, 'us'? Who are you?"

Nausea threatened as the prince's features wavered, softened into feminine curves, and became those of—Marten's mother?

Marten sobbed. He'd been a small child when his mother was murdered, and his recollections of her were vague, but his heart knew what he saw before him now. He reached a hand towards her even as she dissipated into mist, reforming momentarily as his father, but his father as he rarely remembered him, with a sad smile, but a smile, nonetheless.

Again, the soft white cloud shifted, and this time it was Padrus who regarded him with compassion and approval.

"Brother?"

"You give us hope, Marten. All of us. We are all here, those you have loved, and many more. Remember your lessons."

Chel welcomes all souls back into her embrace, until the time they are born again.

He'd heard the words all his life. Now he understood.

Padrus faded out, to become once more the exquisite mask of the goddess. Chel regarded him with compassion. "My son, you have earned your thread in my weave. Now we must strengthen it, lest it snap."

Marten was certain he should feel mortal terror in the presence of the goddess, yet his mind and body remained serene. He gathered the courage his mentors told him he had, to ask the question burning his tongue.

"Why did the priests suggest I open it? Why did you let me?"

"You needed to prove you had the strength to resist such evil."

Bewildered, Marten scrunched up his forehead. "But You know my heart; You know everything. Why did I need to prove anything to You?"

Marten could hear the smile in Her words. "Not to me. To yourself."

"Oh." He regarded the goddess with incredulity. "That's it? You were willing to take a risk of that magnitude, so I could learn a *lesson*?"

Chel's exquisite lips curved into a smile, and Marten glanced down, appalled at himself for questioning his goddess. A feather touch to his cheek raised his head once more.

"You will understand, soon."

The ethereal haze thinned, the face becoming indistinct. A sudden, urgent, thought stabbed Marten. "Wait! Please, wait. I need to know. Is magic truly evil?"

Chel's answer blew softly past his ear, coming from an immeasurable distance. "Magic is born of the soul. That is where you must seek your answer."

And then She was gone. Marten stood alone in his reception room, beside the round table bearing the casket, secure once more beneath its scarlet cloth.

He took a step back, testing. The siren call of the box remained quiescent.

Running his fingers through his unruly hair, he considered what to do next. What did you do, when you'd spoken with your goddess?

A fizzing sound made him spin around, but it proved to be a candle, guttering into a lifeless pool of wax. He glanced up and down the room: only two candles remained of the many burning earlier, and those two were perilously close to expiring.

Apparently, talking to the goddess took a long time; it had been relatively early in the evening when he'd sat down to contemplate his options.

Perhaps his encounter with the demon had taken longer than it had seemed. Marten shuddered. Though somewhat less clear than when first they'd been thrust into his head, the demon's awful memories were embedded in his mind, and would likely haunt him for the rest of his life.

He straightened his shoulders. It was too late to do anything else tonight, and weariness already dragged at his feet. He craved a return to normality after his other-worldly experience, and the notion of sending Davi to fetch Nonni—assuming she could be located—crossed his mind, but he banished it promptly.

Even if he hadn't been exhausted, he wasn't yet ready to resume entertaining other women in his special room. He had no wish to sully the memory of that one special night with Betha; the night that brought gooseflesh and regret each time his mind caressed every precious second.

And besides, he hoped Davi had gone home to rest and recover from whatever ailed him. Marten had never asked another of his guards to fetch one of his special ladies, nor would he. Especially now, when the kingdom at large still believed he was wooing Betha as his potential queen. One could never be certain who might be a player.

He yawned, and headed for his bed chamber. In the morning he would ride to the Temple, and discuss tonight's miraculous events with the senior clergy. Tomorrow would be soon enough.

He barely made it to his bed before sleep claimed him.

35. DAVI

Marten swung into his saddle with ease. Beside him, Davi struggled to clamber astride his mount.

"Are you sure you should be here?" Marten asked.

Davi settled his feet in his stirrups and collected his reins.

"And where else should I be, when my king needs to ride through the city?"

Marten studied his bodyguard. He appeared his usual efficient and intimidating self, ready at any moment to leap into action in defence of the king's person. Only the yellowish tinge to his face gave any hint something wasn't as it should be. Clearly, Davi was determined to ignore his health in favour of duty, and Marten respected his decision.

"Then let's go."

Marten had yet to confide in anyone, even Davi, what had transpired last evening. He wanted to discuss it with priests versed in the ways of the deity, who would hopefully bring more clarity to his conflicted state of mind.

He'd conversed with the goddess. What greater event could happen to any mortal person? At least there were others amongst the priesthood who had similar experience, and those were the clerics he intended to talk to today. He just had to get past Brother Freskin.

Marten was so absorbed in his own contemplations he barely registered his surroundings. As usual, Davi rode in front with two guards, another pair bringing up the rear. Only when Davi called for an unscheduled halt did Marten become aware something was amiss.

They'd reached the lower city, where the buildings crowded close to form narrow streets. On normal days, townsfolk would hug the steps and doorways to allow riders three abreast to pass. Today, the city appeared empty. An ominous hush was punctuated only by the restless shuffling of one of the rear guard's horses.

"What's that?"

Marten's head whipped around. Davi pointed to the right, where a side street funnelled an odd noise towards them. It sounded like the distant roar of a river in full spate.

Davi glanced back at him. "I don't like this. We should get off the street."

Prickles of unease marched down Marten's back. "Agreed, but where can we go? We must be equidistant between palace and Temple. Do you know who lives in any of these buildings?"

Smaller residences lined the surrounding streets. The greater families' mansions all sat in spacious grounds along the wider avenues near to the palace. These must be servants' and craft workers' dwellings.

"I know a place," Davi said. With a decisive aid to his horse, he wheeled the animal around, and urged it towards a side street. For a short while, the dull thud of the horses' hooves on packed earth masked the noise from behind them. However, before long, it rose over them like a tidal wave, and they began to discern individual shouts and cries within the general clamour.

A small figure in skirts scurried across the street in front of them, forcing them to slow down. Marten caught a glimpse of a woman's white face beneath a skewed bonnet before she snatched open a red-painted door and skittered through, slamming it behind her.

A hint of smoke caught at the back of Marten's throat, making him cough.

"What in Chel's name is going on?" he demanded.

One of his guards answered. "I suspect some form of public disorder, Your Majesty. It sounds like a riot I got tangled up in when I escorted a trade caravan to Rylond."

"A *riot?*" Marten had an intellectual understanding of the

word, but the last riot in Kishtan had been during his grandfather's reign, when the populace had finally tried to rise against the tyrant's excesses. The tactic had died a violent death, with mass executions reducing the kingdom's small population even further. "Why now?"

"Sire, we can investigate motives later," said Davi. "Just now, we need to get you into hiding."

Marten bristled. The idea of hiding offended him. Why should he hide from his subjects? Did that not cry of cowardice? Only last evening, his courage had been highlighted by the goddess herself! Should he not turn and face the mob? Show them he stood for goodness and fairness and honest speech.

Two men barrelled around a corner ahead of the royal party. They slid to a halt, dust clouding around their feet. Both of them gaped, before the older of the pair grabbed the other by the shoulder and spun him around, heading back into the alley from which they'd emerged.

"The king! The king is here!"

"Damn it all to Charin's hell! Quickly, my liege, before the others hear them." Davi spurred his horse, and the party raced forward.

"Do you think that means they're after *me*?" Marten yelled over the wind whistling past his face. Shock chilled him despite the warm autumn day.

Galloping alongside, Davi glanced across at him. "I don't know, but we can't take a chance. Nearly there now."

"Turn!" Davi yelled, and then, "Stop!"

The dishevelled party reined to a halt. The horse's sides heaved, and the dust of their sliding stop obscured their surroundings.

"Dismount," Davi ordered, foregoing protocol. "Not you," he gestured at the guards. Confused, but without argument, Marten jumped down from Goldcrest's saddle. He gave the big stallion a hefty pat on the shoulder, proud of the animal's obedience in such odd circumstances.

"Take the horses and ride back to the palace," Davi

ordered. "Send reinforcements. Go!"

With unquestioning obedience to their captain, two of the guardsmen gathered the spare horses' reins and all four rode off, leaving Marten and Davi standing in the street outside a small wooden house.

"Come inside, my king."

Davi took a key out of his pocket and unlocked the solid door, then stood back for Marten to precede him into the dark interior. Had it been anyone else, Marten would have baulked, but he trusted Davi.

Davi pulled the door shut behind them, plunging them into darkness. Marten heard the tumble of the lock, and remained still when his bodyguard slipped past him. Light flared, illuminating a snug kitchen with a square wooden table set before a compact hearth. Davi raised the lantern and beckoned to Marten.

"Come through to the back room. If anyone forces the front door, they might not come further inside if it looks empty."

The back room turned out to be precisely that: a single room containing a bed, with a small desk littered with papers tucked away on the far side, and just enough room for someone to sit on the chair currently pushed beneath it.

"This is your home?"

Davi gave a small grin. "It is. One of the perks of being a royal bodyguard is a choice of accommodation outside barracks. Must admit, though, I never imagined I'd be entertaining my king here."

"Why didn't we ride on with the guards? Wouldn't we have been safer?"

"I don't believe so, sire. There's no telling where the mob is, or if there's more than one. I believe there's a fair chance my men won't make it back to the palace. And those orders I gave? They may, or may not be able to discharge them. We're safer to lie low here until the whole thing passes over. If reinforcements do come, there's no harm done, we can go back then, with a substantial escort."

A metallic clink from the outer room spun them both around. Davi's sword appeared in his hand, though Marten noticed with concern that it wavered.

So unlike Davi's usual sure grip.

"Stay behind me, sire."

Davi pushed past to stand in front of him. The outer door slammed with a heavy thud, and footsteps strode towards them across the wooden floorboards. Marten spotted a relaxation of Davi's shoulders a moment before the inner door opened.

"What—?"

"Praise the goddess it's you." said Davi, and let the tip of his sword sink towards the floor. Marten peered past his bodyguard at a slender man of around his own age. Hazel eyes stared back from beneath a mop of light brown hair.

"Who?" blurted stranger. And then his eyes widened. He transferred his shocked gaze to Davi.

"What's *he* doing here? Do you have any idea what's going on outside?"

"Don't, Jace," said Davi, before he stepped back past Marten, and sank down to sit on the edge of the bed. "I don't have the strength to argue with you. And no, we don't know exactly what's going on. I'm hoping you can enlighten us."

The man's glare raised Marten's hackles.

"The whole city is looking for *him*."

Davi sighed. "Yes, but why?"

Jace's eyebrows shot up to hide beneath his floppy fringe. "Because Master Lorndar's been murdered, and everyone thinks *he's* behind it."

Marten stiffened. He couldn't believe what he was hearing. Why might anyone think he would order the murder of a craft master? What did he have to gain?

He peered at Jace in confusion. "Why in Chel's name would I want Lorndar dead?"

Jace scowled at him. "Because he was stirring trouble. Because he asked for something you didn't want to grant, and you knew the people were behind him."

"That's ridiculous," Marten protested. "I admired his proposal, and I had every intention of acting on it."

"If only you'd told the people that, when they asked," said Davi. As close to an 'I told you so' as he was ever likely to get. Jace took a couple of quick steps to Davi's side, lifted the sword from his trembling fingers, and laid it on the desk.

Impressed by the younger man's tenderness as he whipped a handkerchief from a pocket and wiped Davi's damp forehead, Marten realised Jace must be Davi's lover.

How he longed to have someone—no, be truthful—how he longed to have *Betha* treat him that way. Like they were partners.

"Help me," Jace demanded as Davi doubled over, groaning, in danger of falling off the edge of the bed. Marten grabbed Davi's feet, Jace his shoulders, and between them, they rolled the bigger man towards the middle of the mattress.

"I told him he should be at home, in bed," Jace said gruffly. "He was too ill to go on duty this morning, and now look at him. Too damned stubborn for his own good." He glared at Marten. "Or do you expect your staff to work, even when they're deathly sick?"

"Jace!" Davi barked with much of his customary authority. "Don't speak to your king like that!"

His chastisement was overshadowed by a violent coughing fit. Ignoring the king, Jace perched on the edge of the bed, holding Davi until he could breathe again. Jace's gaze fixated on the grey blanket, and Marten followed his line of sight. His throat tightened when he spotted the red flecks staining the otherwise crisply laundered military bedclothes.

"I sent him home last night. I didn't expect to see him this morning."

"Yet you let him ride out with you."

Davi grabbed Jace's arm, gave it a little shake, "Leave it, Jace. It was my choice."

He coughed again, and scarlet spittle stained his lips. Jace wiped it away.

Davi groaned, and rolled onto his side, clutching his stomach. Marten watched, feeling utterly helpless.

Chel, won't you help him, please? This man is the best friend I could ask for. He doesn't deserve to suffer like this.

"Fetch me a glass of water, will you Jace?" Davi asked. "Please?"

With a scowl that did nothing to hide his fear, Jace slid off the edge of the bed and propped pillows behind Davi to support him. In the enclosed space, he pushed roughly past Marten, and vanished into the kitchen.

"My king." Davi whispered in a frail imitation of his usual voice. Marten perched on the edge of the bed and bent close to listen.

"Take care of him, for me, please? It's the only thing I'd ask of you."

Marten's vision blurred. "I promise, but it won't be for long. You'll be back on your feet in no time. I know how strong you are. And how stubborn."

Davi patted his arm with limp fingers. "Not this time, sire. I just remembered I've seen this before." He turned his left hand over to expose the palm. Angry black lines radiated outward from a nick towards the side if his hand. "Verdank poisoning. There's no antidote can work this late on."

Marten recalled the sliver of wood from the bowl Valaree had destroyed puncturing Davi's hand with enough force to make it bleed. He met Davi's gaze. Acceptance rested in his bodyguard's bloodshot eyes.

Marten's shoulders drooped. "But why?"

A howl of anguish from behind shot Marten up off the bed.

"I knew it!" cried Jace. "It's poison, isn't it? What do we do? There must be a way to fix this!"

Marten's heart cracked as he watched a beautiful compassion transform Davi's pain-ravaged face. Jace flung himself into his lover's arms, weeping. Davi stroked his dark head.

"Shh. I'm so sorry, Jace, there's nothing you can do. There's nothing anyone can do."

"There must be!"

Davi groaned again, and curled up, retching. When he finally caught his breath and Jace helped him straighten a little, a pool of bright blood stained the blanket beside him. Jace flung a terrified glance at Marten.

"*Do* something! You're the king, you have healers. Help him, please!"

"Jace," said Marten, "if there was anything I could do, believe me, I would. Davi's the truest friend I could wish for."

Jace crumpled into tears. "Then do something. Please?"

Tightness stopped Marten's throat. His eyes stung. How could this be happening? Only a short time before they'd been riding together to the Temple to discuss important matters, and now this? What could be more important than the life of a trustworthy, generous friend?

Jace frantically stroked Davi's sweating cheek, all the while staring at the blackened veins leading away from the small hole in his palm.

"It's the Temple, isn't it?" Jace accused. "You told me how that priestess cut you with her magic. Its because of what we are, isn't it? Because you love *me*, instead of a woman."

Davi met Marten's gaze over Jace's bowed head. The dying man's lips curved into a tender smile as he drew Jace's head against his breast. Marten's world darkened to resemble the inside of a bad dream he could not escape. Davi's head moved in slow motion—the tiniest of negatives—before a scarlet bloom pulsed from his mouth.

In the space of a dozen heartbeats, it was over. The light faded from Davi's eyes, though the gentle smile never left his lips. Jace howled in anguish, and Marten stood rooted to the floor even as the world spun around him.

That last gesture plucked at him, demanding attention. What had Davi been trying to tell him?

He stared again at the distorted flesh of Davi's hand, tracing the septic veins back to their source.

He blinked, and narrowed his eyes. Doing his best not to disturb Jace, who clung to Davi's body, rocking it to and fro, Marten bent over for a closer look.

The inky lines led towards the puncture Valaree had caused, but did not, quite, originate there.

Alongside the larger wound, almost obscured by the puffy red flesh, was the tiniest of pinpricks. *That* was where the marks led.

Not a pinprick. A *needle* stick.

Discreet to the end, Davi had furnished Marten with the answer he'd sought for two and half years, while keeping Jace from the knowledge that the king had been the intended victim.

Marten finally knew the identity of the assassin. Had known her all his life.

He and Davi had discussed things in front of her as if she'd been a part of the room's furnishings. She'd worked for his father, his mother. He'd *trusted* her.

Marten remembered the mortified expression on Marganie's face, the apology from her lips, when Davi pricked himself on the needle, oh so carefully concealed in the folds of the king's new cloak.

The distraught weeping of Davi's partner worked its way back into his awareness, and Marten allowed his own tears to fall.

Chel guard you, and comfort you, Davi, until we meet again. You were the truest friend and supporter I could have wished for. Rest well, my friend; you will be avenged, I swear it.

36. CELL

Betha gritted her teeth. She wanted nothing more than to slap Edlund's groping hand away, but she knew it would only earn her more grief. She endured his fondling with a passive expression, annoying him even further.

Edlund brought his lips so close to her ear, she feared he might stick his tongue inside.

"Understand this, girlie: your only way out of here is to become what you pretended to be, and I'm going to make sure you do that. I'm going to enjoy every moment of giving you explicit 'guidance'. Think on that, while you wait for my next visit." He gave her left breast one last squeeze, hard enough to make her flinch, and grinned, wolfishly. "See, we're forming an understanding already." He stood back and waved a hand at her guards. "Make sure she has plenty to eat: we wouldn't want her getting sick, would we?"

Unresisting, Betha allowed the guards to push her into the cell. The solid door clanged shut behind her, but the voices outside intruded.

"Aren't we going to chain her, like the other one?" asked one of the guards—the one who had enjoyed twisting her arm as he'd led her down here.

Edlund answered him. "Only if she tries to injure herself. You heard what the Master said: she's to be kept in good physical health." He put the emphasis on the word 'physical', obviously knowing she could hear him.

"But what about the privy hole? Should we block it up?"

"What, and have the place stinking more than it does now? She's skinny, but not *that* skinny!"

Betha inspected the cell. A light shudder rippled her skin

as she thought about the last person confined within its blank walls. That poor girl, executed in such hideous fashion for the simple crime of conceiving the king's bastard.

In one rear corner of the tiny, square room, the aforementioned privy proved to be no more than a circular hole cut into the wooden floor, with a pair of rough timber boards nailed across either side to reduce the opening to a narrow slit. Betha peered down the dark aperture, shivering in the cold draft that lifted a fetid stench into the already malodorous air trapped in the cell. Thank Chel for the high window that not only let a small amount of light in, but also a modest amount of fresh air to combat the smell.

Edlund was correct—the slit was too narrow, even for her.

An enclosed box ran along one wall, on top of which rested a basic mattress: a bag stuffed with straw. Manacles hung from long chains, offering the unfortunate wearer enough freedom to reach the four corners of the room, and lie on the bed, but preventing any attack on the guards when they opened the door. Betha was grudgingly grateful Edlund had—so far—considered them unnecessary in her case.

She fingered the outline of her concealed dagger. The guards had made a poor job of searching her person. Probably too afraid of damaging her body, after Urien's decree. Her lips stretched into a grim smile; she still had a chance of escaping.

The problem was, would it be in time to save Marten?

Pacing the room, five strides in each direction, she let her frustration and fear flood her mind.

Long ago, she'd discovered fear was a great motivator, and just now she was very, very afraid. Of Charin, of Urien and Edlund, and of what might happen to Marten if she didn't bring her knowledge to him in time.

She had to get out, and quickly. She made another circuit of the confining space. What did she have to work with?

Her small dagger—her only weapon. Her freedom from chains, to allow her to move swiftly should the opportunity present itself. Her feminine wiles, if the guard turned out to be gullible enough. She'd used those before, with great success, but she suspected the taller of the pair who'd brought her here was more of a sadist than a man to be swayed by the promise of a warm female form.

And if they were as scared of Charin as she was, as any intelligent mortal should be, if they had any sense, they would consider her body off limits.

When would they feed her? Had Edlund left yet? How likely was it she would be able to overcome two strong guards by herself, with nothing but a small knife? Yes, she'd had training, but her skills lay less in combat, and more in using her brains to out-think her opponents.

Betha fretted and paced, a grim idea tickling the edge of her mind until she stopped, sat down on the bed, and faced it.

She had another talent; one not shared by any other player, as far as she knew. Marten had forbidden her to use her healing magic, but that didn't change her attitude to pain. Perhaps, when the pain lingered long enough, her body would respond differently, but for now, for her, pain held no horror.

She went over and peered down the privy hole again. If she could remove the two rough planks, the circular hole *might* be wide enough for her to slip through. For a woman, she had unusually narrow hips, which she could probably squeeze down there. There was no doubt her shoulders would not fit as they were, but that was something she could change.

Betha listened at the door. Absolute silence greeted her. She had no idea how long that state of affairs would persist, so she set to work.

Using the edge of her dagger, she worked at prying up the edges of the planks. The sloppy handiwork meant the nails hadn't been driven in flush with the planks, let alone tamped down hard enough to prevent her from getting her knife beneath the wood.

Once she'd raised the nails a little, she changed tools, stretching the dangling chains across the room until she could get one edge of an open metal cuff wedged beneath the wood. She applied all her body weight, meagre as it was, to the other side of the cuff, levering the plank higher off the floor.

She soon discovered the shoddy workmanship extended to the materials. The nails were so short, they popped out of the floorboards much sooner than she'd expected. Caught by surprise, Betha toppled backward, landing hard on her backside. She froze, waiting to see if the guards were close enough to hear, but no one came.

After repeating the procedure to remove the second plank, she inspected the fully revealed circular hole. Betha permitted herself a grim smile.

Quickly, she slipped out of her bulky gown, tied her dagger into a makeshift sheath with the laces of her drawers, and climbed up onto the bed. Reaching up, she knotted a section of one of the chains around her left wrist. Balancing on the ball of her right foot, she put her left against the wall, considering angles and trajectories. If she got it wrong, she might well crack her arm, and she didn't have the time for that, not to mention it would force her to break her promise to Marten.

With a quick prayer to Chel, Betha lunged up and forward, kicking off the wall as hard as she dared. She twisted as she fell, narrowly avoiding landing on her back against the square edge of the box bed. Her arm, cranked into an unnatural angle with her full body weight suspended from it, popped out of its socket with a snap.

Betha inhaled sharply. Pain shot down her arm and into her neck. Pain her mind translated into a thrill of anticipation.

She clambered back onto the bed and untangled her wrist from the chain. Her left arm flopped down limply, sending another jolt of stabbing pleasure surging through her.

Ignoring it, she took the five steps to the edge of the rough hole, and squatted down. She tugged her dislocated arm around in front of her, praying it would be enough. She lowered first one leg, and then the other until they dangled without support, before shuffling forward on her seat bones.

Betha slid into the hole.

As she slipped over the grimy edge, she wished she had more protection than a lightweight shift. Greasy goo clung to the roughly sawn rim; goo she had no desire to identify. The smell intensified, and her legs waved back and forth, unable to find purchase. Cold air whistled around them, raising goosebumps.

Her hips stuck. She thrashed and wriggled, every movement sending confusing messages of pain and pleasure to her brain. Panic welled up, and she bit off a cry. Her muscles tensed—and her body dropped a fraction.

That's it. Stay calm and clench those buttocks. Yes!

She dropped a tiny bit further.

With her dangling, useless arm clasped tightly across her chest, she wormed further into the hole. The awful smell made her want to vomit, but she turned her mind away from that notion. There was already enough muck on her, she was determined not to add to it.

Abruptly, her hips popped free, and she dropped. The rough edges of the hole scraped her arms as she hugged them against her ribcage, but the width of her shoulders blocked her progress. With a desperate tug, she wrenched her dislocated arm further across in front of her.

She slithered through, falling a distance of around her own height to land on her feet in a cold, sluggish water course. She gasped, nerves utterly confused by all the conflicting sensations.

Betha forced herself to straighten up. She could stand almost upright, with the top of her head brushing the roof of what appeared to be a tunnel. The cold water running around her ankles numbed her feet. She splashed towards a glimmer of daylight, and found her way blocked by a grating. She closed her eyes and drew a deep lungful of cleaner air.

First things first, she instructed herself. *Two functioning arms are better than one.*

Back along the passage, she'd passed several square

timber pillars, presumably supporting the building overhead. Shivering, she shuffled back through the icy water until she saw one ahead. She launched into a couple of half running strides, and slammed her distorted shoulder against the column. It snapped back into place with a loud crack.

Her nerves shrieked their muddled messages to her brain, and she stood stock still, panting. This wasn't the first time she'd done this, but last time she'd healed herself within moments. Now her arm felt leaden, and responded sluggishly to commands. Would she have to break her word after all? Or could she still function well enough to escape as she was? She knew she would try anything, rather than renege on her promise.

Anything, unless it meant she wouldn't reach Marten in time.

At least the arm worked a bit, and aside from a dull ache, her body didn't seem to be reverting to what she imagined a normal relationship with pain must be like. Betha released her dagger, and set off along the passageway in the opposite direction to the one she'd taken at first. The glimmer of light coming in from behind her dimmed until she was forced to feel her way in darkness, but quite soon a half moon of light grew before her, and she came up against another grating.

Resolving not to despair, Betha set to work with the point of her dagger, loosening the mortar around the base of the central bar. If she could only pry it loose, she had a slim chance of slipping through.

The point of her dagger snapped off, and she set her jaw, working with more care, despite the urgency. Her shivering turned spasmodic.

If I don't get out of here soon, all this will have been for nothing.

She grasped the metal bar, twisting it from side to side, and eventually she was able to rock it loose. She eyed the gap, wondering if even her slender form would fit, but she had to try.

She was half way through when she heard voices. Edlund!

Chel and Charin, could she be more unfortunate?

"Do the girth up, you lazy oaf! Are you trying to kill me?"

Betha held herself immobile. She was hidden from view by the stable midden, for she realised now that's where she'd come out.

Edlund wasn't looking for her—he was leaving!

Shod hooves rang on cobblestones: more than one horse. Betha slithered smoothly forward, until she cleared the gap she'd created in the grating, and flopped with relief onto the dung heap. Yes, it smelled, but it was less offensive than where she'd come from, and it was blissfully warm.

She burrowed into it a short way, happy to wait for Edlund to leave.

Which he duly did, accompanied by two heavily armed guards. Betha stayed where she was until she could no longer hear the horses' hoof beats, and remained a while longer to ensure no one else was following Edlund. When the stable yard had remained quiet for some while, she crept from her stinky covering, and bolted across the open space, heading for an archway leading into an airy wooden barn.

Never had she been so pleased to inhale the earthy aroma of horse. She'd puzzled over Marten's delight in burying his nose in his horse's mane and inhaling the strong scent, but now she thought perhaps she understood. It wasn't only the smell of horse; it was the scent of freedom.

Most of the stalls stood empty, but she discovered a couple of tall, black horses towards the rear of the building. Presumably these belonged to the men left to guard her. When would their relief arrive? They couldn't be expected to remain on duty indefinitely, even though they obviously expected her to give them no trouble.

She dismissed her concerns; all they did was slow her down. She had no way of answering them, so they were irrelevant.

With a little exploration, she located the tack room, which provided her with a smock and some breeches, as well as a pair of boots five sizes too big for her feet, but so much more practical than her ruined slippers. She did the best she could to dust off the crumbling remains of the dung heap clinging to her skin and hair, but in the end, she settled for putting the clothes on over the top, and basking in the feeling of warmth.

She carried a saddle out and hefted it clumsily up onto one of the animals. Doing the girth up proved to be a challenge, with her left hand unwilling to grip with any strength, but eventually she managed. She thanked the goddess she'd been raised in a house with few servants, and knew how to tack up a horse, even if she hadn't done it for years, and never one so huge as this. She preferred ponies: closer to the ground, and not so likely to crush your foot if they stepped on you.

She heaved a sigh of relief when the animal obligingly lowered his head to receive the bridle, which she slipped over its ears without difficulty.

Now, to get out of the barn without being spotted.

She couldn't leave the way she'd entered. She'd been lucky so far; the stable hand hadn't reappeared after seeing Edlund off, but she was certain if he heard hooves on the cobbles, he would come to investigate.

She turned towards the rear of the barn, and smiled. Double doors, barred at present, offered another exit. She left the horse with his reins looped under a stirrup, and, after a small tussle with the bar, pushed one door ajar, and peeked out.

Outside, a grassy track led away into the woods. Piles of firewood and fodder nestled beneath the building's overhang, suggesting that the track had been made by delivery carts.

Betha pushed the door wider and went back to get her horse. She led him outside and clambered onto a raised platform, probably used for unloading. Her shoulder began to throb, and she winced as she swung her leg over the back of the saddle. It looked so easy, when you watched a competent rider mount, and Betha regretted all the occasions she'd elected to ride in the relative comfort of a carriage, rather than sit on a horse.

At least she had a good idea of the route she needed to

take back to the city. She nudged her purloined mount with her heels, and set his head along the track.

37. RETURN

"What in Chel's name is going on?"

Rustam scanned the palace corridors: empty in all directions.

By keeping their ears open, they'd skirted the obvious trouble in the city streets, and had come close to the Temple grounds without encountering more than a handful of people, all of whom had bolted at the sight of mounted riders. Risada had ridden the few lengths from the mouth of a dim alley to deliver Chayla to a pair of startled Temple priests, but had gleaned little from them in return. All they could tell her was that a craft master had died, and the city was in turmoil.

"Since when did a craft master's demise have such an impact on the general population?" Risada demanded. Rustam could only shrug. He'd been a celebrated craft master before his exile, but he didn't think more than a handful of besotted noble ladies would have mourned his passing if his original sentence had been carried out.

"At least we got here without being seen," Risada continued. "Let's get to my suite the same way, shall we?"

Cradling her sleeping son in her arms, Risada led the way, peeking around corners before permitting Rustam to follow.

As luck would have it, their undoing came from behind.

"Rustam?" Annasala's question bounced around the empty corridor.

Of all people, of course it has to be my sister.

Rustam turned to greet the princess with a jaunty grin plastered across his face.

"Sala! Fancy seeing you here. Do you know what's going on in the city?"

Annasala's brows drew together. "What did I tell you, Rustam, last time I saw you? Are you deaf, as well as irresponsible?"

Rustam produced what he hoped was a winning smile. "Perhaps I am. I thought I heard you say how happy you'd be to see me back home, reunited with my family."

Risada's arm brushed against his as she pushed back past him. "Sala, can we please discuss this? I understand you were angry, but that was with me, not Rusty."

Annasala stalked towards them, her usual royal posture held stiffly, as if it chafed. She stopped barely a length away.

"Why did you not make him stay away?" she asked Risada, ignoring Rustam.

"I tried, believe me. But this little one," Risada ran a finger around the edge of the soft grey blanket the sisters had given her, to expose Halson's cheek, "is his half-brother. As he is yours. Rusty was determined to see him safely back to the palace. He can go now." She frowned meaningfully at Rustam. "Can't you?"

Annasala barely glanced at the baby. "Don't try to distract me, Risada. I made an edict, and good intention or no, Rusty has wilfully broken it." Her shoulders slumped, and she glared at Rustam. "It's the same story all over again: you broke the law to save us, and father forgave you for it. But I can't do the same. Why did you have to come back?"

The quiet after her question stretched. With a heavy heart, Rustam accepted that his sister wasn't going to forgive him. Her mind had been so broken by the usurper, and put back together in distorted fashion by the Temple, and by Valaree in particular, that she wasn't the same young woman he'd grown up alongside. Risada had been correct; he shouldn't have come.

And yet those two years of exile in Kishtan, when he'd believed he was making a new life for himself, had melted into insignificance the very moment he'd stepped back into Risada's presence. When his father informed him of his intention to rescind the exile order, Rustam knew he couldn't return to the half-life he'd been living.

Living without Risada wasn't living. He was never going back to that hollow existence, even if it meant his end. Which sadly was looking ever more likely.

Annasala sucked on her bottom lip, contemplating him thoughtfully. She glanced over her shoulder furtively. "I suppose—"

"Your Highness! Back away from him."

Rustam ground his teeth together. So close. So very close. He was certain Annasala had been about to give ground, but now she was retreating towards Valaree and a pair of palace guards. Could his timing get any worse today?

"Dammit, Rusty!" swore Risada. "Why, oh why, could you not have done as I asked?"

With Valaree and the guards approaching warily, Rustam seized Risada by her narrow shoulders, and gazed deep into her blue eyes. "I trust you. And Chel. You'll find a way. The king can overrule Sala. Don't worry about me; go find Marten."

Remaining passive, Rustam permitted the guards to fold his arms behind his back and fasten manacles around his wrists. The clatter of boots on tiles announced the arrival of a third guardsman at the run, bearing a small bottle containing a brown liquid.

Rustam grimaced. How he detested the taste of hestane.

"Rusty?" Unlike before, Annasala sounded apologetic. "I'm sorry, I must ask you to take this."

He bowed his head to his sister. "I understand. I won't make any trouble; I never intended to."

Valaree stepped forward, brandishing the bottle of hestane, but a fierce glare from Annasala stopped her in her tracks. The princess took the bottle from the priestess, and removed the stopper.

"Take care, Your Highness. Until he swallows, he can still use his vile magic."

"But he won't, will you Rusty?"

The princess held the bottle to his lips, and poured some

into his mouth. He swallowed hastily, then gagged.

"That is without doubt the most disgusting stuff," he said, keeping his tone light. He might be willing to permit them to take him into custody, but he didn't intend to earn any harsh treatment.

His knees sagged. The dose was far less than Hext-al had given him, but still enough to ruin his balance.

"Support him," Annasala ordered as the guards closed in around him. He had a brief glimpse of Risada frowning after him, and then he was half led, half carried along the corridor in the direction of the cells.

Would now be a good time to remind You, dear Chel, that You told me You still have things for me to do? Things I won't be able to do if I'm executed. Just saying.

* * * * * * *

Risada raised her chin and stared down her nose at Annasala. "He's your *brother*, in case you still haven't got that past your prejudices. What would your father say?"

Annasala had the grace to blush. "I know what he is, Risada. That's exactly the problem. If only you'd sent him away, this wouldn't have happened."

Risada stiffened. "Don't you dare put this on me. If you hadn't reinstated his sentence in a fit of pique, we wouldn't be having this conversation. Now I need to find Marten, and sort out this mess."

"Lady Risada."

Risada glared at Valaree.

"The Firestarter is in custody because of his illegal use of magic, not because of anything Princess Annasala may have done. He was given a chance, which he squandered. He will be executed, as the law states, as soon as it can be arranged."

Risada reined in her temper. Arguing with a pious, and potentially dangerous, cleric like Valaree, only ever made things worse. She addressed the princess.

"Where will I find the king?"

Annasala licked her lips, sending prickles of unease racing down Risada's spine.

"We don't know," Annasala admitted. "He rode out towards the Temple before the riot began, and we haven't heard whether he arrived or not."

"The majority of the guard is in the city, looking for him," Valaree volunteered.

Risada resisted the urge to look at her, asking the question without turning to face the priestess. "So nothing will be done about Rusty until Marten's located?"

"The king's permission is not necessary. The edict was rightfully issued by the princess, and will be enacted as soon as the captain of the guard returns to fulfil his duty as executioner."

Wonderful! The guard won't return until they've found Marten, who is Rusty's only hope for a pardon, but the moment they return, the executioner will be available to do his job. Unless...

"Is my maid in the palace?"

Annasala looked perplexed. "Why would I know?"

Risada permitted herself a small snort of amusement. "If old mother Stania is here, you'll know."

Annasala's face cleared. "Oh, *that* one? Yes, she's here. You'd think she was the palace seneschal, the way she organises the staff."

Good. I can leave Halson with her while I sort out this mess.

Risada leaned in to speak quietly to Annasala. "Can I rely on you to inform me, the moment there is news about the king?"

Annasala nodded, her gaze finally fixing on Halson's sleeping form. "Of course. He'll want to meet his heir." She reached a tentative hand towards her little brother, and Risada drew the blanket back a little. Annasala drew a soft finger along the baby's jawline.

"To think, we have the same father."

Risada kept her voice low. "As does Rusty. Please don't

forget that."

The haunted look Annasala lifted towards her gave Risada hope.

* * * * * * *

Risada pushed open the door to Hal's office. She took one step inside, and halted, inhaling the familiar aroma of books, wax, and ink, mixed with a lingering hint of her husband's masculine scent. Her throat constricted.

That she could still smell his presence, a third of a season beyond his death, seemed both a cruelty and a blessing.

She scanned the room. Nothing had changed since the last time she'd stood there. Except for the empty chair behind the desk.

The document-filled shelves appeared undisturbed, and the floor space was still littered with small tables surrounded by the workmanlike chairs where Hal had consulted with his spies and informants. The original ornate furniture had fallen victim to the coup, burned along with most of the personal possessions of the royal family. Even the massive tapestry that had once dominated the wall behind Hal's desk had succumbed to the pretender's wrath.

The huge desk, on the other hand, had somehow survived, and been returned to its rightful place not long after the coup had ended. Parchments still covered most of its surface, arranged in orderly piles, exactly as Hal had left them when they'd set off for Domn to attend Iain's rites. It seemed so long ago. So much had happened, so much had changed, and nothing could ever go back to how it had been before.

Risada threaded her way across the room between the tables. The ghost of an old memory surfaced: how she'd stood behind Hal's desk and studied the approach of the elegant player she'd known only as Charmer. How disgust and despair had gripped her when the acclaimed spy had stepped out of the shadows to reveal his true identity. How she'd despised Rustam, even though she'd never had any close dealings with him, all because, at that time, she'd believed him to be her father's bastard.

What a hypocrite I am, she chastised herself. *I was no different in my attitude toward him then, than Sala is now, and for many of the same reasons.*

With a heavy sigh, she wove her way across the room, and slipped behind the desk. She pulled out the huge padded chair Hal had commissioned to replace the one destroyed by the usurper. She'd always considered the amount of cushioning Hal demanded to be a sign of decadence until she'd married him, and had seen first-hand how much of his day was consumed by sitting at this very desk.

She perched on the edge of the chair. She'd sat here before—most notably that day when she and Rustam had first been introduced—but it still felt wrong. As if she was misappropriating her dead husband's place.

Stop it! Hal left you in charge, he left you everything you need to run this kingdom. Now get on and do it.

She leaned across the table and pulled some blank sheets of parchment towards her.

A small door to the side of the fireplace swung open. Instinct kicked in, and Risada's hand dove for the hilt of her concealed dagger, but before she'd completed the action she identified her late husband's record keeper, and instead beckoned him in.

"It's good to see you, Grendle, come in. We have work to do."

"My lady." Grendle halted before the desk and bowed. Ivory wings of hair framed his face. The remainder, still dark for his age, was pulled back into a neat and orderly braid that reached half way down his back. It was an old-fashioned style, and indeed many of his contemporaries were stooped and frail, but Grendle seemed bent on defying the passing of the seasons.

"I have urgent tasks for you, Grendle. I hope you'll be content to work for me, as you did for my husband? Though I wish he hadn't done so, he entrusted the network to me."

"My lady, I would be honoured."

She gave a single, brisk nod, and cleared her throat. "Then let us get to work."

She wrote her instructions carefully, knowing the reading skills of some of the intended recipients to be meagre. Keeping the letters large, and the words simple, she inscribed a brief note, and copied it until she had three small folds of parchment ready for delivery.

Risada had already considered the consequences of her actions, which would result in her losing the services of three of the best household spies; spies Hal had trained specially for their roles, and relied on for years.

But when she closed her eyes, all she could see was Rustam, languishing in a tiny cell, lolling against the wall in a drugged stupor, awaiting the return to the palace of his executioner. It would be worth it.

She passed the notes across the desk to Grendle.

"Deliver this to Brush, and a copy each to Mouse and Dagger."

"Yes, Mistress."

Hal's—no, *her*—assistant strode from the room, leaving Risada sitting behind the desk that was now her own, contemplating the piles of documents she'd inherited. There was enough to keep her busy for more than a full season, she estimated.

But for now, it could all wait. She pushed back and stood, before turning towards a bookcase that appeared no different to any other. Her fingers moved unerringly to the side of the third shelf down, and tripped the concealed latch. The entire bookcase swung away from her. She lit a lantern, slid past the secret door into the dusty passages that honeycombed the palace, and pushed the bookcase back into place behind her.

If either Annasala, or the priests, had set a spy to watch her door, they would report she'd entered the room but never left it.

She set off into the dark.

38. REUNION

"Sire? Your Majesty, are you in there?"

With reluctance, Marten dropped his hands from where they'd rested on Jace's shoulders in some meagre effort at comfort. Marten took one last, long, look at Davi who, apart from the blood staining his tunic, appeared to be sleeping.

Marten's throat and chest were too tight to answer the call from outside. He dragged his feet across the outer room and put an ear to the door. Urgent hammering vibrated the wood against his ear, and beyond that, he could hear horses shifting restlessly.

He turned the key that Jace had left in the lock, and lifted the latch.

"Praise Chel! You're whole." The speaker, the captain of the palace guard, twisted his head around to yell over the tumult behind. "The king is safe! Praise be to Chel!"

Whole? Marten stared numbly out at the melee beyond Davi's door. *I don't think that quite covers it. I've just lost my best friend. How can I be whole?*

But he was the king. Grief was something he was becoming accustomed to, and duty demanded he consider his people first. He would take time to mourn later.

"Davi," his voice cracked. He cleared his throat as the captain gestured for quiet. He tried again. "My bodyguard has died, defending my person. He will be accorded all honours due his sacrifice." He glanced over his shoulder. "The man he shared his roof with is in there, with him. Anything he needs, the crown will pay for."

There, let them make of that what they will.

Two of the ten soldiers outside were detailed to the task,

and one of their mounts was led up to Marten.

"Have you found my horse?"

"Yes, sire. He came back on his own in a muck sweat, and was being walked to cool off as we rode out to find you."

Marten mounted the narrow bay. The saddle felt hard, and the ears in front of him were too close.

"Then let us get back; I have urgent matters to attend to."

Revenge and justice. If only either of those could bring Davi back.

* * * * * * *

The black horse swished its tail irritably. Betha huffed with annoyance, and drummed her heels against its ribcage yet again.

"You can go faster than this, I'm sure of it!"

The sluggish trot speeded up a fraction.

Frustration added to the pulsing ache in her abused shoulder. It turned out, long-term discomfort did not translate into ecstasy nearly as well as short, sharp pain.

At least she was nearly there. After riding all night, the city had been a welcome sight. Arriving, however, had been a huge shock.

Deserted streets, ransacked market squares, looted shops, all stared at her accusingly. Was she too late? Had Urien already murdered Marten? What other momentous event could have caused such uproar?

Avoiding the noisy mobs was relatively straightforward, but Betha sweated each time she had to change route, sometimes having to double back, or take side roads she didn't know. She'd never had cause to explore beyond the major routes through the city, and the back streets scared her.

Assuming he was still alive, what would become of Marten if she never arrived with her information?

She considered abandoning the horse. In her purloined outfit she'd blend in with the rabble, and the way she smelled, no one would want to come any nearer to her than they had to. On the other hand, on foot, she might struggle to convince the palace guard to let her pass.

She kicked the horse again, to no better effect.

The gate into the palace stable yard yawned ahead, and Betha scrubbed her sleeve over her face. She had no idea if anyone would recognise her, filthy and bedraggled, and wearing such outlandish clothing, but aside from some sideways glances and raised eyebrows, the guards waved her through. She let the horse stop just inside.

"What's caused the unrest?" she asked one of the guards.

He shrugged. "We don't know, madam."

The tightness in her chest eased; it wasn't due to the king's death.

Without doubt, keeping the horse had been the best idea after all. From the neutral form of address, she hadn't been identified beyond being a member of one of the noble houses. Betha urged her reluctant mount to a sluggish jog, and rode on into the main stable yard, where she slithered down from her saddle. She winced as the hard landing jarred her shoulder, but flung the reins at a startled groom, and took off running. Her feet scattered gravel as she raced across the courtyard and into the palace via the huge double doors.

She flew along the corridors, scattering nobles and servants alike, ignoring the vociferous protests and insults thrown after her. At this point, she didn't care what anyone thought, even if they did recognise her.

She barely slowed as she approached the outer doors to Marten's private rooms, ducking beneath the raised arms of the flanking guardsmen and slamming the doors open.

"My lady! He's not—"

Not what? She questioned as she raced across the outer chamber. *Not available? Not willing to see me? He* will *see me; he has no choice.*

With a hefty shove, she thrust the inner door open.

And halted, staring around in bemusement at the empty sitting room. Finally, the half-heard sentence made sense.

He's not here. *Goddess! Marten, where are you?*

"Betha?" Marten's voice carried across the outer chamber behind her, and she spun around to find him hurrying towards her. He looked dishevelled. Not as much as her, but decidedly ruffled, and his already narrow face appeared pinched, with dark rims shadowing his hazel eyes.

What—? Never mind; it can wait.

She grabbed his sleeve and pulled him through the door, slamming it behind him.

"It's Charin, Marten. The benefactor is the god Himself!"

Marten's jaw gaped. His teeth clicked as he snapped it shut. "So *that's* what's going on."

His lack of surprise rocked Betha. Had she not made herself clear? Did he not understand the gravity of what she was saying? She tried again. "The cult isn't pretending, it really is the god, I saw Him myself!"

Marten grasped her by the upper arms, sending tingles racing across her skin. His fingers tightened, and she winced. Concern bloomed on his pale face. "Are you injured?"

He does still care for me.

"Later," she said. "I'll explain later. We have to get to the Temple and find some priests faithful to the goddess. Perhaps, with Chel's backing, they can fight Charin."

Marten shook his head. Betha blinked rapidly. Why did he not seem to understand the impossible position they were in? They had to seek help.

"We can't get to the Temple," Marten explained. "There's a riot out there. Nearly the entire guard is in the city, trying to bring it under control."

"But, but…" Betha ran out of words. Urien had departed the meeting house before her, travelling in a carriage which she'd probably overtaken during the night, not having to stick to the main roads. Likely he would have to abandon that means of conveyance before getting very far into the city which, please Chel, would slow him down. But if he made it through the streets as she had, Marten was doomed. The scheming lord might very well be on his way here now, and if he was able to raise the god…

"Tell me what happened. And for Chel's sake, let's get you cleaned up, you stink like a dung heap. An enemy could smell you coming from a hundred paces."

Cold sweat broke out all over Betha as Marten ushered her towards his private bathing room. There was always water warming over a fire, even in summer, so he had no need to call for a servant unless he wished to. Usually his bodyguard, Davi, helped him. Betha glanced over her shoulder, expecting to see the attentive guard hovering nearby. Where was he? Marten needed all the protection he could get right now, although no one would be able to stand against Charin.

"Where—," she began, but Marten's tight jaw suffocated the rest of her question.

"Not now. I need to hear what you saw."

As she talked, Marten helped her out of her odd collection of apparel. She forced herself to ignore both her impatience at his measured response to her words, and the way her body responded to his touch, battling the distraction of muscles that clenched deliciously, sending spikes of anticipation through her.

Marten frowned at the purple bruising around her shoulder, but gestured for her to continue, apparently unaffected by her nakedness. She kept her story to short, salient points, while Marten poured hot water into the tub. All the while, she fretted about where Urien might be now.

When she related how Charin had executed the girl, she omitted the reason why, and by the grim expression on Marten's face, was glad she had. He didn't need to know he'd lost a child, as well as a lover.

What surprised her, though, was Marten's lack of reaction when she described the terrifying splendour of the god. What had happened to him, to make him so nonchalant in the face of an impossible foe?

Betha finished sponging off the filth, which floated in clumps of little brown flecks, darkening the water. Marten seemed to be considering his next words carefully, and when he uttered them, they perplexed her yet further.

"This is what Chel has prepared me for. I should have seen it coming."

Betha stepped out of tub, heedless that she was dripping all over the rug, and grabbed his chin, pulling it down so she could stare directly into his eyes. She tried to put into her words every fear, every terror of losing him that had gripped her since she'd seen the god manifest, and knew the awful reality of what they faced. "Marten, you can't fight a god!"

He wrapped a huge, soft towel around her shivering body. "Betha, sweet Betha. You've done everything I asked of you. You are a marvel, and I can't tell you how happy I am you made it back, but you should leave now. Get away from the palace, go back to your manor and stay safe. If I survive, you'll be the first person I shall send for, but you can't do anything more here. Your part is done."

"But, the god?"

Marten's mouth folded into a lopsided smile. "I have Chel on my side. She came to me last night, and now I know why."

Betha's vision blurred. "You can't fight Him alone," she protested, brushing away tears. "You'll die!"

"But I won't be alone, don't you see that? Chel will be at my side."

"You'll be dead!" Betha's knees gave way, spilling her onto the thick rug beneath her. "You'll be dead," she repeated. Something inside of her felt broken. "I don't want to live, if He kills you. Don't send me away, I need to be with you."

* * * * * *

Marten hunkered down. Seeing Betha collapsed in a defeated heap at his feet almost undid him. He was trying to stay strong for her. Sending her away was the very last thing he wanted to do, but he wanted her safe. Away from what was coming. He didn't want her to see him fail, and quite possibly die.

For all his confident words, and his efforts at blind trust, he wasn't convinced Chel would aid him. Charin was Her other aspect. How could She fight Herself?

She'd made the point that the lesson he'd needed to learn was about believing in himself. Was that Her way of telling him he had to face the coming battle alone?

He let his gaze roam over Betha's crumpled form. So tiny, so fragile. Yet she possessed an inner strength and integrity he admired beyond measure. He imagined his fingers tracing the curve of her shoulder, the length of her elegant throat. The small, firm rise of her breasts. Fire ignited in his belly as a startling revelation burst into his mind.

He loved her.

His heart didn't care what his head said about her secret magic. He couldn't bear the possibility of being without her, and a fierce strength he'd never felt before surged through him when he thought about anyone hurting her. He still wasn't sure how they could manage things on a practical level, but he knew he would protect her with his life.

Marten gulped, and cleared his throat. "I only want to protect you," he bent close and murmured into her damp hair. "I couldn't bear it if anything happened to you."

She raised wide, bruised-looking eyes, and he knew he was lost.

"You have a strength I could never rival," he said. "Stay with me, and perhaps I can borrow some."

Hope flared in the depths of her azure eyes.

"You mean it?" Her voice was little more than a whisper. "You aren't going to send me away?"

Marten straightened, and held out a hand to help her rise. The towel slipped down to pool on the rug around her ankles. Goddess! She was so beautiful, even with the ugly bruises around her left shoulder. He wanted to kill whomever had done that to her, at the same time as he wanted to crush her in his arms and never let her go.

But there was a god coming for him. He couldn't escape that fate.

With a massive effort he quashed his carnal desires, and picked up the towel. "Here, wrap yourself in that for a moment and I'll see what I can find for you to wear."

Marten hurried to his dressing room before he could change his mind, rummaged in a chest of drawers, and pulled out a white silk blouse, his favourite dark brown leggings that truthfully were on the tight side for him these days, and a pair of soft, lace up boots. All would be far too big for Betha, but she would have to make do.

He blinked hard as he carried the garments back to his bathing room. Davi would have known what to do, how to make it work, even when it shouldn't be possible.

That was another thing that needed attention. If, by fortune, he survived his upcoming encounter with the devious god, he vowed to avenge Davi by dealing with the amateur assassin who'd killed the wrong man.

He helped Betha dress, pulling laces as tight as they would go. He went back to his dressing room for a belt, tied a couple of knots in it to shorten it, and cinched it around her waist to hold everything together.

There. They'd had to roll the sleeves up so many times, the folds bulged around her tiny wrists. Likewise, the leggings above her ankles. And the boots? He hoped she wouldn't trip herself up, but at least she was no longer distractingly naked.

"You're certain the drug is the key?" He wanted confirmation. "Even after his prowess at the tournament?"

Betha shoved one of the slippery silk sleeves further up her arm. "Yes. He must have taken huge doses to survive that afternoon. As soon as his knee bothered him, the god vanished."

"In that case, we need to find his supply and cut it off. We'll start in his suite."

Betha baulked. "That's like walking into a werecat's lair. If he's made it back, that's the first place he'll go."

Marten squared his jaw as he buckled on his sword, and slipped extra daggers into hidden sheaths in his clothing.

"Then we should hurry; we might still beat him to it."

"Shouldn't we find somewhere to defend? Gather the guard and pick a secure place to make a stand?"

Marten smiled grimly. "That's exactly what he'll expect me to do, but I won't put any more innocent lives before mine today." Inside his head, Davi nodded approval. "No number of guardsmen are going to stand against Charin, and anyway, most of them are out in the city, dealing with the riot. No, we're doing this my way."

Without waiting for another answer, he pulled open the door leading back into the outer chamber and marched across the room, trailing Betha in his wake. His gaze snagged on the table bearing the casket.

And there's no way I'm going to risk Charin getting anywhere near that.

39. CONFRONTATION

The door to Urien's suite was unguarded. Marten took that as a good indicator the lord himself was not in residence. He tried the door handle, but it was locked.

"Let me," murmured Betha, pressing close. Marten's breathing quickened.

Concentrate, man. Concentrate.

He watched, entranced, as the woman of his dreams drew a short dagger with a snapped off tip, pressed the blunt end into the gap between the double doors, and fiddled delicately with the angle of the blade. She gave it a sharp jerk, and a quiet snick announced the failure of the lock.

Marten's eyebrows lifted.

"These locks aren't at all secure, you know." She gave a mischievous grin. "They're designed to keep out unwanted guests, not thieves. That's what guards are for."

I'm going to get all my door locks checked, Marten promised himself, even as Betha cracked the door open and peered inside.

"No one here," she confirmed, before giving him a hard stare. "You're absolutely sure you want to do this?"

"Having second thoughts about staying with me?"

For answer, she edged the door a fraction wider and slipped past it. Marten opened it further, so his sword wouldn't catch as he stepped through.

Inside, Marten barely glanced at Urien's utilitarian reception room. He hurried across the bare floor, overtaking Betha with his long strides. He winced at the sharp tap of his boots on the stone flags. Pray Chel they were correct, and Urien wasn't inside the main suite, or by now the treacherous lord would know he had company.

The inner door stood open. Marten's prayers were answered: no one was inside.

"What do these bottles look like?"

"Pocket-sized." Betha held up her thumb and a curved forefinger to demonstrate. "Clear, cut glass, and the potion is dark red."

"That should be easy to find, assuming he keeps a store here."

Betha stared around the large room lined with cupboards, chests, and shelves. "They might be anywhere." She sounded defeated before they'd begun. "And this is only one of his rooms."

Marten set his jaw. He refused to wait for the god to come and attack on His terms.

"Start looking," he ordered, and waved Betha to one side of the room while he took the other. They flung open drawers and cabinets, and swept shelves, discarding their contents onto the floor, heedless of the mess.

"Is this it?" Marten held up one bottle triumphantly even as he reached into the rear of the open cabinet to extract a second.

"You only had to ask," said a silken voice from the doorway. "No need to ransack my rooms."

Marten spun round to face Urien, and his heart faltered. Beside Urien, Edlund grappled with Betha, one meaty fist clamped around her throat, the other tangled in her hair. She clawed at his fleshy hands with her nails, but although he snarled, he didn't relax his grip.

Urien smiled a snake's wide grin. "To think, the king has chosen to pay me a visit, and precisely when I needed to see him." He made an insultingly shallow bow. "If only you'd told me you were coming, I would have had the place prepared."

Marten scanned the debris of their search littering the floor, and then shot a quick glance to each side of where he poised with his muscles tensed for action. A couple of substantial tables and several chairs stood between him and Urien. And the door.

You didn't come here to run. You came here to finish this.

Keeping his eyes fixed on his wily opponent, Marten lofted the two bottles of remedy, one in each hand, to shoulder height. "Looking for these, Lord Urien?"

He snapped his elbows straight, and opened his fingers. The bottles crashed to the floor where they shattered into myriad shards of glass that splattered across his boots. "Oops."

To his dismay, Urien merely smiled, and reached into a pocket. He drew out an identical bottle, still more than half full.

"Fortunately for me, I still have this one."

Making an elaborate show, Urien extracted the stopper, raised the bottle to his lips, and tipped a few drops of carmine fluid onto his extended tongue. With his head tilted back, the blobs of liquid rolled down into his mouth. He swallowed, and smacked his lips.

"Ahh, the sweet taste of victory."

He lifted the bottle for a repeat performance, but Marten was distracted by a commotion beyond Urien. He didn't witness the moment the heel of Betha's borrowed boots landed on Edlund's instep, but he heard the almighty crack, and the accompanying shriek of pain. Urien had barely registered the event when Betha's hand whipped out, sending her broken dagger slicing through the air. It struck the back of Urien's hand.

With a howl, Urien dropped the bottle. Like those Marten had already destroyed, it smashed, splattering the remaining medicine across the rug, and over Urien's feet. Drops of blood from the back of Urien's hand drizzled down to mingle with the like-coloured fluid.

A sliver of hope buoyed Marten's spirits. Unless Urien had another stash close to hand, they'd done what they'd set out to do. The question was, how much had the man already consumed? And how long would the effects last?

"Keep that bitch under control, Ed. Remember, the master still has plans for her."

Marten's mouth went dry. *What plans?*

Face glowing scarlet with a blend of pain and rage, Edlund employed his superior weight to pin Betha against a bookcase. From where Marten stood, he could see little of her slender form, engulfed as it was by the corpulent lord's fleshy body.

Edlund twisted his neck and scowled over his shoulder at Marten. "Couldn't you have done the decent thing, and died in the riot I so carefully arranged for you? It would have been so much neater."

"*You* killed Lorndar?"

Edlund's scowl turned to a smirk. "Well, not personally, you understand. I wouldn't soil myself by dealing with a grubby little tradesman like that. Perhaps if *you* hadn't, he might still be alive."

Marten tasted bile. *He killed Lorndar because I listened to the man. Because I was willing to consider a craft worker's proposal.*

"Enough!" Urien thundered at a startling volume. Marten's knees turned to water as the deity's tell-tale argent glow bloomed into life around Urien, flaring like a candle in a strong wind.

Marten's crumb of hope vanished. *I guess he took enough.*

The glow strengthened, and within its tenuous boundaries a perfect figure gradually coalesced. With no escape and no choices, Marten flipped over the bigger of the two tables, and squatted down behind it.

Chel, if you're going to help me, now would be a good time.

Nothing. No feather-light touch, no comforting warmth, just a chill that trickled down his exposed rear.

"You may try to hide," boomed Charin's awful voice, shaking Marten's bones. "But it will not save you. I have waited a long time for this moment. Come out, and face your end with the pride of your lineage, little king."

Marten peeped over the top edge of the table. "That's your best offer?"

The entire room, and possibly the whole palace, shook with Charin's laughter.

"You have earned yourself a swift death, boy. I might even consider letting you return, one day."

Marten's breath caught. Until this moment, he hadn't considered his future. Could Charin keep his spirit locked away forever? Surely the rebirth of souls was Chel's province, not Charin's?

Charin read his thoughts. "Did you not know, youngling, that my demons feast on mortal souls? Why do you think there are fewer of you now than before?"

Goddess! Is that *why we have fewer children?* Marten felt sick. He gulped a couple of times before raising a retort.

"What will your demons do," he asked, "when you run out of souls to feed them? Will they devour you, too?"

The god replied with a thunderous blast of energy. Lightning bolts slammed into the wood of Marten's defence barrier with such force it shot backward, throwing him to the ground.

That saved his life. The crackling streamers of energy sizzled through the air above where he lay, stunned, on the floor behind what was left of the stout table.

Heavy footsteps cut through the ringing in his ears and he scrambled away to crouch behind the other, flimsier table. One more volley like that, and he'd be burnt to a crisp.

Deadly laughter rolled around the walls. "This is far more entertaining than the last pair."

Marten dared peek around the edge of the table. Charin's head tilted in a parody of musing, a cold smile curving his perfect lips. "My demons ate well, that night. The girl was lusty. And the babe? Such a tender morsel." Charin met his gaze with amusement smouldering in the depthless silver eyes. "You didn't know, did you?"

Marten felt the blood drain from his face. Nonni had been *pregnant*? Oh, dear Chel, this monster had consigned his *child* to oblivion.

Enraged, Marten flung himself to his feet and, brandishing his sword, charged the god. Next moment, he was sailing through the air. His back crashed against the open door of a tall cabinet and he, along with the cabinet, tumbled to the floor. The sword flew from his hand, clattering across the flags to land at Charin's feet.

The god stooped to pick up the blade, the size of a toy in his huge hand. He gave it an experimental swish back and forth.

"Such clumsy weapons you humans create. At least elves temper steel with filaments of their souls." He returned his attention to the king, who was struggling to extricate himself from the smashed furniture. Marten winced and gasped as his abused back muscles spasmed.

"You'd like to die in your own fashion? Is that it?" Charin glanced round. "You!" He pointed a finger at Edlund. "Kill him."

Edlund shrank back, shaking his head. "I'm no swordsman."

"Pah! You are in the service of your god! Do you think I would let you lose?"

All colour drained from Edlund's flushed face. Without warning, the portly lord turned and bolted, displaying an unexpected agility, considering his broken foot. Betha slithered to the floor, gasping, no longer crushed up against the wall by her tormentor's weight.

"Useless bag of flesh."

Charin did not seem particularly put out by the departure of His cowardly servant. He stretched out the hand not grasping the sword and flicked His fingers. An ominously dark slash cut the air.

The ragged edges of the unnatural aperture rippled, as if disturbed by an unfelt breeze, and an acrid odour seeped into the room. Marten squinted apprehensively at the bilious chartreuse glow pulsing within the fissure, interrupted by chaotic flashes of amber and scarlet.

The god contorted His wrist in a sickeningly fluid manner, as if His arm was boneless, and a *thing* crawled through the breach in the air.

Terror drove Marten to his feet. The molten metal stench of the monster evoked memories of the night before. Of the creature in the casket.

If this wasn't the same beast, it was surely its kin.

A huge head came first, horned and tusked, with unblinking eyes of dull ruby. Its tapered snout was topped by a pair of flared nostrils which extended half the length of the skull, their edges fringed with tendrils that writhed as if in constant torment.

The body that followed was serpentine, recalling the shape of the talisman, complete with four stubby legs ending in needle-pointed claws. Gleaming scales of scarlet and emerald rasped over one another as it hauled the length of its body, followed by an elongated, razor-finned tail, through the shrinking gash in the ether.

It slithered to the floor, where it squatted, scenting the air like a hound.

The room heated up. Marten struggled to breathe, the furnace-hot air sucking the oxygen from his lungs. His nostril hairs shrivelled.

He had no idea how to fight a demon.

He tried one last, desperate plea. *If you truly want me to live, please, Chel, I need your help now.*

He imagined the feel of Her arms around him. Recalled the sound of Her voice, the warmth of Her comfort.

But She did not answer.

Marten composed himself. *This must be what you meant, then: that I have the courage to face my death alone. I only wish I knew how this would serve my people.*

He drew himself up, and stared over the head of the hell-beast straight into Charin's silver gaze.

"You are but one side of my deity. I commend my soul to Chel's mercy."

Was that a flicker of uncertainty? Or annoyance? Charin's

exquisite features twisted into a grotesque mask. The creature at his feet whined. Neither moved to attack.

Marten's innards knotted with dread, but a whisper of confidence sparked into life, fed by his growing anger. This demon, or its kin, had devoured Nonni and his child.

He narrowed his eyes at the beast, licked his burning lips, and cleared his throat. Once more, he summoned the sensation of Chel's protective arms around his shoulders, pouring all the strength that memory evoked into his command.

"In Chel's name, demon, begone."

Scales rasped loudly, grating against Marten's ears as the beast thrashed, and keened. Shards of wood from the shattered table spewed outward from its lashing tail, and Marten yelped as a sliver cut into his cheek. He ducked as the beast's whipping tail sheared the air where his head had been but a moment before, and jumped back to what he hoped would be beyond its range.

Still, it made no direct attack. Gathering his courage, Marten repeated his command, louder this time.

"In Chel's name, begone!"

Marten's ears rang with the strength of the creature's angry roar, but to his astonishment its vivid colours began to dull, fading slowly to pastels. The extraordinary heat in the room diminished. The gleaming scales lost their lustre, turning translucent. And then the terrifying body started to shrink. It withered like a plant starved of water, shrivelling to the size of a fist before, with a resounding *pop*, it vanished.

"How?" Charin's rage buffeted him with hurricane force. "No mortal can defy me like that, unless…" His face became vacant for a moment. "Ah, I see *She* has been training you." He gusted a disappointed sigh. "Very well, I shall deal with you myself, after all."

His hands lifted, energy sparking around them in jagged spikes. Marten's hair stood on end, but inside, all he felt was an incredible, calm satisfaction. He had successfully rebuffed Charin, even if he was still going to die. No man could say more.

Firebolts built within the cages of Charin's fingers. His divine lips curved upward—and loosed a terrible scream.

Marten dived sideways as untargeted lightning shot across the room to strike a chandelier and the top corner of a dresser, both of which exploded. He flung a protective arm over his head as Charin shrieked again. The god's celestial body wavered in opacity, with Urien's compact form becoming intermittently visible within the fluctuating light.

He fell to one knee.

With a furious howl, the god vanished. Marten stared in astonishment at the dagger impaling his opponent's left calf.

Behind Urien, Betha sprawled in a crumpled heap inside the door Edlund had left open when he fled.

Marten slipped a knife into each hand. Even crippled, Urien was still dangerous. The hilt of Marten's sword nestled in the injured lord's fist, and his small eyes gleamed with rage. With a growl, Urien reached his spare hand behind himself to jerk the dagger free. The copper taint of free-running blood mingled with the lingering aroma of demon.

"Don't think you're getting out of here alive," Urien snarled as he clambered upright.

Marten didn't waste time replying; he attacked while Urien was still off balance.

Urien swayed out of range of Marten's short knives, taking an experimental swing with his purloined sword. Balanced as it was for Marten's greater height and reach, Urien's aim was slightly off. Marten jumped back out of reach.

Here we go again, only this time, he isn't going to let me win.

Marten hurled one of his daggers as a distraction, and when Urien danced aside, Marten stooped to grab one leg of a shattered table.

Urien's face contorted as he sidled towards Marten. Clearly the pain was getting to him. Or was it a bluff? Marten determined not to take anything for granted.

With a feint to the left, Urien sliced the blade towards Marten's ribcage. The stout table leg blocked the blow, but Urien took the opportunity to snatch a heavy decanter from the shelf beside him, and throw it at Marten's head. Even as he dodged to one side, Marten knew he'd made the wrong move.

He twisted desperately away, and the sword's tip grazed his shoulder instead of impaling it.

Urien grinned. "You're learning. Pity for you it won't be quick enough."

Rotating his sore shoulder, Marten stalked around Urien, staying beyond the shorter man's reach. Urien spotted Marten's objective before he reached it: a small, decorative shield, mounted on the wall above a serving table bearing wine flagons.

"I don't think so."

Urien attacked in a blur of sword strokes, forcing Marten to relinquish his goal. He backed away, seeking anything else he might use to his advantage. An array of gleaming cutlery caught his attention, and he snatched up a handful of meat skewers.

"Planning on a mid-fight snack, are we?"

Marten ignored the jibe. He passed his knife into his left hand along with the table leg, and palmed a spread of skewers in his right. Urien lunged towards the shield Marten had been going after, and Marten threw the skewers after him.

Two of them slammed home, penetrating Urien's upper arm. The sword fell from his limp hand.

Urien shrieked a curse, and Marten ducked, dodging a metal box flying towards his head. Urien plucked the skewers free, and discarded them with a clatter. Then he lunged towards Betha.

Marten yelled a warning, but Betha was still too stunned to respond, her head barely lifted from the floor when Urien grabbed her by the hair.

"I'll cut her throat," he hissed. Crouching over her, he

yanked her head back, and pressed a slender knife against her skin. Marten froze.

Urien narrowed his eyes and gave a lazy smile. "You really fell for the bitch, didn't you? Poor fool. I'm betting you won't stand aside and watch her die."

"Please. You don't have to do this." Marten shuffled his feet, checking for anything beneath his soles that might throw him off balance. He would only have one chance. He dropped the table leg and ran his hands through his hair, palming a tiny throwing dagger from a hidden sheath in one long cuff as he did so. He hugged both hands around the back of his neck.

"I thought your master had plans for the lady?"

His reminder fetched an instant of doubt to Urien's face. An instant Marten seized.

As did Betha.

She grabbed the blade at her throat with both hands, heedless of it slicing into her palms, at the same instant as Marten loosed his throwing knife. It struck home with a meaty *thunk* in Urien's upper torso, and the treacherous lord's shrill scream fetched a satisfying glow of warmth to Marten's belly.

Urien's nerveless hand relinquished the knife he'd held to Betha's throat. With a deft twist, she reversed the blade and plunged the sharp point into his gut. He dropped to his knees, eyes bulging, and hands scrabbling ineffectually at where his own weapon impaled him. His breath came in panicked gasps as Marten closed the distance between them.

The king bent over his duplicitous subject, to peer closely into Urien's glazing eyes.

"Haven't you heard? I enjoy inflicting pain," he said sardonically, and drove the knife deeper into Urien's chest.

Betha elbowed Urien in the ribs and he toppled sideways. His last words bubbled up with a gush of scarlet blood. "Charin will have you yet. He has plans for…"

Urien's final exhalation whistled out, and the blood flowing from his mouth decreased to a trickle, then a few drips. Marten stood over the body. He had to lock his knees to remain on his feet, his muscles trembled so violently.

Nonni. Our child. He killed them. Their souls are gone forever. What sort of monster can do such a thing?

Tears clouded his sight. He blinked quickly before focusing on Betha. Astonishment tangled with grief, and he took a conscious grip on his rapid breathing, forcing it to slow.

We survived.

The tension in his muscles began to fade, draining towards the ground and out through the soles of his boots.

We survived, he repeated to himself. *Chel saw fit to spare our souls.*

Chel's parting words to him the night before echoed through his head. *"Magic is born of the soul. That is where you must seek your answer."*

His gaze rested on the crown of Betha's fair head. His heart ached when he imagined being apart from her. His rage at Edlund, and at Urien, for threatening her, reverberated through his entire being. He would—and had—killed to protect her, and he knew without question, he would do so again.

He pictured Charin, blasting divine lightning from his hands. If that was what the Temple called a miracle, and what Betha's beautiful soul produced was evil magic, then the clerics had it all wrong!

That's *what you were trying to tell me, wasn't it?*

He didn't need a reply from Chel to know he'd finally seen the truth. Magic wasn't either holy or evil, it was just magic. The difference was the user's intent.

He shook his head, astounded he'd been so blinkered, for so long. To think, he'd condemned Betha to suffer when she didn't need to, and she'd stayed true to her promise to him, no matter the cost. Who could be worthier to become his queen than the woman he'd wronged through prejudice and stubborn reaction to events?

Besides, Marten could no longer imagine a future without

Betha. He loved her. He wanted to share the rest of his life with her. And that mattered more to him than any political alliance, the approval of his advisors, or even the religious dictates of the Temple.

Betha stirred, pushing herself up off the floor. Wondering if she would ever be able to forgive him for his stupidity, Marten offered a hand to help her rise.

To his dismay, she shrank away.

"Betha—"

The odour of relaxing bowels rose from Urien's corpse.

Betha sniffed and shuddered. Without a word, she spun, and hurried towards the door with her bleeding hands tucked into her armpits.

"You're hurt!" Marten protested, desperate to explain himself, but terrified of what her reaction might be.

She flung an answer over her shoulder, but her strides never faltered. "So are you."

Suddenly a host of varied pains hit Marten all at once: his shoulder, his back, a gash in his upper arm he hadn't noticed before.

He limped after her. "Slow down!" he implored.

But Betha lengthened her steps, slipped through the door, and vanished into the passageway beyond.

40. GUARDS

Betha fled along the palace's eerily empty corridors, ignoring the pains in her hands and her shoulder. Before, such sensations would have kindled a thrill she'd have savoured at leisure. Now, they were of no consequence, aside from the mess her bleeding palms were making on her borrowed shirt.

She gulped, and increased her speed, racing around corners, heedless of who might be coming the other way. Not since the coup had the palace been this deserted, and even if she did run into anyone she knew, Betha no longer cared how her contemporaries regarded her. All she wanted was to escape her thoughts, her feelings, her desperate love for a man she could never have.

When she'd looked up from Urien's body to see Marten standing above her, tall and strong—a mortal man who'd defied the god and lived—Betha had finally accepted he was beyond her reach. She'd been thinking of him as a potential husband, not as a divinely appointed king. How egotistic of her! Who was she, after all? A lowly widow of a minor House. A nobody. Even if he hadn't rejected her because of her magic, she was too low born to command the love of such a powerful monarch.

No, Marten had done the right thing when he'd dismissed her. She could come to terms with that, though it burned in a manner she assumed must be how others experienced pain.

How did they put up with it? She felt like she was being torn apart from the inside out.

The great double doors of the royal suite loomed before her. A single guard stood to attention outside, and he made no move to stop her as she pushed past him, only saying,

"My lady, there's a—" before she slammed the door in his face.

Betha stumbled to a halt, scanning Marten's reception room through a veil of tears. Why had she come here? Why hadn't she gone to her own rooms? What was she *thinking*?

She turned to leave, just as Marten stepped into the room.

And saw, too late, the dark shadow of a woman hiding behind the open door.

"Ware!" she shrieked.

* * * * * * *

Too many things whirled through Marten's mind at once. His love for Betha, and how her apparent rejection pained him more than any knife or sword cut he'd ever received. Nonni, his child, and their hideous end. Davi's death. Edlund arranging the riot by having Lorndar murdered. Had the guards managed to bring the city under control yet? The palace seemed empty. Presumably his nobles were hiding in their plush, comfortable apartments, while the majority of the guards were out on the streets, striving to restore order.

How many people had been hurt, or died, because he'd not acted swiftly and called a council meeting immediately after Lorndar put his proposal forward?

A solitary guard stood outside the royal suite, the second nowhere to be seen.

"Sire! Mistress—"

Marten cut him off. "Yes, I know," he said. He'd seen Betha enter the suite before the door closed behind her. By the lesser title the guard had used, he mustn't have recognised Betha, dressed as she was in oddments of Marten's own clothing.

He gave the door a hard shove and strode in.

* * * * * * *

Betha's heart lurched as Marten twisted and dipped to one side in response to her warning cry. The tip of the assassin's blade sliced through his tunic, missing his skin by a hair's breadth, but the move threw him off balance, and he staggered a few steps with his hands outstretched. The woman—Marganie, the seamstress, Betha recognised with shock—yanked her dagger free from Marten's clothing and, with a maniacal leer, plunged it towards the king's exposed neck, even as he spun to face her.

Betha flung herself in front of Marten.

"No!" Marten's howl of denial cut through Betha's ears, even as the blade drove into her chest. It slid smoothly between two ribs, stopping only when the short quillions to either side of the hilt kissed her skin.

Sweet agony flared through her body, transforming with shocking speed from the customary exhilaration to something utterly foreign. Her legs failed and she sagged back against Marten. Pain careened along her nerves, radiating outward from the invading metal. The blood pumping through her arteries mutated into liquid torment. Every breath scorched her lungs, pain like she'd never experienced before.

Poison, her stunned mind recognised. *The blade must be poisoned!*

Betha's clouding vision registered a struggle in front of her, and she identified Lady Risada grappling with the assassin.

Why would Marganie want to harm Marten? I don't understand, but sweet Chel, thank you for letting me save him. I've done my duty; my king is safe. I'm ready to return to you.

Her stomach cramped, and a shocking realisation hit her like a gut punch.

Oh goddess, I can't! The baby: I can't let it die. Marten just lost one child, I can't do that to him.

Her whole body convulsed. She could hear Marten's frantic voice, but his words made no sense. She couldn't speak. She couldn't tell him. She couldn't explain why she must break her promise. Her eyes stung as if she cried blood, and the world spun towards darkness. She tried desperately to narrow her focus, to isolate the damage she needed to heal, but like dye spreading through water, the poison permeated her whole body.

Had she left it too late? This was an entirely new challenge; she'd never tried to heal herself from a poisoning. Could her magic even cure her, or would she, by trying, be breaking her word to no avail? Marten would never know, but she would die with guilt shrouding her soul.

I have to try. For Marten.

* * * * * * *

Entering the royal suite in pursuit of the king, Risada evaluated the situation with barely a pause. She whipped out her small dagger and, with her other hand, grabbed Marten's assailant by the hair. She jerked back on the coarse grey strands, astounded when she recognised the aging woman.

Whatever would possess the royal seamstress, Marganie, to attack the king?

"No, no, NO!" Marten's cries swept over her, but she ignored them for the moment, concentrating on securing the scene.

Marganie had not come prepared for a second strike. As soon as Risada held a blade to her throat, all the fight in the old woman died. Her shoulders slumped and her empty hands fell by her sides.

Not a professional assassin, then, but an opportunist. Marganie must hold a grudge against the king. No doubt whatever it was would come out later, when she was questioned, but for now, Marten was safe, and Risada needed him to come with her immediately if she was to save Rustam.

Still, she knew better than to take anything for granted. Marganie might yet be hiding some deadly surprise. Risada wheeled around to face the horrified guard who'd come in behind her to see what the commotion was all about.

"This woman tried to kill the king," Risada stated bluntly. "Bind her, and take her to the prince's rooms. My assistant, Grendle, will show you where to secure her."

The guard's eyes bulged. "Surely, my lady, the cells—"

Risada cut him off. "This is a security matter, which falls under my husband's authority, and now mine."

The guard gave a brisk salute, even though his eyes stood out from his white face. He knew what sort of authority the prince had dealt in.

Once the prisoner was removed, Risada braced herself to deal with the aftermath.

Marten sat on the floor with the unconscious Lady Betha cradled in his arms. He'd plucked the bloody dagger from her chest, and tossed it aside. Tears streamed down his face as he rocked back and forth, repeating Betha's name, over, and over.

Risada caught her bottom lip between her teeth. But for Betha's intervention, she—and the entire royal family—would have died in the fire that destroyed the Great Hall. Risada wondered if Marten knew what a debt of gratitude they all owed the young lady, though she doubted it. Halnashead had kept many of the details of that day to himself, especially after he'd recruited Betha as a fledgling spy.

Marten might not even have any inkling that his uncle had set Betha to watch over him. What was clear, however, was that he'd fallen for the attractive widow.

Risada crouched down beside them. Blood flowed sluggishly from a jagged puncture between two of Betha's ribs. Risada put the tip of one finger to her throat. A faint, erratic pulse still whispered there, but for how much longer?

Wise to Betha's unusual ability, Risada couldn't understand why she hadn't healed the injury yet. Was she hiding her secret from Marten?

Risada gritted her teeth. If that was what Betha was doing, it was going to get her killed, and Risada needed Marten to come down to the cells right away. They didn't have time for this.

"Betha!" Risada snapped out the name, and jostled the girl's shoulder. Her head rolled limply. "Heal yourself, girl. I need Marten to come with me, now."

The king raised a bruised look towards her. "She won't," he said flatly. "I forbade her to use her magic. She's too faithful to disobey me, and now she's going to die. It's all my fault."

Risada stared at him aghast. "What are you saying? Why would you *do* such a thing?"

Marten sniffed. "I didn't understand. I believed magic was evil. Annasala said—"

"Arghhh!" Risada yelled in frustration. "It always comes back to Annasala! Marten. I need your help right now. Please. Rusty's life depends on it."

"I can't leave Betha." Marten shook his head again. "I should have told her to use her magic. I should have told her I love her. I have to stay here and keep telling her, in case she hears me. I have to try."

"Please, Marten," Risada pleaded, "Sala's going to execute Rusty. You're the only one that can overrule her." Desperation tightened her throat. "Please!"

She dared grab a handful of Marten's tunic—an unforgivable assault on the king's person—but she was beyond caring. Rusty was going to die if she didn't bring Marten to the cells. She tugged and yanked, but with no result. Marten ignored her completely, continuing to rock Betha, talking to her, cajoling her, ordering her to heal herself, while his tears mingled with the discoloured blood seeping from her wound.

Recognition gripped Risada in an icy embrace.

"Marten. Marten! The blade was poisoned. I'm sorry, but she's not coming back from that."

But still he refused to respond. Battling the constricting bands squeezing her throat, Risada leant close to his ear, praying to Chel the distraught king would hear her words, and understand them when the inevitable came to pass.

"I'm sorry, Marten. I'm sorry for you, I'm sorry for her, but when this is over, please remember my plea. Rusty will die if you don't come to the cells and stop this execution. I'm going to hold them off for as long as I can, but I need you. *We* need you. Please come as soon as you can."

The calm of resolution settled over her. Marten would either come, or he wouldn't. All she could do for now was to delay things as long as she possibly could.

Before she shut the now unguarded door behind her, Risada spared one last glance for the ill-fated lovers. Betha's love must have been as fierce as Marten's, for her to obey him at the cost of her own life. Annasala's prejudices had wrought unbelievable harm within the royal family, and would do so again if Risada could not find a way to resolve the current situation.

Risada snapped the door closed, and raced as fast as her frustratingly weakened body would allow, to try to save the man she'd finally acknowledged she couldn't bear to be parted from again.

* * * * * * *

Betha swam in a shimmering sea of pain. Sparkling pinpricks relentlessly jabbed at her, both inside and out, and for the first time since childhood, she knew agony, without the expectation of joy. She writhed in desperation, frantic to escape the relentless torment as the invading toxin infiltrated every tissue, every organ, of her body. She was vaguely aware of Marten holding her, restraining her flopping limbs, but she couldn't feel his touch, or hear his voice.

Darkness battled with light, cool dimness offering the sweet temptation of oblivion. Betha's life teetered on the brink of a decision. Nothingness or pain. Agony or blissful limbo.

No! Betha screamed inside her head. *I can't. I mustn't. Oh goddess, it hurts so much I want it to go away—*

A pulsating flicker snagged her attention: the tiniest of

flames, deep inside her belly, waging its own battle for life.

A fierce urge to protect that little spark blasted through the pain.

Marten's baby. My *baby. I have to save my baby.*

The fluttering glint grew steadier, stronger. More stable. A halo of silver light formed around the embryo, forming a protective cocoon that repelled the insidious poison. Betha's racing heart stuttered to a halt before restarting in a slower, more serene tempo. She drew on a strength she didn't know she possessed; the strength of a mother fighting for her child.

The protective shell of light thickened and grew like a snowball rolling down a hill, gathering substance as it goes. Thick tendrils extended from its surface, finger-like protrusions seeking anchor points within Betha's abdomen. Wherever they came into contact with corrupted flesh, they fanned out, blanketing and infiltrating it, overwhelming the dark canker with brightness.

Betha finally grasped what she must do to heal herself. With imaginary fingers, she seized multiple strands of the silver light and thrust them into her veins, flushing the lethal intruder from her blood. The darkness paled, stubbornly clinging on to small spaces within her body cavity, but as the radiance consolidated and expanded, so the corruption grudgingly blanched, until it faded completely away.

Even then, the brilliance continued to grow, overwhelming Betha's inner vision. Sparkles danced across a featureless silver landscape to stretch endlessly in all directions. The scent of her mother's favourite blooms fetched a ghost of a smile to Betha's lips.

"Am I dead?" she asked.

"No," replied a gentle voice. "Your thread continues."

Betha's innards turned to mush. "Chel?" she squeaked. Why would the goddess speak with her? She was a nobody.

A speck of intense lustre resolved into a huge pair of gleaming eyes. Barely distinguishable against the luminous background, nevertheless, Betha knew without doubt it was the deity who watched her.

"Your pattern in my weave is yet to be completed, daughter."

Betha gulped, even though she knew the body she inhabited here, in this special place, wasn't real. "I don't want that future," she dared to disagree, "if it's a future without Marten's approval. I've broken my word; he'll never forgive me."

Although she couldn't see the goddess's hand, she felt the gentle fingers stroke her cheek. "You saved his unborn child."

Her vision blurred. "That may not be enough."

"And yet, it may."

Chel's murmur wafted from a vast distance, and Betha blinked. When she regained her focus, she found herself gazing up into Marten's hazel eyes.

"Praise Chel!" Relief stretched his mouth into a ludicrously wide grin before he leaned over to kiss her forehead. "Betha, I should have told you, I *tried* to tell you. I thought I'd lost you!"

He hugged her so tightly, Betha feared she might suffocate. When he relaxed enough for her to extricate a hand, she reached up and pushed aside a lock of wavy brown hair that had fallen across his face.

"Tell me what?"

* * * * * * *

Slumped on a bench at the back of his cell, Rustam licked his numb lips and stared blearily out through the bars. Hestane gave him vertigo, and a pounding headache, making it hard to focus. Perhaps he was hallucinating? For some reason, his faulty vision insisted on showing him a truly odd assortment of individuals standing guard outside his cell.

And why were they facing a small troop of people dressed in soldiers' uniforms?

If he hadn't known better, Rustam would have sworn his jailors comprised one royal sentry, one gardener, and a kitchen maid. The soldier's crisp and fancily decorated uniform declared it to be an outfit for show, and not for fighting, although the naked sword in the man's hand shone with the threat of a well-honed weapon. The second man, feet encased in oversized, dust-covered boots, sported a few stray hedge clippings embedded in his unruly black hair, above a smock streaked with vegetable sap. The shears dangling from his belt ended in an unusually sharp point, and the hoe held loosely in both hands appeared to have a wicked sharp edge. The scrawny kitchen maid brandished a large pan lid and a gutting knife with alarming confidence.

Rustam rubbed his eyes, but the motley crew didn't go away.

"Stand aside, you three," ordered a familiar voice. Rustam's sister, Princess Annasala. His sluggish gaze wandered over the group of figures standing opposite, crammed up against the rear wall of the corridor. His muzzy brain eventually identified Annasala, along with six soldiers, and Sister Valaree, and it dawned on him the strange trio in front of his cell were keeping the regular guard at bay.

Anger roused him, somewhat. He was sure Annasala had been about to rescind his sentence when Valaree had crashed onto the scene and taken charge. The priestess wielded an invisible hold over Annasala that his sister couldn't, or wouldn't, challenge, even at the expense of her brother's life.

Bastard brother, he corrected himself. Even so, the Annasala of his youth would never have capitulated to another's authority the way this tragically broken version did. If only—

Rustam clamped down on that line of conjecture. 'If only' never got anyone anywhere. The coup had overtaken them all, and the survivors each had their own invisible legacies to contend with.

That didn't salve the pain in his soul, each time he was forced to confront the heartrending transformation of his once brave and independent sister.

Annasala's voice rang out again, and Rustam squinted,

trying to force his wayward eyes into focus.

"Risada, what are you doing? Stop! Come back here!"

A wave of dizziness pulled at Rustam. He squeezed his eyes closed, and when he reopened them, Risada had joined the incongruous trio. Alarm sharpened Rustam's attention.

Risada took up an easy stance alongside Rustam's other defenders. Easy, but potentially deadly. "Please, Sala, think again," she implored. "You don't have to do this. Wait for the king."

Valaree stepped in front of the princess.

"This is the law," said the priestess, chopping the air with a stiff hand for emphasis. "Princess Annasala has every right to condemn this man. The king's presence is not required; any member of the royal family may execute the laws of the land."

Rustam watched Risada's spine stiffen, but she ignored the priestess, keeping her focus on Annasala.

"Then I invoke my own rights, as regent for my son, who is the current heir to the throne. I may not have your royal title, Annasala, but I have some authority, in Halson's name."

"Halson?" Annasala raised her eyebrows. "You named him Halson?"

Risada's voice lowered, became softer. "He is your father's son, Sala. It seemed wholly appropriate. I trust you approve?"

Annasala bit her lip. "I think it's—"

"Enough of this!" Valaree snapped. "We are here to execute this magic user. Family matters can wait."

Rustam tensed, watching Risada's feet slip into a fighting stance. "What's the rush?" she asked. "Afraid you'll lose your chance, if we wait for the king?" She spoke to Annasala again. "Marten has had a change of heart. He can save Rusty. He can save your brother."

"The king would never condone magic," Valaree said hastily, not allowing Annasala to speak. "Not after it was used to kill Prince Halnashead."

The small hairs on the back of Rustam's neck lifted.

Eddies of gathering power spiralled around the priestess, and sparks gathered within her cupped hands.

Blood pounded through Rustam's head. Awe, that Risada was willing to challenge the dangerous priestess in his defence, warred with fear for her life. Valaree's powers were of a nature no assassin's skills could combat.

"Risada!" he called, as clearly as his numb lips would permit. "Don't do this. Don't sacrifice yourself for me. You have a son to raise—"

"Don't you dare!"

Rustam's teeth clashed as his insensate mouth snapped shut. The salty tang of blood told him he'd been too slow to get his tongue out of the way. Using his cuff, he wiped a string of bloody drool from his chin. Hestane was no respecter of a person's dignity.

Risada didn't glance round at him, but there was no question who her words were aimed at. "You got us into this in the first place, with your ridiculous notion of noble sacrifice. Did you ever stop to think how that would make *me* feel? You'd be dead, but I'd have to live with it for the rest of my life. Or didn't that occur to you?"

Rustam dropped his chin as his cheeks prickled with heat. He made no effort to answer Risada's question; they both knew he hadn't thought that far ahead.

Crackling drew his attention back to Valaree. The coruscating light caged between her fingers lit her face from below, lending her terracotta skin a terrifying metallic sheen. Rustam narrowed his eyes to slits, raging inside against his unresponsive body and his blocked magic. There was nothing he could do to save Risada.

"Stop!" King Marten's command whipped through the air.

The glow between Valaree's palms winked out. All the soldiers, including the one standing in Rustam's defence, came smartly to attention. Risada's shoulders slumped. Annasala looked like she wanted to be anywhere but standing next to Valaree.

Rustam sagged back against the wall of his cell. His knees

trembled and he gave thanks to Chel he hadn't tried to stand yet, because if he had, he would have fallen back down.

Marten marched into the floor space separating the two opposing parties and treated each side to the royal glare. Rustam noted some raised eyebrows, and felt his own shooting up to join them as he took in the king's dishevelled appearance, his torn tunic, and streaks of what was almost certainly blood, spattered across both skin and clothing.

"Sire," Valaree began boldly. While Rustam could only see the back of the king's head, the effect of his silent regard was instant. Valaree bowed her head.

"Sister Valaree, your presence here is no longer required." Marten pivoted towards Annasala, before snapping his head back towards Valaree. "In fact, your presence anywhere in the palace is not welcome. Go back to the Temple. I will be discussing your conduct with your superiors."

"Marten, she has the right to be here. I invited her," Annasala protested.

"And I am withdrawing that entitlement."

"You can't do that!"

Marten drew himself up taller, and Rustam's eyebrows twitched upward. When had the meek young man become this self-assured ruler?

"I already have," he said. "And cousin, you would do well to remember who is monarch here."

Annasala's face crumpled. She dipped her gaze to the ground and left it there as Valaree stalked away, escorted by two of the guardsmen.

Marten glanced round at Rustam's defenders and did a double take. He took a couple of steps back, to give himself space to study them in more detail.

"Interesting troops you have there, cousin Risada."

"Indeed," she agreed in a non-committal tone. Rustam watched her whisper a few words to the trio in dismissal before they departed, slipping past Annasala and the remaining palace guardsmen with their heads held high.

Marten watched their exit with an incredulous stare.

"I'm not wrong, am I?" he said. "That *was* my missing door guard."

Despite the wooziness of his drugged state, Rustam almost burst with pride at Risada's self-assurance as she treated the king to a sly smile.

"You didn't think your uncle would leave you without some of his best players close at hand, did you?"

41. THE PRINCE'S PROTÉGÉS

"Well, that's something I hope never to witness again," Marten commented as he shrugged out of his cloak. A pang of sadness hit him when Betha took it from his hands, instead of Davi.

She rubbed her palm up and down his arm, and warmth ignited in his belly.

"I must admit," Betha said, "I didn't expect him to grovel, let alone weep like that."

"Edlund was a bully, and like so many bullies, he was a coward. If he'd stood still and faced his end with courage, it wouldn't have been so messy."

Betha led the way across Marten's reception room. "But it pleased the crowd," she said. "Did you hear them baying for his blood? They got justice for their martyred hero."

Marten snorted. "Lorndar, a hero?"

He pushed his way through the door into his sitting room. Something nagged at the back of his mind, but he had every intention of having a sizeable drink before he faced whatever fresh calamity might have arisen while he'd been overseeing Edlund's execution. He reached for the brandy, a sad smile tugging at his lips as he recalled that the last time he'd shared the bottle had been with Padrus.

He poured two large measures and handed one to Betha. "Lorndar was a troublemaker, but he knew how to appeal to the common folk. I wouldn't have wished him dead, but I must admit, his absence is going to make drafting a new law based on his proposal a lot simpler."

"And the people already love you for it. They're calling you 'the commoners' king'."

Marten canted a bemused glance at Betha as he lowered himself into his favourite padded chair. "They are? I'm not sure how I feel about that title."

Betha bent down to kiss him. "Take the approbation while you can. It only needs another crisis to reverse opinion."

Following a brisk knock, the door swung open to admit Risada, with Halson cradled in her arms. Rustam followed, a step behind.

"Come in, come in." Marten beckoned. He stood up again and reached for a couple of goblets. "Drink?"

"Yes, please," Rustam accepted, even as Risada shook her head.

"Thank you, but I find I need to keep my wits about me when I'm handling this little tyke."

"Handling him?" Betha laughed as she stood on tiptoe to peer into the blanket-wrapped bundle. "What is he: a foal?"

"Rusty would probably have preferred if he was," Risada said, "though I hear he's got one of his own to play with, just as soon as he can fetch the mother back from Shiva." She shot Rustam a teasing grin.

"Nightstalker—my mare—has foaled," Rustam explained quickly. "I got word this morning."

"Would you like to hold him?" Risada offered, lowering Halson for Betha to see more easily. Betha glanced at Marten.

"Go on," he urged. "You need the practice."

Rustam and Risada both stared for a fraction of a second. "You're carrying?" they cried in unison. Marten's chest puffed up with pride.

Betha blushed as she held out her arms to receive the baby. "You're the first to know. Or rather, you're the first people *we've* told. I'm afraid all the cult members know— Charin wasn't quiet when he announced it."

"That's why the wedding's next week," Marten added.

"Congratulations!" Again, Risada and Rustam spoke as one.

Risada showed Betha how to support the baby's body and

head before handing him over. "I'll be the first to admit," she said, "it didn't come naturally to me, but I seem to have perfected the art now, praise Chel."

While the women fussed over the infant, Marten scanned the room with a frown. His eyes slipped over the familiar comfortable chairs, the casual tables, the bright, cheery wall hangings, and the plush rugs scattered over the hard wood floor. Something niggled at him. Something—out of place?

Unable to pinpoint the vague distraction, his mind slid back to the conversation he'd shared with Betha, after she'd rid herself of Marganie's poison.

* * * * * * *

"Tell me what?" Betha asked.

Marten glanced away, shame at his previous attitude flushing through him. "I should never have forbidden you to use your magic. I let grief cloud my judgement. Grief, and Annasala. What am I going to do about her?" He shook his head, dismissing the conundrum of his cousin for later. "What I should have said—and I should have said it as soon as Urien died—was, use *your powers! I never want you to suffer like that again, and I never want to risk losing you."*

Hope kindled inside him in response to Betha's sudden grip on his arm, and he hurried on. "Chel and Charin forced me to see the truth. I've been looking at magic the wrong way. It isn't having magic that makes someone evil, and it's not the Temple's place to decree whether something is divine or not. It all depends on the sort of person you are, and you *are a good person. The best. I nearly allowed my ignorance to destroy you. Can you ever forgive me?"*

A single tear trickled down Betha's pale cheek. Marten brushed it tenderly away.

"It's me who should be begging your forgiveness," she said. He opened his mouth to hush her, but she pressed a fingertip to his lips. "I broke my word, Marten, and I would never have done that if it had been for myself alone, but it

wasn't."

She drew a deep breath, as if sucking in courage to say what she had to next. "I'm carrying your child, my king. Charin declared it to the entire cult."

Light-headedness mixed with a sick feeling in the pit of Marten's stomach. Nonni had been carrying his child too, and yet for her, it had been a death sentence. He swallowed hard.

"Was that what Urien meant, when he said the master still had plans for you?"

Betha shuddered. "Yes. They were going to take the baby, and raise it as a puppet. They needed the bloodline to take over the throne without the upheaval of another coup. But then Risada came back."

"With a new prince." Marten nodded. "And that's when they decided the time was ripe for my death."

"That's why I had to get back to warn you." Betha laid her head against his chest. It nestled into the hollow of his shoulder as if it belonged there, and Marten relaxed and sighed in contentment.

Then he jolted upright. "Risada! She needs me."

Betha kissed the palm of his hand. "Go. Do what you need to do."

Marten sprang up, and sprinted towards the cells with the imprint of her lips lingering on his skin.

* * * * * * * *

Rustam raised his glass in salute to the king, and Marten smiled back.

"My thanks for your timely rescue, sire," said the dancer.

"I'm sorry it wasn't sooner," Marten apologised. "In fact, I'm sorry I didn't put a stop to Sala's nonsense before it got that far. I simply didn't imagine you'd ever want to come back to Tyr-en."

Rustam glanced towards Risada with an expression Marten recognised only too well. He knew it was the same one that covered his own face when he regarded Betha, and suddenly, he understood.

It occurred to him that he might be able to help. Now Rustam was free to live in Darshan again, he needed a job, and Marten had what he considered the perfect position for the former dance master and spy.

"Cousin Rusty, I have an opening for a bodyguard who can double as a valet, and I can think of no one more suited than you. You have both the martial skills, and the flair I'm in need of to replace..."

His words petered out. He couldn't quite bring himself to say it out loud.

Rustam glanced down. "We were sorry to hear of your loss, sire. And I'm flattered, but I fear I must decline. Aside from the likelihood that your subjects wouldn't take a former dancing master seriously as a bodyguard, I've had a better offer."

Marten blinked, but before he could enquire, Risada cut in.

"When Hal tasked me with donning the mantle of Tyren's spymaster, he also suggested I recruit an understudy, in the same way he took me on. Who could be more suitable than his own son?" Her expression became stern. "And besides, he owes me."

Marten watched with amusement as Rustam's face mimicked wide-eyed innocence.

"Me?" he said, with his open hand clapped to his chest.

"Yes, you," Risada replied, struggling to keep a straight face. "I sacrificed three of my best palace players to save your worthless skin. I've had to reassign them to far flung Houses where their faces have never been seen before. You bet, you owe me."

Marten cut his eyes at Risada. "One of those players being one of my personal guards. If Uncle Hal has any more players watching me, I'd like to know."

"I'll give you a list," she promised. Her features softened. "I'm sorry about your bodyguard; he was a good man."

Marten coughed to clear the lump in his throat. "He was. And on that topic, did your research find any clue as to why Marganie wanted me dead?" He frowned. "If she hadn't managed to poison herself while in custody, we could have questioned her."

"You have my apology for that, sire, but yes, Hal's old records held some very revealing facts about your seamstress. Her mother was one of your grandfather's staff— one of those who endured his 'special attentions', shall we call them? She committed suicide when Marganie was a child. It's possible Marganie was Belcastus's get, but that's only conjecture."

Marten winced. "I hope he's rotting in Charin's hell. That man ruined so many lives."

Nearly mine included, Marten added silently, recalling the paranoia that had been his constant companion until Betha slipped into his life.

"I wonder why she chose to attack you when she did, after all her years of peaceful service," Risada mused.

Marten hefted a sigh. It was over now, and he saw no reason to admit to Marganie's previous attempts. The woman's motivation remained the same.

"I think I can answer that," he said. "Before Betha—" he darted a glance at his wife-to-be, and received an encouraging smile in return, "—I had a favourite: a girl called Nonni." He paused again, taking a measured breath before continuing. "She was Marganie's assistant, and I believe she must have said something to make Marganie realise what went on between us."

He pinned Risada with his best monarch's glare. "I trust you can assure me any other captives you take will be thoroughly searched before they have the chance to take their own lives?"

Betha handed Halson back to his mother. "Don't blame Risada, Marten. She was busy saving Rusty at the time. Unless someone had had the presence of mind to strip Marganie of all her clothing, it was always going to happen.

She came here prepared to die, and we should praise Chel she didn't take you with her. I for one, am very grateful for that." She closed the short gap between them, and pulled his head down so she could kiss him.

Marten's eyes closed, the better to savour the sweet taste of Betha's mouth. Her tiny body pressed against his, promising everything he'd ever wanted but always believed he could never have.

Until now.

With Betha wrapped in his arms, Marten dared to anticipate a hopeful future; one where they could be happy together. He opened his eyes to gaze dreamily over her head.

Across the room, the circular table, bearing a rumpled red cloth in its centre, stared back at him. His stomach clenched, and he pointed a stiff finger towards the table.

"Chel's Casket," he choked out. "It's gone!"

EPILOGUE

Brother Freskin watched the wedding from the shadowy cover of the royal portico. When the king and his new queen paraded out of the Temple through the public entrance, on their way to display themselves to the crowd, he took the opportunity to limp back to his room.

His crutches clacked along the floor, fetching a scowl to his face.

His indisposition had been used as the excuse for his non-inclusion in the ceremony—yet another slight he would not forgive.

Suffering a broken leg had not been a part of his plan, though it had provided him with the unexpected bonus of securing the king's sympathy. He could have wished for a less painful way of attaining that, but what was done, was done. No suspicion would attach itself to him now, or doubt about his loyalty to the crown.

Loyalty? Pah! Loyalty belongs to the deity, not to any man.

Things had not turned out quite the way Freskin had foreseen, but the death of that arrogant oaf, Urien, at the king's hand, had left Charin's Cult leaderless. The clerics Freskin had sacrificed to the simulated rebellion, with the intention of panicking the king into opening Chel's Casket, now had a ready-made congregation to annexe. First, they must weed out those who had been identified by the treacherous woman now wed to the king, but that did not, as yet, appear to be too many.

Freskin admired Betha's ambition, though he would savour her downfall once she was delivered of her child. The god still wanted that child, but until Charin selected a new conduit, Freskin was in charge of His followers.

It remained to be seen whether the god would choose the candidate Freskin had been grooming for so very long, but he maintained a quiet confidence in his choice.

All he need do now, was to nudge the god in his preferred direction.

Freskin entered his small room and hobbled over to the small table beside his bed. The presence of the deity vibrated through his bones, making him grit his teeth as his not-quite-healed leg protested with a sharp stab of pain. Disregarding physical comfort as irrelevant, Freskin plucked the covering away from the item squatting on the table top.

He placed his hand on the domed lid of the ancient casket.

Deborah Jay

NOTE FROM THE AUTHOR

Thank you so much for spending your time reading my words. If you liked what you read, would you please leave a short review? Just a few lines would be great!
Reviews are not only the highest compliment you can pay to an author, they also help other readers discover and make more informed choices about purchasing books in a crowded space.
Thank you!

If you'd like to be first to hear about new releases, and be in line for FREE stories, please visit my blog at **https://deborahjayauthor.com/newsletter-sign-up/** and join my newsletter.
For more about The Five Kingdoms and other novels by Deborah Jay, you can find me at:
Blog: **http://deborahjayauthor.com/**
Facebook: **https://www.facebook.com/DeborahJay**
Twitter: **https://twitter.com/DeborahJay2**
Goodreads:**https://www.goodreads.com/author/show/7172 608.Deborah_Jay**
Amazon author page: **http://viewAuthor.at/DeborahJay**

Also by Deborah Jay
DESPRITE MEASURES
The Caledonian Sprite Series #1

Discover a unique eco-urban fantasy with a touch of romance.

On the surface she's a cute and feisty blonde, a slender pocket rocket fitness coach. But Cassiopeia Lake has a secret; she's really a force of nature – an elemental.

Water sprite, Cassie, has lived undisturbed in her native Scottish loch for eons. Now, one encounter too many with modern plumbing has driven her to live in human guise along with her selkie boyfriend, Euan. It's all going fine - until a nerdy magician captures Cassie to be an unwilling component in his crazy dangerous experiment.

Escape is only Cassie's first challenge.

She's smitten by her fellow prisoner, the scorching hot fire elemental, Gloria. But how do you love someone you can never touch?

And what do you do when your boyfriend starts to hero-worship your persecutor? Not to mention that tricky situation of being the prize in a power contest between two rival covens of witches.

So when Gloria's temper erupts and she sets out to murder the magician, can Cassie keep her loved ones safe from the cross-fire, or will she be sucked into the maelstrom of deadly desires and sink without trace?

SPRITE NIGHT
A Caledonian Sprite short story.

When Scottish water sprite, Cassie, volunteers for an anti-fracking protest, the last thing she expects is to find herself at odds with a druid. But with time running out for the local environment, she can't afford to be distracted by the handsome hunk of a Highlander.

Intent on a minor act of sabotage, Cassie is totally unprepared to be caught in the cross-fire of a magical battle. Can she avert catastrophe? Or will she become the very agency of an ecological disaster?

About the Author

Deborah Jay writes fast-paced fantasy adventures featuring quirky characters and multi-layered plots. Just what she likes to read. Living mostly on the UK south coast, she has already invested in her ultimate retirement plan - a farmhouse in the majestic mystery-filled Scottish Highlands where she retreats to write when she can find time. Her taste for the good things in life is kept in check by the expense of keeping too many dressage horses, and her complete inability to cook.

   She also has non-fiction titles published under her professional name of Debby Lush.

Made in the USA
Coppell, TX
01 December 2021